About the Authors

Julia James lives in England and adores the peaceful, verdant countryside and the wild shores of Cornwall. She also loves the Mediterranean—so rich in myth and history, with its sunbaked landscapes and olive groves, ancient ruins and azure seas. 'The perfect setting for romance!' she says. 'Rivalled only by the lush tropical heat of the Caribbean—palms swaying by a silver sand beach lapped by turquoise waters...what more could lovers want?'

Growing up near the beach, **Annie West** spent lots of time observing tall, burnished lifeguards—early research! Now she spends her days fantasising about gorgeous men and their love-lives. Annie has been a reader all her life. She also loves travel, long walks, good company and great food. You can contact her at annie@annie-west.com, or via PO Box 1041, Warners Bay, NSW 2282, Australia.

Award-winning author **Sarah M. Anderson** may live east of the Mississippi River, but her heart lies out west on the Great Plains. With a lifelong love of horses and two history teachers for parents, she had plenty of encouragement to learn everything she could about the tribes of the Great Plains.

When not helping out at her son's school or walking her rescue dogs, Sarah spen with imaginary cowbo which is surprisingly husband. Readers can of cowboys and Indian

G000162376

The Love Islands

COLLECTION

March 2019

April 2019

May 2019

June 2019

July 2019

August 2019

Love Islands:
Secret Escapes

JULIA JAMES

ANNIE WEST

SARAH M. ANDERSON

MILLS & BOON

All rights reserved including the right of reproduction in whole or in part in any form. This edition is published by arrangement with Harlequin Books S.A.

This is a work of fiction. Names, characters, places, locations and incidents are purely fictional and bear no relationship to any real life individuals, living or dead, or to any actual places, business establishments, locations, events or incidents. Any resemblance is entirely coincidental.

This book is sold subject to the condition that it shall not, by way of trade or otherwise, be lent, resold, hired out or otherwise circulated without the prior consent of the publisher in any form of binding or cover other than that in which it is published and without a similar condition including this condition being imposed on the subsequent purchaser.

® and ™ are trademarks owned and used by the trademark owner and/or its licensee. Trademarks marked with ® are registered with the United Kingdom Patent Office and/or the Office for Harmonisation in the Internal Market and in other countries.

First published in Great Britain 2019
by Mills & Boon, an imprint of HarperCollins*Publishers*
1 London Bridge Street, London, SE1 9GF

Love Islands: Secret Escapes © 2019 Harlequin Books S.A.

A Cinderella for the Greek © 2016 Julia James
The Flaw in Raffaele's Revenge © 2016 Annie West
His Forever Family © 2016 Sarah M. Anderson

ISBN: 978-0-263-27551-3

MIX
Paper from
responsible sources
FSC
www.fsc.org
FSC™ C007454

This book is produced from independently certified FSC™ paper to ensure responsible forest management.

For more information visit: www.harpercollins.co.uk/green

Printed and bound in Spain
by CPI, Barcelona

A CINDERELLA
FOR THE GREEK

JULIA JAMES

CHAPTER ONE

Max Vasilikos lowered his tall frame into the leather chair by the desk and relaxed back into it, his long legs stretching out in front of him.

'OK, what have you got for me?'

His UK agent handed him a set of glossy brochures. 'I think there are some good contenders here, Mr Vasilikos,' he said hopefully to this most demanding of clients.

Max's dark eyes glanced briefly, and then he found his gaze lingering on only one of the properties.

An English country house, in warm honey-coloured stone, with wisteria tumbling over the porch, surrounded by verdant gardens and sheltering woodland, with a glimpse of a lake beyond the lawn. Bathed in sunshine, the whole place had an appeal that held his gaze, making him want to see the real thing.

He picked up the brochure and shifted his gaze to his agent.

'This one,' he said decisively.

Ellen paused in the hallway. She could hear her stepmother's sharp voice coming from the drawing room.

'This is exactly what I've been hoping for! And I will *not* have that wretched girl trying to spoil it—again!'

'We've just *got* to hurry up and sell this place!'

The second voice came from Ellen's stepsister Chloe, petulant and displeased.

Ellen's mouth tightened. She was all too aware of the source of their displeasure. When Pauline had married Ellen's widowed father she and her daughter Chloe had had only one aim—to spend his money on the luxury lifestyle they craved for themselves. Now all that was left, after years of their lavish spending, was the house they had jointly inherited with Ellen after her father's sudden death last year from a heart attack—and they couldn't wait to sell it. That it was Ellen's home, and had been in her family for generations, bothered them not in the slightest.

Their hostility towards her was nothing new. From the moment they'd invaded her life Pauline and her daughter had treated Ellen with complete contempt. How could Ellen—tall and ungainly, clumping around 'like an elephant', as they always described her—possibly compare with slender, petite and oh-so-pretty Chloe?

She clumped down the rest of the stairs deliberately now, to drown out their voices. It sounded, she thought grimly, as if her stepmother had hopes of a potential purchaser for Haughton. Despite knowing she would need to resort to legal action against her stepdaughter in order to force a sale through, Pauline obdurately kept the house on the market, and relentlessly went on at Ellen to try to wear down her resistance and force her to agree to sell up.

But Ellen's heart had steeled in that first winter without her father, when her stepmother and Chloe had been disporting themselves expensively in the Caribbean. She would make it as difficult as she could for Pauline to sell her beloved home—the home Ellen had been happy in until the terrible day her mother had been killed in a car crash, sending her father spiralling into a grieving tailspin of loneliness that had made him so dangerously vulnerable to entrapment by Pauline's avaricious ambitions.

As Ellen walked into the drawing room two pairs of ice-blue eyes went to her, their joint expressions openly hostile.

'What kept you?' Pauline demanded immediately. 'Chloe texted you an hour ago saying that we needed to talk to you.'

'I was taking lacrosse practice,' Ellen returned, keeping her tone even. She sat down heavily on an armchair.

'You've got mud on your face,' Chloe informed her sneeringly.

Her gaze was not just hostile, but contemptuous. Ellen could see why. Her stepsister was wearing one of her countless designer outfits—a pair of immaculately cut trousers with a cashmere knit top—her nails were newly manicured and varnished, her freshly cut and styled ash-blonde hair and make-up perfect.

A familiar silent sigh went through Ellen. Chloe was everything she was not! Petite, with a heart-shaped face, and so, *so* slim! The contrast with her own appearance—she was still wearing the coaching tracksuit from the nearby private girls' school where she taught Games and Geography, with her thick, unmanageable hair gripped back in a bushy ponytail and her face devoid of any make-up except the streak of mud on her cheek that Chloe had so kindly pointed out!—was total.

'The estate agents phoned this afternoon,' Pauline opened, her gimlet eyes on Ellen. 'There's been another expression of interest—'

'And we don't want *you* ruining things!' broke in Chloe waspishly, throwing a dagger look at her stepsister. 'Especially with this guy,' she continued.

There was a note in her voice that caught Ellen's attention. So, too, did the discernibly smug expression in Pauline's eyes.

'Max Vasilikos is looking for a new addition to his portfolio—he thinks Haughton might be it.' Pauline elucidated.

Ellen looked blank, and Chloe made a derisive noise. 'Oh, for heaven's sake, don't expect *her* to know who Max Vasilikos is,' she said. 'Max Vasilikos,' she spelt out to Ellen, 'is a stinking rich property tycoon. He's also just had an affair with Tyla Brentley—you *must* have heard of her, at least?'

Ellen had, as a matter of fact. She was an English actress who'd found fame in Hollywood in a hugely successful romantic blockbuster, and the pupils at her school were full of her. But as for this Max Vasilikos... Apart from surmising that with a name like that he must be of Greek origin—well, 'stinking rich' property tycoons were nothing to do with her.

And they would be nothing to do with Haughton either, please God! A cold shiver went down her spine. Someone like this Max Vasilikos would sell it on for a huge profit to a Russian oligarch or a Middle Eastern sheikh who would spend a week or two in it, at best, every year or so. And it would languish, unloved and unlived-in...

Pauline was speaking again. 'Max Vasilikos is sufficiently interested to come and view the property himself. As a courtesy I have invited him to lunch with us.'

That smug expression was in her eyes again. Ellen just looked at her. 'Does he understand the ownership structure of Haughton and that I am unwilling to sell my share?' she asked bluntly.

Pauline waved a hand to brush aside this unpalatable detail. 'What *I* understand, Ellen,' she said bitingly, 'is that if—*if*—he expresses an interest, we will be very, very fortunate. I do *not*,' she emphasised, 'want *you* rocking the boat. Moreover—' she glared at her stepdaughter '—if nothing I can say will make you see sense about selling up, perhaps Max Vasilikos can.'

There was an explosive, choking half-laugh from Chloe. 'Oh, Mummy, don't,' she jeered. 'You simply *can't* inflict *her* on him!'

Ellen felt the jibe, flinching inwardly and yet knowing it for nothing but the truth. No man—let alone one who dated film stars—could look at her with anything but complete indifference to her appearance. She had nothing to attract a man in her looks. Knew it…accepted it. At least, though, she wasn't cruel like her stepsister.

Pauline had turned to Chloe. 'Nevertheless, that's just what we are going to have to do,' she continued. 'Ellen *has* to be there.' Her gaze went back to her stepdaughter. 'We'll present a united front.'

Ellen stared. United? A more fractured family was hard to imagine. But, although it would be gruelling to endure, it would at least, she realised grimly, give her the opportunity to make it clear to this Max Vasilikos just how unwilling she was to sell her share of her home.

With reluctant acquiescence she got to her feet. She needed a shower, and she was hungry, too. She headed for the kitchen. It was the part of the house she liked best now—the former servants' quarters, and the perfect place for keeping out of Pauline and Chloe's way. Cooking was not a priority for either woman.

She'd moved her bedroom to one of the back rooms as well, overlooking the courtyard at the rear of the house, and adapted an adjacent room for her own sitting room. She ventured into the front part of the house as little as possible—but now, as she headed back across the hall to the green baize door that led to the servants' quarters, she felt her heart squeeze as she gazed around her at the sweeping staircase, the huge stone fireplace, the massive oak doorway, the dark wood panelling and the ancient flagstones beneath her feet.

How she loved this house. Loved it with a strong, deep devotion. She would never willingly relinquish it. *Never!*

Max Vasilikos slowed the powerful car as the road curved between high hedges. He was deep in Hampshire country-side bright with early spring sunshine, and almost at his destination. He was eager to arrive—keen to see for himself whether the place that had so immediately appealed to him in the estate agency's photos would live up to his hopes. And not just from an investment perspective. The encircling woods and gardens, the mellow stonework, the pleasing proportions and styling of the house all seemed—*homely*. That was the word that formed in his mind.

In fact… *It's a house I could see myself in—*

The thought was in his head before he could stop it, and that in itself was cause for surprise. He'd always been per-fectly happy to live a globetrotting life, staying in hotels or serviced apartments, ready to board a plane at any moment.

But then, he'd never known a home of his own. His eyes shadowed. His mother had always been ashamed of his il-legitimacy, and that was why, Max thought bleakly, she'd married his stepfather—to try and disguise her child's fa-therless status.

But the very last thing his stepfather had wanted was to accept his wife's bastard into his family. All he'd wanted was a wife to be a skivvy, an unpaid drudge to work in his restaurant in a little tourist town on a resort island in the Aegean. Max had spent his childhood and teenage years helping her, keeping the *taverna* going while his stepfa-ther played host to his customers, snapping his fingers at Max to wait at tables while his mother cooked endlessly.

The day his mother had died—of exhaustion as much as the lung disease that had claimed her—Max had walked out, never to return. He'd taken the ferry to Athens, his eyes burning not just with grief for his mother's death, but with a fierce, angry determination to make his own way in the world. And make it a glittering way. Nothing would stop him. He would overcome all obstacles, with determination driving him ever onwards.

Five years of slog in the construction industry and finally he'd saved enough from his wages to make his first property purchase—a derelict farmhouse that, with the sweat of his brow, he'd restored and sold to a German second-home-owner, making enough profit to buy two more properties. And so it had begun. The Vasilikos property empire had snowballed into the global enterprise it now was. His tightened mouth twisted into a caustic smile of ruthless satisfaction. It even included his stepfather's *taverna*—picked up for a song when his stepfather's idleness had bankrupted him.

Max's expression changed abruptly as his sat-nav indicated that he'd arrived at his destination. Manoeuvring between two large, imposing stone gate pillars, he headed slowly along a lengthy drive flanked by woodland and massed rhododendrons that in turn gave way to a gravelled carriage sweep alongside the frontage of the house. He slowed down, taking in the vista in front of him, feeling satisfaction shaping inside him.

The photos hadn't deceived—everything they'd promised was here. The house was nestled into its landscaped grounds, the mellow stonework a warm honey colour, and sunshine glanced off the mullioned windows. The stone porch with its gnarled oak door was flanked by twisted wisteria, bare at this time of year, but with the promise of the show to come. Already in bloom, however, were ranks of golden daffodils, marching thickly along the herbaceous borders on either side of the porch.

Max's sense of satisfaction deepened. It looked good— more than good. Not too large, not too grand, but elegant and gracious, and steeped in the long centuries of its existence. An English country house, yes, built for landowners and gentry, but also inviting, its scale domestic and pleasing. More than a grand house—a *home*.

Could it become my home? Could I see myself living here?

He frowned slightly. Why was he thinking such things?

Have I reached the age where I'm starting to think of settling down? Is that it?

Settling down? That was something he'd never thought of with any woman—certainly not with Tyla. She was like him: rootless, working all over the world.

Maybe that's why we suited each other—we had that in common.

Well, even if that had been true enough at the time, it hadn't been sufficient to stop him ending things with her. Her absorption in her own beauty and desirability had become tiresome in the end—and now she was busy beguiling her latest leading man, a Hollywood A-lister. Max wished her well with it.

So maybe I need a new relationship? Maybe I'm in search of novelty? Something different—?

He gave himself a mental shake. He wasn't here to ponder his private life. He was here to make a simple business decision—whether to buy this property or not for his extensive portfolio.

Engaging gear again, he crunched forward over the gravel, taking the car around to the back of the house. He drew to a halt and got out of the car, again liking what he saw. The rear façade, built as servants' quarters, might not have the elegance of the front section of the house, but the open cobbled courtyard was attractive, bordered by outhouses on two sides and prettied up with tubs of flowers, and a wooden bench positioned in the sunshine by the kitchen door.

His approval rating of the house went up yet another notch. He strolled towards the door, to ask if it was okay to leave his car there, but just as he was about to knock it was yanked open, and someone hefting a large wooden basket and a bulging plastic bin bag cannoned straight into him.

A Greek expletive escaped him and he stepped back, taking in whoever had barged so heavily into him. She was female, he could see, and though she might be categorised as 'young' she had little else that he could see to recommend her to his sex. She was big, bulky, with a mop of dark bushy hair yanked back off her face into some kind of ponytail. She wore a pair of round glasses on her nose and her complexion was reddening unbecomingly. The dark purple tracksuit she wore was hideous, and she looked distinctly overweight, Max decided.

Despite her unprepossessing appearance, not for a moment did Max neglect his manners.

'I'm so sorry,' he said smoothly. 'I was seeking to enquire whether I might leave my car here.' He paused. 'I *am* expected. Max Vasilikos to see Mrs Mountford.'

The reddening female dragged her eyes from him and stared at his car, then back at him. Her cheeks flushed redder than ever. She shifted the weight of the basket on her hip but did not answer him.

'So, *is* it all right to leave my car here?' Max prompted.

With visible effort the woman nodded. She might have mumbled something as well, but whatever it was it was indistinct.

He gave a swift, courtesy-only smile. 'Good,' he said,

dismissing her from his notice, and turned away to head around the house to the front entrance, his gaze sweeping out over the gardens as he walked. Even this early in the spring he could see that they would be beautiful as summer arrived.

Again he felt that unexpected sense of approval that was nothing to do with whether or not this place would be a profitable investment to make. He walked up to the front door—a massive, studded oak construction—hoping the interior of the house would match the charms of the exterior.

The door opened in front of him—clearly his arrival had been communicated. The female standing there could not, Max thought, have been more different from the one who'd cannoned into him at the kitchen door. She was petite, ultra-slender and immaculately styled, from her chic ash-blonde hair and perfect make-up to her well-tailored outfit whose pale blue hue matched the colour of her eyes. The fragrance of an expensive perfume wafted from her as she smiled warmly at him.

'Mr Vasilikos—do come in!'

She stood back as Max walked in, taking in a large hall with a flagged stone floor, a cavernous fireplace, and a broad flight of stairs leading upwards. It suited the house, Max thought.

'I'm Chloe Mountford. I'm *so* glad you could come.' The daughter of the house—as he assumed she must be— was gliding towards one of the sets of double doors opening off the hall, and she threw them open with a dramatic gesture as he followed after her.

'Mummy, it's Mr Vasilikos,' she announced.

Mummy? Max reminded himself that it was common in English upper crust circles for adult children to use such a juvenile form of address for their parents. Then he walked into the room. It was a double aspect drawing room, with another large but more ornate marble fireplace and a lot of furniture. The decor was pale grey and light blue, and it was clear to his experienced eyes that a top-class interior designer had been let loose in there.

He found himself conscious of a feeling of disappointment—it was all just *too* perfect and calculatedly tasteful—and wondered what the original decor would have looked like. The effect now was like something out of a highly glossy upmarket magazine.

I couldn't live in this. It's far too overdone. I'd have to change it—

The thought was in his head automatically, and he frowned slightly. He was getting ahead of himself again.

'Mr Vasilikos, how lovely to meet you.'

The slim, elegant woman greeting him from one of the upholstered sofas by the fire, holding out a diamond-ringed hand to him, was extremely well preserved and, like her daughter, had clearly lavished money on her clothes and her appearance. A double rope of pearls adorned her neck which, Max suspected, had benefitted from the attentions of a plastic surgeon at some time.

'Mrs Mountford.' Max greeted the widowed owner, his handshake firm and brief, then sat himself down where she indicated, at the far end of the sofa opposite, away from the fire. Chloe Mountford settled herself prettily on a third sofa, facing the fire, at the end closest to Max.

'I'm delighted to welcome you to Haughton,' Mrs Mountford was saying now, in a smiling, gracious tone.

Max smiled politely in response as her daughter took up the conversational baton.

'Thank you for taking the time from what I'm sure must be a dreadfully busy schedule. Are you in England long this visit, Mr Vasilikos?' she asked brightly.

'My plans are fluid at the moment,' Max returned evenly. He found himself wondering whether Chloe Mountford was likely to make a play for him. He hoped not. The current fashion might be for ultra-thin figures, but they were not to his taste. Nor, of course, were women at the other extreme.

His mind flickered back to the female who'd cannoned into him at the back door. Being overweight wasn't a good look either—especially when a woman was badly dressed and plain to boot. A flicker of pity went through him for any woman so sadly unattractive. Then Chloe Mountford was speaking again.

'There speaks the globetrotting tycoon!' she said with a light laugh.

She turned her head expectantly as a door set almost invisibly into the papered wall opened abruptly and a bulky frame carrying a loaded coffee tray reversed into the room. It belonged, Max could see instantly, to the very female he'd just been mentally pitying for her lack of physical appeal.

The unlovely tracksuit had been swapped for a grey skirt and a white blouse, the trainers replaced with sturdy lace-up flats, but her hair was still caught back in a styleless bush, and the spectacles were still perched on her nose. She made her way heavily into the room, looking decidedly awkward, Max could see.

'Ah, Ellen, there you are!' exclaimed Pauline Mountford as the coffee tray was set down on the low table by the fireside. Then his hostess was addressing him directly. 'Mr Vasilikos, this is my stepdaughter, Ellen.'

Max found his assumptions that the hefty female was some kind of maid rearranging themselves. Stepdaughter? He'd been unaware of that—but then, of course, knowing the details of the family who owned Haughton was hardly relevant to his decision whether to purchase it or not.

'How do you do?' he murmured as he politely got to his feet.

He saw her face redden as she sat herself down heavily on the sofa beside Chloe Mountford. Max's glance, as he seated himself again, went between the two young women sitting on the same sofa, took in the difference between the two females graphically. They could hardly be a greater contrast to each other—one so petite and beautifully groomed, the other so large and badly presented. Clearly nothing more than stepsisters, indeed.

'Mr Vasilikos,' the stepdaughter returned briefly, with the slightest nod of her head. Then she looked across at her stepmother. 'Would you like me to pour? Or do *you* want to be mother?' she said.

Max heard the bite in her voice as she addressed the owner of the house and found himself sharpening his scrutiny.

'Please do pour, Ellen, dear,' said Mrs Mountford, ignoring the distinctly baiting note in her stepdaughter's tone of voice.

'Cream and sugar, Mr Vasilikos?' she asked, looking straight at him.

There was a gritty quality to her voice, as if she found the exchange difficult. Her colour was still heightened, but subsiding. Her skin tone, distinctly less pale than her stepsister's carefully made up features, definitely looked better when she wasn't colouring up, Max decided. In fact, now he came to realise it, she had what might almost be described as a healthy glow about her—as if she spent most of her time outside. Not like the delicate hothouse plant her stepsister looked to be.

'Just black, please,' he answered. He didn't particularly

want coffee, let alone polite chit-chat, but it was a ritual to be got through, he acknowledged, before he could expect a tour of the property that he was interested in.

He watched Pauline Mountford's sadly unlovely step-daughter pour the coffee from a silver jug into a porcelain cup and hand it to him. He took it with a murmur of thanks, his fingers inadvertently making contact with hers, and she grabbed her hand back as if the slight touch had been an unpleasant electric shock. Then she ferociously bus-ied herself pouring the other three cups of coffee, hand-ing them to her stepmother and sister, before sitting back with her own and stirring it rapidly.

Max sat back, crossing one leg over the other, and took a contemplative sip of his coffee. Time to get the conver-sation going where he wanted it to go.

'So,' he opened, with a courteous smile of interest at Pauline Mountford, 'what makes you wish to part with such a beautiful property?'

Personally, he might think the decor too overdone, but it was obviously to his hostess's taste, and there was no point in alienating her. Decor could easily be changed—it was the house itself he was interested in.

And he *was* interested—most decidedly so. That same feeling that had struck him from the first was strengthen-ing all the time. Again, he wondered why.

Maybe it's coming from the house itself?

The fanciful idea was in his head before he could stop it, making its mark.

As he'd spoken he'd seen Pauline Mountford's step-daughter's coffee cup jerk in her grip and her expression darken. But his hostess was replying.

'Oh, sadly there are too many memories here! Since my husband died I find them too painful. I know I must be brave and make a new life for myself now.' She gave a resigned sigh, a catch audible in her voice. 'It will be a wrench, though…' She shook her head sadly.

'Poor Mummy.' Her daughter reached her hand across and patted her mother's arm, her voice warm with sympathy. Chloe Mountford looked at him. 'This last year's been just dreadful,' she said.

'I'm sorry for your loss,' Max murmured. 'But I can understand your reasons for wishing to sell.'

A sharp clunk came from the sofa opposite, and his eyes flicked to see his hostess's stepdaughter had dropped her coffee cup on to its saucer. Her expression, he could tell, was tight. His focus sharpened. Beneath his swift glance in her direction he saw her cheeks redden again. Then she reached for the silver coffee pot and busied herself pouring another cup. She did not speak, but the tightness in her face was unabated, even as the colour started to ebb. She took a single gulp from the refilled cup, then abruptly got to her feet.

'I must go and see about lunch,' she said brusquely, pushing past the furniture to get to the service door.

As she left Pauline Mountford leant towards him slightly. 'Poor Ellen took my husband's death very hard,' she confided in a low voice. 'She was quite devoted to him.' A little frown formed on her well-preserved and, he suspected, well-Botoxed forehead. 'Possibly too much so…' She sighed.

Then her expression changed and she brightened.

'I'm sure you would like to see the rest of the house before lunch. Chloe will be delighted to take you on the grand tour!' she gave a light laugh.

Her daughter got to her feet and Max did likewise. He *was* keen to see the house—and not keen to hear any more about the personal circumstances of the Mountford family, which were of no interest to him whatsoever. Chloe

Mountford might be too thin, and her stepsister just the opposite, but he found neither attractive. All that attracted him here was the house itself.

It was an attraction that the 'grand tour' only intensified. By the time he reached the upper floor, with its array of bedrooms opening off a long, spacious landing, and stood in the window embrasure of the master bedroom, gazing with satisfaction over the gardens to let his gaze rest on the reed-edged lake beyond, its glassy waters flanked by sheltering woodland, his mind was made up.

Haughton Court would be his. He was determined on it.

CHAPTER TWO

ELLEN MADE IT to the kitchen, her heart knocking. Having *anyone* arrive to look over her home, thinking he was going to buy it, was bad enough—but…oh, dear Lord… that it was such a man as Max Vasilikos! She felt her cheeks flame again, just as they'd flamed—horribly, hideously—in that first punishingly embarrassing moment of all but sending him flying at the back door.

She had been gawping like an idiot at the devastating male standing in front of her. Six foot plus, broad-shouldered, muscled, and just ludicrously good-looking, with classic 'tall dark stranger' looks and olive skin tones. Sable hair and charcoal eyes, a sculpted mouth, incised cheekbones and a jaw cut from the smoothest marble…

The impact he'd made had hit her all over again when she'd taken in the coffee. At least by then she'd been a fraction more prepared—prepared, too, for what she'd known would be the inevitable pitying glance he'd cast at her as she took her place beside Chloe.

She felt her throat tighten painfully. She knew exactly what he'd seen, and why he'd pitied her. She and Chloe couldn't have made a bigger contrast, sitting beside each other. Hadn't she seen that same expression countless times over the years, whenever male eyes had looked between the two of them? Chloe the svelte, lovely blonde—she the heavy, ungainly frump.

She wrenched her mind away from the image. She had more to concern her than her lack of looks. Somehow she was going to have to find an opportunity to lay it on the line for Max Vasilikos about his buying her home. Oh, Pauline and Chloe might trot out all that sickeningly hypocritical garbage about 'painful memories', but the truth was they couldn't wait to cash in on the sale of the last asset they could get their greedy hands on.

Well, she would defy them to the last.

They'll have to force it from me in a court of law, and I'll fight them every inch of the way. I'll make it the most protracted and expensive legal wrangle I can.

A man like Max Vasilikos—an investment purchaser who just wanted a quick sale and a quick profit—wouldn't want that kind of delay. So long as she insisted that she wouldn't sell, that he'd have to wait out a legal battle with Pauline and Chloe, she would be able to fend him off. He'd find somewhere else to buy—leave Haughton alone.

As she checked the chicken that was roasting, and started to chop up vegetables, that was the only hope she could hang on to.

He'll never persuade me to agree to sell to him. Never!

There was nothing Max could say or do that would make her change her mind. Oh, he might be the kind of man who could turn females to jelly with a single glance of his dark, dark eyes, but—her mouth twisted—with looks like hers she knew only too painfully she was the last female on the planet that a man like Max Vasilikos would bother to turn the charm on for.

'Sherry, Mr Vasilikos? Or would you prefer something stronger?' Pauline's light voice enquired.

'Dry sherry, thank you,' he replied.

He was back in the drawing room, his tour of the house complete, his mind made up. This was a house he wanted to own.

And to keep for his own use.

That was the most insistent aspect of his decision to purchase this place. Its prominence in his mind still surprised him, but he was increasingly getting used to its presence. The idea of having this place for himself—*to* himself. Mentally he let the prospect play inside his head, and it continued to play as he sipped at the proffered sherry, his eyes working around the elegant drawing room.

All the other rooms that Chloe had shown him bore the same mark of a top interior designer. Beautiful, but to his mind not authentic. Only the masculine preserve of the library had given any sense of the house as it must once have been, before it had been expensively made over. The worn leather chairs, the old-fashioned patterned carpets and the book-lined walls had a charm that the oh-so-tasteful other rooms lacked. Clearly the late Edward Mountford had prevented his wife from letting the designer into his domain, and Max could not but agree with that decision.

He realised his hostess was murmuring something to him and forced his attention back from the pleasurable meanderings of the way he would decorate this room, and all the others, once the house was his to do with as he pleased.

He was not kept making anodyne conversation with his hostess and her daughter for long, however. After a few minutes the service door opened again and Pauline Mountford's stepdaughter walked in with her solid tread.

'Lunch is ready,' she announced bluntly.

She crossed to the double doors, throwing them open to the hall beyond. Despite her solidity she held herself well, Max noticed—shoulders back, straight spine, as if she were strong beneath the excess weight she must be carrying, if the way the sleeves of her ill-fitting blouse were straining over her arms was anything to go by. He frowned. It seemed wrong to him that his hostess and her daughter should be so elegantly attired, and yet Ellen Mountford—presumably, he realised, the daughter of the late owner—looked so very *in*elegant.

But then, sadly, he knew that so many women who felt themselves to be overweight virtually gave up on trying to make anything of what looks they had.

His gaze assessed her as he followed her into the dining room, her stepsister and stepmother coming in behind him. *She's got good legs*, he found himself thinking. Shapely calves, at any rate. Well, that was something, at least! His eyes went to her thick mop of hair, whose style did nothing for her—it wouldn't have done anything for Helen of Troy, to his mind! A decent haircut would surely improve her?

As he took his seat at the end of the table, where she indicated, his eyes flicked over her face. The glasses, he decided, were too small for her, making her jaw look big and her eyes look small. And that was a shame, he realised, because her eyes were a warm sherry colour, with amber lights. He frowned again. Her lashes might be long—what he could see of them through her spectacle lenses—but that overgrown monobrow was *hideous*! Why on earth didn't she do something about it? Do something about the rest of her?

It wouldn't take that much, surely, to make her look better? Plus, of course, decent clothes that concealed her excess weight as much as possible. Best of all, however, would be for her to shift that weight. She should take more exercise, maybe.

And not eat so much...

Because as they settled into lunch it was clear to Max

that he and Ellen Mountford were the only ones tucking in. That was a shame, because the roast chicken was delicious—the traditional 'Sunday lunch' that the English loved so much and did so well. But neither Pauline Mountford nor her daughter did anything more than pick at their food.

Max found himself annoyed. Didn't they realise that being too thin was as undesirable as the opposite? His eyes flickered to Ellen Mountford again. *Was* she overweight? Her blouse might be straining over her arms, but her jawline was firm, and there was no jowliness or softening under the chin.

She must have noticed him glancing at her, for suddenly he saw again that tide of unlovely colour washing up into her face. *That* most certainly did nothing for her. He drew his glance away. Why was he thinking about how to improve the appearance of Ellen Mountford? She was of no interest to him—how could she possibly be?

'What are your plans for the contents of the house?' he asked his hostess. 'Will you take the paintings with you when you sell?'

A sound that might have been a choke came from Ellen Mountford, and Max's eyes flicked back to her. The red tide had vanished, and now there was the same tightness in her face as he'd seen when her stepmother had mentioned her bereavement.

'Very possibly not,' Pauline Mountford was answering him. 'They do rather go with the house, do you not think? Of course,' she added pointedly, 'they would all need to be independently valued.'

Max's eyes swept the walls. He had no objection to having the artwork—or, indeed, any of the original furniture. The pieces that had been acquired via the interior designer were, however, dispensable. His gaze rested on an empty space on the wall behind Chloe Mountford, where the wallpaper was slightly darker.

'Sold,' said Ellen Mountford tersely. The look on her face had tightened some more.

Chloe Mountford gave a little laugh. 'It was a gruesome still life of a dead stag. Mummy and I hated it!'

Max gave a polite smile, but his gaze was on Chloe's stepsister. She didn't seem pleased about the loss of the dead stag painting. Then his attention was recalled by his hostess.

'Do tell us, Mr Vasilikos, where will you be off to next? Your work must take you all over the world, I imagine.' She smiled encouragingly at him as she sipped at her wine.

'The Caribbean,' he replied. 'I am developing a resort there on one of the lesser known islands.'

Chloe's pale blue eyes lit up. 'I *adore* the Caribbean!' she exclaimed enthusiastically. 'Mummy and I spent Christmas in Barbados last winter. We stayed at Sunset Bay, of course. There really isn't anything to compare, is there?' she invited, after naming the most prestigious resort on the island.

'It's superb in what it does,' Max agreed. The famous high-profile hotel was nothing like the resort *he* was developing, and the remote island was nothing like fashionable Barbados.

'Do tell us more,' invited Chloe. 'When will the grand opening be? I'm sure Mummy and I would *love* to be amongst the very first guests.'

Max could see Ellen Mountford's expression hardening yet again with clear displeasure. He wondered at it. Out of nowhere, memory shafted like an arrow. His stepfather had been perpetually displeased by anything he'd ever said— so much that he'd learnt to keep his mouth shut when his stepfather was around.

He dragged his mind away from the unhappy memory, back to the present. 'Its style will be very different from Sunset Bay,' he said. 'The idea is for it to be highly eco-friendly, focussing on being self-sustaining. Rainwater showers and no air conditioning,' he elucidated, with a slight smile.

'Oh, dear...' Pauline shook her head regretfully. 'I don't think that would suit me. Too much heat is very trying, I find.'

'It won't be for everyone, I agree,' Max acknowledged tactfully. He turned towards Ellen. 'What do *you* think—would it attract you? Wood-built lodges open to the fresh air and meals cooked on open fires in the evenings?' He found himself unexpectedly wanting to draw her into the conversation, to hear her views. They would be different from her hothouse stepsister's, he was sure.

'Sounds like glamping,' she blurted in her abrupt manner.

Max's eyebrows drew together. 'Glamping?' he echoed, mystified.

'Glamorous camping. I believe that's the contraction it's for,' she elucidated shortly. 'Upmarket camping for people who like the idea of going back to nature but not the primitive reality of it.'

Max gave a wry smile. 'Hmm...that might be a good description for my resort,' he acknowledged.

A tinkling laugh came from Chloe. 'I'd say "glamorous camping" is a contradiction in terms! It would be luxury for Ellen, though—she runs camps for London kids. A million miles from upmarket. Totally basic.'

She gave a dramatic shudder, and Max heard the note of dismissal in her voice.

'Adventure breaks,' Ellen said shortly. 'The children

enjoy it. They think it's exciting. Some of them have never been into the countryside.'

'Ellen's "good works"!' Pauline said lightly. 'I'm sure it's very uplifting.'

'And muddy!' trilled Chloe with a little laugh, and sought to catch Max's eye to get his agreement.

But Max's attention was on Ellen. It was unexpected to hear that she ran such breaks for deprived inner-city children, given her own privileged background. He realised that he was paying her more attention.

'Do you hold them here?' he asked interestedly.

If so, it was something he might keep on with—adding it to the extensive list of charitable enterprises that were his personal payback for the good fortune that had enabled him to attain the wealth he had.

'They're held at my school, nearby. We set up camp on the playing fields,' came the answer. 'That way the children can use the sports pavilion, including the showers, and have use of the swimming pool as well. So they get the fun of camping, plus the run of the facilities of a private school.'

As she spoke for the first time Max saw something light up in Ellen Mountford's eyes, changing her expression. Instead of the stony, closed look that alternated only with the tomato-red flaring of her cheeks when he paid her attention there was actually some animation, some enthusiasm. It made a significant difference to her features, he realised with surprise. They seemed lighter, somehow, less heavy, and not even those wretched spectacles could hide that.

Then, as if aware of his regard, he saw her face close down again and she grabbed at her wine glass, that telltale colour washing up into her face, destroying the transformation he'd started to glimpse. For some reason it annoyed him. He opened his mouth to make a reply, to ask another question, see whether he could get back that momentary animation, draw her out again. But his hostess was speaking now, and he had to turn his attention to her.

'After lunch,' said Pauline Mountford, 'I'm sure you would like to see the gardens here. It's a little early in the season as yet, but in a week or two the rhododendrons along the drive will start their annual show,' she told him smilingly. 'They are a blaze of colour!'

'Rhododendrons...' Max mused, more for something to say than anything else. 'Rose tree—that's the literal translation from the Greek.'

'How fascinating!' said Chloe. 'Do they come from Greece, then?'

'No. They come from the Himalayas.' Her stepsister's contradiction was immediate. 'The Victorians introduced them to England. Unfortunately they've taken over in some places, where they are invasive pests. '

Max saw her eyes flicker to Pauline and her daughter, her expression back to stony again.

Chloe, though, continued as if her stepsister had not spoken. 'And then a little later on in early summer we have the azaleas—they are absolutely gorgeous when they are fully out in May. Masses and masses of them! Mummy had the most beautiful walk created, that winds right through their midst—'

There was an abrupt clatter of silverware from her stepsister.

'No, she did *not*. The azalea walk has been there far longer. It was *my* mother who created it!'

The glare from behind Ellen Mountford's spectacle lenses was like a dagger, skewering the hapless Chloe as Max turned his head abruptly at the brusque interjection. Then his hostess's stepdaughter scraped back her chair and got to her feet.

'If you've all finished—?' she said, and started to grab at the plates and pile them on the tray on the sideboard. She marched out with them.

As she disappeared Pauline Mountford gave a resigned sigh. 'Oh, dear,' she said. 'I do apologise for that.' She glanced at her daughter, who promptly took up the cue.

'Ellen can be so very…*sensitive*,' she murmured sadly. 'I should have known better.' She gave a little sigh of regret.

'We do our best,' her mother confirmed with another sad sigh. 'But, well…' She trailed off and gave a little shake of her head.

It *was* tricky, Max allowed, for his hostess and her daughter to have to smooth over the prickly behaviour of their step-relation, in which he was not interested, so he moved the conversation back to the topic he *was* interested in, asking how far Haughton was from the sea.

Chloe Mountford was just telling him that it would make an ideal base for Cowes Week, if sailing was an interest of his, when her stepsister made another entrance, bearing another tray weighed down with a large apple pie, a jug of custard and a bowl of cream, which she set down on the table heavily. She did not resume her place.

'I'll leave you to it,' she announced shortly. 'Coffee will be in the drawing room.'

Then she was gone, disappearing back through the service door.

'So, Mr Vasilikos, what do you make of Haughton?'

Pauline Mountford's enquiry was perfectly phrased, and accompanied by a charming smile. She was sitting in a graceful pose on the sofa in the drawing room, where they had repaired for the coffee that Ellen Mountford had so tersely informed them would be awaiting them.

Max had been the only one to partake of the apple pie—

no surprise—but he was glad he had. It had been delicious—sweet pastry made with a very light touch indeed, and juicy apples spiced with cinnamon and nutmeg. Whoever had made it could certainly cook.

Had the graceless Ellen made it? If so, then whatever her lack of beauty she could certainly boast of *one* key asset to draw a man to her side. His thoughts ran on. But perhaps being a good cook was not to her personal advantage—not if she overindulged in her own creations.

He gave a little shake of his head. There he was, thinking about that woman again. *Why?* She was nothing to him, and would remain so. He relaxed back a fraction in his seat. His hostess was clearly fishing for whether he wanted to buy this place or not. Well, why not give her his good news right now? He'd made his decision—and every passing moment only confirmed it. It might have been a decision made on impulse, but it was a strong impulse—the strongest he'd ever had—and he was used to making decisions on the spot. His instinct had never failed him yet—and it would not fail him now.

'Charming,' he said decisively, stretching out his legs towards the fire in a fashion that was already proprietorial. 'I believe...' he bestowed a smile on her '...that we will be able to reach an agreement in the region of your asking price—which is a realistic one—subject, of course, to the usual considerations of purchase: a full structural survey and so forth.'

He saw her eyes light up, and from the corner of his eye he was sure that her daughter's had done the same.

'Oh, that is *excellent*!' came Pauline's gracious response.

'Marvellous!' echoed her daughter.

Enthusiasm was in her voice. And relief too—Max could detect that.

It did not surprise him. Being forced to live here with the perpetually prickly Ellen could hardly be comfortable. He did not blame either mother or daughter for being eager to make new lives for themselves. Or even, he allowed, for having preferred to be abroad this last year. Hadn't he himself hightailed it from his stepfather's *taverna* the moment his poor mother had been finally laid to rest?

He pulled his mind away again. He did not want to remember his miserable childhood and downtrodden mother. Nor was he interested in the tense convolutions of the Mountford family either.

He set down his empty cup. 'Before I leave,' he said, 'I'll take a look around the gardens and the outbuildings to the rear. No, don't get up—' This to Chloe, who had started to stand. He smiled. 'My footwear is more suitable for the outdoors than yours,' he explained, glancing at her stylish high heels and not adding that he preferred to keep his own pace, and would rather not have her endless panegyrics about the charms of a property he had already decided would be his.

Though it was only prudent to check out the areas he had not yet seen, he did not envisage there being anything so dreadful as to make him change his mind.

He strode from the room, and as he shut the door behind him he heard animated conversation break out behind him. To his ears it sounded...*jubilant*. Well, his own mood was just as buoyant. Satisfaction filled him, and a warm, proprietorial sense of well-being. He glanced around the hallway—soon to be *his* hallway.

He paused in his stride. A family had lived here for generations. Emotion kicked in him. It was an emotion he had never felt before, and one that startled him with its presence—shocked him even more with his certainty about it. The words were in his head, shaping themselves, taking hold. Taking root.

And now it will be my home—for my family.

The family of his own that he'd never had...the family he *would* have.

A pang stabbed at him. If his poor mother had survived longer how he would have loved to bring her here—make a home for her here, safe from the harshness of her life, cosseting her in the luxury he could now afford to bestow upon her.

But I'll do that for your grandchildren—give them the happy upbringing you could not give me—and I'll feel you smile and be glad! I've come a long way—a long, long way—and now I've found the place I want to call my home. I'll find the right woman for me and bring her here.

Who that woman would be he didn't know, but she was out there somewhere. He just had to find her. Find her and bring her here.

Home.

He started to walk forward again, heading for the baize door that led through to the back section of the house. He would check it out, then go out into the courtyard area, take a look at the outbuildings before making his way around to the gardens and exploring them.

He was just walking down the passageway towards the back door when a voice from the open doorway to what he could see was a large stone-flagged kitchen stopped him.

'Mr Vasilikos! I need to speak to you!'

He halted, turning his head. Ellen Mountford was standing there and her face was stony. Very stony indeed. Annoyance tensed him. He did not want this. He wanted to get outside and complete his inspection of the place.

'What about?' he replied with steely politeness.

'It's very important.'

She backed away, indicating that he should step into the kitchen.

Impatiently Max strode in, taking in an impression of a large room with old-fashioned wooden cupboards, a long scrubbed wooden table, a flagstone floor and a vast old-fashioned range cooker along one wall. The warmth from the oven enveloped him, and there was, he realised, a cosy, comfortable, lived-in feel to the space. No top interior designer had been let loose in here, that was for sure—and he was glad of it.

He turned his attention to Ellen Mountford. She'd taken up a position on the far side of the kitchen table and her hands were pressed down over the back of a chair. Tension was in every line of her body, and her expression was both stony and determined.

He frowned. *Now what?*

'There's something you have to know!'

The words burst from her, and he realised with a deepening of his frown that she was in a state of extreme agitation and nervousness.

He levelled his gaze at her. She seemed to be steeling herself after her dramatic outburst. 'And that is…?' he prompted.

He watched her take a gulping breath. Her cheeks seemed pale now—as pale as chalk. Not a trace of the colour that had so unflatteringly rushed there whenever he'd looked at her before.

'Mr Vasilikos, there's no easy way to tell you this, and for that I'm sorry, but you've had a completely wasted journey. Whatever my stepmother has led you to believe, Haughton is not for sale. And it never will be!'

CHAPTER THREE

MAX STILLED. THEN deliberately he let his gaze rest on her. 'Perhaps,' he said, and he made no effort to make his voice sound anything less than the way he intended it to sound—quelling—'you might like to explain what you mean by that.'

Ellen swallowed, had to force herself to speak. To say what she *had* to say. 'I own a third of Haughton and I have no wish to sell.'

Somehow she'd got the words out—but her heart was thumping like a hammer inside her. Ever since she'd rushed from the dining room, emotions storming, she'd been trying to nerve herself to find Max Vasilikos, get him away from Pauline and Chloe and tell him what she had to tell him. And now she'd done it—and he was not, it was obvious, taking it kindly.

His expression had steeled, and the dark brows were snapping together now. For a moment Ellen quailed. Up till now Max Vasilikos had, she realised belatedly, been playing the role of courteous, amenable guest. Now he was very different. A tough, powerful businessman who was hearing something he did not want to hear.

As she'd delivered her bombshell something had flickered in Max's mind at what she'd said, but it wasn't relevant for the moment.

His gaze rested on her. 'Why not?'

He saw her swallow again.

'What relevance does that question have?'

Max's expression changed. A moment ago it had looked formidable. Now there was a cynical cast to it. 'Perhaps you are holding out for a higher price,' he said.

Ellen's lips pressed together. 'I don't wish to sell Haughton—and I shan't.'

He looked at her for a moment. He looked neither quelling nor cynical. He seemed to be studying her, but she suddenly had the feeling that he'd retreated behind a mask.

'You do realise, do you not, that as only part-owner of this property if any of the other part-owners wish to sell they have the legal right to force such a sale?'

There was no colour in her face. Her cheekbones had whitened. Something moved in her eyes. Some deep emotion. He saw her jaw tense, her knuckles whiten over the chair-back.

'That would take months. I'd drag it out as long as I could. No purchaser would want that kind of costly delay.'

She would make that delay as long as possible, fight as hard as possible. *I won't roll over and give in!*

She felt sick with tension. Max Vasilikos's gaze rested on her implacably. Then, abruptly, his expression changed. His long lashes dipped down over his deep, dark and entirely inscrutable eyes.

'Well, be that as it may, Miss Mountford, I intend to view the rest of the property while I am here.'

She saw his glance go around the kitchen again, in an approving fashion.

'This is very pleasing,' he said. 'It's been left in its original state and is all the better for it.'

Ellen blinked. To go from defying him to agreeing with

him confused her completely. 'My stepmother wasn't interested in doing up the kitchen quarters,' she said.

Max's eyes glinted. 'A lucky escape, then,' he said dryly.

There was a distinctly conspiratorial note to his voice, and Ellen's confusion deepened.

'You don't like the decor in the main house?' she heard herself saying, astonished. Surely property developers *loved* that full-blown interior-designed look?

Max smiled. 'Taste is subjective, and your stepmother's tastes are not mine. I prefer something less...contrived.'

'She's had it photographed for a posh interiors magazine!' Ellen exclaimed derisively, before she could stop herself.

'Yes, it would be ideal for such a publication,' he returned lightly. 'Tell me, is there anything left of the original furnishings and furniture?'

A bleak, empty look filled Ellen's face. 'Some of it was put up in the attics,' she said.

Any antiques or *objets d'art* of value that Pauline had not cared for had been sold—like the painting from the dining room and others she'd needed to dispose of so she and Chloe could go jaunting off on their expensive holidays.

'That's good to hear.' He nodded, making a mental note to have the attic contents checked at some point. There were art valuations to get done, too, before the final sales contract was signed.

For signed it would be. His eyes rested now on the female who was so obdurately standing in the way of his intentions. Whatever her reasons, he would set them aside. Somehow she would be brought to heel. In all his years of negotiation, one thing he'd learnt for sure—there was always a way to get a deal signed and sealed. *Always.*

He wanted this place. Wanted it badly. More than he

had ever thought to want any property... He wanted to make a home here.

He smiled again at the woman who thought so unwisely—so futilely!—to balk him of what he wanted. 'Well, I shall continue on my way, Miss Mountford. I'll see myself out—'

And he was gone, striding from the kitchen and down to the back door.

Ellen watched him go, her heart thumping heavily still, a feeling of sickness inside her. She heard the back door close as he went out. Words burned in her head, emotions churning.

Please let him leave! Leave and—and never come back!

Let him buy somewhere else—anywhere else. But leave me my home...oh, leave me my home!

Max stood in the shade of a tall beech tree overlooking the lake and took in the vista. It was good—all good. Everything about this place was good. He'd explored the outbuildings, realised they'd need work, but nothing too much, and mentally designated some of the old stables for his cars. He might keep some as stabling, too. He didn't ride, but maybe his children would like ponies one day.

He gave a half-laugh. Here he was, imagining children here before he'd even found the woman who would give them to him. Well, he'd have plenty of volunteers, that was for sure—not that he was keen on any of his current acquaintance. And his time with Tyla had been enjoyable, but their ways had parted. No, the woman he would bring here as his bride would be quite, quite different from the self-absorbed, vanity-driven film star bent on storming Hollywood. His chosen bride would be someone who would love this place as he would come to love it—love *him*, love their children...

He shook his head to clear his thoughts—he was running ahead of himself! First he had to buy this place. He frowned. The tripartite ownership structure should have been disclosed to him at the outset, not be delivered by bombshell. His frown deepened.

Well, that was a problem to ponder for later. Right now, he wanted to finish exploring the grounds beyond the formal gardens surrounding the house. He could see that a pathway ran through the long, unmown grass beside the sheltering woodland, around the perimeter of the reed-edged lake. He would walk along it and take a look at what he could see was a little folly on the far side.

My kids would love playing there—and we'd have picnics there in the summer. Maybe barbecues in the evening. Maybe swimming in the lake? I'll get a pool put in as well, of course—probably indoors, with a glass roof, given the English climate...

His thoughts ran on as he emerged from the shelter of the woodland. Then abruptly they cleared. He stared. There was someone over by the folly, leaning against the stonework. He watched as she straightened, and then set off along the path towards him. She was in running gear, he could see that from this distance, but not who it was. He frowned. If neighbours had got into the habit of using the place as a running track he'd better know about it—

Slowly he walked forward on an interception course. But as the runner approached him he felt the breath leave his body. Incredulity scissored through him.

It couldn't be! It just *couldn't*!

It could *not* be the sad, overweight, badly dressed frumpy female he'd pitied—impossible for it to be Ellen Mountford. Just *impossible*.

But it *was* her.

As the figure drew closer, its long, loping gait effortless and confident, his eyes were nailed to it. Tall, long-legged, with dark hair streaming behind like a flag, and a body…a body that was a total knockout—

It was impossible to tear his stunned gaze from her. From her strong, lithe body, perfectly contoured in a sports bra that moulded generous breasts, exposing not an inch of fat over bare, taut-waisted abs, with matching running shorts that hugged sleek hips, exposing the full length of her honed, toned quads.

Thee mou, she wasn't fat—she was *fit*. In both senses of the word! Fit and fabulous!

Every thought about her completely rearranged itself in his head. He could not take his eyes from her. He was in shock—and also something very different from shock. Something that sent the blood surging in his body.

Thanks to the sight of hers…

Greek words escaped his lips. Something about not believing his eyes, his senses, and something that was extreme appreciation of her fantastic physique. Then another thought was uppermost. *How did she hide that body from me?* At not one single point had there been the slightest indication of what she was hiding—and he hadn't noticed. Not for a moment, not for an instant! How had she done it?

But he knew—she'd done it by disguising that fantastic, honed, sleek, fit body of hers in those appalling clothes. In that unspeakable purple tracksuit that had turned her into some kind of inflated dummy, and that shapeless, ill-fitting grey skirt and even more shapeless and ill-fitting white blouse whose tightness of sleeve had had nothing whatsoever to do with her arms being fat—but had simply been because her biceps and triceps were honed, compacted muscle. He could see that now, as she approached more closely.

He stepped out from amongst the trees. 'Hello, there,' he said.

His greeting was affable, and pleasantly voiced, and it stopped her dead in her tracks as if a concrete block had dropped down in front of her from the sky.

Something that was partly a shriek of shock, partly a gasp of air escaped from Ellen. She stared, aghast—Max Vasilikos was the last person she wanted to see!

The emotional stress of the day, the agitation from having had to commandeer him and tell him she would never agree to sell her share of Haughton, had overset her so much that the moment he'd closed the back door behind him she'd headed upstairs to change into her running gear. She'd had to get out of the house. Had to work off the stress and tension and the biting anxiety. A long, hard run would help.

She'd set off on the long route, down the drive and looping back through the woods, then into a field and back into the grounds, taking a breather by the folly before setting off around the lake, hoping against hope that by the time she got back to the house he and his flash car would have gone.

Instead here he was, appearing in front of her out of nowhere like the demon king in a pantomime!

A demon king in whose eyes was an expression that sent a wave of excruciating colour flooding through her.

She was agonisingly aware of her skimpy, revealing attire. Mercilessly revealing her muscular body. She lifted her chin, desperately fighting back her reaction. She would *not* be put out of countenance by him seeing her like this any more than she had been when he'd seen her plonked beside Chloe, and the dreadful contrast she'd made to her stepsister. It was a comparison that was hitting him again—she could see it as his eyes swept over her appraisingly.

'I could see you were totally different from Chloe—but not like *this*!' he exclaimed. 'You couldn't be more unalike—even sharing a surname, you'd never be taken for sisters in a thousand years.'

He shook his head in disbelief. Missing completely the sudden look of pain at his words in her eyes. Then he was speaking again.

'I'm sorry—I shouldn't be delaying you. Your muscles will seize up.' He started to walk forward in the direction of the house, his pace rapid, with long strides. 'Look,' he went on, 'keep going—but slow down to a jog so we can talk.'

He moved to one side of the path. She started up again, conscious that her heart was pounding far more quickly than the exertion of her run required. She found herself blinking. The casual cruelty of what he'd just said reverberated in her, but she must not let it show. With an effort, and still burningly conscious of her skimpy attire and perspiring body, of her hair held back only by a wide sweatband, of being bereft of the glasses she'd been wearing over lunch, she loped beside him.

'What about?' she returned. The thought came to her that maybe she could use this wretched encounter to convince him that there really was no point in his staying any longer—that buying Haughton was off the menu for him.

'I'm making an offer for this place,' he said, glancing at her. 'It will be near the asking price...' He trailed off.

Dismay lanced through her. 'I still don't want to sell my share,' she replied grittily.

'Your third...' Max didn't take his eyes from her '...will be well over a million pounds...'

'I don't care what it is. Mr Vasilikos—please understand—my share is not for sale at any price. I don't want to sell.'

'Why not?' His brows snapped together.

'What do you mean, why not?' she riposted. 'My reasons are my own—I don't want to sell.' She turned her face, making herself look at him. 'That's all there is to it. And I'll make it as hard as I possibly can for you to complete a sale. I'll fight it to the bitter end!'

Vehemence broke through in her voice and she could see it register with him. His eyebrows rose, and she knew he was about to say something—but she didn't want to hear. Didn't want to do anything but get away from him. Get back to the house, the sanctuary of her bedroom. Throw herself down on the bed and weep and weep. For what she feared most in the world would come true if this man went through with his threat!

She couldn't bear it—she just couldn't. She couldn't bear to lose her home. The place she loved most in all the world. *She couldn't bear it*.

With a burst of speed she shot forward, leaving him behind. Leaving behind Max Vasilikos, the man who wanted to wrench her home from her.

As he watched her power forward, accelerating away, Max let her go. But when she disappeared from sight across the lawns that crossed the front of the house his thoughts were full.

Why was Ellen Mountford so set on making difficulties for him? And why were his eyes following her fantastic figure until she was totally beyond his view? And why was he then regretting that she was beyond it?

The question was suddenly stronger in his head, knocking aside his concern about an easy purchase of the place he intended to buy, whatever obstacles one of its owners might put in his path.

* * *

When he reached the house Max went in search of his hostess. She was in the drawing room with her daughter, and both greeted him effusively, starting to ask him about his tour of the outbuildings and the grounds.

But he cut immediately to the chase.

'Why was I not informed of the ownership structure of this property?' he asked.

His voice was level, but there was a note in it that anyone who'd ever been in commercial negotiations with him would have taken as a warning not to try and outmanoeuvre him or prevaricate.

'Your stepdaughter apprised me of the facts after lunch,' he went on.

He kept his level gaze on Pauline. Beside her on the sofa, Chloe Mountford gave a little choke. An angry one. But her mother threw her a silencing look. Then she turned her face towards Max. She gave a little sigh.

'Oh, dear, what has the poor girl told you, Mr Vasilikos?' There was a note of apprehension in her voice.

'That she does not wish to sell her share,' he replied bluntly. 'And that she is prepared to force you to resort to legal measures to make her do so. Which will, as you must be aware, be both costly and time-consuming.'

Pauline Mountford's be-ringed fingers wound into each other. 'I'm so sorry, Mr Vasilikos, that you have been exposed to…well, to this, unfortunate development. I had hoped we could reach a happy conclusion between ourselves and—'

Max cut across her, his tone decisive. 'I make no bones that I want to buy this place,' he said. 'But I don't want problems and I don't want delays.'

'We don't either!' agreed Chloe promptly. 'Mummy, we've just *got* to stop Ellen ruining everything.'

He looked at the pair of them. 'Do you know what is behind her reluctance to sell?'

Pauline sighed again, her face shadowing. 'I believe,' she said slowly, 'that she is a very *unhappy* young woman. Poor Ellen has always found it very...*difficult*...to have us here.'

'She's hated us from the start,' Chloe said tightly. 'She's never made us welcome.'

Pauline sighed once more. 'Alas, I'm afraid it's true. She was at a difficult age when Edward married me. And I fear it is all too common, sadly, for a daughter who has previously had the undivided attention of her father not to allow that he might seek to find happiness with someone else. I did my best...' she sighed again '...and so did poor little Chloe—you did, darling, didn't you? You made every effort to be friends, wanted her so much to be your new sister! But, well... I do not wish to speak ill of Ellen, but nothing—absolutely nothing that we did—could please her. She was, I fear, set on resenting us. It upset her father dreadfully. Too late, he realised how much he'd spoiled her, made her possessive and clinging. *He* could control her a little, though not a great deal, but now that he is gone...' A little sob escaped her. 'Well, she has become as you see her.'

'She never goes *anywhere*!' Chloe exclaimed. 'She just buries herself here all year round.'

Pauline nodded. 'Sadly, that is true. She has her little teaching job at her old school—which in itself surely cannot be advisable, for it keeps her horizons from widening—but that is all she has. She has no social life—she rejects all my attempts to...to involve her!' She levelled her eyes at Max. 'I want nothing but the best for her. If Haughton holds too many memories for *me* to bear, for her

I am sure it is much, much worse. Doting on her father as she did was not emotionally healthy for a young woman...'

Max frowned. 'Did she not want her father to include you in his will? Neither you nor her stepsister?' he asked.

Was that the root of the matter? That Ellen Mountford had wanted everything her father had left to go to *her*, cutting out his second wife and stepdaughter completely?

'That may be so, alas,' confirmed Pauline. 'My poor Edward quite thought of Chloe as his own daughter—she took his name, as you know. Perhaps that led to some... well, perhaps some jealousy on Ellen's part? Possessive as she was about her father...'

Memory stung in Max's head. His mother might have taken his stepfather's name, but he—the nameless, father-less bastard she had borne—had never been permitted to.

Pauline was speaking again, and he drew his mind back to the present.

'You must not think, Mr Vasilikos, that Edward has been in any way unfair to Ellen. Oh, he might have taken steps to ensure that Chloe and myself were taken care of financially, by way of including us in the ownership of this house, but Ellen was left everything else. And my hus-band...' she gave a sigh '...was a very wealthy man, with a substantial stock portfolio and other assets.' She took a little breath. 'Our share of this house, Mr Vasilikos, is all we have, Chloe and I, so I'm sure you will understand why, as well as finding being here without Edward too pain-ful, we must sell. And,' she pointed out, 'of course Ellen's share of the sale price will be handsome.'

Max absorbed the information, keeping his expression impassive. What Pauline Mountford said rang all too true. That open bristling that he had seen from Ellen Mountford in her stepmother's company—

He got to his feet. There was nothing more to be

achieved here right now. 'Well, I will leave it with you. See what you can do to change Ellen's mind and attitude.'

He smiled down at them—the courteous, impersonal smile he used to keep others well-disposed towards him for his own benefit.

Ten minutes later he was heading off down the drive, his glance going to either side, taking in one last sweep of the place. For now. His expression tightened. Whatever was necessary to induce Ellen Mountford to abandon her objection to selling her share of this place would, he determined as he turned out through the drawn-back iron gates on to the road, be done.

With or without her co-operation.

CHAPTER FOUR

MAX HEARD OUT his legal advisor, then drummed his fingers on the polished surface of his mahogany desk. Forcing a sale would indeed be time-consuming, and he wanted to take possession without delay—before summer was over. Which meant getting Ellen Mountford to drop her objections.

He gave a rasp of exasperation, swivelling moodily in his leather chair, his dark eyes baleful. There had been no good news from Pauline Mountford, and he strongly suspected there would not be. If Ellen was as entrenched in her hostile view of her stepmother as she seemed to be, then Pauline was doubtless the last person capable of changing her stepdaughter's mind.

But *he* might be able to.

An idea was forming in his head—he could feel it. An idea to make her *want* to sell up.

Chloe Mountford's voice echoed in his memory. *'She never goes anywhere—she just buries herself here all year round!'*

His eyes glinted. Maybe that was the key that would start to unlock the problem.

Impulsively he summoned his PA. 'Tell me, have I got any particularly glitzy social events coming up soon here in London?' he asked her.

Five minutes later he had his answer—and had made his decision. He sat back in his chair, long legs extended, a smile of satisfaction playing around his mouth. Oh, yes, he'd made his decision, all right. And Ellen herself had given him the way to convince her of it.

That mention she'd made of her surprising involvement in a charity for giving city children a countryside holiday under canvas. That would do nicely. Very nicely. His plan would help him lever Ellen Mountford out of his way—he was sure of it.

And as he settled down to work again, in a much better frame of mind, he became aware that he was sure of something else as well. That, of all things, he was looking forward to seeing her again—and making an end, once and for all, to all that nonsense of hers about looking the unappealing way she did.

I've seen her real body—her goddess body!—and now I want to see her face look just as good as her figure.

The smile played around his mouth once more, and the gleam in his eyes was speculative. Anticipatory.

And for a moment—just a moment—the prospect of finding a way to remove Ellen Mountford's objections to selling him the house he wanted to buy was not uppermost in his mind.

How good could she look? How good could she really look?

The glint came into his eye again. He wanted to find out.

Ellen turned off the ignition and got out. Her car needed a service, but she couldn't afford it. Her salary was wiped out simply paying for the essentials at Haughton—from council tax to electricity bills—and, of course, for the *in*-essentials. Such as the weekly deliveries of hothouse flowers from the local florist, and Pauline and Chloe's regular visits to the local county town for their endless hair and beauty appointments. Their other extravagances—replenishing their wardrobes, their lavish social life and their foreign jaunts to luxury destinations and five-star hotels—were all funded by the stripping out of anything of value still left in the house, from paintings to *objets d'art*.

She hefted out a pile of schoolbooks, becoming aware of the sound of a vehicle approaching along the drive. As the sleek, powerful car turned into the courtyard dismay flooded through her. She'd hoped so much that Max Vasilikos had decided to buy somewhere else and abandoned his attentions to Haughton. Pauline and Chloe had finally lapsed into giving her the silent treatment, after having harangued her repeatedly about her stubbornness in refusing to do what they wanted her to do. Now they had taken themselves off again on yet another pricey jaunt, to a five-star hotel in Marbella while Ellen was just about to begin her school holidays.

Their departure had given Ellen cause for hope that Max Vasilikos had withdrawn his offer—in vain, it seemed. She watched him approach with a sinking heart—and also a quite different reaction that she tried to quash and failed utterly to do so. She gulped silently as he walked up to her, his handmade suit sheathing his powerful frame like a smooth, sleek glove. The dark eyes in his strong-featured face were levelled down at her. She felt her pulse leap.

It's just because I don't want him here. I don't want him going on at me to sell Haughton to him!

That was the reason for the sudden quickening of her breathing—the *only* reason she told herself urgently. The only reason she would allow…could possibly allow—

'Good afternoon, Miss Mountford,' he said. His voice

was deep, and there was a hint of a curve at the corner of his sculpted mouth.

'What are you doing back here again?' she demanded. It was safer to sound antagonistic. Much safer.

Safer than standing here gazing gormlessly at him in all his incredible masculinity and gorgeousness. Feeling my heart thumping like an idiot and going red as a beet-root again!

Her hostile demand met with no bristling. Just the opposite. 'I wanted to see the rhododendrons,' Max returned blandly. 'They are indeed magnificent.' He paused, smiling his courteous social smile. 'Aren't you going to invite me in?' he said.

She glowered at him from behind her spectacles, her thick eyebrows forming that monobrow as she did so, and she was once again, he noted with displeasure, wearing the unspeakable baggy tracksuit that totally concealed her glorious body. Mentally, he earmarked it for the bonfire.

'Would it stop you if I didn't?' she glowered again.

'I doubt it,' he said, and then reached forward to remove half of the tottering tower of schoolbooks from her arms. 'After you,' he said, nodding at the kitchen door.

She cast him a burning look, refusing to say thank you for relieving her of much of her burden, and stomped indoors, dumping her load on the kitchen table. He deposited his share next to it.

'I hope you don't have to get all these marked for tomorrow,' he observed.

She shook her head. 'By the start of next term,' she said shortly.

'You've broken up?' enquired Max in a conversational tone. He knew perfectly well she had, as he'd had her term dates checked, and had timed his visit here accordingly.

'Today,' she said. She looked across at him. He seemed

taller than ever in the kitchen, large though the space was. But then, she knew a man like Max Vasilikos could effortlessly dominate any space he occupied. 'You've wasted your journey,' she said bluntly. 'Pauline and Chloe left for Marbella yesterday.'

'Did they?' he returned carelessly. 'I'm not here to see them.'

Ellen lifted her eyes to him, glaring. 'Mr Vasilikos, *please* don't go on at me any more! Can't you just accept I don't want to sell Haughton?'

'I'm not here to talk about Haughton. I'm here to help your charity.'

Astonishment showed in her face and he went on smoothly.

'I'm confident I can increase your funding, enabling you to run camps more frequently. A national children's charity I support—for advantageous tax reasons—takes on new projects regularly. Yours I'm sure would be ideal for it.'

She was staring at him with an expression of extreme suspicion. 'Why would you do that?' she demanded. 'Do you think it will change my mind about not selling Haughton?'

'Of course not,' he returned equably. 'My only concern is the deprived children. Is that not yours, too?' he countered, with precise gentleness and a bland look in his eye.

She took a breath. 'Well, if you can get us more funding we won't say no,' she managed to get out. There was something about the way he was casting a long look at her that threatened to bring the colour rushing to her cheeks.

'Good,' Max said. Then blithely went on. 'The thing is, though, you'll need to come up to London with me today— make a personal presentation. Time is very short—they have to spend the last of this year's money before the end of the financial year coming up.'

He was hustling her, he knew, and it was deliberate—he wanted to give her no excuse to get out of this.

'What?' Consternation filled Ellen's voice. 'Impossible!'

'No, it's quite all right—it won't inconvenience me at all,' said Max in a smooth voice, deliberately misunderstanding the cause of her objection. He glanced at his watch. 'You go off and get ready while I take another stroll around the gardens—admire those rhododendrons!' He smiled at her, completely ignoring the fact that her mouth was opening to object yet again. 'I'll give you twenty minutes,' he said blandly, and was gone.

Ellen stared after him, open-mouthed. Consternation was tumbling around inside her—shot through with aftershock. Slowly she gathered her composure back, by dint of piling her marking neatly into class rows. Did Max Vasilikos *really* imagine she'd waltz off with him to London for the day, to pitch for more funding for her camping project?

More money would be really helpful right now. We could double the numbers at the half-term session—buy more tents and sleeping bags. Run another week in the summer holidays...

The problem was, though, she thought, as she descended to earth with a bump, that in order to get her hands on the funding she'd have to sit next to Max Vasilikos all the way to London, enclosed in his car. Would she be a captive audience for his determination to wrest Haughton from her?

But the reverse will be true, too. If he goes on at me, then he'll also have to listen to me telling him I'm never going to agree to sell. Never!

Yes, that was the way to think—and *not* about the way the image of Max Vasilikos, seen again now in all its devastating reality, was busy burning itself into her retinas and making her heart beat faster. Because what possible point was there in her pulse quickening? If even ordinary men looked right past her, wanting only to look at Chloe, then to a man like Max Vasilikos, who romanced film stars, she must be completely invisible.

In a way, that actually made it easier. Easier for her to change into something more suitable for London—the well-worn dark grey suit and white blouse that she donned for parents' evenings and school functions, and sturdy, comfortable lace-ups, before confining her unruly hair into a lumpy bun—and then heading back out into the courtyard.

Max Vasilikos was already behind the wheel of his monstrous beast of a car, and he leant across to open the passenger door. She got into the low-slung seat awkwardly, feeling suddenly that despite being invisible to him, as she knew she was, *he* was very, very visible to her.

And very close.

With a shake of her head, to clear her stupid thoughts, she fastened her seat belt as he set off with a throaty growl of the engine. Oh, Lord, was she insane to head off with him like this? All the way to London in the all too close confines of his car? She sat back tensely, fingers clutching the handbag in her lap.

'So, tell me more about this charity of yours,' Max invited as he turned out of the drive on to the narrow country lane beyond. He wanted to set her at ease, not have her sitting there tense as a board.

Gratefully Ellen answered, explaining how she and a fellow teacher had started it two years ago. She also told him about their hopes for expansion, which more funding would definitely enable.

Max continued to ask questions that drew her out more, and as she talked he could see she was gradually starting to relax. The enthusiasm he'd seen so briefly over lunch the other day was coming through again, and she was becoming animated as she spoke. He moved the subject on from the practicalities of the venture to some of its underlying issues.

'How do you find the children respond to the camping?' he asked.

'Usually very well,' she replied. 'They all have to do chores, share the work, and most discover grit and strength in themselves—a determination to achieve goals that will, we hope, enable them to transfer those lessons to their future and make something of themselves, despite their disadvantaged and often troubled backgrounds.'

She became aware that Max was looking at her, a revealing expression on his face.

'Reminds me of myself,' he said. 'When my mother died I had to make my own way in the world—and it definitely took grit and strength and determination. Starting with nothing and building myself up from scratch.'

She glanced at him curiously. 'You weren't born to all this, then?' she asked, indicating the luxury car they were sitting in.

He gave a short, humourless laugh. 'I worked five years on building sites to make enough to buy a ruin that I then spent two years restoring myself and selling on. I took the profit to do the same again and again, until I'd bootstrapped my way up to where I am now,' he told her. His sideways glance was caustic, but there was a trace of mordant humour in it. 'Does that improve your opinion of me at all?' he posed.

She swallowed. She would have to give him his due—anything else would be unfair, however unwelcome he was in her life. 'I respect you for all the hard work you've obviously had to put in to make yourself rich. My only objection to you, Mr Vasilikos, is that you want to buy Haughton and I don't want to sell it to you.'

Belatedly she realised that she herself had brought the subject back to what she did *not* want to discuss—selling her home. But to her relief he did not respond in kind.

'Tell me, how old were you when your mother died?' he asked instead.

Her eyes widened and she stared at him, wondering why he was asking such a personal, intrusive question. Then something he'd said chimed in her head. '*When my mother died...*'

'Fifteen,' she answered. 'She was killed in a head-on car crash.'

'I was the same age when mine died,' Max said.

His voice was neutral, but it did not deceive Ellen.

'She died of lung disease.' There was a slight pause. 'It's not a good age to lose a parent,' he said.

'When *is*?' returned Ellen quietly. It was strange to think of this man, from so utterly different a world from her, having that same tragedy in her life as she did. To think that they, who were so utterly, glaringly unalike, had that in common.

'Indeed.'

He was silent a moment, manoeuvring the car effortlessly around a tight bend, accelerating out of it. When he spoke again it was to return to the subject of the charity and what financial constraints further funding might alleviate.

Ellen was relieved—talking about such deeply felt emotional issues with this man was...*strange*. Yet even though he'd changed the subject, reverted to his smooth, urbane social manner, she felt a curious sense of having somehow touched a chord in him, drawn by the mutual personal tragedy in their lives.

They joined the motorway soon after, and Max could let the car really rip, cruising down the fast lane as if merely out for a stroll. His mind cruised too. Ellen Mountford was definitely losing that excruciating self-consciousness that had dominated her reaction to him up till now, and he was glad of it. It helped that they could talk without looking at each other, and that he had the road to focus on. It seemed to take some of the pressure off her. But there was more to it than that, he was aware. That oh-so-brief mention of his mother—and hers—had been like a flicker of real communication between them. Something that could not have happened between two mere social acquaintances.

He frowned. *Do I want that? Do I want any real communication with her? Why should I? She is merely someone standing in the way of what I am determined to achieve— ownership of a house I want to live in myself. And bringing her up to London is merely the means to that end. Nothing more than that.*

His expression lightened. Of course there was one other reason for bringing Ellen Mountford to London with him. He was all too conscious of that too.

I want to see what she can really look like—when she makes the most of herself instead of the least!

And he would want to know that, he realised, even if she'd had absolutely nothing to do with blocking his way to the house he wanted to possess. Curiosity was mounting within him about Ellen Mountford for herself—not for her house. Across his retinas flickered the recalled image of her in her running gear, showing off that fantastic figure. Which was more than could be said for what she was wearing now—it was no better than the tracksuit. A heavy, badly cut suit and the same ill-fitting white blouse, and those ugly lace-up shoes, which were doing absolutely nothing for her.

A smile flickered about his mouth. What he had in mind for her to wear tonight was quite different…

He dragged his thoughts away and went back into making easy-going conversation with her, taking the opportunity of their passing Windsor Castle to ask something about the British Royal Family. She answered readily enough, and he asked another question to keep her talking.

It dawned on him that she wasn't actually shy at all. Away from her stepmother and stepsister she was noticeably more voluble. Animation lifted her features, lighting up her tawny eyes even behind the concealing lenses of her unflattering glasses, and helping to detract from that damn monobrow of hers which made her look as if she was always frowning. Now that he was seeing her again, he realised, it was clear that actually she didn't look nearly as morosely forbidding as she had when in the company of her stepmother and sister.

So, if she wasn't shy, why the total lack of personal grooming? Why look as dire as she did, considering that she could look so much better?

The question circled in his head as they approached London and headed for the West End, eventually drawing up at his hotel in Piccadilly. His passenger looked at him in surprise.

'I thought we were going to the charity's headquarters,' she said, 'so I can make my pitch for funding?'

Max smiled at her. 'Not exactly,' he said, getting out of the car.

A doorman was opening her door, and as she got out, seeing Max toss the keys to the valet parker, Ellen was suddenly conscious of her plain, dowdy appearance. Utterly unworthy of such a smart hotel—or for keeping company with a man like Max.

'This way,' he said blandly, ushering her inside and guiding her across the swish lobby towards a bank of lifts.

They whooshed upwards, and when they emerged she saw with a frown that they were on the penthouse floor and Max was leading her into one of the suites. She gazed around, confused, taking in the lavish decor of a vast lounge and huge windows overlooking St James's Park. Max was speaking.

'I have not been entirely comprehensive in what I've told you,' he said, his voice bland. He quirked one eyebrow. 'You don't make your pitch now—you make it tonight.' His smile deepened. 'At the ball.'

Ellen stared. 'Ball?' she echoed blankly.

'Yes,' said Max, in that same smooth, urbane manner. 'The annual fundraising ball the charity always holds at this hotel. You'll be sitting on my table, and so will one of the charity's directors. You can have a little chat then, tell him about the camping holidays and what funds you need to expand them.'

Ellen felt the floor disappear from under her. 'I *cannot* go to a *ball*!' she said. The man was mad—completely mad!

'Ah, well,' said Max, his voice as smooth as cream, his smile as rich as butter, 'in that I have to say you are quite, quite mistaken.'

CHAPTER FIVE

ELLEN TOOK A BREATH. Or tried to. There didn't seem to be any breath left in her body because her lungs seemed to be caught in a vice. Horror drenched her—horror at the very thought of being paraded at a *ball* with Max Vasilikos. Her mortification would be exquisite, unbearable—hideous! As hideous as her appearance would be. She felt the colour drain from her cheeks and there was a sick feeling in her stomach.

Max was continuing to speak, still in that same blandly smooth way. 'If you're worried because you have nothing to wear, don't be. I'll have some suitable gowns delivered and you can make your choice. We'll have lunch first, and then afterwards I'll leave you in the hands of the stylists I've booked—it's all arranged. Now...' His tone changed and he walked to the house phone on the desk at the side of the room. 'Time for that lunch. Would you like a pre-prandial drink? You look somewhat pale.'

In fact she looked like a dish of curds and whey, he decided, and without waiting for an answer crossed to the drinks cabinet and found a bottle of sherry, pouring her a generous measure.

'Drink up,' he said cheerfully.

She took it with nerveless fingers but did not drink. Instead she made her voice work, though it sounded like creaky hinges. 'Mr Vasilikos, I cannot possibly go through with this! It's very…kind…' she almost choked on the word '…of you, but…but…no, I can't. It's out of the question. Impossible. Unthinkable.' She swallowed. Made herself look at him. 'Unthinkable,' she said again, trying desperately to put a note of finality into her strangled voice.

It did not work. He simply gave her a straight look. She'd reverted, he could see, to having that grim expression on her face she'd had when he'd gone to Haughton to view it. It didn't suit her—beetling her monobrow and pulling heavily at her features.

'Why?' He gave her an encouraging smile. 'You'll enjoy it, I promise you.'

She swallowed again. 'I'm *not*, Mr Vasilikos, a party animal.' There was strain in her voice, as if she were forcing herself to speak. 'I think that's pretty obvious.'

He was undeterred. 'It will do you good,' he said blandly.

A knock on the door diverted him and he went to open it. Lunch had arrived.

'Come and sit down,' invited Max, and gestured to the table once all the food had been laid out for them and the servers had departed.

Involuntarily, Ellen felt hungry suddenly. She also realised she must have gulped down half the sherry, for there was a taste of alcohol in her throat. She'd better eat something now…

I'll eat lunch, then head off to the station and get home. Maybe if I write to the charity director he'll consider my application anyway.

Because doing what Max was so ludicrously suggesting was out of the question—just totally out of the question.

Thank God he hadn't mentioned me going to the ball in front of Chloe. She'd have had a field day, sneering and mocking me. Laughing like a hyena at the thought of me dressed up for an evening with Max Vasilikos!

Cold snaked down her spine as she made a start on her meal. It was delicious, she noticed absently—a seafood terrine with a saffron sauce, and keeping warm an entrée of lamb fillet. Hunger spiked in her and she tucked in. From the other end of the table Max glanced at her. It was good, he realised, to see a woman eating well. Not that it would put any fat on her—he knew that now. Not with a toned, sleek body like hers. Memory leapt in his head at just how toned and sleek her body was, and how it was that he'd discovered the amazing truth about this woman he'd crassly assumed was overweight.

'Did you go running this morning?' he heard himself enquire.

She looked up. 'I run every morning,' she said. 'Plus I use the school gym and the pool. Taking Games lessons also keeps me pretty active.'

'Hockey?' Max asked interestedly.

She shook her head. 'Lacrosse. A much better game!' There was a note of enthusiasm in her voice that even her dismay at Max Vasilikos's absurd notion of taking her to a ball—a *ball*, for heaven's sake!—could not squash.

Well, she wouldn't be going to any ball—with or without him, tonight or any other night—so there was no point worrying about it. She would just put it out of her head, enjoy this delicious lunch, and then head for the station. Maybe she'd look in at the Natural History Museum in South Kensington, get some more ideas for her Geography classes, pick up some learning material for her pupils. Yes, that was what she would do.

Relaxing slightly at the realisation that of *course* Max Vasilikos couldn't make her go to this ridiculous ball of his, she heard him asking, 'Isn't lacrosse somewhat violent?' He frowned.

She shook her head again. 'You're thinking of men's lacrosse. That can be vicious! But then so can men's hockey. Girls play a gentler game. But it's fast and furious for all that. I've always loved it. Nothing to beat it.' There was open enthusiasm in her voice now.

'Were you in the team when you were at school?' Max asked.

It was good to hear her speak without that note of almost panic in her voice that had been there as she'd reacted to his mention of the evening's ball, and he knew it was necessary for him to back off for a while, let her calm down again. Her forbidding expression was ebbing, too, and that *had* to be good.

Besides, it was, he realised, something of a pleasant novelty to be lunching with a female in his private suite and not have her endlessly making doe eyes at him, batting her eyelashes, trying to flirt and get his attention. With Ellen there was no such tedious predictability. Instead it was refreshing to talk to a woman about keeping fit, exercise and sport—all of which he enjoyed robustly himself. And she was clearly in her element on such subjects, knowledgeable and confident.

She nodded, then answered him. 'On the wing—loads of running there.'

He glanced at her speculatively. 'What about Chloe? Was she sporty?'

He knew perfectly well she wouldn't have been, but he wanted to hear what Ellen would say about the stepsister she so glaringly resented. Would she despise her for not being in the team?

A tight look had formed in Ellen's eyes. 'Chloe wasn't in the sporty crowd,' she said.

Max picked his next words with deliberate care. 'It must have been difficult for her, joining a new school after her mother married your father. She must have looked to you to help her fit in.'

Ellen's expression froze. Memory pushed into her head. Vivid and painful.

Chloe, with her long blonde tresses, her supercilious air of sophistication and her worldly experience of boys and smoking and alcohol and fashion and music and make-up, had been instantly accepted into a bitchy, cliquey set of girls just like her, effortlessly becoming the meanest of the mean girls, sneering at everyone else. Sneering most of all at her hulking, clumping, games-loving stepsister, who'd so stupidly tried to befriend her initially, when she'd actually believed that her father's remarriage might bring him happiness instead of misery and ruin.

Max's eyes rested on Ellen, seeing her expression close up. Had he hit home? he wondered. He hoped so—because it was for her own good, after all, getting her to face up to what was keeping her trapped in the bitter, resentful, narrow life she led, refusing to move on from the past.

She has to let go of her resentment against her stepfamily, stop using her share of their inheritance as a weapon against them. Stop clinging to the past instead of moving into the future. I need to bring her out of herself. Show her the world beyond the narrow confines she's locked herself into—let her embrace it...enjoy it.

And what could be more enjoyable than a ball? A glittering, lavish affair that she might enjoy if only she would give herself a chance to do so! But for now he would not press her. For now he just wanted to keep her in this unselfconscious, relaxed zone. So he didn't wait for an answer to his pointed comment about Chloe, but turned the subject back to an easier topic that she clearly found less uncomfortable.

'What kind of workout routine do you do?' he asked. 'You must use weights, I take it?'

To his surprise she flushed that unflattering red that he'd seen all too frequently on his first visit to Haughton.

'That's pretty obvious, isn't it?' she mumbled, knowing he'd have spotted her developed muscle tone—so mercilessly mocked by Chloe, who jibed at her for being more like a man than a woman—when he'd seen her in running gear. 'But I'm good at them and I enjoy it.'

Was there a defensive note to her voice—defiance, even? If so, Max wondered why. She obviously had a fantastic physique—he'd seen that for himself, and had very much enjoyed doing so! But she was speaking again now, and he drew his mind back from that tantalising vision of her fabulous body when she'd been out running.

'I balance weights with cardio work, obviously, but I'd rather run than cycle. Especially since it's such a joy to run in the grounds at home—' She broke off, a shadow in her eyes. Those glorious early-morning runs she loved to take would become a thing of the past if Haughton were wrenched from her...

'What about rowing?' Max asked, cutting across her anguished thoughts. 'That's a good combo of cardio and strength work. It's my favourite, I admit. Though only on a machine.' He gave a rueful smile. 'When I'm on the water I'd rather swim, sail or windsurf.'

She made herself smile. 'Well, you've got the weather for that in Greece!' she riposted lightly, glad to be away from the subject of her overdeveloped muscles, which so embarrassed her. She knew she was being stupid, feeling self-conscious about it with a man who couldn't care less what she looked like as a woman. Inevitably she was invisible to him in that respect. Much less stressful to blank all that and just talk to him as she'd been doing, about sport and exercise, without any connotations about the impact on her appearance.

'It must be great not to need a wetsuit,' she said enviously.

'Agreed.' Max smiled, glad that he was getting her to relax again.

Deliberately he kept the conversation going along convivial lines, asking her about her experiences in water sport, which seemed to be mainly focussed on school trips to the Solent—definitely wetsuits required. Equally deliberately he waxed lyrical about how enjoyable it was to pursue water sports in warmer climes, recommending several spots he knew well. He wanted to open her mind to the possibilities of enjoying the wider world—once she had freed herself from the self-inflicted confines of her past, stopped clinging to the house he wanted her to let go of.

But with the arrival of the dessert course he steered the conversation back to the reason for her presence here.

As they helped themselves to *tarte au citron* Max was pleased to see Ellen tucking in with obvious enjoyment. *It's a sensual pleasure, enjoying food.* The thought was in his head before he could stop it. And the corollary that went with it. *There are more sensual pleasures than food for her to enjoy...*

The words hovered in his head, but he put them firmly aside. They were inappropriate. All he was doing was introducing her to the delights that could be hers if she embraced the world instead of hiding away from it.

Starting tonight.

He pushed his empty plate away and glanced at his watch. 'We've time for coffee, then a team of stylists are arriving and I'll leave you to them.' He smiled at Ellen.

Her fork promptly clattered to the plate. She was look-ing at him, her former ease vanished, her expression now one of panic. Panic that changed to a kind of gritty stoni-ness. He'd seen that look before, and knew it meant she was locking herself down into herself again.

She began to speak, her voice as tight as her expression as she bit the words out. 'Mr Vasilikos—look, I'm sure you mean well, in your own way, but I really, *really* don't want to go to this ball tonight! It would be…' she swal-lowed '…horrendous.'

He levelled his gaze at her. 'Why?' he demanded simply.

Ellen felt her hands clench the edge of the table as if it might support her. Then she forced herself to speak. To spell out the brutal truth he seemed oblivious to for rea-sons she could not fathom. She had to disabuse him of *any* notion that going to a ball would be anything other than unspeakable torment for her.

'Because,' she said, and it dawned on him that she was speaking as if she were talking to a particularly intel-lectually challenged pupil, 'you said it to me yourself at Haughton, when you saw me running. You said, *"You're nothing like your stepsister Chloe."* You couldn't have made it plainer. And you're absolutely right—I *am* noth-ing at all like Chloe and I never have been. I accept that completely—I've no illusions about myself, believe me. I know exactly what I look like. *That* is why going to a ball, or anything resembling a ball, or any social gathering of any kind at all is anathema to me. The very thought of dressing up and trying to be…trying to be…trying to be *anything* like Chloe—'

There was a choking sound in her voice and she broke off. She felt as if the blood was curdling in her veins—as if Chloe herself were standing there, her mocking peal of derisive laughter lashing at her at the very *thought* of her going to a ball—and with Max Vasilikos of all men! Her eyes tightened shut again, screwing up in their sockets, and her fingers indented into the wood of the table as she gripped it. Then her eyes flew open again.

'I *know* what I am. What I've always been. What I always will be. I'm pushing six foot tall, I've got size eight feet and I've got muscles that can bench fifty kilos. I'm like some gigantic *elephant* compared with Chloe.'

The misery and the self-loathing in her face was contorting her features. Consuming her. Across the table Max had sat back, gazing at her with a new expression on his face. Abruptly he spoke.

'Tell me, do you think Chloe beautiful?' There was a strange note in his voice. Enlightenment was dawning in him like a tsunami in slow motion. Was *this* what was screwing up Ellen Mountford?

Ellen stared. 'What kind of question is that? Of *course* she is! She's everything I'm not. She's petite and incredibly slim, and she has a heart-shaped face and blue eyes and blonde hair.'

The new expression on Max's face did not change. 'And if I described her,' he said carefully, his eyes not letting her go for an instant, 'as…let's see…like a scrawny chicken, what would you say?' Deliberately he chose as harsh a term as she had used about herself to make his point.

She said nothing. Only stared at him, not understanding. Incapable of understanding, Max realised with dawning comprehension. He shook his head slightly. 'You wouldn't believe me, would you?' His voice changed, becoming incisive, incontrovertible. 'Do you not realise,' he demanded, 'that it is only *you* who thinks you are like an elephant?'

She stared at him. Her face was expressionless. Her voice as she answered him toneless. 'Chloe thinks so too.'

She revels in thinking it. Taunts me endlessly. Is vi-

*ciously gleeful about it. Goes on and on about it! Has
tortured me ever since she and her vulture of a mother
smashed my life to pieces—going on and on at me about
how big I am, how heavy I am, how clumping and lumping
and pathetically, pitifully plain and repulsive I am, how
I'm just an embarrassing joke! Someone to laugh at and
sneer at and look down on! Elephant Ellen...*

Max made a sound in his throat and his dark eyes
flashed. 'And has it never dawned on you that Chloe, with
her tiny size zero frame, would consider a greyhound to be
the size of an elephant?' He took a heavy breath and his
eyes bored into her. Something in Greek escaped his lips.

Ellen could only stare at him, her face stricken at the
ugly memory of Chloe's years of merciless cruelty about
her appearance.

'I fully appreciate,' he said, now speaking in English,
spelling out each word carefully, emphatically, so that they
would penetrate her skull, reach deep inside her where
they needed to reach, 'that for whatever reason—the fashion industry, the prevalence of eating disorders and God
knows what else!—extreme thinness is currently regarded
as beautiful. And I fully appreciate,' he went on, not letting Ellen do anything except sit and stare at him with
blank eyes full of helpless misery, 'that Chloe happens to
fit the current description of what makes for a "fashionable" figure. But—'

He held his hand up now, silencing any retort she might
have been likely to make.

'That is entirely and completely irrelevant. Because *you*,
Ellen...' He paused, and a new timbre suddenly underlaid
his voice, resonating through words that echoed in the sudden shift in his expression. 'You,' he breathed, and his eyes
were boring into hers, never letting them go for an instant,
an iota, 'have the body of a goddess. A *goddess*, Ellen.'

There was silence—complete silence. Max let his eyes rest on her, saying nothing more. Watching her react. It was like a slow-motion sequence in a movie. Red washed into her face like a tide, then drained out, leaving it white and stark. Her eyes distended, then shut like the shell of a clam.

'Don't,' she said. 'Please don't.'

But he did. 'The body of a goddess,' he repeated. 'Don't tell me you don't—because I've seen it. I've seen damn nearly all of it. And believe me…'

Suddenly his long, long lashes swept down over his dark, dark eyes and Ellen felt a kind of hollowing out in her stomach that had nothing to do with the tide of misery that had been drowning her and everything to do with the hot, humid memory of how she'd been wearing only a sports bra and brief shorts when he'd seen her out running that time.

'I liked what I saw. I liked it, Ellen…' and now there was a huskiness in his voice '…a lot.'

He shifted in his seat, relaxing now, his broad shoulders moulding the back of the chair, a smile starting to curve his mouth. 'I've seen a lot of women with fantastic figures, Ellen—and my time with Tyla Brentley, especially when I was out in LA with her, supplied that amply!—so I promise you, you can trust my judgement on these matters. And you can trust my word, too.'

His expression changed, and so did his voice.

'My word,' he announced, 'is that I will donate five thousand pounds to your city kids charity today if you will agree to the following. To put yourself into the hands of the team of stylists this afternoon and let them do whatever it is they do. When they've done it, if you still don't want to come to the ball tonight I will let you off and double the five thousand pounds. If you *do* want to come, however, I'll triple it.' He gave a brief, slashing smile. 'Deal?' he posed.

Ellen stared back.

Five thousand pounds... Ten—because of course it *would* be ten! Of course she wouldn't want to go to the ball tonight. No way on God's earth would she volunteer for such an ordeal, however desperately she was scrubbed at by whatever professional make-up artists and the like he had lined up. Yet even as she made that mental averment she could still hear his voice echoing in her head.

The body of a goddess, Ellen.

She heard it, felt it—felt its power. Its temptation.

'Well?' he prompted.

He was holding his hand out across the table. His large, square, strong hand. Into which slowly—very slowly—her own hand seemed to be placing itself, though her head was still reeling with what he'd said to her.

'Good,' said Max. 'So that's all settled, then.' Satisfaction was blatant in his voice. He sat back, withdrawing his hand, moving it towards the coffee pot and starting to pour. 'Cream?' he asked, with a lift of his eyebrow, and poured it in anyway. With a honed, toned body like hers she could drink cream by the bucketload and it would never turn to fat.

Goddess body sorted. Now all that was needed was to sort out the rest of her appearance. Happy anticipation filled him.

People were doing things to Ellen. She had no idea what, and she didn't care. Even about the painful bits that involved tweezers and razors, hot wax and skin peels. She shut her eyes mostly, and let them get on with it, focussing her mind on what she'd do with the ten thousand pounds she'd get for the charity when they'd finished with her.

There were three of them working on her, stylists, beauticians, hairdressers. Whatever they were, they were chattering away. They were all stick-thin, just like Chloe, all wearing ultra-fashionable clothes and four-inch heels, with sharp hairstyles and loads of make-up—which was par for the course, Ellen reasoned, if one worked in the beauty industry. Their conversation seemed to be about clubs and bands, film stars and fashion brands, about which they were intimately knowledgeable.

They looked about twenty and made her feel like thirty. She hoped they were getting paid generously by Max, considering the impossibility of what they were attempting—making her look good enough to go to a ball. Because of course that was impossible. How could it be otherwise?

Dear God, how Chloe would laugh like a hyena if she could see this. She'd be filming it on her phone, posting it to her bitchy friends on social media, and they'd be squealing with laughter. Elephant Ellen, trying to look glamorous! How hilarious! How beyond pathetic!

Cold ran through her at the thought. Well, she'd be spared Chloe's mockery. Because the moment she had that cheque for ten thousand pounds in her hands she'd wipe off all the gunk the stylists were putting on her, get back into her school suit and head home. Back to the safety of Haughton—blessedly hers alone for the next few weeks while Pauline and Chloe were away. Hers to make the most of…the very, very most…

While she could.

Fear bit at her. Max Vasilikos was powerful, rich and ruthless. He'd clearly set his mind on trying to eject her, and he probably had the financial means to do so. It would cost him—but did he care? Maybe he was one of those men who had to win at any price. Wasn't what he was attempting this evening proof of it? Resorting to trying to flatter her into submission?

Telling me I have the body of a goddess!

She heard his voice again in her head, low and husky. She silenced it.

She realised that one of the stylists, who was busy painting her nails a dark crimson—or the nail extensions that had been stuck on—was talking to her.

'You are *so* lucky to be going out with Max Vasilikos tonight.' There was open envy in her voice. 'He's just to die for!'

Mortified, Ellen steeled her jaw. 'This isn't a *date*,' she said, horrified at the implication and trying desperately to sound composed. 'It's a charity fundraiser.'

Her protestation was ignored. 'He took Tyla Brentley last year,' the second stylist confirmed, doing something with long pins and a curling tong to Ellen's newly cut, coloured and piled up hair. 'She was a sensation.'

'Her dress was stunning' said the third, applying yet more mascara to Ellen's eyelashes, having already lavished eyeshadow and eyeliner plentifully upon her.

'It was Verensiana, and the shoes were Senda Sorn,' the first rattled off knowledgeably. 'She wore Verensiana to the film awards this year too—he's her *totes* fave designer. She went with Ryan Rendell, of course—they are *so* an item now!' She sighed soulfully, and then her eyes brightened as she smiled encouragingly at Ellen. 'Don't worry—she is, like, so *totally* over Max Vasilikos now. So the coast is completely clear for you.'

Ellen let them babble on, not bothering to try and refute their insanely wrong assumptions. Nails finished, the stylist dried them off with a hairdryer, before standing back with the other two stylists, who'd also finished whatever it was they'd been doing to her.

'OK,' announced the first stylist, 'let's go for the gown!'

Resigned, Ellen got to her feet, as requested, shedding the cotton robe she'd been inserted into after bathing, standing there in underwear that consisted of a low-cut underwired bra that hoicked up her breasts, plus lacy panties and black stockings—a universe away from her usual plain and serviceable underwear. As for the gown that had been selected for her, she had no idea and didn't care. It wouldn't be on for long anyway—just long enough for her to tell Max to hand over the cheque for ten thousand pounds.

But as she watched one of the trio fetch the gown out of the wardrobe she gasped. 'What is *that*?' she breathed.

'Isn't it *fabulous*?' came the answer.

'But it's…it's…'

'Edwardian,' said one of the others confidently. 'You know—like Victorian, but later. But not flappers like the roaring twenties.' She looked at Ellen. 'Didn't you know it was a costume ball?'

No, Ellen had not known. Had not known anything of the sort.

And right now, as the trio started to help her step into the stiffly draped dark red skirts and draw up the whalebone bodice so that it fitted tightly over her bust, pulling narrow straps over her shoulders to flare outwards in a spray of black feathers, her only conscious thought was that it was going to be hellish getting herself out of the dress again when she changed back into her own clothes. There must be a zillion hooks to undo.

CHAPTER SIX

MAX GAVE HIS bow tie a final twitch. Thank heavens Edwardian male evening dress was not a million miles from modern formal wear. It was very different for women. An anticipatory gleam lit his eye. Oh, he was looking forward to this. He was really, *really* looking forward to it. It would cost him fifteen thousand pounds, but it would be money well spent, he was sure—and not just for the sake of the charity!

Checking his cuffs, he strolled to the drinks cabinet, extracting a chilled bottle of vintage champagne and setting it down by two flutes. The noise at the bedroom door made him turn. It was not the stylists—they'd already gone in a flurry of chatter and on their phones already. Ellen was emerging.

His eyes narrowed. And then—

Yes! He wanted to punch the air in triumph. *Yes, yes, yes!*

He watched her walk into the room in a trail of long skirts. She halted abruptly when she saw him. He saw her face tighten.

'OK,' she said, 'where's this cheque you promised me?'

She spoke brusquely, because Max's eyes were like a hawk's on her, and it made her feel acutely, agonisingly uncomfortable. Even though she hadn't looked at her own reflection yet—she couldn't bear to!—she knew exactly what he was seeing. A big, hulking woman in a ridiculously tightly laced preposterous costume dress, with a tottering hairstyle and a face full of make-up that did absolutely nothing for her—because she had a face for which absolutely nothing could be done and that was all there was to it.

Yet again in her head she heard the peal of Chloe's derisive laughter mocking her…mocking the pathetic attempt to make Elephant Ellen look glamorous.

Well, she didn't care—*wouldn't* care. She only wanted the cheque that Max Vasilikos had promised her, then she was getting out of this ridiculous get-up—zillion hooks or not—and hightailing it to the station and home.

Max smiled his urbane, social smile and reached inside his breast pocket. 'Here you go,' he said, and held the cheque he'd promised out to her.

Awkwardly, Ellen walked over and took it. Then her expression altered and her gaze snapped back to him. 'This is for *fifteen* thousand,' she objected.

'Of course it is,' he agreed affably. 'Because of course you're coming to the ball with me. We're both kitted up—let's have a look at ourselves. See if we look the part.'

He helped himself to her arm with a white-gloved hand—he was wearing evening dress of the same Edwardian era, she realised, but on a man it was a lot less immediately obvious—and turned her towards a huge framed mirror hung above a sideboard.

'Take a look, Ellen,' he instructed softly.

Ellen looked.

And made no response. Could have made no response even if someone had shouted *Fire!* Could only do what she was doing—which was staring. Staring, frozen, at the couple reflected in the mirror. At the tall, superbly elegant and dashing figure of Max Vasilikos—and the tall, superbly elegant and stunning woman at his side.

The dark ruby-red silk gown was wasp-waisted and moulded over her hips to flow in a waterfall of colour the full length of her legs and out into a sweeping train, the body-hugging boned bodice revealed a generous décolletage, and the spray of feathers at each sculpted shoulder matched the similar spray in the aigrette curving around the huge swirled pompadour of her hair.

Curling tendrils played around her face—a face whose eyes were huge beneath winged, arched brows…rich tawny eyes that were thickly lashed and fathoms deep—a face whose cheeks were sculpted as if from marble, whose mouth was as lush and richly hued as damsons.

'Didn't I tell you?' Max said softly to her, because he could see from the expression on her face that something profoundly important and significant was happening to her. She was seeing, for the first time in her life, someone she had never seen before—the strikingly, dramatically beautiful woman that was looking back at her from the glass. 'A goddess,' he murmured. 'Didn't I tell you? In figure and in face…like Artemis the huntress goddess… strong and lithe and so, so beautiful.'

He let his gaze work over her reflection, drinking in face and figure, her beauty fully and finally revealed to him. A frown flickered in his eyes. 'Have you put in contact lenses?' he heard himself ask. What had happened to those wretched unflattering spectacles of hers?

She gave a slight shake of her head, feeling the soft tendrils curling down from her extravagant hairdo wafting softly and sensuously at her jaw.

'I only really need glasses for driving,' she answered. 'But I wear them because—' She stopped, swallowed.

Max said nothing—but he knew. Oh, he knew now why she wore them.

Ellen's eyes slid away. Her voice was heavy, and halting.

'I wear them to tell the world that I know perfectly well how awful I look, and that I accept it and I'm not going to make a pathetic fool of myself trying to look better, not going to try to—'

She broke off. Max finished the painful, self-condemning sentence for her.

'Not going to try to compete with your stepsister,' he said, his voice low.

Ellen nodded. 'Pathetic, I know. But—'

He caught her other arm, turning her to face him. '*No!* Don't think like that!' His expression was vehement, even fierce, as she stared at him. 'Ellen, whatever you've come to think in your head about yourself it's *wrong!*' He took a breath. 'Don't you realise you don't *have* to compete with Chloe? Leave her to enjoy her fashionable thinness! You...' His voice changed. 'Ah, *you* have a quite, quite different beauty.' He lifted a hand to gesture to her reflection. 'How can you possibly deny that now?'

Ellen gazed, her mind still trying to keep on denying what Max was saying to her—what the reflection in the mirror was telling her. That a stunningly beautiful woman was gazing back at her. A woman who was...*her*...

But that was impossible! It *had* to be impossible. It was *Chloe* who was lovely—*Chloe* who possessed the looks that defined beauty.

And if it was *Chloe* who was lovely, then she, Ellen, who was everything that Chloe was not—not petite, not blonde, not thin, not with a heart-shaped face, not blue-eyed, not *Chloe*—could only be the opposite. If it were *Chloe* who was lovely—then she, Ellen, could only be *un*lovely.

That was the logic that had been forced on her—forced on her with every sneering barb from Chloe, every derisive glance, every mocking jibe from her stepsister—for years… Those vulnerable teenage years when Chloe had arrived to poison her life, poison her mind against herself, destroying all her confidence so that she'd never even tried to make something of herself, instead condemning herself as harshly as her stepsister condemned her. Believing in Chloe's contempt of her. Seeing herself only through Chloe's cruel eyes.

But how could the woman gazing out at her from the mirror with such dramatic beauty possibly be described as unlovely? How could a woman like that be sneered at by Chloe, mocked by her, treated with contempt by her?

Impossible—just impossible. Impossible for Chloe to sneer at a woman such as the one who was gazing back at her now.

Emotion swept through Ellen. She couldn't give a name to it—didn't need to. Needed only to feel it rush through her like a tide, sweeping away everything that had been inside her head for so many years. And now Max was speaking again, adding to the tide sweeping through her.

'You can't deny it, can you?' Max repeated. His eyes were fixed on her reflection still. 'You can't deny your beauty—your own beauty, Ellen. *Yours*. As different from Chloe's as the sun is from the moon.'

He gave a laugh suddenly, of triumph and deep satisfaction.

'We shall drink a toast,' he announced. 'A toast to the goddess revealed.' He drew her away, towards the tray of champagne, opening the bottle with skilled long practice and filling the flutes to hand one to her.

Ellen took it numbly, her eyes wide, as if she was in a dream. A dream she still could not quite believe was reality after all.

Her eyes flickered back to her reflection in the mirror. *Is it really, truly me? Can it be—?*

Then Max's gloved hand was touching her wrist, lifting his own foaming glass, and she looked back at him, still with that bemused expression in her eyes, as if she dared not believe the truth of her own reflection. He held her gaze, not letting go for an instant.

'To you,' he said. 'To beautiful Ellen. Beautiful, stunning Ellen!'

He took a mouthful of champagne and she did too, feeling the bubbles burst on her tongue, feeling a glow go through her that had nothing to do with champagne at all...

He smiled down at her. 'Tonight,' he told her, his mouth curving into an intimate smile, his lashes dipping over dark eyes lambent with expression, 'every man will envy me—you'll be a sensation.'

The word echoed in her head. A sudden memory stung like a wasp in her mind. She lowered her champagne glass, her fingers gripping it hard suddenly.

'Those girls—the stylists—they said you brought Tyla Brentley here last year—that *she* was a sensation.'

Max heard the sudden panic in her voice, that demon of self-doubt stabbing at her again. He wanted to kick it into touch without delay. He gave a deliberately dismissive shrug. 'Of course she was,' he said indifferently. 'Her fame guaranteed that. And Tyla adores men gazing at her. It flatters her insatiable vanity.'

Even as he spoke he knew his words were true. He, too, had once fed that vanity—until he'd realised that Tyla's self-absorption meant it was impossible for her to think of anyone but herself. His wealth had been useful to her, coming as it did with the person of a male whose looks could complement her own, and she had known with her innate instinct for self-publicity that she and he together made a couple that would always draw both eyes and attention, gaining precious press coverage to help her build her career. Tyla's belief in herself, in her own charm and beauty, had been total.

The very opposite of Ellen.

She was looking at him doubtfully still, as if she could not believe his indifference to having once squired a Hollywood film star. He wanted that doubt gone—completely— and so raised his champagne glass to his lips, deliberately letting his gaze wash over her.

'Tyla's got a good body—no doubt about that—but…' And now he let something else into his gaze that he knew from long experience had an effect on all females. 'But I can promise you that she had absolutely nothing on you. If Chloe,' he said 'is a tiny little Chihuahua…' he made his voice amused, deliberately exaggerating her stepsister's petiteness '…then Tyla is a…a gazelle, I guess. But *you…*' Once more his gaze rested on her, sending her the message he wanted…*needed*…her to get. 'You, Ellen, are a lioness!'

He grinned at her, and tilted his champagne glass to her in tribute.

'And lionesses gobble up little dogs and antelopes for breakfast!'

He toasted her again, his eyes becoming serious now, holding hers, sending home his essential message to her, the reassurance she needed—the reassurance that he would give her whatever it took. He would make sure of that. His eyes rested on her, their expression intent. Suddenly it seemed crucially important that Ellen believed him, and believed in her own newly revealed beauty. And it was for a reason that had nothing to do with his plans for Haughton. For a reason he was only dimly aware of—and yet it seemed to be forcing itself into his consciousness with an insistence he could not ignore.

I want it for her sake—not for mine. I want it so that

she can be happy—happy in her own body, finally. I want that for her.

'Be proud of what you are,' he told her. 'Be happy in your body. Your fantastic body! Strong and lean and lithe—'

She felt gloved fingertips glide down the bare length of her upper arm.

'And with great muscle tone!' he finished approvingly.

Ellen's eyes flickered uncertainly. 'Maybe I need a shawl over my arms,' she ventured. 'I'm too muscular—'

Max rolled his eyes, shaking his head. 'Uh-uh! Remember—think lioness!' He let his gaze liquefy again, knowing the effect it would have, the effect he wanted right now. 'Think Artemis. Think goddess. Think beautiful...' There was a sudden husk in his voice that he had not put there deliberately at all, but which came of its own powerful accord. 'Very, very beautiful.'

The wash of his warm gaze over her was instinctive, and he felt it resonate with a warming of his blood, too, that surged in his body powerfully, unstoppably.

His eyes were holding hers, not letting her go. Ellen felt her breath catch in her breast, felt her heartbeat give a sudden surge, felt the surface of her skin tighten as if an electric charge were spreading out through its whole expanse, radiating out from her quickened heart rate. She could feel her pupils flare, her lips part—felt faint, almost, heard drumming in her ears...

The world seemed to slow down all around her.

And then the sound of the suite's doorbell ringing broke the moment. For a second Max just went on staring, unable to relinquish his gaze on the woman whose beauty he had revealed to her—and to himself. Then, with an exclamation in Greek, he dropped his hands, strode to the door and yanked it open.

As he saw who it was he relaxed immediately. 'Ah,' he said. 'Come in!'

Ellen turned, dazed, her pulse hectic, still blinking, breathless from that strange, powerful moment that had hummed like charged plasma between them. She saw a neatly suited man walk in, a briefcase handcuffed to his wrist. She blinked again. What on earth…?

'So,' she heard Max saying as the man set his briefcase on the table, unlocking it, 'what have you brought us?'

The man opened the lid and Ellen gasped audibly. It was jewellery, carefully nestled in black velvet liners, glittering in every hue—diamonds, emeralds, sapphires and rubies.

Rubies...

Ellen's eyes went to them immediately—it was impossible for them not to. She felt her breath draw in sharply as her gaze fixed on the ruby set, deep and glowing, a necklace, bracelet, earrings and a ring.

Max saw her focus on the set. Her expression was fixed, and for a second—just a second—he thought he saw something fleeting cross it, like a sudden convulsion. Then it was gone, and he was speaking.

'Ah, yes,' he said. 'Rubies, definitely. Ideal for your gown.'

The jeweller started to lift the pieces. 'As you can see,' he told them, 'their setting is of the period, and original. If I may…?'

He carefully lifted the necklace—a complex design of several loops of different lengths, with pendent rubies from each—and as he placed it around Ellen's throat the necklace occupied a considerable amount of the bare expanse of flesh between her throat and the swell of her breasts. He fastened the necklace, then held up a large hand mirror so she could see herself.

She gazed, her expression strange, and that fleeting look passed across her face again as she lifted her hand to touch the gems.

'Perfect,' said Max, well pleased. 'Let's get the rest of it on so we can see the final effect.'

Ellen still had that strange expression on her face. Max found himself wondering at it. He watched her hold out her wrist as the jeweller fastened the glittering bracelet around it and handed her the earrings. As he lifted the ring he paused, glancing doubtfully at Ellen's large hands.

'It will fit—just,' Ellen said.

She sounded sure of it and took the ring, pausing to glance at the inscription inside, which Max could see but not read, before carefully working the ring over her knuckle. It did, indeed, just fit—as she had forecast. She looked at it on her finger for a moment, the same strange, fixed expression on her face.

Then it was gone. She got to her feet. There was something different about her, Max fancied—some subtle change had come over her. There was an air of resolve about her—confidence, even. But then he was taking in the impact of her appearance, finished to perfection now with the glittering ruby parure that went so superbly with her Edwardian gown and hairstyle.

Beautiful!

That was the woman standing there, with her upswept hair, gems glittering, her toned, honed body sumptuously adorned with the lustrous ruby silk of her gown. He reached for his champagne glass and drained what was left, prompting Ellen to do likewise. They set their flutes down and Max turned to Ellen, holding out his arm to her.

'Time,' he said, and he gave her a little bow, his eyes glinting with pleasure and anticipation and appreciation, 'to take you to the ball.'

* * *

Walking into the hotel's ballroom, its rich red and gold decor a perfect complement to her black and ruby styling, Ellen tightened her hand on Max's sleeve. Being at his side, she thought, her own generous figure seemed completely in proportion. His height easily topped hers by several inches—his wide shoulders and broad chest saw to that. Unconsciously, she seemed to straighten her shoulders further, and her hips moved with regal ease, her chin held high, as she walked beside Max with her athletic gait.

She should have felt nervous—but she didn't. Oh, the glass of champagne had helped, but it was not the bubbles in the champagne alone that were gliding her forward, filling her with wonder and elation.

She could see eyes going to her as they made their entrance, and for the first time in her life she experienced the oh-so-pleasurable thrill of knowing she was turning heads—for every reason a woman could dream of. Because she looked—*stunning*.

They both did.

As they walked past a mirror she caught their joint reflection and could see exactly why people were pausing to look at them. They were both tall, both sleekly groomed, with stunning looks, male *and* female, between them. Surely even Max and the glamorous Tyla Brentley could not have turned more heads?

We make a fantastic couple!

The thought was in her head before she could stop it. Urgently she sought to suppress it, then gave in. Yes, she and Max *did* make a fantastic couple—but it was for tonight only, for the purposes of this glittering charity bash. That was what she had to remember. And one other vital thing.

He's only doing all this to soften me up—to try and persuade me to give up Haughton to him.

But even though she knew it was true she didn't seem to mind right now. How could she when what he'd given her this evening was something she had never thought she would ever possess in all her life? Freedom from the malign hex that Chloe had put on her so many years ago.

Self-knowledge flooded through her, washing away so much of the blindness that had clouded her image of herself for so long. The blindness that she had allowed her stepsister to inflict on her.

I let Chloe have that power over me. I let her control my mind, my image of myself, my sense of worth.

It seemed so strange to her now, to think of how defiant she'd always been with Pauline and her daughter—and yet they had controlled her at this most basic, potent level. But no longer—never again! A sense of power, of newborn confidence swept through her. Unconsciously she lifted her fingers to the necklace, touching the jewels around her throat. Beautiful jewels to adorn a beautiful woman. A woman worthy of a man like Max Vasilikos.

She looked up at him now, easily a head taller than her, and smiled. He caught her expression and answered it with his own. Long lashes swept down over his eyes and he patted the hand hooked into his.

'Enjoy,' said Max, smiling down at her.

And enjoy she did. That was the amazement of it all.

Time and again her fingers brushed at her necklace, or grazed the gold band around her finger beneath its ruby setting—and every time she did she gave a little smile, half haunting, half joyous.

As Max had promised her, sitting to her left she found one of the host charity's directors, who listened attentively as she told him about the camps she ran, then nodded approvingly and told Ellen he'd be happy to help with her funding.

Glowing, she turned to Max. 'Thank you!' she exclaimed, and it was heartfelt.

And she was not just thanking him for setting her up with this funding, or his cheque for fifteen thousand pounds. It was for lifting Chloe's curse from her shoulders—setting her free from it.

His eyes met hers and, half closed, half veiled, they flickered very slightly. As if he were thinking about something but not telling her. He raised his glass of wine to her.

'Here's to a better future for you,' he murmured.

The corner of his mouth pulled into a quizzical smile, and she answered with one of her own in return, lifting her glass too.

'A better future,' she echoed softly.

At the edge of her consciousness Haughton loomed, still haunted by Pauline and Chloe, the dilemma insoluble. But the house she loved so much, the home that she longed only to be safe, seemed far, far away right now. Real—much more real—was this moment…this extraordinary present she was experiencing. All thanks to Max, the man who had made it possible for her.

For an instant her gaze held his, and she felt bathed and warmed by the deep, dark brown of eyes fringed by thick lashes, flecked with gold. And then for an even briefer instant, so brief she could only wonder whether it had been real, there was a sudden change in them, a sudden, scorching intimacy.

She sheared her gaze away, feeling her heart jolt within her as if an electric shock had just kicked it. As if it were suddenly hard to breathe.

All through the rest of the meal, and the speeches and the fundraising auction afterwards, she could feel the echo of that extraordinary jolt to her heartbeat, flickering in her consciousness as port and liqueurs, coffee and petit fours circulated. Then, on the far side of the grand ballroom an orchestra started up.

'Oh, how lovely!' she exclaimed as the music went into the lilting strains of a slow waltz, ideal for an Edwardian-themed ball.

'It's Lehár!' exclaimed one of the women at their table, delighted.

'So it is!' agreed Ellen, starting to hum the composer's familiar melody—the waltz from *The Merry Widow* operetta.

'Well, I think this calls for audience participation,' said the charity director at her side, as all around them at the other tables guests were getting to their feet to take to the dance floor. 'Will you do me the honour?' he asked Ellen with a smile.

But he was forestalled. Max was standing up.

'I claim the first waltz,' he said, catching Ellen's elbow and guiding her to her feet. His rival conceded gracefully. Max bore Ellen off.

She was in a state of consternation, aware that her heart was racing and that she felt breathless. Taken over.

But then Max has taken me over all day, hasn't he? I've done everything he wanted, all the time!

Well, now she was going to dance with him, and she wasn't getting a choice about it. Except—

'I have *no* idea how to waltz!' she exclaimed. 'And I think the Viennese waltz is different from the English waltz anyway. And I—'

He cut her short. 'Follow my lead,' he instructed, and simply took her into his arms and swept her off.

Into the dance.

Into the irresistible, lilting music that wafted them around the ballroom floor.

She felt her long, heavy silk skirts become as light as

a feather, swirling around her legs as Max whirled her around until she was dizzy with it, until all she could do was clutch helplessly at his shoulder, hang on to his hand for dear life as he turned her and guided her and never, never let her go.

'You see? It's easy.' He smiled at her. 'Much easier than you feared.'

And she knew, with a little skip of her heart, that it was not just the waltzing he meant.

It's all been so, so easy. The lifting of the hex. Her transformation tonight. Putting on this gorgeous costume, being swept away in his arms...

Joy filled her—a wonderful sense of carefree elation as if, simply by whirling her around like this, he had whisked away all that oppressed her.

And for tonight he has! I know that I will have to go home tomorrow, back to all the difficulties and the stress and the fear of losing Haughton. But for tonight I will waltz my cares away.

The music ended with a flourish, and the cessation of the swirling made her head spin instead. But then she was joining with the others in applauding the orchestra, its players in historical costume as well, and their leader was turning and bowing, introducing the next dance they were going to play.

It was a polka, and Ellen's eyes widened again.

Max didn't let her speak. 'Just follow my lead,' he instructed again.

And once more she did. It was just as well, she thought absently, that she was pretty fit, for the dance was vigorous and not a few couples finished panting. But Max wasn't the slightest out of breath, and neither was she.

'Thank goodness for early-morning runs!' she exclaimed.

'It's hot work, this elegant dancing,' Max agreed, running a finger around his distinctly damp collar.

Ellen smiled. 'My father used to say that *his* father, when they went to dances before the war, had to take spare collars with him because they wilted during the night.'

Max laughed. 'Well, I envy you your bare shoulders and arms, I can tell you. Will it cause a scandal if I shed this very hot evening jacket, I wonder?'

'You'll be blackballed instantly!' she warned him with a laugh.

'Oh, well, I'm just a foreigner and a parvenu, so I won't care,' he riposted, and took her back into his arms as the music started up again.

It was a much slower waltz now, and Ellen was relieved. Or at least she was until she felt Max's hand tightening at her waist. It was hard to feel much through the whalebone bodice, but there was something in the way he was imprinting his hold on her that made her breath catch despite the slowness of the music. Made it catch again when she saw the expression in his eyes, looking down at her. She felt colour run out into her cheeks. She tried to stop it, tried to hope that he would take it only for heat, no other reason. She tried to pull her gaze away, but it was hopeless...

'Glad you came to the ball?' he asked, a faint smile ghosting at his mouth.

His long lashes swept down over his eyes and he smiled at her. Were there gold flecks in those eyes? She could only gaze into their depths, captivated and entranced.

Her lips parted in a wide, joyful smile. 'Oh, yes! It's just...*wonderful*! All of it. Every bit!'

A wicked glint gleamed in Max's eyes. 'Even the whalebone in your bodice?' he asked.

'OK,' she allowed. 'Not that.'

'Though it *does* give you the most superb figure,' he

said, and now...oh, most definitely...now there were golden
flecks in his eyes.

He pulled a little away from her so his eyes could take
in the glory of her narrowed waist, the full roundness of
her hips, and then, moving upwards, the generous curva-
ture of her breasts. His gaze lingered...then he dragged
them away.

No. The voice inside his head was stern. No, he must
not. This evening was about liberating Ellen Mountford
from the chains that weighed her down. Freeing her from
the mental burdens that blighted her life, made her want to
hide herself away in her safe place, her childhood home,
where she could moulder away, never emerging into the
world.

Well, she was emerging now, all right. Male eyes were
all over her. Max had seen that the moment he'd walked
into the ballroom. They were on her still, and he didn't
blame them.

Mine are too...

No. The stern voice inside his head came again. No—he
must not permit that. This evening was for *her*, not him!
Oh, it was for himself too—of course it was—but only
because showing Ellen how wonderful her life could be
once she joined the world, instead of hiding herself away
at Haughton, would mean that he could acquire what he
was set on acquiring. Which was not Ellen Mountford—it
was the house she would not willingly sell to him.

But you could have her as well...

The siren thought was in his head, as sinuous and seductive as the slow pulse of the music he was moving to.

Ellen was in his arms, her body so close to his, her
weight pressing in on him as they turned, his arm around
her waist, her rich ruby mouth smiling up at him. Tempting him...

The music ended and he was glad. He led her back to their table and immediately the charity director was on his feet. Ellen was led away, and Max watched her go. Was there a reluctance in her now? Would she rather have not danced again but sat with him and watched the dancers? He didn't know—knew only that there was a kind of growl inside him...a growl that made him reach for the cognac bottle and pour himself a glass.

The two other couples at the table were taking a break as well, and were chatting, drawing him into their conversation. He joined in civilly but his gaze, he knew, kept going back out to the dance floor, searching for Ellen.

I want her.

That was the voice in his head now. Stark, blunt and simple. His jaw set. He could want her all he liked, but fulfilling that want would lead to complications.

The question was—did he care?

And right now, watching her in another man's arms—this woman he'd released from the bondage of her mental chains, freed to revel in the natural beauty that was hers—and feeling that deep, primal growl rising in him again, he knew as the fiery liqueur glazed his throat and fuelled his heated blood that he didn't care at all...

CHAPTER SEVEN

THE WORLD WAS whirling pleasantly around her—oh, so pleasantly! Ellen felt herself swaying slightly, as if she were still dancing, humming a waltz tune, hearing her long silk skirts rustling. The ball was over, midnight long gone, and now she was back up in the penthouse suite. The orchestra was still playing in her head. And everything was wonderful! Oh, just *wonderful*! Her gown was wonderful, her hair was wonderful, the dancing had been wonderful, the evening had been wonderful!

Max had been wonderful...

She gazed at him now, blood singing in her veins. He was twisting open a bottle of water, looking so tall, so strong, so utterly devastating in his Edwardian evening dress, and her eyes just drank him in as the room swirled around her and the music played in her head and on her lips. All she wanted to do, all she longed to do, was to be back in his arms, dancing and dancing...

'Drink this—and drink it all,' Max's deep voice instructed her as he came to her and handed her a large glass of water. 'You'll thank me in the morning, I promise you.'

'I feel fine,' she said. 'Absolutely fine.' Still, she gulped down the water, never taking her gaze from Max—wonderful, *wonderful* Max!

How gorgeous he is—how incredibly handsome and gorgeous and wonderful and devastating and...

Then she yawned—a huge, exhausted yawn. Her eyes blinked.

'Time for bed,' said Max.

But not, alas, with him. He knew that. The champagne, the wine, the liqueurs she'd drunk made that out of the question. Should he regret it? He shouldn't, he knew, but he did all the same.

Maybe it's for the best. That was what he needed to tell himself. Remind himself of all the complications that might arise were he to follow what he knew his body wanted right now...the new-found desire that had swept over him.

I want to celebrate her new-found freedom with her. I want to take the final step of her liberation with her. I want to be the man who does that—

Well, not tonight. Frustration could bite at him all it liked, but that was that. And he—he'd be back in his own bedroom in the hotel suite, heading for a cold shower.

But first he had a real ordeal to get through. One that was going to test him to the limits.

'Hold still!' he instructed her, catching the back of her shoulders to steady her.

It was a mistake, for the warmth of her bare skin under his palms was an unwise sensation for him to feel right now. He pulled his hands away as if burnt, made his fingers drop down to the fastenings of her dress instead. *Thee mou*, there were a million of them! As he started the finicky work of undoing them he could feel the effort of not thinking about what he was doing.

Don't think about how her beautiful bare back is emerging...how she's dropped her head, exposing the tender nape of her neck caressed by tendrils of her chestnut hair...

*how easy...how tempting it would be to lower your mouth
and graze that delicate skin with your lips. No, don't think
about any of that—*

He swallowed heavily, dropping his hands away. 'Done!'

She turned, oblivious to the punishing, disciplined self-
control he was exerting, her unfastened bodice held up
only by her hands pressed to her half-exposed breasts,
her feathered shoulder straps collapsing down her arms
as well. A sigh of happiness, of bliss escaped her, and her
eyes were clinging to his.

'This has been,' she announced, 'the most *wonderful*
night of my life.'

Her lips were parted, her eyes glowing, her face lifted
up to his. She swayed towards him in the motion of a
dance, with intoxication in her blood, unconscious invitation in her glorious goddess body.

And he was lost. Totally, completely lost. Could resist
her no longer.

His hands fastened on her upper arms and he hauled
her to him. Drew her smiling parted lips to his and took
his fill. He could not resist it—just could not.

Tasting first, he glided his lips across the velvet softness
of hers, taking possession of her mouth, tasting her bou-
quet like a rich, radiant wine. Then, as his kiss deepened,
he opened his mouth to hers and she came with him—
came with him every iota of the way—moving her mouth
on his, opening to him, tasting him, taking her fill of him.

He could feel her full breasts pressing against the cotton of his shirtfront, feel her nipples start to peak, feel desire flare through her, fuelled by the wine in her blood, the
champagne in her veins, the music in her head.

Hunger for her leapt in him, seared through him. He
knew his body was surging, engorging, knew that desire
and need and all that could burn like an inferno between

a man and a woman was igniting within him now. Knew that in seconds the conflagration would take hold—unstoppable, unquenchable.

With a groan, he let her go, wrenching his mouth from hers, pulling his hands away, stepping back from her.

There was a dazed expression on her face, the bewilderment of loss in her eyes—her huge, widened eyes—and their pupils were flaring with desire, arousal...

He shook his head. Held up his hands. Stepped further back.

'Goodnight!' he said.

His voice was shaken, he could hear it, and he could feel the heat in his body still, the fullness still there, but he had to beat it back, subdue it. Whatever primal hunger was possessing him, he had to defeat it. To indulge himself now, when far too much wine and champagne was coursing through her, would be unforgivable.

For a second a stricken look was there in her eyes—a look that somehow pierced him like a stiletto blade in his throat—and then, like the sun coming out from a cloud, dazzling in its brightness, she smiled. Her face lit up once more.

'Goodnight!' she breathed. 'Oh, *goodnight*!'

He backed to the door. He did not want to do this. Did not want to leave. But he had to. Had to get back to his room—had to get that cold shower sluicing down over his body...*had* to!

As he reached the door she lifted her hand from one side of her bodice, dangerously exposing yet more of her sweet, succulent flesh, a final torment for him, and then, with another dazzling smile, an insouciant, joyous gesture, she kissed her fingers and blew the kiss to him.

'Thank you!'

They were the last words he heard before he got out through the door and pulled it shut, to keep him safe.

Safe from the only thing in the world he wanted to do right now…

Go right back in and sweep her into his arms.

Ellen was asleep, but someone was making her wake up. A hand was on her shoulder, gently shaking her. She shrugged it off, nestled back down into her pillows, but the hand returned. Someone said something to her, but she didn't know what. It was foreign. Greek?

Greek!

She bolted upright, only just having the presence of mind to clutch her bedclothes to her, her eyes flaring open. Max Vasilikos, freshly showered—she could tell from the damp hair feathering his forehead and the towelling robe that emphasised the Mediterranean tan of his skin—was sitting on her bed.

'How are you feeling?' he enquired. His voice was urbane, equable—and amused.

She pushed her hair out of her face. It seemed to her to be softer than it usually was, and finer, and less heavy. She blinked, looking around her, dragging her gaze past the figure of the man sitting at the foot of the bed, with his dark eyes resting on her speculatively and a curve at his sculpted mouth that suddenly made her very, *very* aware of her state of dishevelment.

'Um—fine,' she got out.

Was she fine? she wondered. She blinked. Yes, she did seem to be OK. Memory came rushing back, tumbling into her head like a series of snapshots. The ball—that fantastic, gorgeous, wonderful ball! Chatting away to all those people over dinner. Dancing with Max.

Kissing Max…

Colour flared in her cheeks as memory flooded her, intense and vivid.

He kissed me! Max Vasilikos—the man who made me beautiful and waltzed the night away with me!

Max saw the colour flare and knew what she was thinking. It was what he was only too conscious of himself. His night had not been peaceful. It had been disturbed by dreams. Dreams in which there had been no need to tear himself away from the woman he'd been kissing.

No—don't think about it now! Not when he was sitting on her bed and she was only a metre away from him, her naked body shielded only by the sheet she was clutching to her, her lush hair tumbling wantonly around her shoulders, her smeared mascara making her eyes smoky and deep…

He got to his feet, stepping away from the bed. Well away. 'I've ordered brunch,' he told her. 'So have a wake-up shower and come on through.'

She nodded, and waited till he was well clear of the room before getting up.

It was strange, she thought as she caught her reflection in the mirror of the en-suite bathroom… She was so used to her body, so used to thinking it large and muscular and unattractive. And yet now— Her eyes held her own naked reflection. Saw it for the very first time not through Chloe's eyes, but through someone else's completely.

Max's eyes…

Tall, with sculpted shoulders, taut arms, generous breasts, flat abs, toned glutes, strong quads, long legs. A goddess body?

And her face still held the beauty conjured from it by those skilful magic-making stylists last night. Her fingers lifted uncertainly to her hair. Whatever those chattering women had done to it, it was amazing. Its colour was so much richer, glowing in the lights around the vanity unit, and it felt so light on her head, yet it waved in lush tresses down over her shoulders, softening her face, her jaw, caressing her neck. She touched her mouth with her fingertips—elongated nails still crimson with varnish—and felt a smile part her mouth.

A goddess indeed...

She heard Max's words in her head, felt his eyes on her, his hand on her spine as they'd waltzed.

The melody played in her head again. Happiness filled her. Whatever her worries, whatever her woes, this...*this* would always be with her now.

He made me beautiful.

He might be trying to take her beloved home from her, but he had given her something she had never thought to have—something that Chloe's cruelty had taken from her, that her own self-doubt, self-criticism had *let* her stepsister take from her.

And Max—wonderful, wonderful Max!—had now restored it to her.

With a smile of wonder and gratitude still playing on her lips she piled her hair up, pinned it loosely, and stepped into the shower unit. Brunch beckoned—and so did the thought of seeing Max again.

Even if only for what was left of the morning.

A pang smote her. She swallowed as the hot water plunged down over her shoulders, rousing her to full wakefulness. Suddenly the thought of leaving him, of returning home to Haughton, seemed like the worst thing in the world.

But the ball is over—and it's time to go home.

For the first time in her life she did not want to.

Max was already seated at the table when Ellen emerged. He was clad, like her, in a white towelling robe. Seeing him like that seemed suddenly very...intimate.

Into her head came the memory, vivid and real, of how he had kissed her.

Oh, she might have been intoxicated—with champagne and wine, with music and wonder—but that could not dim the searing memory.

Instantly she reproved herself fiercely.

It was just a kiss! Don't make anything of it! It was only a kiss. It meant nothing—just a way to say goodnight.

Yet even as she told herself that she could feel the colour flare in her face. Busily, she sat herself down, hoping Max hadn't seen. Didn't know the reason for it.

It would have meant nothing to him—think how many women he's kissed in his life! With looks like his...

And one of those women—the most recent—had been a film star. To a man used to kissing film stars—used to doing a whole lot more than kissing!—bestowing a goodnight kiss on *her* was...well, nothing.

But not to me.

Her eyes flickered a moment. No, it had not been nothing to her...

To me his kiss was the ultimate breaking of Chloe's vicious hex. The one I gave in to—was too cowed to fight, to deny. I gave her an easy victory. A victory she revelled in!

Her expression steeled. But no more. Chloe's cruel mental domination of her was over. She had to keep it that way.

She looked across at Max. His eyes were resting on her with an expression in them that was half glinting, half veiled. She met it square-on, refusing to let any self-conscious memory colour her cheeks. Then she looked at the lavish brunch spread out before her. She was instantly hungry.

'Mmm...eggs Benedict. My favourite,' she announced appreciatively.

She took a generous helping and got stuck in. Max was

doing likewise—well, he had a big frame to fill, and muscle burned more calories than fat…not that there was a trace of fat about him. He was lean and powerful and devastatingly attractive, and the way the tan of his skin contrasted with the white of his robe, the way there was really quite a lot of chest exposed in the deep vee…

She gulped silently and focussed on her food.

'No sign of a hangover?' Max enquired. She didn't look hungover in the slightest, and she shook her head, making her long wavy tresses resettle on her shoulders and waft around her cheeks. He felt satisfaction go through him. Those stylists had been worth their weight in gold! Even with all the make-up now scrubbed off, the changes they'd made were glaringly noticeable—most of all the taming of her fearsome, frowning monobrow.

She wasn't frowning now at all. 'Nope,' she said. 'All that water you poured into me before I flaked out did the trick!'

'I told you you'd thank me in the morning,' he replied with a glint in his eyes.

She made herself look at him, pausing in her eating. 'I *do* thank you,' she said 'I thank you for…for everything!'

She didn't have to spell it out. He knew. He smiled at her down the length of the table. Then raised his glass of orange juice to her. 'To the new you, Ellen—and may the old one be banished for good!'

He took a draught of the juice, setting down the glass. 'Now,' he opened, sounding businesslike, 'what we need to get done today is sorting out your wardrobe. Fabulous though you look in Edwardian costume, it's not for every day,' he finished lightly, with another smile. 'So, when we've eaten it'll be time to go shopping.'

A troubled look shadowed her face. 'I really need to go home,' she said.

Max raised his eyebrows. 'What for? It's not term-time—'

'Yes, but… Well… I really ought to…'

He gave an airy wave of his hand. No way was Ellen going to beetle off back to Haughton and bury herself there again! Not yet—not by a long way! He hadn't done with her…

Deep in his abdomen he felt an oh-so-masculine response kick in. He'd had to relinquish her last night—anything else would have been inexcusable—but the impulse he'd experienced then, the overriding rush of desire, had in no way been attenuated. His mind was made up—the long, sleepless, frustrated hours of the night he'd just spent had given him conviction of that.

A romance is exactly what she needs. It will show her how wonderful life can be if she just emerges from her shell, tastes all that life can offer now that she knows how beautiful she is. She can start to shed the burden of bitter resentment, knowing that her deep, dark, disturbing jealousy and envy of her stepsister is quite unnecessary.

And with that burden of resentment lifted—well, then she wouldn't need to keep trying to thwart Pauline and Chloe by refusing to sell her share of Haughton. Wouldn't need to keep trying to punish Pauline for marrying her father and Chloe for having the beauty she thought she herself was denied.

'So,' he said decisively, 'it's all settled. There's absolutely no call for you to head off straight away, so we'll definitely go shopping.'

She was still looking at him with a troubled expression. She wanted to tell him that even if she didn't actually need to go back home today shopping for clothes was the last thing she could afford. Her salary was wiped out paying for her living expenses and Pauline and Chloe's extravagances! But even as she thought it she felt rebellion stir. If *they* could fund their lavish lifestyle by selling off paintings from Haughton, well, so could she!

In the deep pocket of her robe she could feel the weight of the jewellery she'd worn last night, which she would hand back to Max as she must, however reluctantly...

A stab of anger bit at her, hardening her resolve. Her expression changed as she made her decision. Max saw it and was glad.

He was even more glad, later that afternoon, when she emerged from the changing room of one of the most upmarket fashion houses, finally looking the way her natural looks deserved.

It hadn't been completely plain sailing—she'd balked as they'd walked in, a look of near panic on her face, and he'd had to steer her firmly towards the serried racks of clothes.

'I don't think there'll be anything to fit me!' she'd said nervously, her eyes casting about at the stick-thin customers who all seemed to be Chloe clones.

Doubt had suddenly assailed her. She'd been wearing, perforce, the dowdy old-fashioned suit she'd worn yesterday, and there, surrounded by elegance and fashion, she'd felt her fragile new-found confidence waver. Panic had bitten at her throat.

They're all looking at me—wondering what on earth a lumpy frump like me is doing here! Wanting me to get out, to stop inflicting myself on their eyesight!

The old, painful, mortifying self-consciousness had come back, drowning her, trying to send a tide of humiliated colour back into her face. The urge to run out of the shop, to take herself off to the station, to rush back down to Haughton, seeking its refuge, hiding there in solitude, safe from condemning eyes, had almost overpowered her.

Then Max had spoken, ignoring her protestation. 'This will suit you,' he'd said decisively, reaching for a knee-length dress in warm caramel, soft jersey with a draped neckline. 'And these.'

He'd taken a teal-blue dress and a tailored jacket off the rack. He'd handed them to her and then started sorting through the trousers, pulling out a black pair and a chestnut-brown pair, before picking up a couple of cashmere sweaters. He'd guided her to the changing rooms.

'In you go,' he'd said, and he'd given her the rest of the clothes and a gentle push. He'd had no intention of letting those chains start winding themselves around her mind again.

As she had headed, still reluctantly but obediently, into the changing rooms he'd beckoned to a sales assistant, giving her a particularly engaging smile. 'We're going to need a lot more clothes,' he'd said, nodding at Ellen's back.

The sales assistant had cast an expert eye over her, taking in the tight, ill-fitting suit. 'Definitely.' She had nodded and glided off, returning with a large selection of separates, plus shoes, belts and some costume jewellery.

With a smile at Max, who'd settled himself comfortably into one of the leather chairs conveniently placed nearby for attendant males, complete with magazines about cars and fitness to while away their time while they waited for their womenfolk, she had whisked them into the changing room.

It had taken quite some time for Ellen to emerge…

CHAPTER EIGHT

'TELL ME,' MAX SAID, 'how are you with helicopters?'

Ellen stared. 'Helicopters?'

'Yes. I've got one on standby,' he informed her. 'There's a property out in the Chilterns I want to take a quick look at, and a helicopter is the fastest way.'

'I've never been in one,' Ellen said.

Max grinned. 'Great—a new experience. You'll love it.'

He bore her off towards the kerb, where his car was hovering. He wasn't giving her a chance to object, just as he hadn't given her a chance to run out of that fashion house. When she'd finally emerged from the changing room he'd wanted to punch the air, like he had the night before. And now she had looked—fantastic!

Straw-coloured trousers neatly hugged her trim hips, and a casual cashmere sweater in oatmeal superbly moulded her generous breasts. A long jacket and a swish leather handbag completed the outfit.

Behind her came the sales assistant, with more clothes, and they all totted up to a good half-dozen or more capacious carrier bags.

His driver climbed out of the car to put the bags in the boot as Max helped Ellen into the back of the car.

She was in a daze—no doubt about it. She'd handed over her credit card, wincing at the huge total, but then tightening her mouth in defiance. Another watercolour would have to be sold—but this time *she* would get the benefit of it.

And it was money well spent—she'd seen that the moment she'd taken in her reflection, seeing not frumpy, lumpy Elephant Ellen but a tall, good-looking, athletic, fashionably dressed woman who could stride through the world with assurance and poise. It was a good feeling—a brilliant feeling!

A bubble of happiness rose in her, as if she'd just drunk a glass of champagne. She was going to enjoy this—enjoy *everything*! Including the novelty of a ride in a helicopter.

Her eyes widened in excitement as the noisy machine rose into the air, skating high above the River Thames. London became increasingly miniature, and then was left behind as the countryside approached. She gazed spellbound as they flew, then circled over the property Max wanted to assess.

It was another large country house, Victorian gothic in style, and far larger than Haughton. Only then did a shadow cross her eyes, for it reminded her of the danger to her home. Oh, he could buy anywhere he liked—so why insist on buying the one place in the world she so desperately loved?

Conflicting emotions swirled in her. Max had been so *good* to her, and even though she knew why he was doing it, it did not detract from the gift he had given her.

I will always, always be grateful to him.

It was a gratitude she voiced yet again that evening, as they dined in the Michelin-starred restaurant at the hotel.

'All I've done, Ellen,' he said, and smiled, 'is show you what was always there—that's all. You've always been like this—but you hid it. And now you don't any more. It's as simple as that.'

His eyes washed over her, liking what they saw. She was wearing the teal-blue dress he'd instinctively known would suit her, and it did—much to his satisfaction—and her hair was loosely gathered into a chignon at the back of her head. Her make-up—another purchase that day—was not as striking as it had been for the ball, but it gave her smoky eyes and long lashes and a soft, tender mouth...

He dragged his gaze away, returning to his study of the wine list. The arrival of the sommelier diverted him some more, and when he was done with his discussion and selection he turned back—to find Ellen looking around the dining room and getting the attention from male diners that she well deserved. He was glad to see it—it would do her good.

All the same, he reached out to touch her arm, with an atavistic instinct to show the other males she was spoken for.

Her gaze came back to him. 'So, will you buy that place you looked at this afternoon?' she asked.

As she'd glanced around the room she'd become conscious that she was being looked at by other men, and whilst it had given her a little thrill of confidence in her new appearance it had also, with her not being used to it, been somewhat disconcerting. She was grateful to have Max with her. He seemed...reassuring.

How odd that Max Vasilikos should seem reassuring to me—yet it's true.

A thought flickered through her mind. Could this man who had wrought this seismic revolution within her, with whom she'd spent the most amazing twenty-four hours in her life and still counting, really be the same man who was threatening Haughton, threatening to wrest from her all that she held most dear? It was hard to think of it.

'Maybe.' He was answering her now. 'Of course I'll need to look over it in person. But it ticks a lot of boxes. It's on at a good price, I like the look of it and it's close to London.'

'Much closer than Haughton!' she heard herself say quickly.

Max's eyes veiled. 'Haughton is quite different,' he said. 'I have...*other* plans for it.'

'*If* you manage to buy it!' Ellen riposted, her chin going up.

But even as she spoke she wished she hadn't. She didn't want to talk about Haughton, about how he wanted to buy it. For now—just for now—she only wanted to enjoy the present, this wonderful time with him. Nothing more than that. All the difficult, painful stuff could be left to one side. For now at least.

He gave a guarded smile. 'As you say,' he murmured, offering nothing more than that.

The sommelier returned with his choice of wine and he busied himself sampling it, nodding his approval.

He glanced across at Ellen. 'So,' he said, 'did you enjoy the helicopter ride?'

'It was amazing!' she exclaimed. 'A completely new experience.'

His long lashes dipped over his dark eyes. 'Well, new experiences are what you *should* be having, Ellen. Lots and lots of amazing new experiences!'

Was there a subtext to what he was saying? He was conscious of it. He was determined for her to have experiences with him... But he also wanted to indicate to her how her life could, and would, open up once she was free—not just of the chains that had made her think herself plain and unattractive, but of those that bound her to a house that had become a weapon against her stepmother and stepsister.

'Tell me,' he said, taking the subject further, 'when were you last abroad?'

She thought. 'Um... I took a school team to the Netherlands in the autumn term,' she recollected. 'And I did a field trip to Iceland with some sixth-formers—that was extraordinary. The geology and geography is breathtaking!'

Skilfully Max drew her out, and then equally skilfully drew her into contemplating where in the world she might yet like to go, exchanging his own views and experiences with her as their food arrived and they started on their meal.

An idea was forming in his head, but it would be premature to voice it now. He *could* sound her out, however, in general...

'And what about sun, sea and sand—tropical beaches and all that?' he ventured. 'Or did you do all that as a child in holidays with your parents?'

She shook her head. 'No, my mother preferred cultural destinations—so I've been to places like Florence and Paris and so on. Done all the museums and art galleries. I'm not sure I'd like to go back to those places again,' she said. 'They'd have sad memories for me now.' A shadowed look permeated her expression.

He nodded in sympathy. 'I've never gone back to where I was raised except once. And that,' he said, 'was to buy out the *taverna* my mother once slaved away in. I bought it, and now run it as a place to train unemployed young men—of which Greece now sadly has all too many—in useful skills.'

She looked at him. 'Would you never live in Greece again? Never settle there?'

He shook his head. 'I've let it go, Ellen. Cut my ties to a painful past and made a new life for myself. A better life by far! One I'd never known I'd dreamed of until I started to make the dream come true.' His eyes rested on her, his expression intent, challenging. 'Maybe, Ellen, it's time for you to do the same. Make a new life for yourself. Think about the future instead of clinging to a past that is gone.'

He'd spoken deliberately. It had to be said, after all. For her own sake as well as his.

She needs to be free—free of her chains. Free to move on. She needs to see the truth of that.

But a mutinous look had closed down her face and her eyes dropped, refusing to meet his gaze. 'This isn't a subject for discussion,' she said tersely. 'I don't want to sell you Haughton and that's that.'

Inside her head thoughts were teeming. She was immediately wary, reminding herself just who this man was and why he was interested in her, in spending time with her.

He's a stranger who wants to buy your home—and he'll use any means to get it. Including all this that he's doing for you now. Oh, he may have given you a priceless gift, freeing you from what that witch Chloe did for so long, but don't think it's for your sake he's done it—it's for his. That's why he's done it.

From the corner of her eye she saw the waiter approaching with their dessert and was glad of the diversion.

For a moment Max went on gazing at her, fulminating. Her constant obdurate stonewalling was frustrating. Then, with an intake of breath, he let it go. He'd made his point—he would let it be. He hoped she would take it on board internally, even if she did not accept it yet. Besides, he thought as he rested his gaze on her closed face as she doggedly focussed on her food, he wanted to dismiss the subject himself. He didn't want to think about the house she was refusing to sell, or her convoluted reasons for that. No, what he wanted to think about right now was something far more immediate.

The effect that she was having on his libido.

He'd been resolutely repressing it all day, but now, sitting opposite her, with her newly revealed beauty playing havoc with his senses, he knew without a doubt what he wanted to happen between them.

Even if she didn't own a single brick of the house I want to buy from her I'd still be doing this—still be spending the day with her, the evening with her.

And the night too…?

His eyes drifted over her face, visually caressing the curve of her cheek, the length of her lashes, the sweep of her hair, the lush, inviting richness of her mouth whose sweetness he had tasted so tormentingly as he'd bade her goodnight. He tore his gaze away, only for it to slip downwards, to see how the soft material of her dress shaped and pulled across the generous swell of her breasts, and into his head leapt the memory of how they had danced last night, her body so intimately close to his. He wanted to feel her in his arms again, closer and closer still…

He reached for his glass of wine, started to speak again to take his mind back into safer territory for the moment. Besides, he wanted to remove that fixed, closed look on her face. Wanted to see it soften again, become animated with interest and engagement with him. Wanted to see her smile at him again.

'So, tell me,' he opened decisively, 'this eco-resort of mine in the Caribbean—do you think it's the kind of place that would appeal to someone keen on an active holiday?'

It was a deliberate trail—something to catch her attention, make her look at him, take her away from that dark mental interior where she brooded on her father's resented second marriage. It seemed to work, for she lifted her head, blinking for a moment.

'What sort of activities will there be?' she asked.

Max waved a hand expansively. 'Well, water sports, definitely. Nothing motorised—that would be out of keeping—but sailing, windsurfing, kayaking…that sort of thing. Snorkelling and scuba diving, of course—the reef is notable, and I'm hiring a marine ecologist to advise me on the best way to preserve and nurture it. All the sports will have to be outdoors, but to be honest there probably isn't room for a tennis court. Plus it would require a hard surface—again, out of keeping. We'd run beach volleyball maybe,' he finished.

He found himself on the receiving end of an old-fashioned look. 'Well, that would be popular as a *spectator* sport—for the male guests, certainly,' she commented drily.

Max's riposte was immediate. 'It would be popular with me if *you* were taking part, even more certainly.'

The sweep of his long lashes over his revealing glance gave him the satisfaction of seeing her dip her gaze as his compliment registered. He followed through seamlessly.

'So, does it tempt you to come out and check over the place yourself? Try everything out before the first guests arrive later in the season?'

Ellen stared at him. 'Go to the Caribbean?' she said, as if he'd suggested a jaunt to Mars.

Max lifted a hand nonchalantly. 'Why not? You've got time before term starts again, haven't you? Plenty of time to cross the Atlantic.'

She opened her mouth, then closed it again. Gave a slight shake of her head as if that was all she could manage. He let it go. He'd planted the idea—he would harvest it later. When the time was right.

He started to talk about coral reef conservation. It was as good a subject to pass the time as any. He was enjoying the meal, enjoying spending this convivial time with her—no doubt about that. And there was even less doubt that he was looking forward to what he wanted to happen afterwards…

The elevator, when they walked into it some time later, seemed too small, too empty. And as it whooshed them up to the top floor of the hotel Ellen could feel her stomach dropping away. But it was not just from the effect of the lift. No, it was caused by the man she was sharing it with.

He stood a few feet away from her and gave her a quick smile as the doors opened, waiting for her to emerge. The soft, deep carpet of the penthouse-level corridor muffled all sound. It was completely deserted. A strange sensation of electricity started to run in her veins, along her nerve fibres, just as it had throughout dinner, in little jolts and quivers, every time she'd let her eyes rest on him.

Inside the suite, only a table lamp was lit, creating an atmosphere that was…intimate.

'Nightcap?' Max asked, strolling towards the drinks cabinet.

For a second—just a second—Ellen heard in her head the answer that she could give—*should* give. *Thank you, but no. It's been a long day. I really must turn in.* But instead she heard her voice saying, 'Lovely.'

She walked to the sofa. She could feel her heart thumping in heavy slugs, feel that electric current setting off again, humming through her veins. Carefully she lowered herself down, deliberately kicking off her shoes, tucking her legs under her and resting her elbow on the sofa's arm. A moment later Max was placing a small measure of liqueur on the coffee table in front of the sofa and then lowering himself on to the far end, his free hand cupping a cognac glass. It was a large sofa, but it suddenly felt very, very small.

She took a tiny sip of the sweet, orange-scented fiery liquid—no more than a sip, for it was strong, she knew, and she'd already drunk wine at dinner. A supreme sense of self-consciousness filled her—but not like anything she'd ever known before. This was nothing like the embarrassingly awkward consciousness of her ungainly body, her unlovely appearance that she was so bitterly used to feeling.

No—this was utterly different.

A lioness—that's what he called me last night!

And that was what she felt like—with her lithe body toned and honed, not an ounce of excess fat on it, yet rounded and womanly. She was supremely conscious of the way her hip was indenting the cushions of the sofa, the way the soft jersey of her dress was stretched over her breasts. Breasts that seemed fuller, somehow...heavier.

She felt the alcohol creaming in her bloodstream, heating it. Making her feel different...oh, so different. Free...bold...daring.

Daring enough to sit there with the devastating homage to manhood that was Max Vasilikos, whose lidded eyes were resting on her, whose sensual smile was playing around his mouth. His long lashes were veiling but not concealing the expression in his deep, dark eyes. That thrill came again in her...electricity crackled along her nerve fibres. She was no longer the person she had been—she was someone else now. Someone new.

Someone a man like Max could desire?

Because why else was he sitting there so close, so intimately, his eyes holding hers as if by a silken thread that was drawing her towards him, closer and closer yet? Why else—unless he desired her?

Wonder and hope welled up in her. Was this truly happening? All those long, lost years when she'd been trapped in despising her body, her face...were they really over?

Was it possible that she could now reach out and take what was surely every woman's right—could taste and enjoy the sensual pleasures of the flesh?

A memory pressed at her of her time at university, studying sports science, when all about her everyone had been pairing off, partying…and she had not dared. She'd felt excluded, forbidden from trying to join in. Had drawn back and hidden away, feeling herself unworthy—for who could want a woman like *her*? Men could only possibly want women like Chloe…who was the total opposite of herself.

I banished myself—did not dare to try and claim the place that every other woman was claiming.

But now—oh, now she *did* dare! She *did* dare to lean back into her end of the sofa, to relax and take a deep, easing breath.

And the absolute proof of her right to dare was the expression in Max Vasilikos's eyes now, as he twined his gaze with hers. The dim light cast shadows, created an atmosphere that was as heady as the liqueur she was sipping. She felt relaxed, languorous. And yet that low electric current was humming all the time, fuelling the charge that was building up in her, circuit by circuit.

Desire quickened in her veins. Desire made her eyelids heavy. Her breathing was shallow, her awareness of the sheer, raw physicality of Max becoming heightened… super-aware, ultra-aware.

I want this! I want what is to happen. I want it with all my being. To taste what I have denied myself so long…what I have never dared to take…

Yearning filled her, fusing throughout her being.

He moved first.

Wordlessly he placed his cognac glass on the table. Wordlessly he reached to remove her glass from her hand

and do likewise. Wordlessly he curved his hand around the nape of her neck. Silently, his heavy-lidded eyes lambent upon her he drew her lithe, pliant body towards him.

And as his mouth closed over hers in the sweet heat of his kiss there was only one conscious thought left in her head.

If Max Vasilikos desires me, then I am desirable indeed!

And then all conscious thought fell from her.

Now there was only sensation—sensation so strong, so overpowering, so arousing, so incredible, so blissful, so pleasurable, so *fantastic* that there was room for nothing else at all in her entire existence. His kiss was as skilled as it was consuming, unhurried—leisurely, even—as touch by touch, graze by graze, his mouth explored hers, slowly at first, skimming her lips, then deepening moment by expert moment, deepening until she was lost, yielding to what he was arousing in her, igniting in her, as each touch of his lips set new fires within her. Fires that he stoked, and stroked as his fingertips explored the nape of her neck, grazed the tender lobes of her ears, as his mouth moved to nuzzle at them softly, sweetly, arousingly.

She felt her breasts engorge and strain, and then a hand was cupping one, and a whole explosion of sensation ignited within her. A soft gasp sounded in her throat as he coaxed her cresting nipple to exquisite arousal. Her hand pressed against the hard-muscled wall of his chest, fingers splaying out, finding as if by instinct the shirt buttons, reaching between, within, slipping one and then another undone as if this were a skill that had been innate inside her all her life.

She heard him groan as her palm slid across the bare skin of his chest, slid down to where his belt snaked around his hips, eased along the rim of it. And he groaned again, his hand tightening on her breast, his mouth devouring hers now.

Excitement ripped through her, raw and intense. She pulled her mouth away, gazed at him, lips parted, eyes flaring, spearing her free hand into the hair that feathered at the base of his skull, shaping it with her fingers. There was an urgency in her now. A sense of power. She felt ripped, pumped, with adrenaline flowing in her, strong and purposeful. She knew what she wanted. *Who* she wanted.

A lioness seeking her mate…

His mouth curved into a smile. A smile of triumph. She knew it, gloried in it.

Their eyes twined together as they half lay upon the sofa that was suddenly much too small.

With a single fluid movement he got to his feet, scooping her up with him. She gave a cry that was half a gasp, for she knew just how much she weighed, even though it was muscled mass, not fat, but it didn't faze him in the slightest. As if she were a feather he carried her through to his bedroom, lowered her down on the bed. But he didn't come down beside her, remaining on his feet.

He wasn't idle, though. He was shrugging off his unbuttoned shirt, ripping the tie from him, ripping everything from him. Her eyes widened—how could they not?—and then, belatedly, she started to work off her own dress.

A hand stayed her.

'Oh, no,' growled Max. 'That's for *me* to do.'

He drew her back to her feet, utterly shameless in his own nakedness, his own rampant arousal. And she, because of that, was shameless too, standing there in front of him, fully clothed, her hands reaching up to her head, pulling off the hairclip so that her tousled locks fell with a single sensuous shake of her head, rippling down her back.

She heard him growl in satisfaction, saw his eyes flaring in the near darkness, for the only light came from the dim lamp in the lounge beyond. It was all the light they needed, and now he was stepping towards her, his hands catching at the hem of her dress, drawing up the soft jersey material in a slow, unstoppable movement until he'd eased it clear off her shoulders and freed her from it, casting it unwanted to a nearby chair. Now it was just her, with her hair rippling down her back, and the underwear she stood in.

But not for long.

Her own hands reached behind her back and she unhooked her bra deliberately, displaying herself, her eyes holding his all the time, her chin lifted, lips parted, knowing *exactly* what she was doing. Her breasts were freed, the bra discarded to the floor, and she stood there, showing her body to him as he was showing his to her.

His expression changed. 'My beautiful lioness...' he said, and his voice was low, deep, husky. His hand reached forward and the tips of his fingers simply grazed across her peaked nipples, so that they flowered even more, and a whisper of delight, of pleasure so exquisite, rippled through her so that she gasped and her head fell back, her long tousled hair brushing across the lower reaches of her arching spine.

He cupped her full, engorged breasts, heavy in his hands, and then his mouth found hers again, slowly, sensuously, with an intensity of arousal that she knew, with a kind of glory inside her, was the beginning of ultimate consummation.

She let him press her down upon the bed, let his body come over her, felt the crushing, arousing weight of him. He was kissing her still, one hand still enclosing a breast, the other now despatching the last remaining obstacle to his imminent possession. She lifted her hips as he discarded her panties and then she let his hand slide between her thighs, parting them for him. Whirls of pleasure rose within her, each one more intense than the last. A mist descended over her consciousness. She was no longer a thinking being—only a feeling one. Giving herself to the ultimate sensation.

He nestled himself within the apex of her body, and she felt with a mix of shock and exultation just how ready he was for this. How ready *she* was...

He took her hands, lifted them above her head so that the peaks of her breasts lifted too, and she gazed up at him. He smiled. Slow, intimate—possessive.

With an instinct older than time she felt her hips lift a little, straining towards him, yearning for his possession. His name was on her lips. An invitation—a plea. His smile deepened. And then, in a sudden fluid movement, he pulled away from her—only a fraction, but it was enough to cause alarm to flare in her eyes. Until she realised what he was doing—reaching into the drawer beside his bed... finding protection. *Her* protection.

She shut her eyes—there were things that even as a lioness she could not cope with! She heard him laugh, as if he realised that. A kiss nuzzled at the tip of her nose.

'Safe to peek now,' he said.

Amusement was in his voice, but it was only on the surface. Below was something deeper, and far more primal. She opened her eyes, looked deep into his, and even in the semi-darkness the naked desire there, the raw arousal, shocked her like electricity jolting through her body— her inflamed, aroused body.

For one long moment he gazed down at her. 'My lioness,' he murmured. 'My strong, beautiful lioness!'

And then, with a slow, deliberate tensing, he lowered himself to her as her thighs parted for him, as her hips lifted to his, as her body opened to his. Taking possession of her.

As she did of him.

There was tightness, but no resistance. She drew him into her, her body welcoming his, glorying in it, her delicate silken tissues gliding him in, sending a million nerve endings firing, shooting volley after volley of pleasure through her.

How could it be so good—so good to feel like this? How could this fullness be so incredible? This fusion, this melding of their flesh?

She dimly realised that for a moment he did not move, with supreme self-control, letting her body accommodate itself around him, letting her revel in the fullness of their fusion, letting her body reach the same level as his, poised at the brink.

Her hands were on his shoulders, braced against him, and his hands were bearing his weight, for he did not want to crush her. He wanted to see her face—a face that was raised to him in wonder, in beauty—in the moment before the ecstasy took her…took him…

And then, with the slightest shift in muscle, he moved, letting himself release.

He saw it happen in her face, saw her eyes distend, and then he was beyond everything but his own conflagration which swept up through him like a firestorm, burning him to ashes. Burning her with him.

She cried out in wonder, in amazement, in pleasure, and the sound of her cry shook him to his core. Her spine arched, her hips straining at him, nails clutching at his shoulders, head thrown back so that he could see the ecstasy that was in her face, the wonder and the joy. He felt her body thrash around him, pulsing with consummation, felt her thighs straining taut against his, and then his arms were around her, holding her, cradling her, keeping her safe within his embrace as her body burned.

And then slowly, oh-so-slowly, she slackened in his arms—slowly, oh-so-slowly, she stilled, her eyelids fluttering, her breath ragged, her skin dampened with a silken sheen. He held her tight against him, still half possessing her, then slackened away from her. He smoothed her hair, so fine and soft, and spoke to her in his native tongue. He knew not what he said. And she was like one who had gone beyond—gone far beyond, to a place she had never been before.

He held her while her taut muscles relaxed, released their tension, became soft and lax. She was letting him rock her gently, oh-so-gently, and he held her, still murmuring to her, as he brought her back slowly, carefully… oh-so-carefully.

He kissed her forehead, with scarcely any energy left in him to do so, and then a great lassitude swept through him. An exhaustion of the senses, of the passions. He turned her in his arms, her body still damp, her eyes still glazed, and kissed her bare shoulder, nestling her into him, holding her close and safe and warm against him.

'Sleep,' he said, his voice a murmur. 'Sleep now…'

He saw the ghost of a smile cross her mouth. It was all that she could manage and he asked for no more—not now. She had given all and taken all, and now they would rest, exhausted and complete, embraced by each other.

Sleep took them both.

CHAPTER NINE

ELLEN STIRRED. SHE was cradled against hard, warm muscle, and an arm lay heavily around her. She could feel Max's breathing, low and steady, feel his breath on the nape of her neck. As she came to wakefulness her own limbs felt heavy, tired, and there was an ache between her legs. Yet it was not pain. Oh, no, not pain...

A sense of wonder suffused her. Was it real to be lying here in the dim morning light, with Max's arms around her, holding her so closely? Could it possibly be real? But it was—oh, it *was*. That was the wonder of it—the miracle. That after all those long, miserable years of thinking herself repulsive, repellent, all the misery, the dreary self-torment, was over.

Gratitude flooded her. She knew why Max had done this, knew what his reasons were—to wean her away from clinging to the home she loved so much, that he could only see as her hiding place—but she didn't care. How could she care when his strong arms were warm around her? When her body had discovered the bliss he could arouse in her? No, whatever his motives, she could only be grateful for this wondrous, incredible gift that he had given her—the gift of knowing herself to be desirable.

It was gratitude that she gave voice to when Max awoke and made love to her again, bringing her once more to a peak of ecstasy that left her breathless with wonder. Then another appetite struck, and they wrapped themselves in voluminous bathrobes, padded through to the suite's dining area to partake of a large and filling breakfast.

She caught his hand, staying him. Her eyes huge. *'Thank you...'* she breathed.

He turned her hand in his, winding his fingers through hers, turning them towards him. Amusement danced in his eyes, but there was another expression there too.

'Oh, the pleasure was all mine—be very, *very* sure of that!'

He kissed her nose, lightly and humorously, squeezing her hand, his free hand brushing the loosened locks of her hair caressingly. She was gazing up at him wide-eyed, with that wonder in her expression that did strange things to him. There was wonder in him, too. He'd awakened her senses—but she had awakened in him senses he had not known he possessed.

Satisfaction—deep, consuming and very...well, very *satisfying*—creamed through him. Whatever his original motives for setting Ellen free from the chains she was bound with, he knew with absolute certainty that what had happened between them—what was still happening—was for quite different reasons. For reasons that had only to do with him being a man and Ellen being a woman, desiring him and being desired.

That is all we need. All I want.

He sat himself down opposite her, reaching for her glass and filling it with fresh orange juice from the jug on the table. His eyes rested on her, appreciating what he was seeing—her loose, tousled hair, the deep vee of her robe exposing the swell of her breasts, the softness in her face, in her eyes, the deep, sensuous glow of a woman who'd spent a night of passion in his arms.

He poured his own orange juice and drank it in one draught, setting down the glass. She was sipping hers in a more genteel fashion, and her gaze was flickering to his, as if she wanted to feast on him but felt a touch of shyness yet. Hunger rattled in him—and not just for the croissants nestling in their napery. He helped himself to one, tearing it open with strong fingers. Then his eyes went back to hers, holding them.

'We need,' he announced, 'to get hold of your passport.'

Ellen started. She'd been in a daze, wanting only to let her eyes gaze across the table at him, to drink him in—the way his jaw was roughened right now, and how enticingly piratical the dark shadow of regrowth made him look, and how there was that glint in his eyes again that could melt her bones like water, and how the towelling robe he wore with such casual ease was so incredibly white against the gold tan of his smooth, half bared chest, and how his strong, lean forearms were reaching for that croissant with fingers that had stroked her body to shuddering ecstasy.

'What?' Her eyes widened in confusion.

'Your passport,' Max repeated. His expression changed, become amused. 'So we can visit my eco-resort in the Caribbean. I told you over dinner last night that I needed to go out there.' Long lashes dipped over his dark eyes. 'Surely,' he said softly, 'you did not think that a single night with you would be enough—did you?'

He watched his words sink in. Words that he had already formed in his own head as soon as he'd awoken. A single night with this woman? No, not enough! Not anywhere *near* enough!

Across from him he saw her reaction—saw for the fraction of a second indecision hover in her eyes and then vanish.

Her face lit, and inside her head words were singing suddenly.

Go with him! Go with him while he wants you—because he does want you. Because this time is the most wonderful of your life so far. So seize it—seize it all. Take what you've never had before and wring from it every last drop. After all, why not?

Max Vasilikos had given her a gift she had never, never thought to possess—the gift of her own beauty. The gift of himself desiring her.

Wonder, joy and gladness filled her to the brim.

'There are no walls!' Ellen exclaimed as they walked into the room. It was situated in one of the cabanas that had already been constructed, at one end of the resort, and was cantilevered over a low, rocky bluff that jutted right out over a sheltered bay on the tiny islet.

'Just mosquito nets,' agreed Max. He strolled up to the missing outer wall, where an area of decking gave some outside space to meld interior and exterior seamlessly. 'Like it?' he asked as Ellen walked up to join him, resting her hands on the balustrade above the tumbling rocks.

A little wooden staircase to their left led down to the white sand beach a few metres below. An azure sea lapped lazily, beckoning to her with seductive allure.

She twisted her head to look at him. Made a face. 'Oh, no, it's awful—honestly, how could you bring me to such a place? I mean, there isn't a nightclub for miles, and there's no gourmet restaurant with a signature chef, and, I mean, there isn't even a *wall*, for heaven's sake!'

In the hours it had taken them to arrive here the very last remnants of her shyness and uncertainty in his company had vanished. Gone completely. Now she was at ease with him, daring to laugh with him, be confident with him, to tease him as she was doing now.

He kissed her to silence her and they both laughed into the kiss, and then Max tightened his hold and deepened his kiss. 'There is, however,' he told her, 'a bed—a very large, king-sized bed—and the mattress is very, *very* high spec... I promise you.'

It was, too, and suddenly all jet lag was gone, and energy and the fires of arousal leapt within her, dismissing all other thoughts.

'I wanted to swim in the sea,' was her last muffled cry as he swept her off to the bed.

'Later...' Max growled.

Afterwards, as they lay exhausted in each other's sated embrace, it came to him that for a woman who had only a handful of days ago regarded herself as completely repellent to the male race, she was, in fact, taking to this like a natural. As if she'd been born to be in his arms...

Ellen waded out of the water, feeling the heat of the sun on her body immediately, even through her sopping wet T-shirt. Her snorkel and mask dangled loose in her hand.

'Lunch?' asked Max, glancing at her and admiring the way the wet T-shirt material clung to her generous breasts. Desire stirred in him. Maybe they could wait for lunch for a while?

'Definitely,' agreed Ellen, dashing his hopes, or at least deferring them until a post-lunch siesta.

Ellen glanced fondly at him. The days had slipped by, one after another, each one glorious. They'd swum and snorkelled, sailed and kayaked, and Ellen had done a beginner's dive while Max, with years of experience, had gone for a serious deep water session.

She'd accompanied Max as he'd inspected the resort site, talking to his project manager, the architect and the work crew who came across from the main island, where they lived. It had been revealing to see him with his staff, because even the most junior of the work crew got a word of appreciation from him, and she'd been able to see they regarded him as a good boss.

That said a lot about a person...things she could admire, respect. No mere venal money-grubbing property developer was he—his values were those she could share and approve of.

'There are places in the world where new construction is fine—and places where it isn't,' Max was saying now as they relaxed, replete after dinner cooked over an open firepit, down on their little beach, leaning back against a rock with the water lapping gently a few metres away and overhead the tropical stars wheeling their slow arc across the midnight sky. 'Places where we should tread lightly on the land, as I'm trying to do here, or not tread at all— places where we should save and repair what is already there, conserve what earlier generations have built.'

She glanced at him, liking what she'd heard him say. 'Maybe being Greek helps—growing up amongst so much antiquity?'

But her words drew from him a glance that seemed, she felt, to admonish her.

'We cannot live in the past—it is not healthy to do so. Sometimes,' he said, 'we have to let go. Let go of the past and make a new future for ourselves! A new life.'

Ellen's eyes slipped away. Discomfort snagged in her, and she wished he had not said that. This was the first time he'd referred to the underlying reason he was in her life at all. Up till now there had been no mention of it— as if that troubled situation thousands of miles across the ocean did not exist. And certainly it had not intruded into what they had here.

Here, she knew—with a gratitude that in itself was revealing of how much she did not want to think of anything beyond this bliss—she could merely revel in what was happening. Day after day, just her and Max—wonderful, *wonderful* Max!—who'd transformed her, transformed her life, and to whom she would be grateful always! Walking barefoot on the sand, hand in hand beneath the sun, beneath the moon and stars. All cares and concerns far, far away.

But now he was reminding her of them. Making her think about them…making her face them once again. She didn't want to hear him say such things. He'd made no mention before—none at all—of what was for this brief space of time an ocean away. Nor did she want him to.

I don't want this time with him spoilt in any way at all. I don't want to think about Haughton, how desperate I am to keep it. Nor to be told that I should let it go…

But Max was speaking again, gazing up at the starry night sky.

'I remade *my* life,' he was saying. 'My mother's death forced me to do so. I wish so much she'd lived to see what I've achieved, but it was not to be.'

His gaze flicked back to her, trying to read her expression in the dim light. But he could not see it. And nor could he bring himself to tell her how struck he'd been by the house he wanted her to yield to him—how it had called to him immediately, arousing in him for the first time in his life an urge to cease his wandering, rootless lifestyle.

Instead he focussed on what he so wanted her to realise for herself. 'Do you not think,' he ventured carefully, weighing the impact of each word upon her, 'that your father's death is also a turning point for *you*? Allowing you to be free at last to do what you want with your life?' He chose the word 'allowing' specifically. 'Allowing you,' he finished, his eyes on her, 'to move on. To claim your own life for yourself?'

With a sweep of his hand he indicated the whole expanse of the beach, the starry tropical sky, the lap of the gentle waves.

'It's a good life, isn't it?' he said softly. 'Here—and everywhere! The whole world lies before you, Ellen, and now you know how beautiful you are, how desirable, what is stopping you from walking out into that world? Living your life. *Your* life, Ellen—unfettered and untrammelled. Not trapped in an unhappy past.'

She let him speak. She knew why he was saying it—knew it was because he wanted her to stop fighting him, stop clinging to Haughton. Knew that he truly believed it would be for her own good. But she could make no reply. Inside her, like a festering wound, was all the bitterness she felt about what Pauline's marriage to her father had done, and it could not be so easily lanced.

I don't want to think about them—what they did to my father, to me—not while I'm here, having this precious time with Max. I don't want to tell him what they're like, how vicious and ruthless they are—greedy for everything they can get their hands on. I don't want this idyll with Max spoilt.

So she looked away, giving a slow shake of her head, closing her eyes momentarily. Shutting out what he was telling her. Then she felt his hand on her arm, not pressing firmly, almost as a message to her.

'Think about what I've said…' His voice was low, compelling. 'That's all I ask for now.'

He paused, instinctively knowing that he must say no more now, that she must ponder his words, let them soak into her. Make sense to her.

He shifted his position, hooking his arms loosely around his splayed bent knees. 'So,' he said, his tone quite different now, 'what shall we do tomorrow? How about if we take the catamaran out?'

Gratefully, Ellen followed his lead. This was the Max she wanted. Carefree and easy-going. Revelling in the days and nights they spent here.

And she was grateful, too, the next day—to experience the thrill and the speed of skimming over the azure swell as she clung to the tarpaulin between the twin hulls of the wind-hungry vessel, with Max commandingly at the helm.

'Enjoying it?' he shouted to her over the rush of wind.

'Fantastic!' she yelled back, and then gave a cry, snatching more tightly at the tarpaulin, as with a careless answering laugh Max spun the helm, heading right into the wind, and the catamaran tacked with a lift of one hull before coming about again.

Exhilaration filled her as he headed downwind back to shore. With easy strength she helped him haul the vessel up on to the beach, then flopped down on the hot sand.

Max lowered himself beside her. Her eyes were shining, her face alight. There was sand in her hair, and it was windblown and tangled. A memory of how Tyla had hated getting her hair in a mess sifted through him—how she'd fussed endlessly about her appearance, wanting him and every other man to admire her constantly. Desire her.

His eyes softened. Ellen—his own beautiful lioness— was fit and fabulous. She'd believed no man could desire her, and even now that he had convinced her how very, very wrong that misconception had been, so that she now finally accepted the truth of her own appeal, there was still no trace of the fussing and self-absorption that Tyla had indulged in endlessly.

How easy that makes her to be with—she accepts my

desire for her as naturally as breathing now, returns it with an ardour that takes my breath away!

And it was much more than simply the time she spent in his arms, breathtaking though that was. It was her enthusiasm, her sheer enjoyment of everything—from food, to sunbathing, to swimming, to gazing up at the stars— everything they did together.

I like being with her. I like her company—I like her thoughts and views and opinions. I like it that she likes this simple place and that she does not yearn for bright lights and sophisticated glamour. I like her laughter and her smiles.

She was smiling now—smiling right up at him as he loomed over her.

'Good fun?' He grinned, and she laughed again exuberantly. 'You can sail her tomorrow,' he promised, and then busied himself with kissing her.

From kissing her it was an easy progression to sweeping her up into his arms and carrying her up to their open-air room, making use, yet again, of the very large bed.

His last conscious thought, barely forming in his head, was just how good it was to make love with Ellen—how very, *very* good. And then there was no more thought, no more conscious awareness of anything at all, only rich, sating fulfilment.

Max's hand was resting lazily over Ellen's warm, sand-speckled thigh as they lay in partial shade on their little beach, having breakfasted on their terrace after an early-morning workout at the open-air gym in what would shortly be the reception and central services area of the resort. They were sunning themselves, waiting for enough wind to rise so they could take out the catamaran.

It was their penultimate day there, and Ellen was only

too conscious of a sense of deep, aching reluctance for this blissful, wondrous time to end. She could feel a little tug on her insides—a sense of yearning for this time not to be over, not to be done with. She glanced over the sparkling azure water to the curve of the tiny bay edged with vivid glossy foliage. The fronded roofing of their wooden cabana was barely visible, blending into the verdant greenery.

She gave a low, regretful sigh. These past days—one slipping effortlessly into the next, so that she'd all but lost count of them—had been so wonderful. So idyllic. They had been cocooned on this lush tropical island, living as close to nature as they could. Away from all the rest of the world, away from all its problems and difficulties.

A little Eden—just for the two of us. And I was Eve— woman new-made. Discovering for the first time just how joyous being a woman can be.

New-made, indeed—and from Adam's rib. A smile tugged whimsically at her mouth.

Max made me—he made me a woman, sensual and passionate.

Oh, he'd done it for his own purposes, his own ends— she had no illusions about that. He had been perfectly open about wanting her to discover what life could be like beyond what she knew he saw as the prison of her childhood home. The place that had trapped her in misery, in the past, in her bitter feud with Pauline and Chloe. But she didn't care. How could she? His motives could never detract from the effect his liberation had had on her. The wondrous, glorious gift he had given her!

The gift of his own desire for her.

And hers for him.

Her eyes went to him now with familiar pleasure as he lay beside her on the sand, dark glasses shading his eyes so that she did not know if he was dozing or awake.

It was the latter. 'Why the sigh?' he asked, turning his head towards her.

'Oh, I guess it's just that I… Well… This time tomorrow we'll be heading back to London.'

She felt his gaze on her through the opaque lenses. 'You've enjoyed it here?'

There was a little choke in her voice. 'Of *course* I have! It's been idyllic.' It was all she could manage to say.

'Yes,' he agreed, 'it's certainly been that.'

His hand moved a fraction on her thigh, and he turned his head away to look up into the sky. She could hear a pause in his silence. Then he spoke.

'Tell me…'

His voice was different—almost, she thought, speculative.

'What do you think about Arizona?'

She frowned in surprise. 'Arizona?'

'Yes. Or actually it might be Utah. I'll have to check.' He turned his head towards her again, pushing his dark glasses up on to his head. 'Ever heard of Roarke National Park?'

She shook her head, still frowning slightly.

'Well,' Max continued, 'it's not as well-known as the more famous National Parks in the American West, such as Zion and Bryce—let alone the Grand Canyon. But, anyway, the lodge there is hosting a seminar on sustainable tourist development which I've a fancy to go to.'

He paused again, his eyes suddenly unreadable.

'So what do you say? Shall we head there next? We can fly from Miami. Once the seminar's done we could add a few days' hiking, maybe. Pick up boots and kit when we're there. Does it appeal?'

She was silent. Then suddenly she propelled herself up on her elbow, looking down at Max. '*Yes!* Oh, yes.'

In an instant her heart was singing, her mood soaring into the stratosphere. More time with Max—oh, yes, more time!

A grin split his face. 'Great,' he said.

He reached up a hand to her nape, drawing her mouth down to his, letting her hair fall like a veil around them. Satisfaction filled him. And a sense of triumph. Another new place, another new experience for Ellen to savour—to tempt her to stay out in the wonderful world that could be hers if she left her past behind her.

And, best of all, another stretch of time to enjoy all that she bestowed upon him.

His kiss deepened, and soon all thoughts of taking the catamaran out that morning faded completely.

CHAPTER TEN

ROARKE NATIONAL PARK proved to be an experience ideally suited to Ellen. She loved it—loved the wild beauty of the American West, loved even more experiencing it with Max.

They flew in to Salt Lake City, then drove down through the increasing grandeur of the landscape as it rose in a vast stone flight of inclined steps from the south. The park itself was still relatively quiet at this early time in the season, with parts of it still closed by snow, but in the sheltered canyon it was warmer, and the sunlit orange sandstone rock was a vivid contrast with the deep blue of the sky and the dark green of the pines.

The timber-built lodge fitted into its remote setting perfectly, blending into the landscape, a tribute in itself to the kind of design that worked best in places where nature was pre-eminent. And Ellen found the seminar fascinating—as fascinating as learning about the geology and geography of the park and the wider landscape beyond. Already she was planning a field trip here, making appropriate notes with which to broach the project with her headmistress on her return.

She made no mention of that to Max, however. She did not want to trigger another attempt by him to persuade her to abandon what he was so convinced were the confines of her life at Haughton. She did not want that upset. Wanted only to enjoy this time with him to the hilt.

And enjoy it she did.

As he'd promised, after the seminar they kitted themselves up with hiking gear and took to the trails that were open at that time of year.

'Boy…' she breathed as they reached the summit of one trail that had ascended up out of the canyon and on to a rocky plateau where the chill wind seemed only cooling after the heat generated by their hard-pushed muscles. 'You don't need a gym at this place, do you?'

Max gave a laugh, leaning back on a rock to take a long draught of water from the flask that hung around his neck—an absolute necessity for hiking, as they'd been firmly instructed by the rangers—and she did likewise.

'No, indeed,' he agreed. 'We're going to feel it in our legs tomorrow, though, I suspect. But it's worth it ten times over.'

'Oh, yes.' She nodded, her eyes sweeping out over the grandeur of the wilderness that stretched as far as the eye could see and much further still. Her gaze came back to Max. 'Thank you,' she said.

He smiled, warm and affectionate. 'I knew this was a good idea,' he said. He lowered his backpack to the ground. 'Right, that hike's made me starving—time for lunch.'

They settled themselves on a sun-warmed rock in the lee of a boulder that sheltered them from the keening wind and companionably started on the packed lunch prepared for them. Ellen lifted her face to the sun. Happiness filled her. Complete and absolute happiness.

Her eyes went to Max.

You…you make me happy. Being with you makes me happy. Whether we're making love or sitting like this, side by side in the silence and the grandeur of nature's gift to us. It's being with you that makes me happy.

Yet even as the thoughts filled her head their corollary came. If being with Max made her happy, what would being *without* him make her?

For being without him was what awaited her. It had to—there could be no escape from that. In days they would be heading back to England.

And even if it were not mere days...even if it were weeks...even months...at some point I would have to be without him.

Shadows clouded her mind and through the shadows words pierced her. Pierced her with painful knowledge.

The longer I am with him, the harder being without him will be.

There was a little cry inside her head as the piercing knowledge came. Instinctively she sought to shield herself. To hold up a guard against the thought that must come next but which she would not permit. Dared not permit.

Fiercely she fought back.

Enjoy only this! Enjoy this for what it is and don't ask for more.

Yet even as she adjured herself to be cautious she knew with sudden certainty that it was already too late for caution. Awareness opened out within her like a physical sensation, and the words that went with it took form in her consciousness—loud and unstoppable.

Am I falling in love with him?

She pulled her mind away, tried to silence the words. Sought urgently to counter them. To deny them. No—*no*—she *wasn't* falling in love with Max. She was only *thinking* she was!

And it was obvious—wasn't it? Max was the first man in her life...the only man to have made love to her, embraced her, kissed her, spent time with her. It was obvious that she should fancy herself falling in love with him! What female *wouldn't* fancy herself falling in love with him when he was so incredibly attractive, so devastating, from his deep, dark eyes and his curving smile to his strong, lean body?

That was all it was—just a natural and obvious reaction. It was only that, nothing more—it was nothing real… just her imagination.

Beside her, Max was packing away his now empty lunch box and fishing out his phone.

'Selfie time,' he announced, hooking one arm around her while holding out his phone ahead of them. 'Big smile!' he instructed, and set off a flurry of shots of them both. 'There,' he said, showing her the images.

Ellen smiled, but she could feel a pang inside all the same. A sudden sense of impending loss.

This is all that's going to be left of my time with him— photos and memories.

She took a steadying breath. Well, she would deal with that when she had to. Right now, as Max slipped his phone away and got to his feet, hefting his backpack on to his broad shoulders again, she would make the most of this time with him. So she got up too, and set off after him on the descent.

More hiking, cycling along the paved valley trails and even horse riding—with Ellen discovering the novelty of a Western saddle—comprised their days, and dining at the lodge in rustic comfort passed their evenings. Roaring log fires in the lounge and no TV or other electronic distractions all added to the ambience and mood. Yet all the same the days passed, one by one and ineluctably, taking them nearer to their return to the UK.

Ellen's mood, as they finally headed north to pick up their flight from Salt Lake City, became increasingly sombre as mile after long mile ate up this last time of being with the man who had so utterly transformed her.

Inside as well as outwardly.

An ache caught at her. Soon they would be parting. One plane journey away and she would be heading back to Haughton, and he—well, he would be heading to whatever was next on his busy schedule. This time tomorrow he would be gone from her life.

A silent cry went up inside her. And a savage admonition.

You went into this with your eyes open. You knew why he was doing it, what his reasons were—so don't bewail it. Think of it as...as therapy!

She shut her eyes, blocking the sight of him from herself. There would be other men in her life now. He had made that possible. Made her see herself as desirable, as beautiful. That was the gift he'd given her, even if he'd given it to her for reasons of his own. From now on she knew that men would desire her—

But even as she told herself that she could hear that voice cry out again in silent anguish.

But what man could I desire after Max? What man could ever compare to him? Impossible—just impossible! No one could ever melt me with a single glance, could make love to me as he does, could set the fires racing through my veins as he can! No one! No one else ever will.

A shiver went through her, as if she had stirred ghosts from a future that had not yet happened but was waiting to happen. A future without Max Vasilikos in it. An empty future.

No, she mustn't think like that. A future without Max in it would not be empty. Could not be—not while she had to fight for her beloved home, keep it as long as she possibly could, safe from those who wanted to take it from her. Including Max.

Her face shadowed. Here, on the far side of the Atlantic, she had been able to forget that it was he who wanted to oust her—for her own good, as he believed—but that bitter truth was not something she must ever forget.

And it was a truth that loomed larger with every hour on the plane as they flew back to the UK.

Her mood had darkened as they flew into the night, and she had slept only patchily and uncomfortably. She knew she had a sombre air about her as they arrived at Heathrow in the bleak early hours of the morning. She was facing the end of her time with Max and the resumption of her battle for her home.

After the tropical heat of the Caribbean, and the crisp, clean air of the American west, the wet spring weather of the UK was uninviting and drear as a chauffeured car drove them into London through the rush hour traffic.

Ellen sat huddled into a corner, groggy from the red-eye flight, and Max let her be, busying himself with catching up on his emails on his laptop. Thoughts were racing across his mind.

As they stepped out on to the pavement outside the hotel he shivered extravagantly. 'It's freezing!' he exclaimed. He ushered her inside the hotel, and as they reached the warmth of the lobby said, 'Thank goodness the Gulf is our next destination!'

He didn't notice Ellen's sudden start at his words, only guided her into the elevator. Back in his suite, he elaborated, watching as room service departed after setting breakfast out for them.

'I've just had confirmation via email that my appointment with the business adviser to the Sheikh there is the day after tomorrow. It will be a bit of a rush, but we can fly out tomorrow. You can cope with that, can't you?' He smiled. 'We'll stay on—go camping in the Arabian desert. Stargazing, camel rides, dune-bashing—you'll love it.' Then his expression changed. 'What is it?' he asked.

Concern was in his voice. Ellen was just looking at him in consternation.

'Max… Max, I can't,' she said.

He frowned. 'You've still got a while before your next term starts,' he said.

She shook her head. Her expression had not changed. 'It's not that,' she said.

'Then what is it?' he demanded.

There was an edge in his voice he could not suppress. Emotion was starting up inside him. An emotion he did not want to feel, but that was happening all the same. Why was she hesitating like this? Making objections? Didn't she *want* to come out to the Gulf with him?

Because I certainly want her to come with me. I don't want to let her go—not yet. Definitely not yet.

Emotion swirled within him. He was certain—two hundred per cent certain—that he had no desire whatsoever to part company with Ellen now. That conviction had been growing with every passing day they'd spent together, and had come to a head on their overnight flight, when he'd realised he did not want their time together to end yet.

She'd been a revelation to him—a total revelation. Not just in her new-found physical beauty, which had knocked him for six from the moment she'd walked out looking so incredibly fantastic in that Edwardian ballgown, but ever since… And, no, not just in that respect. But more—oh, *much* more!

I like being with her. She's good company. Fun, intelligent, with a great sense of humour. She's easy-going, undemanding. She enjoys everything, is good-tempered, isn't self-obsessed or demanding of my attention—though I'm more than happy to lavish it on her because I so enjoy being with her.

The litany ran on in his head, concluding with the most obvious reason of all. In bed, he and she set off fireworks!

Ardent, passionate, sensual, sensitive, affectionate...

The litany set off again. And was cut brutally short as she shook her head again. He saw emotion flash across her face, then vanish. There was something different about her suddenly. Something that reminded him, with a sudden flicker of concern, an inward frown, of the way she'd looked when he'd first gone to look over Haughton and succumbed to its charms. As if she were locked inside herself. Shutting out the world. Shutting *him* out.

And he didn't want that. He didn't want it at all.

OK, he allowed, trying to rationalise her reaction, so she was jet-lagged. Flying the red-eye was never a fun experience. But her wavering was more than just sleep deprivation and grogginess. His thoughts raced on swiftly. Was it because although *he* was two hundred per cent sure he had no desire to call it quits between them, *she* might not realise that? Was she feeling uncertain about him? About what they had between them?

He took her hand in his, squeezed it tight. Time to reassure her.

'Ellen—we are *good* together. Never doubt that. So let's go on making the most of it until your term starts. Don't cut this short unnecessarily—come with me to the Gulf! I want to show you as much of the world as I can. I want—'

But she tugged her hand free, stepping a pace away from him, her face working. Emotions were swilling within her—a turbulent mix. All the way back on the flight it had been worsening with the knowledge that her time with Max was ending. And it *must* end. That was the blunt truth of it. She would be back at school, and Max would either be pressing ahead with his proposed purchase of her home—although Pauline would have to start legal proceedings against her to force a sale—or else he would be backing off and leaving Haughton alone.

Whichever he did, her time with him would have ended. And while part of her—the part that had her heart leaping at the thought of what his words meant—was saying, *Go with him now—take these last few days with him!* she could not let herself listen to it. A few more days and then she would be back here again, just as she was now, and their time together would be over.

Better for it to be over now. Because the longer you are with him, each and every day, the worse it will be for you when it's finally over. The more you will fear that you're falling in love with him—which you must not do. You must not!

Because whether she was falling in love with him, or whether it was just an obvious reaction to her first romance, it was going to hurt, doing without Max—it was hurting already...had been hurting all the way across the Atlantic...this prospect of her time with Max running out, reaching its close.

I'm going to have to do without him. I'm going to have to go home, back to my life, and keep fighting for Haughton to the bitter end.

So she had to crush down the rush of joy that came from the knowledge that Max wanted to spend more time with her.

She sought for the right words to say to him. 'Max, I can never thank you enough for what you've done for me. *Never!*' Emotion filled her voice, though it was low and strained. 'You've given me a gift I never thought to have—

and this time with you has been…*miraculous*. I'll always be grateful to you—'

He cut across her. 'I don't want your gratitude! I want you to come to the Gulf with me, make the most of our time now, before your term starts again. It's not too much to ask of you, is it?'

His tone was persuasive, compelling, but there was an edge to it as well. Didn't she *want* to be with him for longer? That bite of emotion came again, and with it another spiralling upwards of frustration.

She was staring across at him, her hands lifted as if— damn it—as if she were holding him at bay. Ellen was holding him off—

Emotion bit in him again, more painful this time.

'Max—it isn't that. It's…it's just that it'll only be post- poning the time when I have to get back to Haughton. And it seems to me that it might as well happen now, rather than in a few days' time, when I'll just be right back here, facing the same situation. I *have* to go back to Haughton. And it isn't just because term is starting, it's because it's where I *want* to be—'

She broke off. Echoing bleakly in her head were the unspoken words—*while I still have it*.

But that was too painful even to think—too painful to say to the man who was trying to take it from her. Even though she knew that if it was not him who wanted to buy it at some point someone else would, and Pauline and Chloe would force the sale through, and she would lose the place she held so dear to her. The place where all her happiness was centred.

Yet even as the clutch of emotion that always came when she thought of Haughton gripped her, so did another.

All my happiness? And what of the happiness I've had with Max? What of that?

But her mind sheered away. Whatever happiness she'd had with Max, it was never, ever going to be anything other than temporary. How could it be otherwise? He'd transformed her into a woman who could finally indulge in her own sensuality—a gift she would always be grateful for, just as she'd told him. But for him...? Well, she was just a...a novelty, maybe, made all the more intriguing by the revelation of her desirability for him. Whatever her appeal for him, she had to accept that she was no more than a good companion, in bed and out, while they were together.

'We're good together,' he'd said, and it was true.

But it did not make it anything more.

Time for me to go home.

She shook her head, her expression anguished now. 'I just want to go home, Max,' she said. 'It's all I want to do.'

Even as she spoke she could feel that anguish spearing her. Yes, she wanted to go home—to be there while she still could, before it was torn from her—but it was not all she wanted. She wanted Max—oh, how she wanted him, to be with him—but even if she stayed now it would only be putting off what must be the inevitable end, only be making it worse for herself. So best for her to go now— go now and have precious time at the home that she could only lose in the end.

He saw her expression and hated seeing it. Hated hearing her say what she had said. Telling him she didn't want to be with him—wanted instead to return to the place he was trying to free her from. Frustration boiled up in him—more than frustration. It was an emotion he did not want to name, *could* not name. It boiled over. He stepped towards her, closed his hands around her arms, fastening her to him.

'Ellen, don't do this. Your obsession with Haughton

isn't healthy. It's poisoning you. Chaining you to a life you should not be living!'

His voice was urgent, his expression burning. Here they were, not an hour back in the UK, and she was already reverting to what she'd been like when he'd first known her. He had to stop that—right now! He had to make her see what she was doing to herself. Had to convince her, finally, that she *must* set herself free from her self-imposed chains. Chains that were as constraining and as deadly as those of her belief that she lacked beauty or desirability had been.

He took a shuddering breath, surged on with what he *must* say to her now to set her free.

Free to seize life with both hands. Free to take all it offers. Free to be with me—

Words were pouring from him. He could not stop them. He'd tried to be gentle on her during their time together, tried to ease her into seeing how she had to let the past go, not cling to it, had to move forward with her life, not stay trapped in the mesh of resentment she so obviously felt about her father's remarriage, unable to free herself of it. He had to make her see that now—in all its stark, unvarnished truth—or she'd just go right back into it all again. And be lost...

Lost to *him*...

An even greater urgency fuelled his words. 'You call it home—but it's a tomb, Ellen. *Your* tomb. Don't you see? You've buried yourself in it, clung to it, and you go on clinging to it because you can use it as a weapon against Pauline, who dared to marry your doting father and give him a second chance of happiness—'

A cry broke from her but he did not stop. Could not stop.

Frustration surged in him, boiling up out of the long, sleep-depriving red-eye flight that had taken them from their passion-filled carefree travels together to land them back here.

Ellen—*his* Ellen—whom he'd freed from her self-imposed mental prison of thinking herself unlovely and undesirable, was now determined to go straight back to the destructive life he'd released her from. He couldn't bear to let it happen. He had to make her see what she was doing to herself, consumed by bitterness as she was. It was a bitterness that was destroying her. Changing her from the wonderful, carefree, passionate woman she'd been when she was with him. Changing her back into the embittered, resentful, anger-obsessed person he'd first encountered.

He couldn't let that happen. He couldn't!

He plunged on. 'Ellen—look at yourself. You've let your anger and resentment eat into you. For years and years. You never gave Pauline and Chloe a chance—you never wanted them to be part of your family. You were fixated on your father—understandably, because of the loss of your mother—but now you've become obsessed with punishing them by hanging on to Haughton.'

She thrust him away, lurching backwards. Her eyes were wide and distended. Emotion battered at her. Stress, weariness and anger rushed up in her.

'It's my *home*, Max! Why *should* I sell it so that someone like you can turn it into a hotel? Or sell it on to some oligarch or sheikh who'll only set foot it in once a year, if that!'

He shook his head vigorously. 'That *isn't* what I want to do with Haughton. What I want is—'

She didn't let him finish. Dear God, why was he choosing now, of all times, to lay into her again? Why couldn't he just leave her alone? Stop going on and on about it?

'I don't *care* what you want! I don't care because I will fight you to the last—fight Pauline and Chloe to the last.

Haughton is my home, and all I want—*all* I want—is to live there in peace!'

Max's hand slashed through the air. Exasperation and anger and emotions that were far more powerful than both of them fuelled his outburst. 'Then do it! Just damn well *do* it! Stop your venomous, vengeful feud with your step-mother, which is twisting you and poisoning you, and buy them out.'

He saw her freeze, his words stopping her in her tracks.

'Buy them out...' It was not a question, not a statement. Merely an echo. Her face was blank—quite blank.

He took a heavy breath. 'Yes, buy them out. If that is how you feel, Ellen, then simply buy their share from them so they can make a new life for themselves some-where miles away from you, since I'm sure they feel the same way themselves. And then there'll finally be an end to this sorry saga. God knows I've tried to show you how good your life can be, but while you cling to your ven-detta, keep punishing Pauline and Chloe, the poison is destroying you.'

He shook his head. He was beating it against a brick wall, he could see. He turned away, pouring himself a cup of coffee and knocking it back, as if to restore energy lev-els that were suddenly drained dry. Could *nothing* make her see what she was doing to herself?

There was the lightest touch on his arm. Ellen was there, drawing his attention. He put down the drained cup and turned.

There was something strange in her expression—some-thing he'd never seen before. And it chilled him to the core.

Her voice, when she spoke was thin...thin like a nee-dle. 'You said I should buy out Pauline and Chloe's share of Haughton...' Something flared in her eyes like a black flame. *'What with?'* The words were spat at him.

Exasperation lashed from him. 'Ellen, don't be melo-dramatic,' he said crushingly. 'You could easily buy them out if you wanted. Pauline told me that you'd inherited everything else your father left—his stocks, his shares, all his other assets. She told me herself he was a very wealthy man.'

He saw her face whiten like a bone. Bleach-white. The hand on his sleeve seemed to spasm. But when she spoke her voice was very calm. Too calm.

'Let me tell you something, Max.'

Her hand dropped like a dead weight from his arm. There was something odd about the way she was look-ing at him. Something that made him think of a mortally wounded animal.

'Do you remember the night of that Edwardian ball? The jeweller who arrived with all that jewellery for hire? Do you remember I chose the rubies immediately?'

There was something wrong with her voice too, and it made Max frown.

'It was not just because they went with my gown. It was because—'

And now there was definitely something wrong with her voice—with her eyes—with her white face and stiff-ened body.

'Because they once belonged to my mother. I recog-nised them instantly—especially the ring. It was her en-gagement ring. And it was my great-grandmother's before that—as was the rest of the parure. My mother liked the old-fashioned setting. But Pauline did not.'

And now Ellen's eyes had a different expression in them—one that Max found was causing the blood in his veins to freeze.

'So she sold it. She sold a great deal of my mother's jewellery, only keeping what she liked. Or what Chloe liked. They both like pearls, as it happens, in particular. The double pearl necklace Pauline was wearing when you came to lunch was my father's tenth anniversary present to my mother, and the pearl bracelet Chloe wore was given to me by my parents for my thirteenth birthday. Chloe helped herself to it—said it was wasted on me. Wasted on me because I was nothing but a clumsy great elephant, an ugly lump, totally *gross*. And she never, ever missed an opportunity to remind me of that! Wherever and whenever. She made me a laughing stock at school for it, and has gone on laughing ever since—she's mocked me mercilessly ever since her mother got her claws into my poor, hapless father!'

Max saw her take a breath—just a light, short breath—before she plunged on. There was still the same chilling light in her eyes, in her voice.

'When Pauline married my father he was, indeed, a very wealthy man. It was his main attraction for her, his money—she just loved spending it. And so she spent and she spent and she *spent*! She spent it all. *All* of it! She spent it on endless holidays to expensive places—spent a fortune on interior designers both at Haughton and for the flat in Mayfair she insisted on. And she spent it on couture clothes for herself and Chloe, and on flash cars that were renewed every year, and more and more jewellery for themselves, and endless parties and living the high life at my father's expense.

'She burned through the lot. He sold everything in the end—all his stocks and shares, and some of the most valuable paintings. He cashed in all his funds and his life insurance, just to keep her in the luxury she demanded for herself. He died with almost nothing except Haughton—and he left two-thirds of that to Pauline and Chloe. Pauline made sure of that when he had to make a new will once he'd remarried. Made very, *very* sure!

'So you see, Max—' there was a twisting in her voice now, like the wire of a garrotte '—there is absolutely *nothing* left of my father's wealth except what Haughton represents, so it would be hard for me to buy out Pauline and Chloe on my teacher's salary. That goes on paying for groceries and council tax and utility bills—and for my stepmother and stepsister's essential expenses. Like having their hair done. Their little jaunts abroad, of course, are paid for by systematically selling off the antiques and paintings left in the house.'

Her voice changed again, becoming mocking in its viciousness.

'To be fair to them, that's how I've decided I'm going to pay for the clothes I bought here in London. After all, why *shouldn't* I get just a fraction—a tiny, minute, minuscule fraction—of what my father's wife has taken? And by the same token, Max...'

The pitch of her voice chilled his blood once more, and the venom in her eyes was toxic.

'Why shouldn't I be just a tiny, teeny bit...*reluctant*... to let that pair of blood-sucking vampires sell my parents' home out from under my feet? *Why damn well shouldn't I?* Because it's all I've got left. They've taken everything else—everything! They bled my father dry and made his life hell—*and* mine! And I will loathe their guts for it till my dying day.'

A shuddering breath escaped her, as if she were at the end of all her strength.

'So now, if you don't mind, Max, I'm going to go back to the place where I was born and raised, where I was once entirely happy until those...*vultures*...invaded it. The home I so fondly thought would one day be mine to raise my own family in, where I'd live out my days, but which is now going to be torn from me by my grasping, greedy, *vile* stepmother and stepsister, because it's the only thing left they can take. And I'm going to make the most of it—the *very* most of it—until the law courts, or the bailiffs, or your security guards or whatever it damn well takes drive me out of it.'

Her face contorted. She whirled around, seizing up her suitcase. He watched her stalk across the room, yank open the door, slam it shut behind her. Watched her while he stood motionless.

Quite, quite motionless.

CHAPTER ELEVEN

HAUGHTON WAS BATHED in watery sunlight, turning the house and gardens to pale silver, but as she stepped inside misery filled Ellen to the brim—for her father's ruin, her stepmother's avarice, for her angry parting with Max, for parting with him at all.

And for the loss of her home, which must come—now, or later, come it must.

As she went into the kitchen she could feel a dull, dread awareness forcing itself into her consciousness. A new, bitter truth pushing itself in front of her.

I can't go on like this. I just can't—not any longer.

Stark and brutal, the words incised themselves into her consciousness. She felt a pit of cold, icy water in her insides, a knot of dread and resolve. She had to face it—accept it. She could not stay locked in her vicious, destructive battle with Pauline and Chloe. It was a battle she could not win in the end. A battle that was indeed twisting her, deforming her.

I can't stop them taking it from me. I can't stop them and I can't go on the way I have been. So all I can do is give in. Give up. Give up my home.

More words echoed in her head, stinging even more painfully. Max calling this house a tomb. *Her* tomb. She felt her hands clench as if in desperate denial. But his accusation stabbed again. Forcing her to face what he had launched at her. Forcing her to face another truth as well.

I've changed. Max has changed me—changed not just my outer appearance but what is inside as well. I'm not the same person any more. Being with him, seeing the world with him, has changed me. He's opened my eyes to the world beyond here, given me the means to make the most of it, to stride through it with confidence and assurance.

I won't have him and I won't have Haughton—but I will have myself. And that must be enough. It must be enough because it is all that I can have now.

She knew it, accepted it—had no choice but to accept it.

But it was with a heavy heart and a sick feeling of dread and painful anguish that she went to make the phone call she knew she must make.

Max sat with an expression of polite interest on his face, as his meeting with the Sheikh's development minister proceeded. The meeting was going well, mutual benefits from his proposal were being agreed, relations were all extremely cordial and everyone all around was very pleased.

But Max's thoughts were far, far away, burningly consumed by a project that was small fry compared to the one being set up here, but ultimately far more important to him. One that was crucial to his future. His UK head of legal affairs had phoned him just as he'd arrived for his meeting and Max had mentally punched the air with relief.

The meeting finally over, with an entirely satisfactory conclusion, Max walked out to his waiting car. The heat of the Persian Gulf engulfed him. So did spearing emotion.

Ellen should be here. She should be at the hotel, by the pool. I'd join her and then enjoy a sundowner as the day cooled, looking forward to dinner together followed by an early night.

Then tomorrow we'd explore the souks of the old city, with the scent of a thousand spices and the fragrance of frankincense everywhere we went, with gold glinting from a hundred stalls! We'd cruise along the coast at sunset in a dhow, watching the sun set over the city like a ball of crimson flame.

The next day we'd drive into the desert, camp out in the Empty Quarter, sleep under the stars burning holes in heaven's floor...

He tore his mind away. He must not indulge in such wishful thinking. He must only look to the future now—must get back to his hotel, phone London, get matters expedited, concluded with all possible haste. No delays could be tolerated. The rest of his life depended on it.

Ellen glanced at her stopwatch, lifted her whistle to her lips and blew sharply to call full time on the match that was taking place on the pitch in front of her. She shivered. A cold wind was blowing, seemingly straight off the tundra hundreds of miles to the north—the Canadian spring was later to arrive than the English one.

But she was grateful that her headmistress had looked to her to accompany the school's lacrosse team's visit to a school in Ontario at short notice when a fellow games teacher had had to pull out. Even more grateful for the invitation she had just received from the principal here—to spend the summer semester as an exchange teacher.

New horizons, a new life—Max would approve.

She sheered her mind away. *No—don't think of Max. Don't think of anything to do with him.* He was gone, out of her life now—gone from everything that had ever been anything to do with her. Except... She felt emotion twist inside her like a spasm, except from the one place on earth she had sought so desperately to keep—the place that a single phone call to her solicitor had severed from her for ever.

Maybe here, as she forged a new life for herself, she might start to forget the home she had lost. Maybe here, in the years to come, she might forget the man who had given her more than she had ever thought to have—who now possessed what she had feared so much to lose. Maybe. But she could not believe it. Because there was only one place on earth she wanted to call home. Only one man on earth she wanted to share it with.

Max! Oh, Max, why am I missing you so much? Why do I want only to rush back to you? To go with you wherever in the world you go, for however long you want me? Why do my dreams torment me? Why does longing fill me— useless, hopeless longing for some fairy-tale world where it would all have been different?

A world in which Haughton was hers. In which Max was hers.

But what was the point of such longings? What would be the point, now, in standing here in the cold wind, in this alien land, and dreading a future on her own, without Haughton, without Max? What would be the point of admitting that what she had tried to pass off as merely a predictable reaction to the first man in her life was so much more?

What would be the point in admitting she'd fallen in love with him?

Max turned the powerful car on to the long curve of the gravelled drive, flanked at either side by a crimson blaze of rhododendrons, misted with bluebells along its verges, until the vista opened up to reveal the lawns and gardens beyond, and then the house itself, with the pale mauve of wisteria coming into bloom tumbling over the porch.

Haughton was, indeed, looking its best in the late spring sunshine. Satisfaction overflowed in him.

He had achieved exactly what he wanted, and as he parked his car in the kitchen courtyard his mind went back to the first time he had done so.

I fell in love with this place the moment I saw it and nothing has changed.

Except that Haughton was now his.

Satisfaction curved his mouth into a smile, putting a gleam into his dark eyes as he strode up to the back door. Haughton was *his*. His to do exactly as he wanted! With no more blocks or obstacles or impediments.

His keys were at the ready—after the completion of his purchase they were in his possession—and he unlocked the back door, glancing briefly into the kitchen where Ellen had hurled at his head her refusal to sell her share of the property unless it was forced from her by a court of law. Yet again satisfaction filled him. Well, that had not proved necessary.

He walked down the stone-flagged corridor to push open the green baize door and walk out into the front hall. It was chilly there, with no heating on yet, but that would be easily remedied. He paused, and gazed around, feeling the silence of the old house lap at him.

It's waiting. Waiting for its new owner to take possession. To live here and make a home here. To love it as it wants to be loved, to cherish it and value it.

Into his head came the memory of how he'd stood on this very spot, recognising his self-discovery, his sudden determination that he should make a home here for himself—recalling the moment he'd first felt that overpowering urge so strongly.

For a fleeting moment regret showed in his eyes for what he had done. Then it was gone. He had done what he had done, and it was what he had wanted to do. He would allow himself to feel nothing but satisfaction at having accomplished it. Nothing but that. He would have no regrets at how he had achieved it—at the price that had been paid for it. None.

He strode to the front door, throwing back the bolts and locks and opening it wide. Only one more signature was required to fulfil his purpose, to achieve what he wanted to do. And that would be supplied soon—very soon. He stood and watched over the gardens. Waiting…

Ellen sat in the back of the taxi taking her from the station to Haughton. A grief so profound she could not name its depth filled her. This was to be her very last time walking into the house that had been her home—that was hers no longer. Now, after landing that morning from Toronto, her charges having been safely bestowed upon their waiting parents, she was coming here only to remove her own personal possessions and the few keepsakes she still had from her parents before returning to Canada.

Everything else was included in the sale. A sale that had been conducted at breakneck speed the moment she'd made that fatal phone call to her solicitor to yield victory to Pauline and Chloe.

Now all that remained was for her to put her signature to the contract. She'd be calling in at the family solicitor on her way back to the station. Where Pauline and Chloe were she did not know and did not care. They'd signed the contract and taken themselves off—presumably to await the transfer of their share of the sale price into their accounts and then spend it as lavishly on themselves as they had spent all the rest of her father's money.

She closed her eyes. She must not let bitterness and anger fill her again. *She must not!* Max had been right—

those harsh emotions had eaten away at her for too long. Now she had to make a new life for herself. A life without Haughton. A life without Max.

She felt her throat constrict, felt pain lance at her.

I've lost my home and I've lost my heart as well. I can bear neither of them, and yet I must.

'Stop! Please!'

The words broke from her as the taxi driver turned between the stone pillars on to the drive. Startled, he braked, and Ellen fumbled for money, pressing it into his hand and scrambling from the vehicle.

Dragging her pull-along suitcase behind her, she started along the drive. Emotion poured through her, agonising and unbearable, a storm of feelings clutched at her heart. Soon...oh, *so* soon...all that would be left to her of her beloved home would be memories.

I was happy here once. And no one can take those memories from me. Wherever I go in the world I will take them with me.

She took a searing breath. Just as she would take the memories of her time with Max—that brief, precious time with him.

I had Haughton for a quarter of a century and I had Max for only weeks. But the memories of both must last my lifetime.

An ache started in her so profound it suffused her whole being with a longing and a desire for all that she had lost— the home she had lost, the man she had lost.

As the massed rhododendrons in their crimson glory gave way to lawn she plunged across the grass, cutting up towards the house, her eyes going immediately to its frontage.

This is the last time I shall see it! The last time...the very last time! The last time—

She stopped dead. There, standing on the porch, was a figure—tall and dominating and already in full possession.

It was Max.

Max watched her approach. He'd timed his own arrival perfectly, having obtained from her school details of the flight she'd be on, and calculating how long it would take her to reach here. He had the paperwork all ready.

As she reached the porch he could see her face was white, the skin stretched tight over her features. He felt emotion pierce him, but suppressed it. No time for that now. He must complete this business as swiftly as possible.

'What are you doing here?' The question broke from Ellen even though the moment it was out she knew how stupid it was. What was he doing here? He was taking possession—as he had every right to do.

His long lashes dipped down over his eyes. 'Waiting for you,' he said.

He stood aside, gesturing for her to step into the house. *His house. That's what it is now. Not mine—not once I've completed the final step that I must take and put my signature on the contract for my share. That's all he is waiting for now.*

She swallowed. Anguish seared her. Dear God, why did he have to be here? Why must she endure this final ordeal? *How can I bear it?*

How could she bear to see him again? How could she bear to feel that terrifying leap in her pulse, which had soared the moment her eyes had lit on him? How could she bear to have her gaze latch on to him, to drink him in like a quenching fountain after a parched desert?

He was crossing to the door to the library. 'Come,' he said to her, 'I have the paperwork here.'

Numbly she followed him, her suitcase abandoned on

the porch. She was incapable of thought. Incapable of anything except letting her eyes cling to his form. She felt weak with it—weak with the shock of seeing him again. Weak with the emotion surging in her as she looked at him.

He went to her father's desk and she could see the documents set out on it. He indicated the chair and, zombie-like, she went to sit on it, her legs like straw suddenly.

She looked at him across the desk. 'I was going to do this at the solicitor's later today,' she said. Her voice sounded dazed.

He gave a quick shake of his head. 'No need,' he said, and picked up the pen next to the paperwork, holding it out to her.

Ellen took a breath, ready to sign. What else could she do?

Do it—just do it now. It has to be done, has to be faced, has to be endured. Just as seeing him again has to be endured.

She lowered the pen to the paper. Then, abruptly, before she could start to write, she stopped. The enormity of what she was about to do had frozen her.

She lifted her head to stare helplessly up at Max.

'Ellen—sign the contract. Go on—sign it.'

There was something implacable in his face now. Something that made her eyes search his features. Something, she realised, that was making her flinch inwardly. Making her forcibly aware that this was a man who dealt in multi-million-pound deals as casually as he ordered a bottle of vintage wine. That to him this purchase was nothing but small fry—a drop in the ocean—when it was the whole ocean itself to her.

Did he see the flash of anguish in her eyes, hear the low catch of her breath—suspect the emotion stabbing at her now? She didn't know…knew only that he had placed both his hands, palms down, on the edge of the desk opposite her, that his tall frame was looming over her. Dominating, purposeful.

She tried to remember how different he could be—how he had stood at the helm of that catamaran, facing into the wind, his dark hair tousled, his smile lighting up the world for her. How laughter had shaken his shoulders as they'd laughed at something absurd that had caught his humour. How his dark eyes had blazed with fierce desire as he'd swept her into his arms and lowered his possessing mouth to hers...

'Just sign,' he said again, wiping all the anguished memories from her. His eyes bored into hers. 'It's for your own good,' he said.

His voice was soft, but there was a weight of intent in it that pressed upon her.

She lowered her head, breaking the crushing gaze that was bending her to his will. His words echoed hollowly. Forcing her to accept their truth. The truth as he saw it—the truth as he had made *her* see it. She could not go on as she had sought to do, locked in a toxic, unwinnable power struggle in the bitter aftermath of her father's death.

Slowly, carefully, she set her signature to the document before her, on the final page of it. The only clause visible was full of incomprehensible legal jargon she did not bother to read. Then, swallowing, she sheathed the pen and put it down. It was done—finally done. She had no claim on what had once been her home. Now it was just one more property in Max Vasilikos's investment portfolio.

Emotion twisted inside her. Impulsively she spoke. 'Max! Please... I know that the future of Haughton is nothing to do with me...' She swallowed and her voice changed, becoming imploring. 'But this was once a happy family home. Please—think how it could be so again!'

She saw a veil come down over his eyes. He straightened, took a step away, glanced around the room they were in. The original dark panelling was still there, and the serried ranks of books, the smoke-stained fireplace with its hearthrug and her father's worn leather chair. Then his eyes came back to her.

'When I first came to Haughton,' he said slowly, 'my plan, if I decided to buy it, was to realise the value in it and likely sell it on, or rent it out for revenue. But…' His eyes flickered to the tall windows, out over the gardens beyond, then moved back to her again. 'But as I walked around, saw it for myself, I realised that I did not want that.'

He looked at her. His expression was still veiled, but there was something behind that veil that caught at her, though she did not know why.

'I realised,' he said slowly, and now a different note had entered his voice, 'that I wanted to keep this house for myself. That I wanted to make this house my home.'

He looked at her. The veil was impenetrable now, and yet she gazed at him fixedly still.

'I still want that—for it to be a home,' he said.

For just a fraction of a moment his eyes met hers. Then she pulled her eyes away, closing them tightly. Emotion was sweeping up in her.

'I'm glad.' Her voice was tight with emotion. 'Oh, Max, I'm glad!' Her eyes flew open again. 'It deserves to be loved and cherished, to be a happy home again.'

There was a catch in her voice, a catch in her heart. To hear that this was what Max wanted—that Haughton would be protected from the fate she'd dreaded for it— was wonderful! And yet her heart ached to know that he would make a home here for himself…only for himself.

Until one day he brings his wife here!

Images forced themselves upon her. Max carrying his

bride over the threshold, sweeping her up the stairs…his threshold, his stairs, his bride. Max running effortlessly on untired limbs around the pathway beside the lake, taking in his domain, making it his own. Max surrounded one day by children—a Christmas tree here in this hall, where she had once opened her childhood presents—their laughter echoing as hers had once done.

Max's children. Max's bride and Max's wife. Max's home.

And she would be in Canada, or any place in the world. For where she was would not matter—could not matter. Because she would be without Haughton.

Without Max.

Pain lanced at her and she got to her feet, scraping her father's chair on the floorboards. She faced Max. He was still standing there, his expression still veiled, still resting his gaze on her.

'Yes,' he said. 'It does. It does deserve that.'

He spoke the words heavily, incisively, as if they were being carved into him. He looked at her, held her eyes unreadably for one last moment longer, then spoke again.

'And I hope beyond all things that it will be *my* home—'

She stared at him. Why had he said that? It *was* his home now—her signature had made it so.

But he was speaking still. 'That, however, depends entirely on you.'

Bewilderment filled her. There was something in his eyes now—something that, had the sombreness and the despair of the moment not overwhelmed her, she would have said was a glint.

'You should always read what you're signing before you sign it, Ellen,' he said softly, and his eyes were still holding hers.

'It's a contract of sale,' she said.

Her voice was neutral, but she was trying desperately in her head not to hear the seductive, sensuous echo of his naming of her, that had sent a thousand dangerous whispers across her skin.

'Yes, it is,' he agreed.

'Selling you my share of Haughton.'

'No,' said Max, in measured, deliberate tones. 'It is not that.' He paused. 'Read it—you've signed it…now read it.'

Numbly, she turned back the pages to reach the opening page. But it was full of legalese and jargon, and the words swam in front of her eyes.

Then Max was speaking again. 'It *is* a contract of sale,' he said, 'but *you* are not the vendor.' He paused. 'I am.'

CHAPTER TWELVE

MAX'S EYES WERE holding hers and not letting them go—
not letting them go for an instant…a single second.

'You see…' he said, and he spoke in the same measured
tones, but now there was something else in his voice—
something that was an emotion rising up to break through,
an emotion that was possessing every cell in his body. 'You
see, I am selling you the two-thirds share of Haughton I
have already purchased from your stepmother and stepsister. Which, Ellen—' and now the emotion broke through
finally, unstoppably, blazing through him, lighting up his
eyes with the fire he had banked down with every ounce of
his strength since he'd watched her walk up to him across
the lawns '—which I now restore to *you.*'

For one last moment he held on to his self-control.

'I've given you a very good price,' he told her. 'I believe even on your teacher's salary you can afford to pay
me a hundred pounds. How does that sound? I hope it's
acceptable—because you've just put your signature to it.'

She wasn't saying anything. She was just staring at him
as incomprehension, shock, disbelief, all flashed across
her face.

'I don't understand…' It was a whisper, faint and
scarcely audible.

For one long, timeless, endless moment the tableau held.

Max standing there, his face expressionless, and she seated across the desk from him, as white as a sheet with shock etched across her features. Then, like a dam breaking, all the emotions Max had been holding in check burst from him.

'Did you truly think I would take your home from you—after you'd ripped the scales from my eyes?'

He took a shuddering breath, making himself calm. His gaze was on her, holding her like a magnet.

'The moment you hurled what you did at me, before you stormed out, I knew there was only one thing to do. Only one! And now...' A sigh of profound relief went through him. 'Now it's done. I put my legal team on to it straight away, the minute you'd gone, and they got hold of your stepmother out in Spain and told her I'd buy their share even without yours.'

A hard, cynical look entered his eyes.

'She jumped at the chance like I was dangling a diamond necklace in front of her. My lawyer phoned me their agreement when I was in the Gulf, and then I knew, finally, that I was free to do what I have just done.' He paused, and an expression moved across his face that showed all that had possessed him until this moment, the driving urgency to accomplish what he had. 'Make Haughton safe for you,' he finished.

She heard him, yet still she dared not believe what he was saying. Dared not believe that she had just bought her beloved home back for herself—for a song—for a gift...

For of course it *was* a gift! How could it be otherwise at so paltry a price? A gift that Max had given her—a gift so wonderful, so precious that it took her breath away, squeezed her lungs so tight she could hardly breathe, could hardly feel the beating of her heart, though it was hammering in her chest.

'Why?' It was the only word she could say, as faint and low as her breath could make it. 'Max—*why*?'

She took a searing breath through the constriction in her throat and made herself speak again, forced the words from her though they were still low and faint.

'Why should you care what Pauline and Chloe did to my father and me? Why should you give me so fabulous a gift?'

He was looking at her still, and the expression in his face made the hammering in her heart pound in her ears.

'Why?'

His voice echoed hers. But he gave her no answer. Only strode around her father's desk, catching at her hand and drawing her to her feet. Her legs were like jelly and she had to cling to his arm lest she collapse, so overpowering was the shock shaking her.

In her head she kept hearing her own voice, saying over and over again—*Haughton is mine! It's mine! It's mine! Dear God, it's mine for ever now!*

It was a paean, an anthem, ringing in her head like bells. She gazed helplessly up at Max. At the man who had done this, made this happen. Into her head, flashing like a strobe light, came the memory of the moment Max had given her that first wonderful, miraculous gift—the moment when he'd shown her her reflection the night of the ball, transformed beyond recognition. Made beautiful by him.

He freed me from Chloe's hex—and now, oh, he's freed me from Pauline's too!

Emotion overwhelmed her. Gratitude and wonder and so much more.

'Why?' His voice came again, husky now. He caught her other hand, held it, cherished it. He towered over her, his strong body supporting her stricken one. 'Oh, Ellen—

my beautiful, lovely, passionate, wonderful Ellen… Have you really not the faintest idea why?'

He held her a little way from him, the expression on his face rueful.

'Did you not hear me when I told you that the moment I saw this house I wanted to live here? That something about it called to me? That after all my years of wandering, never having had a home of my own, having existed only on sufferance at my stepfather's *taverna* and having lived in hotels and apartments anywhere in the world, I had finally come across a place that urged me to stop…to stop and stay. Make my life here.'

Now the rueful expression deepened.

'That was what drove me so hard to buy it—to make it mine. What drove me to do all I could to achieve that aim. Including…' his eyes met hers wryly '…whisking you off to London to show you how good your life could be if only you would let go of the place I wanted for myself.'

He gave a regretful sigh.

'I went on and on at you. I know I did. But you see…' and now a different note entered his voice '… I'd sought an explanation for your stubbornness, your refusal to agree to sell your share, from your stepmother and stepsister.' His eyes shadowed as he remembered that scene in the drawing room when he'd made his initial offer for Haughton. 'And they told me that you'd become obsessed with the house, that you'd never accepted Pauline's marriage to your father, that you had rejected them from the very first, seen them as interlopers, invaders.'

He gave a shake of his head.

'I remembered my own childhood—how my stepfather never wanted me, never accepted me into his home, always resented my presence even though he made use of it. I was always the outsider, the unwanted brat of my mother.

Maybe,' he said slowly, 'that was why I was so ready to believe what Pauline and Chloe told me. So, while I could make allowances for your reaction to your father's remarriage, all I could see was how that resentment was poisoning you….chaining you to this place. Making you think it was the only way you could punish Pauline for marrying your father, seeking to take your mother's place.'

He felt Ellen draw away slightly. Her eyes were full of grief. Her voice when she spoke was low and strained, her glance going to her father's empty chair by the hearth.

'I was *glad* when my father told me he was marrying again. So glad! He'd been grieving for my mother and I desperately wanted him to be happy again. If Pauline made him happy, then I knew I would be happy. I tried to welcome them, tried to befriend Chloe…' A choke broke in her voice. 'Well, I told you how they reacted. But even then if they'd only made my father happy I could have borne it! But within months of marrying Pauline my father realised that her only interest in him was his money.'

Her mouth set.

'He was powerless to do anything about it. If he'd divorced Pauline she'd have taken half of everything he had—forced him to sell Haughton and split the proceeds. So he kept on paying out and paying out and paying out. I had to hide from him all the spite and venom that came from them—hide from him how Chloe had tried to make my life hell at school, and how she constantly sneered at me because I'm tall and sporty, told me how repellent I was because of it until I believed her completely…'

Her voice broke in another choke before she could continue.

'I had to hide it all from my father because he'd only have been hurt all the more, worried about me more, and felt yet more trapped by Pauline. So when he died I was almost relieved, because finally I didn't have to pretend any longer. I could find my backbone and resolve that even though I knew it was impossible to stop Pauline and Chloe from getting their claws into Haughton eventually I would do everything in my power, for as long as I could, to make it as hard and as expensive as possible for them to force a sale.'

She took another choking breath.

'I was—just as you said—using Haughton as a weapon against them—my only weapon.' Her gaze shifted again, became shadowed. 'But when I came back here after leaving you I knew…' She paused, then made herself go on. 'I knew that I'd changed—that you'd been right to say that I was poisoning myself in my battle against them. That it was time…finally time…to let go. They had won and I had lost and all I could do was leave and make a new life for myself somewhere else. *Anywhere* else.' She took another searing, painful breath. 'This—today—was to be my very last visit, my last sight of my home.'

He drew her towards him again and his voice was gentle…very gentle. 'And now it is yours for ever.' His eyes poured into hers. 'No one can ever threaten it again.' His mouth curved into a smile. 'Look around you, Ellen—it's yours, all yours.'

A strangled sound was torn from her throat, and then a sob, and then another, and then tears were spilling from her eyes and Max was wrapping his arms around her, and she was clinging to him, shaking with emotion, with the relief and disbelief that all this was really true, that all the stress and fear and anguish at losing her home was over—over for ever. Because Max—wonderful, kind, generous Max—had made her dream come true. Haughton was hers, and it was safe for ever now.

He held her while her body shook with the tears choking from her, convulsing her, while her hands clutched at him and she was finally purged of all that her stepmother and stepsister had done to her for so long. And when she was finally done he stroked her hair with his hand, murmured things to her in Greek.

She didn't know what they were, but knew that he was the most wonderful man on earth. And that she had now taken from him something he had wanted from the moment he'd first set eyes on it.

Her thoughts whirled in her head, troubling her. She lifted her face from his shoulder, looked up at him with an anxious look.

'Max, I still don't understand. You've given me this miraculous gift and I still don't understand *why*. Why would you do it when you've told me yourself that you fell in love with Haughton and wanted to make your home here? How can you bear to give it away to me like this?'

He looked down at her, his deep, dark eyes holding an expression she could not recognise.

'Well, you see, Ellen, I'm forced to admit that I am a shamefully devious character.' He cradled her to him, his hands resting loosely around her spine. '*Shamefully* devious. Yes, it's absolutely true that I was…devastated…' his voice was edgy suddenly '…when I realised how wrong I'd been about you—about your behaviour towards Pauline and Chloe over this house—how deceived I'd been by their appearance of solicitude towards you, how disgusted I felt at their exploitation of your father and their cruelty to you. It made me absolutely determined to redress this final wrong, to restore your home to you, out of their clutches. But…'

His voice changed again, softening now, taking on a hint of wry humour.

'But even while I was set on being the one to save

Haughton for you, because you love it so much and have been through so much because of it, I also knew perfectly well that I had... Well, let's say an ulterior motive all along.'

There was a glint in his eyes now, blatantly visible. It did things to Ellen's insides that even the flood of emotion over regaining her home could not quench—things that took her back instantly to the time she'd spent with Max abroad, setting loose a quiver inside her, a quickening of her pulse that made her all too aware of how Max's body was cradling hers, of the lean strength of him, the taut wall of his chest, the pressure of his hips, the heat of his body...

'I told you when you signed my contract restoring Haughton to you how much I was still hoping to make it my home,' he was saying now, 'but that it would depend entirely on you. So...' He raised a quizzical eyebrow. 'What do you think? Could you bear to share Haughton with me?'

She looked at him, not understanding. 'Do you mean some kind of co-ownership?' she ventured.

He shook his head. 'No, I don't want you ever to have to worry about not owning Haughton one hundred per cent,' he said. 'I was *thinking*,' he went on, and now the glint was even more pronounced, and she felt a sudden tightening of the arms around her spine, 'of a *different* way to make this my home.'

'I don't understand...' she said again. But her voice was weaker this time. Her whole body was weaker.

'Then maybe,' said Max, 'this will make things clearer.'

He let her go suddenly, and she felt herself leaning back on the desk as his hold on her was relinquished. She clutched the edge of the desk with her hands. Saw him reach into his jacket, draw out a tiny square box. Felt her heart rate slow...slow almost to a standstill. The breath in her lungs was congealing.

Before her very eyes she saw him lower himself upon one knee and look back up at her.

'Will you…?' he said, and his eyes pinioned hers as she gazed down at him, her own eyes widening until they could widen no further. 'Will you, my most beautiful, most wonderful, most lovely and fit and fabulous and incomparable Ellen, do me the honour, the very *great* honour, of making me the happiest of men? Will you…?' he asked. 'Will you marry me?'

He flicked open the box and her eyes went to the flash of red within. She gave a gasp.

Max quirked an eyebrow again. 'I'm sort of hoping,' he said, 'again quite shamelessly, that this might help persuade you.'

He took the ring out, got to his feet, lifted Ellen's nerveless left hand and held it. His other hand held the ring. The ring she'd worn at the Edwardian ball that had changed her life for ever. The ring that had been her mother's engagement ring, given to her by her father. The ring that had once belonged to her grandmother and her great-grandmother.

'How did you get it…?' Her voice was faint again.

'I bought the ruby parure you wore to the ball. And by the same token I also bought back all your mother's jewellery that Pauline and Chloe helped themselves to—it was in the fine print of the terms and conditions of their sale contract. As for everything else—all the other jewellery and antiques and paintings they sold—I've got a team searching them out and I will buy them all back as and when we find them.' And now that glint was blatant again. 'You see, Ellen, I want to do absolutely everything in my power to persuade you to do what I want you to do more than anything else in the world—and, my sweet Ellen, you haven't actually answered me yet.'

Was there tension in his voice, lacing through the humour, turning the glint in his eyes to something very different?

She gazed at him. Her heart was suddenly in her throat—or something was. Something huge and choking that was making it quite impossible for her to do anything at all except gaze at him. And force out one breathless whisper.

'Did…did you just propose to me?' she asked faintly.

A tidal wave of disbelief was sweeping up through her—the same as when he'd told her he'd gifted his newly acquired share of Haughton to her.

A rasp broke from Max. 'Do you want a replay?' he said, and he started to go down on his knee again.

She snatched at him to stop him. 'No! No—*no*!'

He halted, looked at her quizzically. 'Is that no, you won't marry me?' he asked her.

She shook her head violently. She could not speak. Emotion was pounding her, crashing in on her consciousness, overwhelming her.

'So, that's a yes, then, is it?' Max pursued. He paused. 'I'd just like to clarify this, if you don't mind. Because it is, you see, somewhat important to me.' His expression changed suddenly. 'It's going to determine my entire future happiness.'

She swallowed. That huge, choking lump was still in her throat, and the tidal wash of emotion was still pounding in her.

'Why…?' The single word was faint, uncomprehending.

'Why, what?' he said blankly.

His self-control was under the greatest pressure he'd ever experienced in his life. Even worse than that very first night of the revelation of her beauty to him, when she had offered her mouth to him and he had swooped upon it with all the hunger of a starving man—and then, with the feast before him, had had to draw back, let her go and get the hell out of her bedroom before he'd succumbed to the most intense temptation he'd ever known.

Even worse than that…

'Why…?' She swallowed. 'Why are you asking me to marry you?'

And Max lost it. Finally lost it. It had all been just too damn much. Too damn much from the moment Ellen had laid into him in his hotel suite, telling him the truth about the vultures who were feeding off her. In that single instant he'd known exactly what he was going to do—and he'd spent the last fortnight pulling out every stop, racing to get the paperwork done, the contracts drawn up and completed, and to drive down here to do what he had just done. Hand her back her home and gain her for himself.

'Will *this* help you understand?' he demanded.

He swept her up to him, his strength easily crushing her against him, his mouth swooping down on hers. And instantly she went up in flames, her mouth opening to his, melding with his. Her arms wound around him, her fingers spearing into his hair. She was hungry for him. Desperate for him. When finally he released her she was shaking, breathless.

Max's hands splayed around her face. 'I've fallen in love with you,' he said.

His voice was quiet but there was an intensity in it, a strength that came from the very core of his being.

'Somewhere along the way I've fallen in love with you. Oh, I admit that my motives in taking you to London were entirely self-interested—you knew that…knew I was seeking to open your eyes to what your life could be like beyond the narrow confines you'd imprisoned yourself in with your vendetta against your stepmother and stepsister once you'd discovered your own beauty. But once I'd discovered it too—and helped myself to it!' His voice was wry. 'Once I'd whisked you off to enjoy it to the full... Well...' Warmth infused his voice now. 'It dawned on me that I was enjoying your company in a way I'd never experienced with any other woman.'

'Even Tyla Brentley?' Ellen breathed.

A dismissive sound came from his throat. 'Tyla was lovely to look at, glamorous to be with—and totally self-absorbed. You... Ah, *you* were utterly different. Even before you had your makeover I knew that. You're intelligent, clear-sighted, and I approve of your efforts with all those deprived city children.'

He dropped a kiss on her nose.

'We had a good time together, Ellen, on our travels. We were good together—incredibly, fantastically good. And when you stormed off I wasn't just appalled to discover how vicious your step-relations were, I also knew I desperately didn't want you to leave me! I knew I *had* to try and get you back—get you back so we could go on being good together. Good together for the rest of our lives, Ellen— that's what I so hope for.'

Something changed in his voice again now, and an urgency speared it.

'And if somewhere along the way you happen...just happen to come to feel for me what I feel for you... Well...'

She didn't let him finish. She reached up her hand, snaked it around the back of his head, hauled his mouth down to hers again. She pressed her lips hard against him to silence him. Then, as she drew back again, emotion burst in her.

And so did a storm of weeping.

For the second time in a handful of minutes she clutched at him as wave after wave of emotion swept through her yet again—and again and again. Max loved her—he *loved* her! He'd given her the inestimable gift of her home to her, and he'd given her a more incomparable gift as well.

Himself. His heart. His love.

'Max! Oh, Max!' It was all she could say. But it seemed to satisfy him.

As she finally came down on the other side of the tsunami inside her he patted her back and reached for the ring box, sitting abandoned on her father's desk.

'That's *got* to be a definite yes,' he told her, with satisfaction in his voice and the love in his eyes pouring out over her, embracing her and caressing her.

'Of *course* it is!' She gulped. 'I kept telling myself that because you were the first man in my life of course I'd get the idea in my head that I'd fallen in love with you—but it wasn't just that. It was real. Completely real what I was feeling for you. When I stormed out on you it was tearing me to pieces, and being out in Canada, facing the rest of my life without Haughton and without *you*—I... I just couldn't bear it!'

Tears threatened again, spilling into her watery eyes.

'And now I've got both—I've got my beloved home and I've got something even more desperately precious to me.' Her face worked. 'I've got *you*. And you, my dearest, most adored and most *wonderful* Max, are my heart, my life— the love of my life.'

'Excellent!' he said, and his satisfaction was total now. 'So,' he said to her, taking the ruby ring from its case, 'do we finally get to the ring bit now?'

He took her hand again and, not waiting for an answer, slid the ring carefully over her finger. But he did not relinquish her hand. Instead he gazed down at her.

'When I first walked into this house I knew it was the place I wanted to call my home,' he told her. His face was serious now—completely serious. 'I had a sudden vision… a vision of myself here, with the woman I love, making our home here together, raising our family here together.' His eyes had a rueful glint in them again. 'I thought that I would have to bring her here, having found her some-where out in the world beyond. And yet all along—' His voice changed, and there was a crack in it, he knew. 'All along she was here. Waiting for me to find her. Waiting,' he said, 'to find *me*.'

He paused minutely.

'And now,' he said, 'we're done with waiting. Done with finding. We can just enjoy, Ellen. Enjoy the rest of our lives together.'

His mouth lowered to hers and he kissed her softly, gently, before withdrawing. He felt her fingers tighten-ing over his as his lips brushed hers, felt the sudden con-stricting of her throat, saw the misting of her eyes as he drew his head away.

'So…' he said, because he wanted to make sure—to make absolutely, totally sure of his future happiness…a happiness that was already flooding through him, soak-ing through every cell in his body, radiating from him like a beacon. 'Have we finally got everything sorted? I love you, you love me, and we're going to marry and live here together in this house we both love, make it a home again, for you and for me and for all the children we are most definitely going to have! A happy family home for a happy family—just as we both wanted. Did I leave any-thing out?' he asked.

Ellen leaned into his shoulder. Her sigh was pure happi-ness. 'No,' she said. 'I think you've just described heaven on earth.'

Max smiled. A warm, approving smile that melted her all the way through.

'That's what I thought,' he said. He dropped another kiss on her nose. 'I do like to be right,' he told her.

He straightened up.

'OK, it's a lovely day—actually the best day in my entire life so far—let's get outdoors. Let's get into the sunshine—the sunshine of our lives, my adored, beautiful goddess and lioness.'

She looked at him. 'Can I be *both*?' she queried, with a teasing smile in her eyes.

Max's mouth quirked, his expression doting. 'You can be everything you want, my beloved, providing you go on loving me.'

He started to lead the way out of the library and across the hall, his hand wound in hers and hers in his. Side by side and shoulder to shoulder.

'And you me,' said Ellen.

He paused at the door. 'Deal,' said Max, and kissed her once again.

Then, with a squeeze of her hand, he opened the front door and they stepped through it, into the sunshine, into the happiness of their life together, into their love for each other.

EPILOGUE

MAX WRAPPED HIS arm around Ellen and drew her closer against his shoulder as they leant back against the sun-warmed stone. They were sitting on the step of the little folly, looking out over the lake to where the setting sun was turning its reedy waters bronze. Ellen gave a sigh of deep contentment as she nestled into Max's sheltering embrace, her knees drawn up and slanting against his thighs.

'You're really sure you're OK with us spending our honeymoon here at Haughton?' she asked him, glancing up at his profile.

He nodded, his gaze going to her. 'My beautiful, adored Ellen—don't you know that I am happy wherever *you* are? And if you are happiest here, then here we shall stay for all our days,' Max finished with a fond smile, and let his lips brush across her hair.

'Maybe,' she mused, 'I feel that if I ever leave Haughton I'll return to find that this heaven was only a dream, and I'm back here again with Pauline and Chloe still trying to sell it from under my feet and force me out,' she said.

Max shook his head. 'Oh, no,' he said decisively. 'This heaven is real, believe me. And as for your stepmother and stepsister—well, they'll never set foot on your property again, I promise you. If they even come back to the UK I'll know about it!'

She looked at him quizzically. 'Are you really keeping them under surveillance?' she asked.

'I'm keeping tabs on them, yes,' Max admitted. 'So that wherever in the world they go, if they try and home in on anyone wealthy but vulnerable, like your father was, then their target will be warned. Of course,' he went on, 'it could be that they won't need to target money any more—they have pots of their own. And I don't mean just their ill-gotten gains from selling me their share of Haughton!'

Ellen's quizzical look intensified and Max elucidated.

'I just happened to mention to them, at some point while I was acquiring their share of Haughton, several new property hotspots that were emerging, where substantial profits could be made. They seized on it, and my latest information is that they're now investing substantially. However, if they're prudent they'll take on board that where there is the chance of high return there's also the chance of being wiped out financially.' He smiled, and it was not a wholly benign smile. 'Let's just say that if they *do* get wiped out financially...well, I for one will not be weeping.'

Ellen looked away, out over the lake. She had come so close to losing her beloved home that it was hard to feel any concern at the prospect of Pauline and Chloe losing the money they'd made on selling up to the man who'd saved Haughton for her.

'Karma,' she murmured now.

'Yes, indeed,' agreed Max. 'And it was fate, too, that brought me here...let me find you here.'

He turned his head to look across the lake, beyond the lawns, to the mellow stone house that was now home to both of them, safe and secure for ever, for themselves and for their children to come. Contentment filled him. With his free hand he reached sideways to lift the bottle of champagne from its ice bucket.

'Time for a refill,' he said, and Ellen picked up her empty glass and held it tilted while he topped it up, then held his glass while he did likewise.

He set down the champagne bottle and raised his brimming glass, clinking it against hers.

'This is to us,' he said, and now his eyes wound into hers, his love for her glowing like an eternal flame. 'To our marriage, to our lives together, to our love—and to our beautiful, most precious home.'

'To us,' she echoed. 'To you, my darling, wonderful Max, who has made all my dreams come true!'

He dropped a kiss on her upturned face, then took a deep draught of champagne as she did likewise.

'It's going to be quite a busy honeymoon,' he observed. '*Un*decorating the house from all that interior design, getting it back to the way it used to be… It's great,' he added, 'that so much of the original furniture got stashed in the attics.'

'We *will* need new curtains, though, and soft furnishings,' Ellen commented.

'We'll choose them together. Did I tell you?' He cast a wicked look at his bride. 'I've always had a thing about spots. I think curtains made from a polka dot fabric would be ideal…' He trailed off.

She laughed. 'Let's save that for the nursery, maybe,' she said.

He cast her an interested look. 'Are you trying to tell me something?'

His voice was casual, but Ellen was not deceived.

'Well, no,' she admitted. 'But maybe this time next year? That should give my headmistress time to sort out maternity cover.'

'You really want to go on teaching?' Max asked.

'Oh, yes,' she answered. 'I can't just be the idle wife of a rich man! And besides…' it was her turn to throw him a wicked look '…if I don't teach Games I might go off the boil about exercise in general. I might run to fat,' she said dulcetly. 'And *then*,' she finished dramatically, 'you wouldn't love me any more!'

A growl came from Max and he set down his champagne glass, removing hers at the same time. His arm around her shoulder tightened, and with his free hand he cupped her face.

'My goddess—my lioness—you could turn into a morbidly obese rhinoceros and I wouldn't love you an iota less. Don't you realise it's *you* I love, and to hell with anything else?'

'Oh, Max!' She gave a little choke, feeling her eyes misting suddenly.

How blessed she was—how unutterably blessed—that Max should love her!

He kissed her, warm and tender, deep and passionate.

Increasingly passionate.

Gently he drew her down upon the stone floor of the folly, and their bodies were limned with the light of the setting sun as desire flared between them—rich and ardent, sweet and eternal. Desire that was the manifestation of a love that would not end—that *could* not end. That could only bind them, each to the other, all their days…

* * * * *

THE FLAW IN
RAFFAELE'S REVENGE

ANNIE WEST

An enormous thank you to
dear Abby Green
who heard my plot ideas then asked
why I didn't combine them.
I loved our rare chance to talk stories!

And a huge thank you to
Franca Poli
for your support and patient assistance
with your lovely language.
Any errors are mine.

PROLOGUE

RAFFAELE PETRI POCKETED his credit card and left the waterfront restaurant. Ignoring the stares, he nodded his thanks to the waiter. The service had been excellent, attentive but not fawning, the tip well-earned.

Raffaele hadn't forgotten how it felt to depend on the goodwill of rich foreigners.

He paused, his eyes adjusting to the sunshine. The sea glittered as it slapped the whiter-than-white yachts. The salt tang was strong on the air and he breathed deep, relishing it after the overpowering perfume of the women who'd tried to catch his attention from the next table.

He sauntered past huge yachts and motor cruisers. The Marmaris waterfront was packed with ostentatious displays of wealth. Just the place to invest, if his research was right, which it always was. This trip to Turkey would be profitable and—

A bray of laughter froze his footsteps. The hoarse, distinctive sound ran up his spine like dancing skeletal fingers, pinching his skin.

Raffaele's breath rushed in like the snap of a spinnaker in a stiff breeze. The laugh came again, yanking his attention to a towering multistorey cruiser. Sunlight polished the chestnut hair of the man leaning from the upper deck, shouting encouragement at two women on the promenade.

The ground beneath Raffaele's feet seemed to heave and buckle, mirroring the tumble of his constricting gut. His hands rolled tight as he stared at the florid man waving a champagne glass at the women.

'Come on up. The bubbly's on ice.'

Raffaele knew that voice.

Even after twenty-one years he recognised it.

That smug tone, that hoarse laugh, had crept through his nightmares since he was twelve.

He'd given up hope of finding him. He'd never known the man's name and the slimy villain had disappeared from Genoa faster than a rat leaving a scuttled ship. No one had listened to a skinny twelve-year-old who'd insisted the foreigner with hair the colour of *castagne* was to blame for Gabriella's death.

Gabriella...

Fury ignited. The wrath of thwarted retribution, of loathing and grief.

The blast of emotion stunned him.

He'd spent his life perfecting the art of not feeling, not caring for anyone, not *trusting,* since Gabriella. But now... It took everything he had merely to stand still and take in the scene.

Keenly he catalogued everything, from the guy's features, grown pudgy with age and self-indulgence, to the name of the cruiser and the fact his staff, neat in white shorts and shirts, spoke English as only natives could. One of them offered to help the women aboard.

Girls, Raffaele amended, not women. Both blonde, both in their teens, though one was made up to look ten years older. Raffa was an expert on make-up and on women.

The Englishman's tastes hadn't changed. He still liked them young and blonde.

Bile rose. Raffa's heart thrashed with the need to climb aboard and deliver justice for Gabriella with his fists. There was no doubt this was the same man.

But Raffa was no longer an impulsive, grieving kid.

Now he had the power to do more than beat the man to a bloody pulp. That thought alone held him back. Even so, it was a battle to rein in his need for instant vengeance.

'Ciao, bella.' He strolled forward, curling his mouth in a half smile the camera, and millions of women the world

over, loved. Not for a second did he lift his gaze to the middle-aged man above them.

'Lucy—' The taller one nudged her companion. 'Quick. Turn around. He looks like… He couldn't be…could he?'

Two pairs of eyes widened as he approached. Twin gasps of excitement. The one who'd spoken smiled wide while her companion looked dazed.

Raffa was used to dealing with besotted fans. But instead of a nod of acknowledgement before moving on, he increased the wattage of his smile in an invitation that had never once failed.

The taller girl stepped closer, pulling her friend along, the boat and its owner forgotten. They didn't even blink as the man above them called agitated instructions for them to come aboard.

'You look just like Raffaele Petri. I suppose people say that all the time.' Her voice was breathless and young. Too young for the man on the boat. Or for Raffa. The difference was that with him she'd be safe.

'That's because I *am* Raffaele Petri.'

Twin gasps met the announcement and the smaller girl looked as if she might faint.

'Are you all right?'

She nodded, goggle-eyed, while her friend dragged out her phone. 'Do you mind?'

'Of course not.' The world was full of amateur photos of him. 'I was going to get a coffee.' He gestured to a street leading away from the waterfront. 'Care to join me?'

The girls were so busy chattering as they walked that only Raffa heard the Englishman's abusive yells. He'd been deprived of his afternoon's amusement.

Soon he'd be deprived of everything that mattered to him.

The Englishman wouldn't escape again. Justice would be sweet.

This time Raffa's smile was genuine.

CHAPTER ONE

'STOP PULLING MY LEG, Pete.' Lily leaned back from the desk and shifted her grip on the phone. 'It's been a long day. You might be just waking up in New York but it's bedtime in Australia.'

Looking towards the window, she saw the reflection of her office in the glass. Her house was too far from town for street lights and the stars wouldn't show till she switched off her lamp. She rubbed her stiff neck. Completing this project within deadline and to her own exacting standards had been tough.

'No joke.' Pete's usually laid-back voice with its Canadian accent sounded excited. 'The boss wants you here and he never jokes about business.'

Lily straightened in her seat, her pulse thudding. 'You're serious?'

'Absolutely. And what the boss wants, the boss makes a policy of getting. You know that.'

'Except Raffaele Petri isn't my boss.' Even saying his name aloud seemed somehow ridiculous. What could she, ordinary Lily Nolan, living in a rundown farmhouse an hour south of Sydney, have in common with Raffaele Petri? 'He doesn't know I exist.'

Petri inhabited a stellar plane ordinary mortals only dreamed of or read about in gossip magazines, while she…

Lily dropped the hand she'd lifted to her cheek. She hated that old, nervous gesture.

'Of course he knows. Why do you think you've had so much work from us? He was impressed with your report for the Tahiti deal and asked for you on every one since.'

Lily blinked. She'd never imagined Signor Petri himself

reading her research reports. She'd assumed he had other things to do with his time, like indulging himself at the world's most luxurious fleshpots.

'That's fantastic, Pete. I can't tell you how pleased I am.' Despite her recent success, the size of the loan she'd taken to buy this house and expand the business kept her awake at night. But after years feeling like an outsider she'd been driven by the need to establish her own place in the world, something *she'd* achieved and could be proud of. Even though it meant moving across the continent from her anxious family. She needed this to turn her life around.

Tight muscles eased. If Signor Petri had personally commented on her work—

'Excellent. You'll find the contract in your inbox. It will be great finally putting a face to the voice once you're working here.'

'Whoa. Wait a minute.' Lily shot to her feet. 'I meant I'm pleased to have what I do valued. That's all.' She drove herself to excel and knew her service was first class, but it was reassuring having it confirmed by her most influential customer, especially now she had this mortgage.

'You *don't* want to accept the boss's offer to work here?' Pete's hushed tone made it sound as if she'd refused mankind's only chance to find a cure for cancer.

'That's right.' The thought of being in a city, surrounded by millions of people, being *seen* by strangers every day, made her flesh crawl as if she were breaking into hives. She even avoided driving into her small town when possible, opting to have her groceries delivered. Working in New York, constantly facing curious stares, would be a nightmare. It was one thing to be confident about your work and your worth, quite another to run the gauntlet of constant public interest.

'You're joking. Who wouldn't want to work for Raffaele Petri?'

Lily threaded her fingers through her long hair, pushing

it from her face. 'I already work for him, off and on.' Her contract work for his company had been so lucrative it had made her enormous mortgage possible. The prestige of his name on those regular contracts had convinced even the cautious loans officer. 'But I'm my own boss. Why would I want to change that?'

Her independence, her ability to *control* her life, meant everything. Perhaps because her world had been impacted irrevocably by a single, senseless event that had robbed her of so much.

A moment's silence told her how bizarre her attitude seemed.

'Let's see. The kudos for a start. Work for him and you can walk into any job you like. He only employs the best. Then there's the salary. Read the contract before you reject it, Lily. Chances like this don't just come along.'

His tone was urgent. But Lily knew what was right for her.

'Thanks for your interest, Pete. I appreciate it, really I do. But it's not possible.' She forked her hand through her hair again, for a millisecond wondering what opportunities she might have pursued if her life had been different. If *she* were different.

She dropped her hand, disgusted with herself. She couldn't change the past. Everything she wanted, everything she aspired to, was within her grasp. All she had to do was work towards her goals. Success, security, self-sufficiency. *That* was what she wanted. Not jostling with commuters or being a drone in a corporation. Or hankering after places she'd never visit.

'Lily, you can't have considered. At least think about it.'

'I have, Pete, but the answer is no. I'm happy here.'

At first she thought the chirruping noise was the dawn chorus. Each morning magpies and cockatoos greeted the first light. But this was too monotone, too persistent. Groaning, Lily opened her eyes. It was still night.

Pulse thundering, she groped for the phone. No one rang at this time unless it was an emergency.

'Hello?' She struggled to sit up, shoving her pillow behind her back.

'Ms Lily Nolan?'

The pulse that an instant ago had sprinted in her arteries gave a single mighty thump. The deep male voice was foreign, rich and dark like a shot of espresso.

She groped for the bedside light and squinted at her watch. Minutes to midnight. No wonder she felt groggy. She'd only slept half an hour.

'Who's speaking?'

'Raffaele Petri.'

Raffaele Petri!

To her sleep-addled senses that voice sounded like liquid seduction. She frowned and pulled the neck of her sleep shirt closed. Male voices didn't affect her that way. But then how many sounded like this?

'Are you still there?'

'Of course I'm here. I've just woken up.'

'*Mi dispiace.*' *I'm sorry.*

He didn't sound sorry. He sounded...

Lily shook her head. If it *was* Raffaele Petri this was business. She couldn't afford to think about how potently male he sounded. Even if her hormones were dancing at the sound of that deliciously accented voice.

'Signor Petri—' She raked her hair from her face, shuffling higher in the bed. 'What can I do for you?'

'Sign the contract and get here *subito.*'

Lily choked down her instinctive response. The only place she was going *subito*, immediately, was back to sleep.

'That's impossible.'

'Nonsense. It's the only sensible course of action.'

Lily breathed deep, letting the chilly night air fill her

lungs as she sought calm. He wasn't only her client, he was her most important client.

'Did you hear me?'

'Yes.'

'Good. When you've arranged your flight give my assistant the details. He'll organise for you to be met at the airport.'

This must be how Renaissance Italian princes had sounded. As if every word they spoke was law. Imagine having such confidence you'd always get what you desired.

'Thank you, but I won't be contacting Pete.' She cleared her throat, her voice still husky from sleep. 'I was very flattered by your offer, Signor Petri, but I prefer working for myself.'

'You're turning me down?' His soft voice raised the hairs on the back of her neck.

Had anyone ever denied Raffaele Petri what he wanted?

Lily's heart thudded. She was on dangerous ground.

Widely touted as the most beautiful man in the world, he'd become famous as the golden-haired, outrageously handsome face, and body, that had turned designer casual into a style men around the globe aspired to emulate. No doubt he'd had women saying yes all his life.

But he had far more than looks. After leaving modelling he'd defied the critics and proven himself über-successful in business. Wealthy and powerful, Raffaele Petri was clearly used to instant compliance.

'I'm very flattered by the offer—'

'But?' That purr of enquiry barely concealed a razor-sharp edge.

Lily drew in a slow breath. 'Unfortunately I'm not in a position to accept.'

Silence. Long enough for her to wonder if she'd burned her bridges. Fear skated through her. She needed the work his company sent.

'What would have to change so you'd be in a position to accept?'

Damn the man. Why couldn't he just accept no?

'May I ask instead why you want me?' For a nanosecond heat surged at the unintentional double meaning of her words. But the idea of Raffaele Petri wanting her for anything other than work was so utterly unbelievable it rapidly faded. 'I was told you were happy with my research and our current arrangement.'

'If I were unhappy with your work I wouldn't offer you a job, Ms Nolan.' His clipped tones twisted her tension higher. 'I want you here on my team because you're the best at what you do. Simple as that.'

The heat suffusing her this time came from gratification.

'Thank you, Signor Petri. I appreciate your good opinion.' She'd love to ask about a testimonial but the throbbing silence told her this wasn't the time. 'Please know I'll continue to offer the best possible service.' She wriggled back against the pillow.

'That's not enough.'

'Sorry?' What more could he want than her best?

'I'm starting a significant project.' He paused. 'I need my team on hand and bound by the utmost confidentiality.'

Lily stiffened. 'I hope you're not implying I'm a security risk. Every contract I accept is completed in strictest confidence. I safeguard my research and my clients.' She never shared details of clients without permission. Which was why it would have been a coup to have a testimonial from him on her website.

She'd begun as a researcher for a private enquiry firm but the cases got her down. She'd found her niche when she widened her horizons—from staff checks to analyses of businesses and commercial trends. Lately it had been the viability of new ventures or businesses ripe for takeover.

That was where Raffaele Petri came in. The man was like a shark scenting blood before his competitors. Every time she investigated a business for him she'd discovered vulnerabilities and problems. It was the magic of the man that, once he acquired them, he turned those businesses into some of the most successful in the leisure industry, from a glamorous resort in Tahiti to a marina and yacht-building company in Turkey.

'If I doubted your ability to keep a secret I wouldn't hire you.'

Lily released a breath, relief rising.

'But,' he added, 'I can't afford risks. This team will be the best of the best. And it will be in New York. I need you here.'

Pride swelled. Lily had never been *needed*. Never stood out. Looks, school grades, sport, she'd always been average, never in the limelight until—

Lily shook her head in self-disgust at that old neediness. It was a spill over from her teenage years when she'd felt no one really wanted her, that to her family she was only a burden and a worry. And to her friends an embarrassing, constant reminder of a disaster they'd rather forget. She'd hated that awareness of being included out of duty rather than because her peers wanted her around.

His words made her long to say, *Yes, of course, I'll be in New York tomorrow.*

Imagine exploring the Big Apple. Imagine…

She swallowed hard. It wasn't possible. Facing the curious eyes of all those strangers, seeing them stare in fascination or hurriedly turn away. She wouldn't put herself through that anymore.

'I'm used to working with your staff from a distance. I'm sure—'

'That's not the way this project will proceed, Ms Nolan.' His words were staccato, tiny darts pricking her skin. 'I won't tolerate failure on this one.'

Lily opened her mouth to say that if his project failed it wouldn't be down to her.

'Yes, Ms Nolan? You were saying?'

'I'm sorry I can't accommodate you, Signor Petri.'

'I'll double the salary. And the bonus on completion.'

Lily's eyes widened. She'd been curious enough to check the contract and the salary had staggered her. It was more than she'd earn in two years. The thought of four years' income in one hit was so tempting. It would solve her financial worries...

'Changing your tune, Ms Nolan? I thought you might.' That voice was smug now, making her want to hiss her displeasure. At him for thinking she could be bought? Or at herself for being tempted despite knowing it couldn't happen?

Part of her still hankered after adventure, travel, excitement. But she'd had to push those dreams aside when her life had derailed at fourteen. She'd been robbed of her best friend, her carefree youth, her 'normal' life. She'd even missed out on things everyone else took for granted like flirting with boys and dating.

She shook her head, long tresses slipping over her cheeks. Curse the man for stirring longings she'd put behind her years before.

She loved her home, was proud she'd saved enough to be buying it. But it was more than that. Lily *needed* the security and peace it provided. The sense of refuge.

'No, Signor Petri. That was the sound of surprise but not agreement.'

'Interesting, Ms Nolan. Most people would jump at this opportunity. Why aren't you? A family, is that it? You have a husband and children perhaps?'

'No! I don't—' Lily clamped her lips shut before she blurted out anything else. Instinctively she felt safer keeping her private life private from this man.

'No family? I thought you sounded a little young for one.'

Lily's eyebrows arched. At twenty-eight she wasn't so young. Or was he implying she didn't sound professional?

Or maybe he's just winding you up. This man enjoyed playing with her, like a cat with a trapped mouse.

Like a bully wielding his superior power.

Lily's chin shot up. 'I suppose age becomes important when one reaches…*mature* years.'

A little huff of sound reached her over the long distance. A gasp of irritation or, could it be, stifled laughter?

She shouldn't have said it. The veiled reference to his age, five years her senior, was indiscreet and possibly ruinous. But she refused to sit like a pincushion to be needled.

'Fortunately I'm not quite in my dotage, Ms Nolan.'

No, he wasn't. She kept seeing photos of him at glamorous functions. Always with a sophisticated woman on his arm, but never the same one.

'So if you don't have a family·to tie you there it must be a lover.' His voice dipped low, like dark treacle rolling through her veins to eddy in her belly. Lily drew her knees up, pressing them to her chest, trying to kill the unsettling sensation.

'My private life is no concern of yours, Signor Petri.' Did he hear the wobble of fury in her voice?

'But it is, Ms Nolan, when it comes between me and what I want.'

'Then it's time you discovered you can't always get what you want.' The words poured out. 'I decide when and where I sell my services.'

Lily scrubbed a shaky hand over her face, her chest heaving. This was going from bad to worse. Anger and anxiety curdled her insides. And self-disgust. She needed to stay calm, no matter what the provocation.

'I assume you don't normally speak to your clients in that suggestively sexy voice.' His own voice was far too sultry. 'It would give them the wrong idea about what services you sell.'

Lily almost dropped the phone.

Suggestively sexy?

He had to be kidding! No man had ever called her sexy.

Of course he's kidding. He's playing with you, searching for your weak spots.

And finding them!

Curiously, the realisation calmed her, despite the burn of annoyance.

'There are reasons I can't work for you in New York, Signor Petri, but—'

'Name three.'

'Sorry?'

'I want to know why you reject my offer. Come on, three sound reasons.' The words shot out, quick and demanding, and before she knew it, Lily was answering.

'I don't have a passport for a start.' She winced. That made her sound like some country hick to a man who travelled the world as easily as she travelled it vicariously via the internet.

'That's one. What else?'

'I can't afford to rent a place in New York.'

'Not even with the bonus I'm offering?'

'I have commitments here. Any money I earn goes to those.'

'And the third? What's your third reason?'

Because she couldn't stand the thought of working in an office with other people? Because she wouldn't put herself through all that again?

Because she preferred solitude? She had a good life and an exciting business plan and no bullying magnate was going to disrupt those on a whim.

'You don't answer, Ms Nolan, which makes me think it's the most important reason of all. Or you don't have one.'

Sheer strength of will stopped Lily from blurting a response. He wasn't going to goad her again.

'Is it a lover holding you back?'

'You have no right to quiz me like this.'

'I have every right when it stymies my most important deal.'

Despite his monumental arrogance, Lily's ears pricked up. She was fascinated by this man's business acumen, his ability to see opportunities before anyone else. She'd love to know what this secret project was.

'You want my advice?' She was in the process of saying 'No' when he spoke over top of her. 'Ditch him, Ms Nolan. Find yourself a man who won't obstruct such a brilliant opportunity. You've got real talent. You shouldn't let him stand in the way of it.'

For a second Lily gawped. Raffaele Petri was beyond belief. If she had a partner she'd never leave him on the say-so of some self-important stranger.

'I wasn't aware you were an expert on relationships, Signor Petri. Aren't your girlfriends famous for being short-term?'

Lily gasped as she heard her thoughts slip out. She'd just scuttled her future with his company. But his behaviour, his whole attitude, was offensive.

A crack of laughter sounded on the line, resolving into a warm chuckle that did strange things to her insides.

Lily stiffened as fire tongued her sensitive flesh. A hot shiver ripped through her as if a warm masculine hand, rather than a disembodied voice, caressed her. She swallowed hard, horrified at her instantaneous response.

Wasn't it enough that the man looked like a Greek god come to life? Did he have to sound irresistible too? Lily pressed the heel of her palm to her sternum, trying to ease her heart's wild pounding.

She detested bullies. Her response was inexplicable.

Except it wasn't. She was a young, healthy woman, with the physical urges that went with that. Her hormones didn't care if he was a saint or the devil incarnate. All they cared about was that they'd been deprived of anything like excitement or satisfaction for far too long.

'Don't laugh at me!' Her words rapped out, too short, too sharp.

In the sudden silence she realised what she'd revealed. He knew he'd got to her.

Raffaele Petri might be a bully but he was clever. All the world knew he came from the backstreets of some large Italian city. His business success was a commercial miracle.

'What if I'm laughing at myself? Finally being called on my defects.' His voice held an edge but she couldn't tell if it was amusement or banked fury. 'My decrepit age. My lack of emotional staying power. What else, I wonder?' He paused. 'Have you been investigating me, Ms Nolan?'

Despite the rich cadence of his voice, Lily heard the threat in that low purr of sound.

'I haven't, Signor Petri. Your business, yes, before I agreed to work for it. But as for a personal profile...' She shook her head, her hair swirling. 'That wasn't necessary.'

'Because the paparazzi do such a thorough job of portraying someone's life, don't they?'

Lily frowned. Was that emotion? Had she hit a nerve?

'The passport can be fast-tracked. I'll get my people onto it. Accommodation will be arranged. Plus I'll have the contract altered to include the increased salary and bonus.' He paused, which was as well, because her head was spinning. His abrupt change of subject left her floundering. 'Appealing enough for you?'

The silence that followed was thick with expectation. He was waiting for her to agree before he hung up and dealt with whatever issue was next on his list.

Except Lily wasn't some problem to be fixed.

'I appreciate the offer, the very handsome offer,' she choked out, her fingers clamping the phone. 'But it won't work for me. I'm happy to do whatever I can from here—'

'But that won't work for *me*.' His voice sent a trickle of foreboding down her backbone.

For ten seconds there was silence. For twenty. But Lily

refused to back down. What he asked was impossible for her and she had too much pride to explain why.

'You leave me no choice, Ms Nolan. We'll find someone else to be principal researcher.'

Lily eased back against her pillow, shaky as the tension gripping her body finally began to abate.

'And my company won't hire you again.'

Lily couldn't stifle a hiss of shock. Air locked somewhere between her throat and her lungs as her body froze. Stars scattered her vision, dimming to pinpricks till, with a sagging release, her lungs began pumping again.

Without his business, hers was dead in the water. Four months ago she'd have weathered the setback but not now. Not since the loan and the expansion.

If she couldn't meet the repayments she'd lose everything—her work and her home. The life she'd so painstakingly built.

'Did you say something, Ms Nolan?'

Lily gulped to clear her throat but couldn't think of a thing to say.

'It won't take long for my dissatisfaction with your service to get out, either. You'd be surprised how fast news spreads. Continental boundaries don't mean anything and I have contacts around the world. From Melbourne to Mumbai, London to Los Angeles.'

Again that lethal pause, allowing her time to process the bleak scenario he'd painted. Her name would be mud with the really big enterprises, the internationals she'd set her sights on to make her expanded business a success.

'You'll go out of your way to blacken my name?' Her voice was a thin scratch of sound but at least it was steady. Unlike the rest of her. She shook as if with fever.

'I'll be sure to mention it whenever appropriate.' In other words he'd take delight in savaging her reputation.

Hatred coiled, tightening in her belly. Hatred as she'd only ever felt once before, for the guy who'd changed her life in an instant—from carefree to a grim round of medical treatments. Her hand lifted to her face.

Swallowing hard, Lily turned the nervous gesture into a defiant flick of the wrist, sending her long hair flying back from her face. Deliberately she set her chin, staring at her face reflected in the window.

One thing Raffaele Petri didn't know—she was a fighter. She'd survived far worse than he could dish out and emerged stronger as a result.

She lowered her hand, smoothing the quilt as she dragged in aching breaths. She opened her mouth to speak but he beat her to it.

'Of course if you were to change your mind...'

Fury swamped her. He knew she had no choice.

Even so, part of her brain noted that the snake in the Garden of Eden must have sounded like this. No hissing, no sharpness. Just a lush, seductive roll of sound that invited her to go against everything she knew and trusted. To take the plunge, even though it must end in disaster.

'You're nothing if not predictable, Signor Petri.' She pressed the phone to her ear but heard no response. 'Textbook bullying, in fact.'

Still nothing. His silence infuriated her but she refused to give him the satisfaction of hearing her rant. She looked at her hand, fisted so tight in her lap it was hard to prise open. When she did she saw scarlet crescents where her nails had scored.

'Very well, Signor Petri. I'll work for you.' Her lungs ached as she released the breath crammed in her chest. 'But you can change the contract to three times the original salary. Ditto with the bonus. Have it in my inbox tomorrow and if it's satisfactory I'll sign.' She paused, trying to control her sharp, shallow breaths.

To her astonishment he didn't disagree.

'I'll see you in New York, Ms Nolan.'

Not if I see you first.

She might be stuck working for him but she had no illusions he'd be part of the project team. He'd be sunning himself in the Bahamas or skiing in Switzerland or whatever the wealthy did when they weren't harassing ordinary people. Somehow she'd deal with the travel and all those people. She'd do the job, take his money and come back to build her future here as she'd planned.

She'd get through this.

'Goodbye, Signor Petri.'

'Not goodbye. *Arrivederci*, Ms Nolan.'

CHAPTER TWO

RAFFA GOT TO the office after a breakfast meeting.

Across the large room he saw an unfamiliar figure—long hair, loose shirt, loose trousers and flat shoes. The clothes were resolutely unfeminine but the body beneath all that unflattering drabness wasn't. Femininity was there in the way she moved, despite her rigid back and high shoulders.

It had to be Lily Nolan. The area was off-limits to all but his hand-picked team.

She'd been tense on the phone that night too. Uptight and angry, yet that husky, just-awake voice had done things to him no woman had in years.

He frowned at the unwanted memory.

Raffa's eyes narrowed on the rhythmic swish of hair down her narrow back as she walked away. It all but reached her waist. Not blonde or black or even dark but simply brown. A brown so ordinary and unremarkable it looked uncompromising, as if she spurned most women's desire to improve on nature with eye-catching colour.

He turned into his private office and took a seat, gesturing for his assistant to do the same. Through the glass walls he saw Lily Nolan talking with someone by the door to the conference room. Her body language radiated stress, right down to the fist clenching at her side.

Had he made a mistake bringing her here? He'd wanted her because of her talents, her often brilliant insights and her professionalism. He knew she'd go the extra mile to meet his needs.

But that night on the phone her obstinacy, the way she challenged him as no one else dared, had piqued his interest. He'd accepted her outrageous terms because every refusal she gave made him more determined to win.

The knowledge he'd acted on a whim had annoyed him ever since. He never allowed himself to be sidetracked. He'd got where he was by grabbing every opportunity to build his wealth and success. Even if some of those opportunities were unpalatable, they'd been necessary. He was never impulsive.

'How's our newest staff member fitting in? Any problems?'

'No, nothing like that.'

Was that a flush on Pete's boyish face? Raffa felt his eyebrows cinch together. The woman had been here less than a day. Surely she hadn't seduced his PA already?

'She's hit the ground running. She must be jet-lagged but she's already got acquainted with our set up here. Now she's meeting the rest of the team.' Pete swivelled his head towards the conference room, his gaze fixed.

Raffa realised it wasn't adoration on his assistant's face but something he couldn't read.

'Yet she makes you uncomfortable?'

Pete's face mottled red. Embarrassment? Lust?

'Of course not.' The words tumbled out too quickly. 'She's very professional.'

Professional. It sounded like faint praise. Especially since in the past he'd overheard Pete laughing with the woman over a long-distance connection.

'But?' Raffa fixed him with a stern gaze. His policy was to remove problems the instant they arose. If this woman disrupted the smoothly oiled workings of his team he'd take action immediately.

Pete shrugged. 'You know how it is when you know someone only from a distance. You build up a picture in your mind. The reality can be…different.' He gestured abruptly to the tablet he carried. 'About the review of the

Hawaiian hotel. Will I bring that forward? You'd mentioned a snap inspection to keep them on their toes.'

Raffa surveyed his PA, reading his discomfort. It was probably as Pete said—the deflating reality of the first face-to-face meeting. But Raffa never left anything to chance.

He'd planned to leave the rebellious Australian alone today to get on with the job for which he was paying such an exorbitant salary. And he would—after he'd checked her out.

'We're busy wrapping up some other projects but anything you need on the legal side, let me know.' Consuela Flores gave a brisk nod and smile from the end of the conference table and Lily felt herself sink back in her seat, a grateful answering smile on her face.

Among the group she'd be working with, the middle-aged lawyer had proved the easiest to deal with. Her severe demeanour, magenta power suit, expensive pearls and stiffly lacquered hair had made Lily wary. Here was an imposing woman for whom appearance as well as performance was important. Yet after a millisecond of silence when they met and that brief, predictable widening of the eyes, Ms Flores had treated Lily like everyone else around the table.

Lily had wanted to hug her for that.

This morning had been tough, every bit as difficult as she'd feared. Her hands were clammy, her chest weighted and her pulse still too fast. Forcing herself into the office had been a major test of nerves already strung out from the stress of travelling.

'Thanks, I appreciate that. For now, though, I suspect it won't be legal expertise I need. There'll be a lot of digging first.'

Consuela nodded. 'I'm glad it's you doing the digging. Your reports for the Turkish deal made our work much easier. There's nothing like heading into negotiations well-prepared, with no lurking pitfalls. Now you're onsite we can touch base as anything arises.'

Lily's smile grew, the clamp on her chest easing a little.

Only the knowledge she was up to this job, more than up to it, had got her across the Pacific, across the United States and into this building, when all she wanted was to lock herself inside her home and not budge.

She could do this, no matter how horribly far out of her comfort zone she felt.

No, she wouldn't just do the job. She'd excel! Her work meant everything. It was the one part of her world where she had complete control, complete confidence.

Which made it all the more infuriating that she'd been nauseous with nerves today. Fronting up at the office was the most difficult thing she'd done in years.

See what happens when you lock yourself away all the time?

Now it's you with the problem, not them.

Lily banished the voice in her head. She didn't have time for self-doubt.

'I'm looking forward to working with you too, Consuela.'

She darted a glance around the table. The woman from finance in retro-trendy glasses quickly turned her head as if she'd been watching the lawyer, not Lily. But she was too slow. Besides, the distressed twist of her lips, as if she felt ill, betrayed her.

Further down the table the guy from acquisitions flushed as Lily turned to him. Like Pete, Raffaele Petri's PA, he found looking at her embarrassing. Beside him the older man from systems management didn't even try, instead staring past her shoulder.

Lily sat straighter, determined not to be daunted.

Yet that didn't stop the sick feeling in her stomach, or the churning memories of her previous forays into office work. Each one a disaster. Eventually she'd given up trying and decided to work from the seclusion of home.

The fingers of her right hand twitched but she repressed the urge to raise her hand to her face. It had taken years to cure herself of the habit and she wasn't starting again now. No matter how exposed she felt before these strangers.

'I appreciate you all making time to meet me on my first day. I'll look forward to working with you.'

Liar!

'I have a question, though.' Lily looked to Consuela. 'We all have different areas of responsibility, but is there a team leader? Without coordination we'll have problems.'

'That would be me.' The masculine voice curled around her like warm smoke.

Her heart jolted and a prickling spread across her skin.

She'd only heard that voice once but its echo had lurked in her subconscious since, visiting in those moments between waking and sleep when she was most vulnerable.

Was that heat flushing her cheeks?

It couldn't be. She'd spent half her life being gawked at. She'd lost the ability to blush in her teens.

Reluctantly she turned her head.

It was a good thing she was sitting.

Raffaele Petri's face was known around the globe. Yet the photos hadn't prepared her. Tall, taller than she'd expected with his Italian heritage. Wide shoulders, slim hips, long legs—the epitome of masculinity in its prime. Oddly his casual jacket and open-necked shirt emphasised rather than detracted from the power she sensed in him. He didn't need a three-piece suit to stamp his authority.

Chiselled features that looked too close to perfection to be true. She'd assumed those photos had been airbrushed. Yes, there were crinkles around his eyes, as if from time in the sun, but perversely that only made him more attractive. Hair the colour of dark old gold, tidy but hinting at tousled. Enough to make her fingers twitch at the thought of touching. The hooded cast of his eyes looked languorous until you met that piercing blue stare.

Lily swallowed over a ball of sandpaper in her throat. Meeting his gaze was a palpable experience, as if he'd reached out and taken her hand. Sizzling heat ran through her as those eyes held hers—compelling, electric.

It wasn't just that he was ridiculously handsome, she realised as she forced a slow breath out. He was...*more*. Even from the other side of the conference table she felt the crackle of energy, the sense he was a man who made things happen.

Unhurriedly he surveyed her, cataloguing everything from the hair brushing her cheeks to her face, her throat and down as far as was visible above the table.

The old resentment rose, that he should scrutinise her like some animal in a cage. Till she realised she'd done the same—taking in his appearance in minute detail.

The knowledge sapped her anger, leaving her winded as his gaze lifted.

'At last we meet, Ms Nolan.'

So that explained it.

Realisation slammed into Raffa like a fist to the chest, so strong it felt like recognition. An unexpected hit of adrenaline.

But recognition implied a link with the woman on the far side of the table. That was nonsense, even if the memory of her husky voice and feisty attitude had intruded at the oddest times these past weeks. The pulse of energy he felt could only be satisfaction at getting to the bottom of his PA's discomfort.

Lily Nolan's long hair framed an oval face that should have been, at best, ordinary. Brown eyes, a mouth neither thin-lipped nor lush, an unremarkable nose. Beautiful she wasn't, but she might have been pretty if it weren't for the wide swathe of tight, shiny skin that ran from her temple down one cheek to her jaw.

Scars faded with time. How long had she had this? The colour wasn't livid and she'd had plastic surgery. It must have been a hell of a sight before that.

Not a knife wound. He'd seen enough in his youth to realise no knife marked like this.

A burn? Some other trauma?

'Signor Petri.' That familiar voice stirred something unaccustomed that for a heartbeat distracted him.

He circled the table, arm extended.

She hesitated then pushed her chair back to stand. Her long, buttoned-up shirt fell loose around her slim frame. Again her choice of clothes hit him. A deliberate attempt not to fit in? To make the point she was here under sufferance? As if he cared what his staff wore so long as they did their work.

Her hand clasped his. Smooth and cool and small.

She just topped his shoulder in her flat shoes, tilting her head to meet his eyes. At the movement her hair slid back off her cheek, revealing more of that shiny, scarred flesh. But it wasn't the blemish that drew his attention, it was the bright challenge in her eyes.

'I believe this is where I'm supposed to say it's a pleasure to meet you, Signor Petri.'

A gasp from the other side of the room reminded him of the staff still there.

Raffa held her hand in an easy grasp, not ready to let go.

'That's right,' he murmured, bestowing a small smile. He'd won their little contest of wills and could afford to be gracious.

Yet he saw no softening in that stern expression, no easing in her rigidity. Not even a hint of response in those serious eyes.

Surprise flickered. It was rare to find someone genuinely unresponsive to his charm.

Lily Nolan grew more interesting by the moment.

'It's definitely a pleasure to meet you, Lily.' He widened his smile just a fraction, lingering on her name. 'I've been looking forward to having you here as part of the team.'

Silence for just a moment too long. 'So I gather, since you went to such lengths to get me here.'

Another muffled sound came from nearby but Raffa didn't turn. He didn't care what anyone thought.

'You were certainly elusive.'

He waited, expecting her to pull her hand from his. Instead she stood, unmoving but for the fine vibration coursing from her hand to his. She was wound up tight, bottling in strong emotion.

Yet her eyes met his directly, nothing but challenge to be read there.

This woman would make a hell of a poker player. She betrayed no hint of weakness or discomfort.

His gaze zeroed in on a minuscule movement at the corner of her mouth. For a moment he wondered if it could be the scar pulling at her mouth, till he remembered there'd been no distortion of her lips when she spoke. The tiny flicker of movement was what then? Her biting her cheek?

'Did you want me for something now?' She looked pointedly at their joined hands and Raffa felt amusement bubble. She was so patently determined to be unimpressed. So ostentatiously unaffected by his looks or position. Perversely he liked it.

How long since he'd done anything, gone anywhere, and been treated like an average Joe?

It was a novelty he hadn't known he craved till a slip of a woman with muddy brown eyes looked at him as if he wasn't anything special.

'As a matter of fact, now is the perfect time to brief you in more detail about my expectations.' He turned and nodded to Pete. Moments later his stalwart PA had emptied the room and closed the door on them.

If Lily Nolan was intimidated she didn't show it. Her hand lay unresisting in his, as if making the point his touch was immaterial to her.

Who was this woman? She'd intrigued him from their first contact.

Raffa's world and the people in it were predictable. Mostly they wanted something from him—reflected fame, an 'in' to the best circles, business opportunities, sex. Everyone wanted something.

Except this woman who didn't want him at all.

Was that why she fascinated him? Because he'd grown bored?

Raffa released his hold. He had more significant things to concentrate on than the novelty of an employee who resented his authority.

Yet he admired the way she slowly slid her hand away, not snatching it, though he'd touched her far too long. Nor did she move back, but stood, taking stock as he did.

His eyes dipped to her loose, unattractive clothing. She'd gone too far with the dressing down, the not being just another cog in his corporate wheel.

Unless she dressed that way because the scar on her face wasn't the only one. Did she have other injuries that made it uncomfortable to wear fitted clothes? The thought stirred discomfort.

Because he'd brought her here against her wishes? The idea was ludicrous. Whatever her problems, he wasn't responsible for them. He employed her at an outrageously high salary and hitherto unheard of bonuses.

'Take a seat.' He gestured to the chair she'd vacated and sank into one beside it. He was determined to understand this woman. Then he could push her from his thoughts and get on with business.

She sat watching him, feet flat on the floor, hands clasped loosely. For all the world as if he, not she, was the one whose work had to impress.

Raffa felt his lips twitch. If ever he needed another negotiator on his acquisitions team he could do far worse than Lily Nolan.

Lily read that quirk of his sculpted lips and knew she amused him.

An icicle of frozen rage jabbed her side. She wanted to cry out but kept her mouth closed and her face calm. She'd weathered enough pity, horror, revulsion and sympathy to last a lifetime. A self-important tycoon who laughed at her because she wasn't a perfectly tailored, respectful employee hardly mattered.

Or was he amused by how unfeminine she looked? His inspection had raked her from head to toe.

Remarkably, though he'd surveyed her damaged face his gaze hadn't lingered longer there than anywhere else. Almost as if her scar were no more significant than the shape of her nose or the comfy shoes she'd grabbed rather than teeter in the unaccustomed heels she'd bought in a moment of weakness. As if a pair of shoes would transform her into just another office worker!

Not with her face.

Was that what amused him? The difference between his bronzed beauty and her marred features?

She swallowed hard, tasting sharp bitterness. She was jumping to conclusions. Raffaele Petri was selfish and ruthless. She had no proof he was shallow and cruel.

But the day was young.

It wouldn't be the first time someone had used her as a foil for their own beauty. In her final year at school a couple of new girls had befriended her, both beautiful, blonde and bubbly. For the first time in years Lily had felt accepted and valued. Till she overheard them discussing how letting her hang out with them made people see them as sympathetic and even prettier than they were.

Lily shoved the memories away, drawing back her shoulders, imagining strength streaming through her spine and lifted chin. Whatever his game, she was his match. She might not be much to look at but she'd developed a strength of purpose few could equal.

Silence stretched but she refused to fill it. If this was a test of willpower he'd be disappointed.

Eyes the colour of the Pacific Ocean met hers, piercing as if reading her thoughts.

'You're settled into your office?'

She nodded. 'Yes, thank you. Pete showed me around.'

To her horror she'd discovered the floor full, not of little rabbit-hutch cubicles where workers could hide from public view, but of spacious glassed-in offices that reduced noise levels but left everyone on show.

Worse was the fact her office was beside Pete and Raffaele Petri. The idea of working with this man watching her made something shrivel inside.

'And your accommodation? It's comfortable?'

Lily nodded. The size and luxury had overwhelmed her, reminding her she was a country girl, out of her depth in sophisticated New York. Fortunately jet lag had got the better of her last night before she'd had a chance to explore properly and feel like too much of a misfit. This morning she'd overslept and had to rush to get ready. All she'd really seen was the sybaritic black marble bathroom and the inside of her suitcase as she hunted for clothes.

'Yes, thank you. It's quite sufficient.'

'Sufficient?' His mouth kicked up in a smile that did strange things to her pulse, turning it from steady to riotous. It was bad enough when he'd smiled before. He'd looked so compellingly handsome he'd stolen her breath. But this was different—genuine, and more powerful for it.

'What's so amusing?' She sat straighter.

His eyes zeroed in on hers and a fizzle of heat zapped her bones. 'I've never heard my penthouse described as merely *sufficient*.'

CHAPTER THREE

'YOUR PENTHOUSE?' LILY COULDN'T hide the shock in her voice. 'I'm staying in your *penthouse*?' Her fingers dug at her chair's leather arms.

'No other floor has a roof garden or swimming pool.' He surveyed her as if analysing a curious specimen.

For the second time that day she felt almost like she were blushing.

'I didn't open the blinds. It was late and I was jet-lagged and—' She snapped her mouth shut before she blurted out any more. She'd had a vague impression of a spacious sitting room, of stylish furnishings, but she'd never dreamed...

'Never mind, you'll see the roof garden later.'

Lily shook her head. 'There won't be a later. I can't stay there.'

'But you said the accommodation was perfectly adequate.' This time his mouth didn't curl in a smile but she knew he was laughing at her. How could he not be when she was too thick to realise she'd spent the night in a Manhattan penthouse?

'It's your home. It wouldn't be appropriate.'

Raffa couldn't imagine any of the women he'd dated turning down an opportunity to move into his apartment, even if just the guest quarters. They'd see it as a stepping stone to more.

He'd known Lily Nolan was different from the moment she picked up the phone and spoke in that sultry midnight voice. It had evoked a fragile tendril of something—not quite arousal, but definite interest.

She continued to pique his interest. She was…refreshing. Intriguing. Not because of her damaged face or appalling clothes. He, of all people, was the last person to judge on looks.

How many years since he'd found any woman interesting?

He leaned closer, registering her subtle shift as she compensated by pressing back into her chair.

Did she dislike men or just him?

The fact he wondered pulled him up short.

He wouldn't be distracted into musing on Lily Nolan's likes and dislikes. But he *did* need to ensure he'd made the right decision, bringing her here. Too much rode on this.

'If I think the arrangement appropriate then who's to say otherwise?'

'Are you perverse with everyone or just me?' She spoke slowly, enunciating each syllable with clipped precision. 'I can't live in your home.'

'Is it your privacy you're concerned about? Are you worried I'll invade your space?'

The paparazzi labelled him a playboy because he wasn't seen with the same woman twice. No one knew that was due to boredom and a dislike of being the object of any greedy woman's avarice. These days his reputation for carnal pleasure owed everything to the fantasies of those he *hadn't* taken to bed. He hadn't desired a woman in years.

They always wanted something from him. Always had.

He hated how that made him feel.

Surely Lily Nolan didn't think he was so desperate he'd sexually harass his staff?

'The guest wing is separate, with its own entrance. There's a lock on the door connecting to the rest of the penthouse so you'll be quite alone.' In light of experience, *he* should be worried about *her* intruding.

Yet she remained silent. Indignation rose.

The sensation made him pause. Raffa couldn't remember the last time he'd felt it.

Because he always got his own way?

Or because there was little except business that he cared about, including what people thought of him?

'The arrangement is temporary. My PA had organised accommodation but there was trouble with burst pipes yesterday. The place is badly water damaged.'

'I could stay at a hotel.'

'You could, but you said you couldn't afford that. Something about spending your salary on other things.'

Her eyebrows lifted as if she recognised his curiosity and was surprised by it.

Dannazione! He was surprised by it!

'You couldn't have put me up somewhere else?'

'Because I'm rolling in cash?' She had a point. It would have been the work of a moment for Pete to make alternative arrangements. But Raffa was already financing her New York stay in style. Besides, having her close meant a chance to satisfy his curiosity.

'I didn't get rich by wasting money, Ms Nolan. The guest suite is empty and convenient for your work here. I can be sure you'll be on hand, doing what I want you to do, not off sightseeing.'

For a moment her eyes glowed and he could have sworn the temperature in the room rose a couple of degrees. But her temper didn't ignite. She really had phenomenal control.

Raffa refused to consider why he enjoyed testing it.

'You may recall I didn't want to come to New York. If you're concerned I'll get distracted I could go home and work there.'

He shook his head. 'You'll stay where you are till the other apartment is ready. I'm paying top dollar for your services. I want to be sure I get my money's worth.'

'You don't trust me?' Her head angled as if to view him better.

'I don't trust anyone till they prove themselves.'

Her gaze sharpened. 'You were the one eager to have me here.'

He shrugged and steepled his hands, elbows on the arms of his chair.

'Based on past performance, I judge you to be the person I need. But this project is more important than any you've done. Nothing will be left to chance.'

Lily looked into those bright blue eyes, felt the intensity of that searing stare and knew they'd reached the heart of things.

She felt the change in him. The quickening, the sizzle of energy.

Their conversation up to now had been skirmishes. Maybe he kept all new staff on their toes till he was convinced of their worth. Though why he'd take such a personal interest in her she couldn't fathom.

'Why is it so important?'

The furrow on his tanned brow disappeared as he leaned back. 'I won't brook failure on this.'

As far as Lily knew he never failed. Raffaele Petri had a nose for a good deal and a reputation for success. He also had an unerring instinct for what would appeal to the wealthiest clientele. That was how he'd built his fortune, with elite resorts, clubs and now marinas servicing those who demanded the best in everything. The rich always had enough to spend on themselves despite economic downturns that affected people like her, struggling to make a go of things.

'This man I'm to focus on, Robert Bradshaw...'

'Yes?'

'Can you tell me about him?'

'That's your job. I want a full report—his business interests, friends and connections. Everything.' Raffaele

Petri's expression didn't alter but Lily heard something in his voice that made the hair at her nape rise.

She had the disquieting certainty she was venturing into dangerous waters. Once more instinct yelled at her to back out. But she had no choice. He'd destroy her reputation if she reneged on this job.

'It would help if you told me something about the project.'

He regarded her, unblinking, and she shivered. It was said Raffaele Petri could seduce a woman with a glance from those stunning ocean-blue eyes. Not that he'd ever turn his fabled seduction skills on her. But what she read there now was hard calculation. Shrewdness as if he assessed her, deciding how much to share.

Not much, if the firm set of his sculpted jaw was an indication.

Lily stared back, trying to ignore the tremor of feminine response fluttering through her belly and the teasing trickle of heat in her blood.

What a time for her hormones to wake up from hibernation!

She breathed deep, corralling her thoughts. 'My other commissions for you have been to research companies or commercial trends, even localities.' They had been to determine if a site or company would be a good investment. 'This time it's about a man.'

Still he said nothing, as if waiting to see how far she could go connecting the dots.

Exasperation rose. 'Is there a particular angle I'm to focus on?'

'I told you. Everything. The size and nature of his income. His business associates. His interests, his weaknesses and habits. Who he sleeps with. The lot.'

Was it imagination, or did that stare harden?

She didn't imagine it. His voice when he'd said 'who he sleeps with' was different, his Italian accent stronger, like rich chocolate coating a lethal stiletto blade. She fought to repress a shiver. Whoever Robert Bradshaw was, whatever he'd done, she'd hate to be in his shoes.

In that instant Lily felt what she'd understood only intellectually before: Raffaele Petri would be a dangerous enemy.

Just as well she was too insignificant to be his enemy.

'I see.' She didn't, but clearly he wasn't going to enlighten her. 'Okay. I'll do the best I can.'

'That's not good enough. I need to know you'll deliver the goods.'

'You'll get your report, Signor Petri. But it will take time. This is a broad brief.' She waved one hand, trying to look brisk and organised, despite the chill sinking between her shoulder blades. 'His commercial interests and associates I can uncover. I'll do a thorough check on all those. His property and lifestyle, ditto. But there are limits.'

'Limits?' Dark eyebrows rose as if he'd never heard the word.

'I'm a researcher, Signor Petri, not a private detective. If you want information on this man's personal life, you'd do better hiring one of those. They can stake out his residence and give you an account of his comings and goings.'

He was already shaking his head. 'I learned long ago not to trust them. I want results, not excuses.'

Surprised, Lily leaned forward, then froze as she registered a warm, spicy scent. It teased her nostrils, sending shockwaves of delight to her belly.

It made her think of photos she'd seen of this man years ago. He'd lain half naked on a rumpled bed, jaw shadowed and his arms raised behind his head in a pose that accentuated the impressive musculature of his chest and arms. The sight had coaxed millions of women to buy decadently expensive aftershave for their men.

Was that what she smelled now? Lily inhaled, wondering at the art of producing a fragrance that seemed so purely natural, like hot male flesh and forbidden longing.

Abruptly she pulled back, trying to remember her train of thought.

That was it. When had he used private detectives in the past, and why didn't he like them?

His expression made it clear he wouldn't answer.

She shrugged. 'It's up to you. I'm just warning you that there are limits to my capabilities.'

'Yet you once worked in a private detection firm, even received some training.'

Lily stared. He knew *that* about her? She tried to recall how much detail she'd included on her résumé, but what really surprised her was that he'd read it personally.

'It was a long time ago and I didn't qualify as a private investigator. The work didn't suit me.' She'd got sick of grubbing around in people's personal lives. Commercial research was much less seedy.

'But you have the skills. I want everything, from Bradshaw's finances to his phone records.'

Lily laid her hands in her lap, maintaining her aura of calm despite the alarm bells going off in her head.

'Unless you have a warrant, phone records are protected.' She paused, breathing deep. 'Obviously you're not talking about hacking into phone company records.'

Those straight, decisive eyebrows rose. 'Aren't I? But I understood you included hacking in your skill set.'

Lily reared back, her seat sliding away from the conference table. 'How did you know that? It was years ago.'

Her breath came in staccato bursts. It had been years since anyone had mentioned her one brush with the law. She'd been just a kid, bored from being alone so much, cut off from her friends by the regime of medical treatment and surgery she'd undergone. And by the fact that to a lot of her schoolmates she'd become a freak. Not just because of her scars, but because she'd been the one to survive. She'd wondered if they felt guilty because secretly they'd have preferred it if her popular friend Rachel had lived, not her.

Emotion tugged at her like an ocean current, threatening to pull her under.

Instead she focused on Raffaele Petri—so strong and arrogant and utterly in control. She'd bet he'd never felt overwhelmed or insecure. Surprisingly, that worked. Her racing pulse slowed.

'I chose the best for this project team, with the best skill set. Your short-lived career as a hacker was impressive. It's a wonder you got off so lightly.'

Lily crossed her arms over her chest. 'I was underage. And I did no damage.'

'No, just managed to break into one of the best protected and encrypted government databases in the world.'

'If you hired me to break the law, think again, Signor Petri. I won't do that for any client.' She sprang to her feet and paced away.

That was better. At last he read something definite in Lily Nolan. Not just anger but indignation and surely a little fear?

He didn't want to scare her. But she'd sparred with him for so long he'd begun to wonder what it would take to probe past her control. Even when she was angry she'd been coolly poised, a challenge, a mystery he couldn't resist prodding.

Not now. Now Raffa saw the woman behind the mask of calm self-sufficiency.

What he saw heightened his interest.

Lily Nolan's eyes flashed fire as she turned to face him. Her lips moved in what he was sure was an unconscious pout of defiance. A pout any red-blooded man would respond to.

Except he was her boss.

He never harassed his staff.

Besides, he wasn't into kissing. He'd perfected the art from necessity but never really enjoyed it. It was a tool like any other to get what he wanted.

Raffa stilled, surprised at his blurring thoughts. He didn't want to kiss Lily Nolan. The idea was farcical.

He wanted to understand her. Label and catalogue her so she no longer took up even a scintilla of his brain space. Then he'd move on to more important things.

Yet now he'd provoked a reaction he wanted more. Contempt welled. Had he turned into what he'd always abhorred? A wealthy man so self-absorbed his only delight was toying with others?

'You have scruples, Ms Nolan.'

She strode back to stand close, hands on her hips.

'There are lines I won't cross, Signor Petri. Breaking the law is one.'

Spoken like a woman who'd never experienced real need. Raffa's mouth tightened. He knew precisely the depths to which poverty and desperation could drive people.

Or was that the excuse he used to justify his past?

'Not even for money?'

Those eyes weren't muddy brown now. They looked almost pure amber, rimmed with honey brown, and they met his with quiet certainty. 'Not even for money.'

Slowly he nodded. 'Good. Then presumably you can't be bought by a competitor to betray confidential information.'

A furrow appeared on her forehead. 'Was all this some elaborate test of my honesty?'

Raffa shrugged. Easier to let her believe his interest was so straightforward than try to explain something he didn't understand himself.

If her report was insufficient, he'd have to ignore his prejudice and hire a detective. At least now he wouldn't be sucked in by nebulous 'promising leads' that required just a little more time to produce results.

Years ago, when he'd begun making decent money, he'd

spent lavishly on fruitless investigations. Older than his years in most ways, his desperation to find the man responsible for his sister's death had made him gullible in this one area.

Now he knew better. He didn't trust investigators.

He didn't trust anyone.

Raffa pushed his chair back and stood. 'We'll meet when you've completed your initial report.'

By that time this fascination would have worn off. She'd be just another employee.

CHAPTER FOUR

THERE WAS NO SOUND, no disturbance, but suddenly Lily knew she was no longer alone.

Her spine tingled from her scalp to her tailbone. Her skin drew tight and she realised she'd frozen, fingers on the keyboard, waiting.

Slowly she lifted her head.

There he was, one shoulder propped against the door-jamb, legs casually crossed at the ankles. The only man whose presence she could sense with unerring accuracy.

Every time.

Even before he looked at her.

Even when he never looked at her.

It was a sixth sense, something primitive, buried so deep in her animal instinct as to be inexplicable. Yet it happened whenever Raffaele Petri got near. Lily was always the first to notice his presence. Her senses were on alert when he was nearby, even if he wasn't talking to her.

Now he watched her with a heavy-lidded look that made her blood surge.

She'd thought him stunning in the casual trousers and jackets he wore in the office. But in formal clothes... Her eyes widened. He looked like some sinfully gorgeous fallen angel wearing a tuxedo and a lazy half smile. The bow tie loose around his collar added a decadently raffish air.

'Working late again?'

Lily nodded and cleared her throat. Ridiculous that he had this effect after more than a month, but there was no mistaking the excited pump of her heart or that sudden breathlessness.

It did no good to tell herself millions of other women

had the same reaction. Or that she made a fool of herself. All she could do was ensure no one, most especially the man before her, guessed.

'But obviously not to impress the boss.' He crossed his arms but Lily kept her eyes on his face, refusing to dwell on the way the gesture emphasised the impressive symmetry of his broad-shouldered, slim-hipped frame.

'You think not?' Her voice worked after all.

What she'd give for an interruption! These days other members of staff were in and out of her office regularly. To her surprise, after their initial shock they'd accepted her as one of the team—so different from her other work experiences. Maybe because she'd been so focused on this project she hadn't had the leisure to stress about their reactions?

Yet a frantic glance through the glass walls told her they were alone. Everyone had gone home long ago.

'I know not.' He straightened and, to her alarm, stepped into her office.

'You're a mind-reader now too?' The words blurted out.

'In addition to what?' He stopped a couple of paces from her desk, sucking all the oxygen out of her office. 'No, don't tell me. I'll enjoy the challenge of working it out.'

Lily sat back, letting her hands drop to her lap. His words were light, as if he viewed their interactions as some sort of game.

Well, she wasn't playing.

Especially since his light tone didn't match that assessing scrutiny.

'How do you know I'm not trying to impress you with my diligence?' Better to stick to concrete issues than try to guess what was going on in that brilliant, convoluted mind.

He shrugged, the fluid movement innately Italian.

'You never look to me for approval. You don't hang about my office asking questions or showing off your success with what you've unearthed about Bradshaw.'

Lily's mouth twitched, a smile hovering at the implication he'd been impressed. But she was too much on edge to allow her lips to curve up. If she let down her guard with this man, she sensed she might never be able to resurrect it.

No matter how charming he could be, Raffaele Petri was dangerous. He'd forced her here. He'd unleashed a sexual awareness in her that terrified her. Every day and every night he'd loomed in her thoughts, a forbidden temptation when she should have been focusing on work or sleep or anything but mortifyingly sensual imaginings.

'You see the end results anyway.' Carefully she laced her fingers together as if relaxed. 'What would be the point of hanging around your office showing off every little success?'

Those sculpted lips stretched in a smile that tugged a sexy crease down one tanned cheek.

Heat drilled from Lily's lungs to her belly, cramping her abdominal muscles and stirring sexual arousal, instant and unmistakable.

That was why she needed to be vigilant. Raffaele Petri didn't just have the power to make or break her. He made her crave things that were impossible.

'You're paying for the best.' It had taken her a long time to develop self-confidence about her work and she refused to play coy about something that meant so much. 'I'm not so needy I require a pat on the head every time I do well.'

If she'd aimed to deflect his attention she'd erred. Instead of backing off, he surveyed her through narrowed eyes.

'Sometimes it's not about a pat on the head,' he murmured. 'Sometimes people just want my attention.'

Lily looked up into that bright, deliberate gaze, sifting his words.

Seeking attention.

From him.

Why? As soon as she asked the question she had the answer. Because they were attracted to him. Because they wanted him to notice them, respond to them. Just as a tiny, unstoppable part of her had fantasised he might—

She moved so abruptly her chair slid back from the desk, rolling till it crashed into the wall.

Lily found herself standing, her stomach churning so hard she tasted bile. He'd touched too close to her own secret desires and made them seem all the more pathetic. As if he suspected the attraction she couldn't quell.

Her right hand lifted in that old, compulsive gesture she'd taken years to vanquish. At the last moment, just before her fingers reached her scarred face, she remembered, forcing it back down, planting both palms on her desk. Her hands were damp against the wood, her throat jammed with distress.

It wasn't just that Raffaele Petri would never find her attractive. *No* man would.

She was experienced enough to accept that, after several painful experiences where she'd tentatively reached out to a man and had to endure horrified, embarrassed rejection. Yet some foolish part of her still fantasised.

It wasn't him she was angry with, but herself.

'You mean they want you to notice them because they're attracted to you?' Her voice was raw, stretched tight.

'It's been known to happen.' Again that fluid shrug, but she was beyond noticing how appealing it was. She was too caught up with the burn of shame and self-consciousness.

'You're annoyed I haven't fallen over myself to get your attention?' She almost choked on the words. Pride was her only lifeline and she clung to it tenaciously. 'You do realise there are some people who aren't bowled over by your beauty, Signor Petri?' Her tone made it clear she was one of them.

If only that were true! Daily exposure to Raffaele Petri had done nothing to inoculate her against his golden good looks. Instead it had given her a respect for his incisive decision-making and his ability to get the best out of his team. She'd discerned fairness and even a self-deprecating humour she found far too appealing.

The sound of laughter sliced her thoughts. Rich and warm, it encircled her like a caress. There was nothing calculated about it, or about his expression, and Lily had the impression that for a moment she saw Raffaele Petri as few did. For, despite his approachability to his staff, he usually exuded a sense of being utterly self-contained.

'You're absolutely right, Lily.' Her pulse gave a throb of pleasure at the sound of her name in that deep, lush voice. 'And an antidote to my overblown ego. Not everyone finds me attractive. It's good to know you're one of them. It makes working together much simpler.'

Lily breathed out slowly. Had she really fooled him? Maybe all those years masking her feelings and learning not to show vulnerability had stood her in good stead.

'What is it you want from me?' He hadn't singled her out again since her first day in the office, yet she hadn't been able to shake the feeling he noticed her almost as much as she did him. That he was aware of her, even when his attention was on something else. Not that he was attracted to her, of course, just assessing.

'Honestly?' Eyes of searing blue met hers and heat feathered her skin. 'I find you…interesting. Different.'

She snorted. This time she didn't stop her hand as it rose to her face. But, instead of touching scarred flesh, she deliberately pushed her hair back, tucking it behind her ear, revealing the whole marred side of her face.

Her chin angled higher as her gaze challenged his, defiant. 'Oh, I'm definitely different.'

'You think I'm talking about looks?' His eyebrows flattened in something close to a scowl.

It was her turn to shrug stiff shoulders. The movement had none of his beautiful fluidity. 'What else?'

He shook his head. 'I don't know.' For a moment he

looked almost perplexed. 'But it's got nothing to do with the way you look.'

Lily didn't know whether to be relieved or ridiculously hurt.

'Perhaps it's because I don't beat a path to your door.'

His eyebrows rose. 'If you had your way we'd be a hemisphere apart.'

Lily crossed her arms, projecting an ease she didn't feel. 'You're too used to people chasing you.'

'You think this is about ego?' He paused as if considering. 'Perhaps. But it's more too. I like the lateral way you think. The combination of solid, thorough research and inspired leaps of imagination. I saw it in your report on the Tahitian project and the ones since.'

Lily felt her strain ease, her muscles loosening. Professional accolades she'd accept gratefully. It was when they veered off work that discomfort grabbed her.

'I like that you're not afraid to voice your opinions.'

'I don't see any yes-men on your team.'

'Ah, but you take your independence to a fascinating new level. It's obviously a point of honour.'

'There's nothing special about me, Signor Petri. I'm merely a professional, used to being self-employed rather than having a boss.'

For too long he regarded her with that steady gaze she suspected saw too much.

'Maybe you're right.' He lifted his hands, closing the collar of his formal shirt then deftly tying the black satin bow tie.

Lily watched, fascinated to realise such a process could be so enthralling. Not just the fact he managed a bow tie with impressive ease and without a mirror, but that the action should be almost…arousing.

'Lily?'

She blinked. 'Yes?'

'I asked if it's straight.'

'Almost, just at a slight angle.'

'This way?' He twitched the black silk and she shook her head. 'Well?' An expressive eyebrow lifted. 'Can you help?'

She looked at the tie, askew against snowy linen and golden flesh, and felt something drop in her belly. She didn't want to touch Raffaele Petri. She didn't want to go near him.

But refusing wasn't an option. Briskly she stepped around the desk. She was close enough to inhale his signature scent of rich spices and warm male skin. That warmth enveloped her as she reached out and twitched his bow tie into place.

'There.' She kept her gaze fixed below his chin, ignoring her wobbly knees and the curious hollow sensation in her chest as if someone had scooped out all the air. 'Enjoy your evening out.' Then she turned back to her seat and her work.

It was only eleven-thirty when Raffa got home. Tonight's function had been more cloying than usual. His companion had pretended there was more to their night out than the mutual convenience of being seen with a suitable partner.

He strode through the living room, not bothering with lights. Moonlight streaming in made it easy to see the single bottle on the bar. Moments later he tossed back a mouthful of grappa, its heat punching through his impatience.

He was sick of the posturing and pretence, being part of the same well-heeled crew trying so hard to enjoy themselves. But he'd hoped to see Robert Bradshaw so he'd forced himself, pretending he gave a damn for 'society.'

Since he'd identified the man responsible for Gabriella's death he itched to bring him down. He had no hope of proving Bradshaw's guilt in court after all this time, but he'd see the man who'd seduced and discarded his sister utterly ruined.

But Bradshaw hadn't been there, probably nervous about facing so many creditors. Given the information Lily had unearthed, Raffa suspected he'd gone to ground on his private island, the one his family had owned since they'd traded in slaves and sugar. His homes in London and Cannes had been sold to pay debts and the New York apartment was next. No doubt he was licking his wounds, scheming how to recoup the fortune he'd inherited and squandered.

Raffa's fingers tightened on his glass as anticipation rose. It was time to take the game to Bradshaw. The decision lightened Raffa's mood. He'd grind Bradshaw into the dirt and enjoy every moment.

Discarding tie, shoes and socks, then yanking the top buttons of his shirt undone, he slid open the door to his roof terrace and stepped out. Raffa turned his face to the light breeze and stalled mid-step.

He wasn't alone.

Someone sat on a sun lounger by the pool. Someone staring not at the garden, or the Manhattan view, but the glowing screen of a laptop.

What was *she* doing here?

It had to be Lily Nolan. No one could get past security to his private space, except the woman in his guest suite. The woman who drew the curtains as soon as she got in each night to shut herself off. He'd wondered if she was agoraphobic. That might have explained her reluctance to come to New York. But here she was, with the city laid out before her, relaxed as if her eyrie position didn't bother her in the least.

So it wasn't the view she'd been shutting out, but him— her only neighbour on the penthouse level.

Intriguing.

A now familiar trickle of heat spilled through his veins. A sensation he felt whenever Lily Nolan interrupted his thoughts. He still hadn't found a name for it. Not arousal

or excitement. Nor mere curiosity. More a charged awareness, as if he waited for...

Raffa shook his head. He wasn't waiting for anything
from Ms Nolan, except another report, this time detailing
Bradshaw's Caribbean island resort built around an old
plantation estate.

She didn't hear him approach—was too absorbed in
what she was doing. Surely not work at this time?

What he saw fascinated him. For the first time she didn't
wear loose trousers and a shirt buttoned to the throat. Her
feet and legs were bare. His gaze travelled along lissom
thighs and shapely calves as she sat with legs bent to support her laptop. Her arms and shoulders were bare too and
free of scar tissue.

He'd wondered if she carried more scars under her long
sleeves and trousers. The thump of his pulse felt like relief
that her injuries weren't worse.

Her swathe of long hair was tucked back. She wore a
tank top and shorts and looked potently alluring.

Every woman he met projected an image—sophisticated, provocative, flirtatious, or brisk and professional.
Raffa halted, enjoying the silvery light on her naked limbs,
relishing the tantalising charm of a sexy woman who wasn't
deliberately projecting anything.

Raffa felt a sharp, unmistakable tug of response low
in his groin.

It was almost eclipsed by the quake of shock that ripped
through him an instant later, making his eyes widen and
his belly clench.

How long since he'd felt sexual arousal?

It seemed a lifetime since the thought of sex made him
feel anything but impatient or...tainted. For all its transient
pleasure, and Raffa had known plenty of that, sex was a
transaction, intimacy a calculated risk.

He frowned, his gaze stuck on Lily Nolan and the innocent simplicity of her sex appeal.

Even when he was young there'd never been anything innocent about sex. Simple, yes. But never innocent.

His gaze swept from her hair, dark in the moonlight, to her marred cheek, delicate throat and long limbs. The tug of awareness sharpened to coiling, gut-grabbing tension.

He'd thought he didn't give a damn what Lily Nolan looked like. He'd been wrong.

It was true her scar meant nothing to him. What difference could that make when even the most glamorous beauty failed to stir him? Yet the sight of Lily's supple bare limbs, her ripe breasts and delicate collarbone...

But it wasn't merely that she had a sexy body. He'd seen more than his share of those.

His response was as much to do with the fact that this was Lily Nolan. The woman who'd defied, intrigued and surprised him for six weeks. Even before that, when they'd spoken on the phone, there'd been something, a fizz of energy in his veins that made him feel different—more *alive.* More *real.*

Raffa's frown became a scowl. He didn't do flights of fancy or self-doubt.

Yet he'd always been honest with himself. It had been the only way to keep his head on the tumultuous ride from poverty to success, from obscurity to being one of the most recognisable men on the planet.

Which was why he accepted that it was, remarkably, desire weighting his lower body, sexual interest spiking for the first time in years. More important—it wasn't a reaction merely to an appealing body but specifically to Lily Nolan.

He drew a sharp breath as heat stabbed, keen as a blade.

She must have heard his indrawn breath, swinging her head around and stiffening, hands grabbing the computer.

'You!'

Raffa's mouth twisted wryly. 'Don't sound so pleased to see me.'

Lily Nolan was guaranteed to keep him grounded. Far

from falling at his feet, she viewed him as a necessary encumbrance.

If he believed in good triumphing over evil, in redemption, he'd be tempted to think she'd come into his life to save him, from his ego if nothing else.

But it was a lifetime since Raffa had believed in anything but himself.

'It *is* my home.' His gesture encompassed the garden and penthouse.

'But you went out.' She snapped her mouth shut as if to prevent more words bursting free.

'I see. That's why you sneaked out here. You thought I'd be out of the way.'

Predictably her jaw angled up. 'I didn't sneak anywhere. You told me I had access to the garden.'

'A privilege you've never used unless you believed me safely gone.' He paused, watching her compose her face, wiping away the signs of shock and replacing them with her habitual mask of composure. It annoyed him to realise how much he wanted to peer beyond that facade.

'I thought you'd appreciate privacy. Especially in the evening when you might be…entertaining.' She looked beyond him towards the door to the penthouse.

'Thoughtful of you,' he murmured, 'but unnecessary.' He didn't explain that he never *entertained* at home. He valued his privacy too much.

Besides, the memory of the permanently drawn curtains in the guest wing spoke not so much of giving him privacy but herself. Why did Lily Nolan conceal herself? What secret did she protect?

How hard would it be to unravel that protective web she'd woven around herself? To discover the Lily Nolan who warded him off with her fierce concentration on work? He hadn't missed how she removed herself from his company when possible. How she kept her distance, calling him *Signor Petri* when others used first names.

Tonight he'd get answers.

'What are you working on?' Maybe she'd surprise him and reveal she spent her evenings playing online games.

Her hand went out as if to close her laptop, but his hand shot out, covering hers.

Raffa's pulse throbbed hard. He'd only touched her once, the day they'd shaken hands, but strangely there was a beckoning familiarity to her smooth flesh beneath his.

A second later her fingers slid away and she sat, cradling her hand as if stung.

Interesting.

And far more convenient to concentrate on her reaction than his own.

Raffa angled the screen to see it better. 'Consumer buying patterns in Brisbane? What's that got to do with Bradshaw? I wasn't aware he had interests there.'

'He doesn't.' The screen was pulled from his grip and closed. 'This work isn't for you.'

'You're moonlighting?' She was so close he inhaled that delicate scent he'd noticed before. Subtle yet sweet. It reminded him of crisp, cool days and…pears? That was it—ripe, luscious pears.

She shifted away, further down the lounge seat. Did she somehow register the abrupt spike of adrenaline flooding his bloodstream? The sharpening of his senses now she was within touching distance.

Raffa applauded her good sense in moving.

Yet he grabbed another chair and hauled it over, sitting so he faced her, knee to knee.

Playing safe had never been his style.

CHAPTER FIVE

LILY FOLDED THE laptop on her knees as if it might protect her from his keen gaze.

She felt vulnerable out here, away from the office. Away from her clothes! With that thought her nipples tightened into needy pebbles against the cotton of her sleep top.

How long before her body stopped responding to this man as a virile, spectacular male? She longed for the day she could relegate him to a mere colleague like the ones she worked with daily. The ones who, to her surprise, were becoming friends.

Lily swallowed a groan. Caught half naked by Raffaele Petri. Thankfully he hadn't turned on the lights.

Not that he needed lights. The moon was bright. Enough for her to have difficulty keeping her gaze off the tantalising V of skin revealed by his partly unbuttoned shirt. The combination of formal clothes and rumpled hair, bare feet and open shirt made him look even more potently masculine than usual. Every nerve centre relayed shock waves of pleasure at the sight.

How could her body betray her so?

'Moonlighting implies I'm going behind your back,' she snapped, stress tightening her vocal chords. 'That I'm cutting corners on my work for you. That's not so.' Better to focus on that than her body's tingling excitement.

'So what *are* you doing?'

She drew a deep breath, marshalling her thoughts, and was surprised to intercept a flicker of movement as his gaze dropped to her chest. Instantly her nipples budded tighter as if trying to push closer to him.

Lily told herself it was a reaction to the breeze.

'I told you I had responsibilities that meant I couldn't come to New York, but you forced my hand. This—' she waved a hand at the laptop '—is one of them. A job for a business looking to expand in Brisbane. I was checking a draft report from my assistant.'

'Assistant? I thought you worked alone?'

Once more Lily was unsettled that Raffaele Petri had taken time to learn about her.

'I recently expanded my business. There's a good market for high-quality research.' He said nothing and she felt compelled to fill the silence. 'I'm not cutting corners on your work. I'm doing this in my own time.'

'At midnight? That's no way to run a business.'

It stung that he of all people should lecture on her gruelling work schedule. As if her exhaustion didn't remind her every day when she dragged herself out of bed, almost drip-feeding coffee to keep going.

'You think I don't know that?' She shook her head, finally breaking free of his gaze and turning to look over the diamond-sprinkled velvet of the city at night. Even now, with Raffaele Petri evoking desires she had no business feeling, she couldn't quite get over the fact she was *here*, in New York, the city she'd never believed she'd visit. What wouldn't she give for a chance to explore? To wander and be part of the anonymous crowd? Yet, despite her growing ease with her colleagues, that was a step too far.

'I don't have a choice. Not since I was blackmailed into coming here despite my other work commitments.'

'*That's* why you were reluctant to leave? Not because of a man?'

Lily almost snorted in derision. A man? That was a laugh. There'd been no men in her life. They weren't exactly lining up outside her door, besotted by her looks and charm. Not even when she'd been fourteen and fresh-faced had she been that popular with boys. She'd been too ordinary, too easily overlooked. And later she was noticed for the wrong reasons. She'd learned the hard way not to confuse sympathy for interest.

'Several men, actually.' She watched, surprised, as he stiffened. Was it imagination or did his eyes narrow? 'That retailer in Brisbane. The HR manager of a security firm wanting checks on potential staff. The head of a planning authority—'

'Clients, you mean.'

'Yes. And all important. Which is why I use my spare time working for them.'

'But none are as important as me.'

True. None had the same power to make or break her business.

'*All* my clients are important. They expect results and I'd already promised to deliver. I don't take on work I can't complete to the best possible standard.'

'Even if the projects bring in a pittance compared with what you're doing for me?'

Lily tried not to grind her teeth. Good thing he was so arrogant. It would counteract this powerful attraction.

Shame it hadn't worked yet.

'You'd be surprised. Some of my clients even rival you.' She'd recently done work for a man who could reasonably be called Raffaele Petri's rival. Luca De Laurentis was another entrepreneur providing vacation services to the rich. 'For my business to expand it makes sense to cultivate as many sources of income as possible.'

Slowly—perhaps reluctantly?—he nodded.

'When you say expand, what do you mean? There's only so much you can do, even if you go without sleep.'

'Is it so hard to take me seriously as a businesswoman? To see me as an employer?' Umbrage thickened her voice. Her work, her professional success, meant everything. They were all she had. She'd long ago realised she'd never have a family of her own.

He shook his head. 'You're the most serious-minded

person I know, Lily.' Inevitably there it was again, the tiny thrill of delight as he turned her name into something exotic with that mellow voice and mouthwatering accent. 'It's just that you obviously prefer to work alone.'

'You mean I'm not a team player?' She read criticism in his words.

'No, not that. I've seen how meticulous you are about sharing information, making sure everyone's up-to-date. More that you prefer to be alone.'

Lily swallowed, her throat tight. He was right. Over the years she'd developed a taste for her own company. Surely he could understand that.

Or maybe not. People stared at him all the time, but it was in admiration, not horror at how he looked.

'Well, you'll be interested to know I employ two other people.' Albeit part-time, and both still learning the ropes. But for Lily this was a major step forward.

'Why?'

She frowned. Hadn't he listened? 'You said yourself there's a limit to the work I can do alone.'

'Why expand? Why build up a company rather than accept a permanent job here, for instance?' His voice resonated with genuine curiosity.

Lily stared into that gorgeous fallen-angel face. No one else, not her family or friends or even her bank manager, had bothered to ask.

Something faltered inside her. She found herself on her feet, staring at the beautifully lit pool. Yet she couldn't distract herself from stirring disquiet. Her heart thumped high in her chest and she knew it was because his interest made a difference. What he thought mattered.

Despite their differences she respected him—his business acumen, his drive, even his sometimes brutal honesty. And the fact he'd never once seemed fazed by her looks. He treated her not as scarred Lily Nolan but, she realised in shock, as someone strong enough to stand up to him. As an equal, despite their imbalance of power.

She should end this conversation. It bordered on the intimate. Yet their isolation in this moon-washed garden and the sense of familiarity made it seem almost normal.

It struck her how far she'd cut herself off from those who cared about her. In Australia she'd crossed a continent to get away from her family's loving but claustrophobic over-protectiveness, moving from Fremantle, on the west coast, to the east. Since then she'd focused on work. She had no bosom buddy, no confidante. No one close to share her hopes and dreams.

'I want to build something for myself.' The words tumbled out.

To her surprise he nodded. Only a tiny inclination of the head but it seemed to bridge the distance between them.

'I want…' How did she put it into words? 'Security, the safety that comes from success, but more too. I want…'

'Recognition.'

Lily's eyes widened. 'How did you know?'

His shoulders lifted and her gaze slid across that wide, straight expanse of powerful muscle and bone. 'It sounds familiar.'

'You?' It didn't seem possible. 'But you already had recognition before you started your business.'

His lips curved in what should have been a smile.

'To be recognisable as a face, or a body, plastered across the media in advertising campaigns isn't quite the same as genuine recognition.'

'Recognition for your achievements, you mean?'

Again that nod.

Was it naive to admit she'd never thought of the difference before? Raffaele Petri's phenomenal media presence had seemed the epitome of success. To be so watched, adored and admired…

It was as if he'd read her mind. 'Being known because

of how you look isn't an achievement.' His eyes held hers and phantom heat washed her scarred face. 'Being someone because of your actions, your success, is something else.'

Understanding stretched between them. An understanding she'd never before shared. It felt momentous. Lily sank back onto her seat, watching him avidly.

'Is that what drove you to build your business? The need to make your mark?' She admired him for that. It would have been easy to continue modelling. To move from that field where he was in such demand and strike out on his own must have taken grit as well as talent.

'Maybe. I wanted to take charge of my future. That's hard when you're dependent on the whims of advertisers and fashion gurus, likely to be out of style next year because they're hungry for a new face.'

She blinked, astounded that he shared such information. He wasn't a touchy-feely sort of guy. She'd seen him affable and relaxed but he could as easily intimidate with a look.

Was he too affected by the intimacy of the half-darkness, high above the city?

'I can't imagine you out of modelling work for long.' It wasn't just his staggering good looks. He had a magnetism Lily couldn't resist, no matter how she tried. And she'd tried. For over a month she'd fought the compulsion to watch him.

He laughed, the sound a soft ripple skating along her bare arms. 'It's a cutthroat business. Don't let the gloss fool you.'

'So you took to real estate as a safety net?' That was how he'd started his enterprise.

'You could say that. I was determined to make myself safe.'

'Safe?'

Again that quirk of the lips that should have been a smile, but which felt, in the dimness, like something else.

'I was born poor. It takes a lot of money to stop worrying you'll lose everything and end up in the gutter again.'

Lily nodded. She knew he didn't come from money. But the gutter? Was that just a figure of speech?

'Building my business meant I could choose my direction, doing things the way I want, not dependent on others.'

'I know what you mean.'

He sat back, and even in the semi-darkness she felt his piercing regard.

Lily held her breath, waiting for him to continue. He didn't. He looked perfectly relaxed, watching her. But he sat closer than in any meeting. There was nothing between them except a few scant inches of space.

Abruptly the elusive feeling of companionship dissipated.

The silence grew and Lily's lungs tightened with the effort to breathe normally, not gulp down huge draughts of warm air, scented with that man and spicy deliciousness she'd come to associate with him.

'What are you thinking?' she burst out when she couldn't bear the silence.

His mouth quirked up again and this time she spied amusement. 'I'm thinking how similar we are.'

He had to be kidding! They were galaxies apart.

'We're both loners.' He ticked the point off one finger. Lily watched, fascinated that he lumped himself with her there. Raffaele Petri was always surrounded by people. In the office he was the hub around which everyone revolved, eager to meet his needs. She'd seen enough media reports to know that out of the office he was surrounded by glamorous, beautiful people, drawing them like a magnet.

But how many is he close to?

The question had never occurred to her before.

'We both want the security of success.' Another tick. 'We both want to make our mark, rather than have the world judge us on how we look.'

Lily sucked in her cheeks on a hiss of shock, blinking at those knowing eyes. She'd never mentioned the problem she'd had since her teens—of people not seeing her, just her scarred face.

It stunned her that he'd picked up on that.

Why had she thought he wouldn't get it? Because he wasn't interested in anyone but himself? Yet he'd continually surprised her with what he knew about her.

Because he was so handsome?

For the first time it struck her that he carried a burden too—far easier, of course, since his looks must have opened doors. In a weird way they were linked—judged by people because of their faces—his utterly gorgeous and hers downright ugly.

Slowly Lily released her breath, and with it some of the tautness in her shoulders and neck.

She nodded. He'd put into words something she'd never admitted. That she still fought to be judged as someone other than the woman with the appallingly scarred face.

That was why, until now, she'd enjoyed working from home instead of in someone else's office. When people couldn't see her they treated her like anyone else—no pity or sneaking stares or embarrassment.

Working here in New York was the first time in years she'd begun to relax with others. Were the people here remarkable or did her hard-won confidence in her work mean she was less concerned with their initial reaction? Whatever the cause, she felt more relaxed and accepted than she'd expected. It irked to admit it but her forced move had been good for her.

'We've both set up our own businesses too. That's another point in common.' It didn't matter that his was a multinational empire and hers a fledgling company carrying brand-new debt. The principle was the same. 'Did your previous career help you get started?'

His laugh was short. 'Not in the beginning. I wasn't

taken seriously. I was a face, not a businessman. No one understood how single-minded I'd had to be to get where I was.'

'I suppose people think modelling is easy.' She had.

'Modelling?' He shifted in his seat, his head swinging up, and she had a curious feeling she'd missed something. 'Let's just say I paid my dues to climb out of the hole where I started life.' His face hardened. 'Getting investors to trust me with their assets was tough. Everyone expected me to fail.'

'But you didn't.'

'In the beginning, when I needed advice and investors, no one would touch me. Later it was different. People wanted a part of what I'd built, but by then I was used to working alone.' He shrugged. 'Maybe being forced to go solo was a good thing. It made me more determined to succeed and learn from my mistakes.'

'Did you make many? Mistakes?' Lily leaned forward, her hands clasped between her knees.

'Plenty. I had money, I'd been careful about saving, but I overextended myself with a project that ran into problems. It was touch-and-go for a while.'

Lily knew the feeling. 'But you succeeded.' Fervently she hoped she could too.

He lifted one hand, palm up, in a gesture that seemed wholly Italian. 'It was the only option I'd accept.'

Didn't that say it all? Raffaele Petri was a man who, as Pete said, made it his policy always to get what he wanted. Did she have the same determination to succeed?

'You make it sound easy.'

'Not easy. Straightforward. I refused to accept failure. I did whatever it took to succeed.'

Could she do that? She was trying. How hard she was trying!

Perhaps it was ridiculous to take solace from the example of the man who'd disrupted her plans, the one forcing her to work twice as hard as usual just to keep on top of her obligations. Yet she felt buoyed.

'Have you considered narrowing your market?' His query dragged her out of her reverie.

'Sorry?'

'Your market. It seems very broad. You're doing personnel security checks. You've taken a job for a small business plus some project for a planning authority. Then there's your work for me, which is in a different ballpark. I'm asking if you need to specialise and become the best at what you do instead of being all things to all people.'

Lily surveyed him with surprise. Instead of anger that she wasn't devoting all her efforts to his project, he was interested in her business? Offering advice? It was too good an opportunity to ignore.

'Specialising would cut off some lucrative income.' Like those security checks she didn't particularly enjoy.

'Lucrative long-term or short-term?'

She hadn't thought about it like that. 'Lucrative enough to pay the bills while I build my name in the areas I want.'

'And do you have a plan for the transition from doing everything to doing only what you want as your core business?'

Lily hesitated. Her business plan had been based on doing more of the same. General expansion rather than targeted. Her focus had been on building income to make the enterprise as secure as possible.

'I see.' He sat back.

So did she. 'There's a gap in my planning, isn't there?'

She didn't feel defensive. This shadowy version of Raffaele Petri, sitting easily with her in the garden, wasn't nearly as daunting as the one she worked with daily. She could almost pretend to forget her attraction to him. Despite her quickened pulse and the tingle of awareness, she felt easier with him than ever before. As if he were no longer a threat.

Amazing what a little moonlight could do. Or was it because his interest was in her work, not her?

'It sounds like you need to revisit your strategy. Unless you want to be stuck in a rut, tendering for every job, whether it interests you or not.'

Lily dragged her fingers through her hair, letting it slide away over her shoulder. 'I've had enough of that, working at things that don't interest me.'

Even in the moonlight she saw his eyebrows rise. 'Does that apply to what you're doing for me?'

Quickly Lily shook her head. 'No, I love that.' She paused, wondering if she sounded too eager. But he'd acknowledged she never ran to him seeking kudos. 'The projects are complex enough to be fascinating. I—' She paused. 'Signor P—'

'Raffaele. Or Raffa. Surely we've gone past formality.'

Lily wished his face wasn't half-shadowed. There was a note in his voice she couldn't recognise. It kicked her pulse into high gear.

Reluctantly she nodded. 'Raffaele.' She stumbled over his name. Not because she couldn't say it, but because it felt like an illicit pleasure on her tongue. As if she'd crossed some boundary. Heat spiked in her chest. 'Is there a chance you could…?'

'A chance I could…?' He leaned forward and she felt the waft of warm air as he exhaled. Lily blinked, overwhelmed by his sheer physical presence. The stark male beauty that even pale moonlight couldn't diminish. The challenging mind. The fizz of attraction.

Yet most appealing of all was the way he talked to her. He made her feel…important. As if she genuinely interested him.

Lily's gaze fell to those powerful hands at his knees. Her blood tingled as for one decadent moment she wondered how it would feel if he lifted a palm and put it on her bare flesh. A quiver of exultation coursed through her. Till sanity returned.

The very fact he was so close, discussing corporate planning of all things, proved he had no interest in her physically. It was her mind, her plans he was curious about.

She was glad. It was what she wanted, to be taken seriously as a businesswoman.

Yet Lily couldn't help wondering what it would be like, just once, to be desired by a man.

She gulped down a sudden restriction in her throat. She didn't do self-pity. Far better to focus on what she *could* get out of life.

'I wondered if you had any advice. About how or when to make that switch from taking every job to something more targeted.'

Her nerves stretched with the growing silence. But just when she'd decided she'd gone too far, he spoke.

Raffa watched Lily expound a point, gesturing, the light catching the small scar on the back of her hand. It caught the larger scar on her cheek too. But not even that detracted from her lit-from-within animation.

When she talked about her business it was with an enthusiasm most women reserved for a lover. An enthusiasm he found hard to resist.

True passion was rare.

How many would-be entrepreneurs had approached him to give them a start up? How many established businessmen had tried to entice him into a shared deal? He was adept at resisting, going his own way.

Yet here he was, caught up in Lily Nolan's enthusiasm for a solid, but nevertheless tiny enterprise.

Or, more accurately, caught up in watching her, enjoying the change from buttoned-up, defensive worker bee to a woman who even in this gloom shone with an inner glow. A woman who made him wonder what she'd do if he stretched his arm out and hauled her onto his lap.

Her effervescence was a turn-on. It was no hardship to discuss business plans with her. He'd been genuinely interested, but beyond that was an edge that had nothing to do with commerce and everything to do with the fact that for the first time in recent memory he found himself contemplating taking a lover.

Lily Nolan?

It was a crazy idea.

'When will that report on Bradshaw's Caribbean property be complete?'

She looked surprised at his question. Understandable given it had nothing to do with their discussion. 'Tomorrow. I've got one more thing to check in the morning.'

'Excellent. You can have ten days off when it's done. That will give you time to work through your other responsibilities.' He gestured to her now dormant laptop. The sooner she got on top of those, the sooner he could have her to himself. He needed her. For her expertise, he assured himself.

'Ten days? But I've only worked for you a short time.'

Raffa's mouth kicked up. Who complained about time off? 'Don't worry. I'm getting my money's worth from you and I intend to keep doing so. When you start back we'll be in a crucial stage of the project and I'll want you available twenty-four-seven.'

Slowly she nodded. 'Well, I *am* on the premises, so I'll be available.'

Raffa shook his head. 'We won't be in New York. We'll be in the Caribbean, on Bradshaw's home turf.'

She stilled, her eyes widening. 'We?'

'That's right. We. I want you where you can be most useful.'

This was a sensible business decision. It had nothing to

do with the tug of attraction he felt towards Lily Nolan. Almost nothing.

She opened her mouth, the same tight expression settling on her face that he'd become used to before tonight. It didn't bother him. Now he knew something of the vital, intriguing, oddly innocent woman behind the facade.

He looked forward to seeing more of that woman. To learning her secrets.

'And, before you object, this is a requirement, not a request. Finish what you have to. I don't want you bringing other work. I want you completely at my disposal.'

CHAPTER SIX

'THAT'S IT FOR NOW. Thanks, everyone.' Raffaele ended the video conference with a final word to Consuela in New York about a contract.

Lily eased back in her seat, stretching. She was tired, but good tired. Working with Raffaele was intense—satisfying, but a challenge to keep up. Just as well she'd been well prepared for the meeting.

He was a dynamic entrepreneur but his restless energy since they'd arrived on Bradshaw's island was electric. There must be a personal element to this. She sensed it in the grim twist of Raffaele's mouth when the other man was mentioned, and his insistence on breakneck speed, as if completion couldn't come fast enough. Yet even now he was cagey about the details of his plan, as if it were too important to share in full.

'Right. Time for a break.'

She looked up to find he'd shut the screen and was watching her. His stare made her feel abruptly *un*professional.

Lily worked hard *not* to think of him as a desirable man. But it was like trying to pretend the sun didn't shine out there on the white sand of this island paradise. The mere sight of his sinewy, powerful forearms, dark gold beneath rolled-up sleeves, made her stupid heart thud.

They were alone in his spacious bungalow, set a little apart from the other accommodation spread through the leafy resort gardens. The rest of the team were thousands of miles away in New York and Lily felt a flicker of guilt that she alone had travelled here with him. Even her smaller bungalow was gorgeous, with its plantation-style furnishings, four-poster bed and ocean views.

'Dinner at the poolside café, I think.'

Lily could imagine him there. With his burnished good looks and casual white cotton shirt and trousers, he'd be right at home amongst the bikini-clad beauties.

She averted her gaze, gathering her gear. 'Enjoy yourself. I'll start following up—'

'Later, Lily. It's time to eat.' That mellow voice trailed through her veins.

She fixed on a smile. 'I'll grab something in my room. I want to get this down while it's fresh.'

To her surprise he came to stand before her, crossing his arms and planting his feet wide, owning the space.

Her pulse danced that silly little jig. No matter how often she saw him, he still had the power to enthral her. She should be immune to Raffaele Petri. But since that night on his rooftop her defences were in tatters.

He'd taken time to advise her on her fledgling enterprise. She'd never had a mentor and eagerly soaked up his suggestions. He'd been kind, discussing her insignificant start-up company.

Who'd have thought Raffaele Petri could be kind?

There'd been more too. He'd told her about his own business. For the first time she saw her research in a wider context. It was exciting to feel part of something bigger than her own narrow goals. He'd made her feel valued, as if she *belonged*. It was rare and satisfying.

Above all was the heady sense he saw her not just as an employee but as a woman interesting in her own right. He made her feel he saw *her* as no one else did. She was human enough to want him to admire what he saw.

'That can wait. Food first. Leave your stuff here and collect it later.'

He was inviting her to eat with him? Excitement buzzed.

Or was that horror at the thought of sitting at the resort's most public venue beside the most gorgeous man on the planet? With all those beautiful people looking on?

Her shrinking stomach warned it was both.

'Thanks, Raffaele.' She paused, savouring his name. 'But I'd prefer to eat alone and get my thoughts together.'

'In your room?'

She nodded, scrambling up from the low seat.

To her consternation he didn't step away and she found herself toe to toe with him, close enough for the heat of his body to brand her. For that evocative scent of his to inveigle its way into her nostrils.

Awareness shuddered through her—real, alive, all-consuming.

The daunting truth was that she wanted him as a woman wanted a man. It was laughable. He'd been supportive and, yes, kind, but there was no way he'd ever—

'Hiding again, Lily?'

Her chin tipped up as if yanked on a string. She met gleaming eyes and read knowledge in them. Her breath froze and splintered in her lungs.

'I don't know what you're talking about.' He couldn't know how she felt about him. Could he?

Raffa scented her fear. He'd learned to recognise it early, a legacy of growing up in the rough end of a derelict neighbourhood. He wanted to tell her it was okay.

But it wasn't okay, not if what he suspected was right. His hands clenched as he strove not to reach for her. The impulse to reassure, to comfort was so unexpected and strong, it shocked him.

He'd been many things to many women.

But a comfort? Never.

Yet he persisted. His suspicion had grown so strong he'd found himself pondering it rather than his plans for Bradshaw. Nothing, he vowed, would deter him from justice for Gabriella. For her sake, and for Lily's, he needed to sort this so he could focus again.

'We've worked together long enough for me to be able

to read you, at least a little.' He'd never met anyone so self-contained. It made him itch to discover her secrets. 'I know you're scared.'

She froze. He sensed the tightening of her slim frame as her eyebrows rose. 'I don't know what you mean.'

He gave her full marks for bravado.

'You think I haven't noticed that you hide away?' He shook his head. 'You never go out. Ever. In New York you stayed in the office or in the guest suite. When other staff talk about what they did on the weekend or meet for a drink after work, you don't join in.' He'd been too absorbed in his plan for justice to realise at first how insular she was. But, once he did, it was glaringly obvious. Like the way she concealed herself behind that long hair.

'You *know* I don't have time for that.' She waved a hand dismissively. 'I'm working full-time for you and trying to keep my business afloat back home.'

True, but that wasn't the whole story.

'You've got time to eat with me. Here. Now.' He paused. 'Unless you're afraid of that too?'

'Too?' Lily shifted as if to step away but he blocked her exit.

'I saw you on the beach at dawn.' At her surprised look he shrugged. 'You're not the only early riser.'

Instantly suspicion, or was it fear, clouded those amber-brown eyes.

'You were staring out to sea, even waded knee-deep in the water a couple of times. But you didn't go in. Why was that? I could tell you were yearning to.'

She'd stood there in another long-sleeved shirt with cargo pants rolled up around her knees and it had struck him how she deliberately camouflaged that lithe, luscious body he'd seen in his garden.

He'd been about to approach her when he'd noticed her expression, illuminated in the peachy morning light. It was a look of such longing, such regret, it stirred discomfort. As if he'd intruded on something utterly personal.

The melancholy of that lone figure, arms crossed over her chest, just as now, had stayed with him all morning.

'I wasn't *yearning*. I was admiring. The view was spectacular.' She hitched a quick breath that betrayed discomfort, her gaze skittering away. 'Besides, I didn't bring a swimsuit.'

'You came to a Caribbean resort and didn't bring a swimsuit?' Disbelief dripped from each syllable.

Her chin jerked even higher. 'I don't own one.' She hurried on before he could interrupt. 'I'm here to work, not swim, remember?'

'I see.' She was finding excuses again. More than ever, he wanted to lay them bare.

'What do you see?' Anger vibrated in her voice and Raffa felt a little of his edginess ease. He preferred her angry to fearful or dejected. Watching her this morning, reading infinite sadness in that longing gaze, had felt like a sucker punch to the gut. He'd felt…lost, something he hadn't experienced since he was twelve and Gabriella had left him.

'That you're afraid of the water. Can't you swim?'

'Of course I can swim. I grew up on the coast. Learning to swim was compulsory.'

Raffa stared at her set features, reading the truth in her expression. Now they were getting somewhere.

He lifted his hand, gesturing to her scarred cheek. 'What happened? Was that from an accident in the water? Is that why you don't swim?'

Lily gasped and shifted back but she couldn't escape because of the couch behind her.

'Lily?'

'That's none of your business.' Her voice rose half an octave.

'Perhaps not. But it's time someone asked.' Clearly her

injury had affected more than her face. It was a crying shame that a woman so full of spark and energy should conceal herself.

Why was he making it his mission to interfere?

He was selfish to the core. Since when had he taken an altruistic interest in anyone?

'Just because you employ me doesn't give you a right to pry.'

Raffa said nothing, merely stood and waited.

He'd almost given up on an answer when the words burst from her. 'It wasn't a swimming accident. A jealous thug decided to make a point with a flask of acid.'

Raffa recoiled at the brutal words. He couldn't help but imagine the fiery burn on tender flesh, the howling pain. The shock and suffering. Nausea swirled in his belly and rose as bile in his throat. His heart pounded his ribs.

What sort of man attacked a defenceless woman?

Another like Robert Bradshaw.

Raffa's hands curled into fists, tension radiating up his arms to his shoulders and neck.

'Your boyfriend?' His words slid from between gritted teeth.

She shook her head, her long hair slipping around her cheeks. 'My best friend's. I was just in the wrong place at the wrong time, sitting beside her at the cinema. Rachel bore the brunt of it but my injuries kept me in and out of hospital for a long time while they tried to repair the damage.' Her voice was brittle.

It struck him how tough it must have been, not only badly injured, but in such a random way. How had she ever felt safe again?

He wanted to soothe her, haul her close and reassure her.

As if he had any experience of comforting a woman.

As if she'd accept his touch! She glared at him with the same distrust he'd once seen on a half-wild dog. As if she'd bite his hand if he came close.

'So why don't you swim?' There was something there, some reason she wouldn't go in the water. He'd seen it on her face in the dawn light. 'Is it the same reason you try to disappear?'

'Disappear? I'm here, aren't I?' Her voice told him he was on the right track. Defiance tinged with fear.

'Not all the time.' Did she even realise how often she tried to blend into the background? 'Sometimes, when you're passionate about a discussion or a new work direction, you forget to take a back seat. Then you're vibrant and persuasive and...*present*.' *He* always noticed her, but he also saw the way she tried not to attract attention. 'But it seems to me you're worried about being seen.'

She said nothing, yet he heard the snatch of indrawn air, saw the sudden lift of her breasts as her breathing turned shallow.

Her vulnerability made his chest clench.

'That's it, isn't it? The reason you wear those cover-up clothes.'

Her eyes narrowed to a gleam of amber fire. 'We can't all afford designer gear.'

'It's not about designer labels, Lily. You've got an attractive body yet you hide it as if you're ashamed. Did you even bring shorts or a sleeveless top here?'

Her silence said she hadn't. His suspicion grew to a certainty as so much became clear. Horror furrowed his gut at the implications.

'No summer clothes, no swimsuit, because you don't want anyone seeing you. You won't go in the water in case you attract attention. Even at dawn when you thought there was no one to see, you wouldn't risk it.' Her silent watchfulness told him he'd hit the truth. 'You want to take cover behind your drab clothes in the hope you won't be noticed.' Raffa was torn between incredulity and pity as he met that stubborn narrowed stare.

'It doesn't work that way, Lily.' His voice grated. He was

staggered at how much he felt for her. 'Don't you realise the more you try to hide, the more obvious you become? The more people watch and wonder? You think they don't see you hiding behind that long hair or those drab clothes? That they don't notice you avoiding them?'

'Who do you think you are to tell me what to wear or how to behave? If I want to wear my hair loose or wear long sleeves, that's my choice.' Her shimmering gaze scraped him from hairline to jaw. 'Even if it displeases a fashion expert like you.'

'And when it stops being a choice? When you deny yourself the pleasure of swimming because you're afraid, not of anything in the water, but of being seen?' Raffa tasted a dull, metallic tang on his tongue. 'That's not choice, Lily. That's when fear has taken over your life.'

The heel of her hand jammed into the centre of his chest, as if she could push him away. Or she needed an outlet for the emotions she'd bottled up so fiercely.

'Don't you *dare* lecture me!' Her voice was a gasp, her breathing too fast, too shallow. 'You have no idea what it's like.'

At the sight of her distress something turned over deep inside. He felt her quiver with the force of her emotions. How long had she dammed it all up? Energy radiated from her in sharp surges that zapped like electricity.

'Then tell me.' He clamped a palm over her hand, holding it to him, feeling the shudders rippling through her. He doubted she noticed.

She shook her head, her hair swirling silk-soft against his hand.

'Tell me, Lily.'

Finally her gaze meshed with his. Those eyes were like amber starbursts now, rimmed with honey-brown. Startling, unique, mesmerising.

'What do you want me to tell you? That for half my life people have looked at me as if I were a freak? They can't help but stare. And they talk to me slowly, in soft voices, as if they're so *sorry* for the way I look they think it's affected my ability to think. Then there are the ones who won't even look at me. They'll have a whole conversation staring at a point over my shoulder to avoid seeing the scar on my face.'

'In one day I lost not just my face but my youth, my friend, my fearlessness. The bliss of being *normal*.'

She laughed, the sound off-key, tugging a chord in his belly. 'You have no idea of the jobs I had to give up because of the way people see me. A baker gave me work out of sympathy but lost customers because people didn't want me serving them. Perhaps it made them lose their appetite.'

Raffa tightened his hold, his jaw setting.

'The job in the property office where the other girls couldn't be comfortable working with someone who looked like me. Something about my presence was just too…unsettling.' Sarcasm laced her words and he couldn't blame her.

'But that's not the case now.'

'Sorry?' She looked up at him as if he spoke another language.

'However livid your scar once was, and however stupid some of your old work colleagues. That doesn't apply now.'

She snorted. 'You're going to tell me my scar has suddenly disappeared?'

'I'm telling you that, whatever it looks like, you're a different woman now to the one you were then. You're confident, capable and successful. You can stand up for yourself now. As for the scar—' He lifted his free hand and pushed her hair back behind her ear.

Instantly she stilled, the vibrant energy diminishing to a low-grade hum as if someone had flicked a switch.

Her breath, warm and sweet, feathered his face as he surveyed that taut skin. Raffa tried to imagine how angry it must once have looked, how shocking. But he'd grown so used to it he had trouble seeing it as anything but part of her.

'I've seen far worse,' he said finally.

With an audible snap she shut her mouth, wrenching her hand from his.

'I can't tell you how much better I feel after hearing that!'

Raffa's lips curved at her waspish response. He'd never met anyone so ready to attack in order to defend themselves. It had intrigued him from the first. 'I'm not being patronising, just truthful.'

'And this truth is meant to make my life easier, how?' She tilted her head in mock consideration, her hands going to her hips.

'Let me guess. I'll be so excited that the mighty Raffaele Petri has announced he's seen worse that I'll cut my hair, put on a bikini and spend the rest of my time here chatting up strangers. And, miraculously, no one will notice that one side of my face looks like something out of a horror movie.'

She thrust out her chin, invading his space. 'Get real, Raffaele. Would you touch a woman who looked like this? Of course you wouldn't.'

She opened her mouth for another jibe then shut it when he lifted his palm to the taut skin of her cheek. He heard a hiss and felt her whole body rise with her quick intake of breath. She stared up at him, eyes wide.

He moved his hand over warm skin, exploring, learning the contour of cheekbone and jaw, scar and unblemished skin that was petal-soft. Finally his thumb discovered the rapid tattoo of her pulse. So vital, so fascinating.

Her sweet fruit scent filled his nostrils as he leaned closer, surveying her brilliant eyes, drawn by the inexplicable sense of anticipation trembling between them.

Then, abruptly, she was gone, sliding away from his touch. A few angry strides and she was across the room, shoulders heaving.

He stood where she'd left him, oddly bereft.

What had just happened?

'You have no idea what my life has been like with this scar. Don't you dare tell me it's all okay. I don't need your condescension.'

Raffa was dazed by the emotions she'd evoked. Pity. Protectiveness. Arousal. Anger. And something else.

He'd been trying to help. And what did he get for his pains? That would teach him to try being altruistic!

'Of course, you're the only one in the world whose life has been affected by the way they look.' The words were out before he knew it. 'You need to get over yourself, Lily. That scar can't blight your whole life. Not unless you let it.'

Her gasp was loud in the silence. Once more her hands found her hips and her chin lifted imperiously, like a queen surveying her dominions. Or, given that kindling look, judging some insubordinate slave.

'Get *over* myself?' She shook her head, her stunned eyes never leaving his. 'I don't know what's more insulting. That you pretend I've somehow done this—' she gestured to her face '—to myself. Or that you're looking for sympathy because you've been judged on your looks. Sympathy from *me*?' Her tone said it all.

She was right. Raffa had no grounds to complain. Even if his looks had led him to places, to actions he regretted. He'd have done anything to escape grinding poverty and what he'd done…well, others would say he'd been supremely fortunate. Even if it meant he carried a taint that time couldn't erase.

He'd done what he had to and escaped more lightly than many. As for his looks—he might have been used, and even, some would say, abused, because of them. But he'd made his fortune with his face and emerged triumphant.

Yet in the dark recesses of his soul he acknowledged unexpected kinship with Lily and her problems. Both judged because of the way they appeared.

The difference was that she carried her scars on the outside. His were internal.

'You're absolutely right. I've no cause for complaint. I've got everything a man could want and more.' He didn't add that having everything money could buy didn't counteract the hollowness at the core of a world centred only on himself. The suspicion, too late, that such hollowness would eventually consume him.

'But believe me, Lily, if you don't make a change soon, you won't be able to. Either you let that scar define you or you make the life you want in spite of it.'

Raffa turned on his heel and strode to the door, willing down the tumultuous boil of feelings. He wasn't interested in emotion. He wasn't interested in scars, real or psychological. He was here for a single vital purpose. It was time he got on with it.

He needed to forget the murky...*feelings* Lily evoked and concentrate on Robert Bradshaw. Justice and revenge were much simpler.

CHAPTER SEVEN

NOTHING HELPED. LILY HAD paced her bungalow half the evening, reliving the conversation, coming up with scathing retorts, and still Raffaele's words scraped like a blade scratching flesh. Like the memory of acid on her cheek.

Work hadn't helped. Not that she'd done any work for *him*. She'd dragged out her laptop and spent hours on tasks for her business.

All night she'd worked, but no matter how busy she was, she couldn't stop his words in her brain. Or the fear, deep in her roiling belly, that he might be right. It had stopped her sleeping, despite her exhaustion.

These last years it should have been easier to face the world, especially since surgery had diminished the horror factor of her injury. Yet, perversely, each trip into town had become more difficult than the last. Travelling was a nightmare of self-consciousness, and forcing herself into that New York office every day...

Lily shook her head, hair sliding reassuringly across her cheeks. She'd had to face down panic attacks just to get through the door.

You think they don't see you hiding behind that long hair or those drab clothes?

She stilled. He'd all but accused her of being a coward. She who'd weathered such pain, such grief, and then had to face the unmistakable, if unspoken, blame of the whole community when *she'd* been the one to survive rather than Rachel. Vibrant, pretty, life-of-the-party Rachel, star of the swim squad, the debating team, academically gifted, on her way to stellar success in whatever field she chose.

Rachel, her best friend.

Lily gulped down a sob that shook her from her shoulders to her soles.

She didn't do self-pity. She didn't!

She'd faced medical treatments and long convalescence stoically when all her peers were enjoying themselves. Hadn't she forced herself to succeed, refusing to give up when one job after another failed? She'd been determined to stand on her own feet, not be a burden to her worried parents and protective brothers. She'd worked like a slave to establish her own business, carve success and security.

Security away from the world.

A continent away from her family and the last of her friends.

The air rushed from her chest as if she'd been stabbed in the lungs. She felt herself deflating, crumpling, her knees collapsing till she sagged onto the edge of the bed.

It hurt to breathe. Blackness clouded the edge of her vision like churning storm clouds. Spots of white burst around her as the world turned grey, then darker. Her head swam. Any second now the blackness would consume her.

Then, with a huge, juddering heave, her lungs opened up, drawing in air that seared all the way down her aching throat. The grey retreated. The room, with its pale furnishings and bright tropical accents, came into focus. Through the window she saw the golden bloom of dawn fringe the horizon, spreading across the water towards her.

Raffaele was right.

She was scared. More than scared—she was petrified.

When had it happened?

She'd been so busy forcing herself to face the world, the need to find a job, build a career and be independent from her worried, loving parents. She hadn't noticed when wariness had gradually become withdrawal, independence had turned to isolation and the comfort of her own home had become a cage.

Reluctantly, each muscle protesting, she turned her head.

Across the bed lay strewn the items she'd tossed there last evening when her rage had been white-hot. A staff member from the resort boutique had brought them in glossy, silver-ribboned bags. Only one person could have sent them.

A broad-brimmed hat, a bright skirt of some soft fabric that slipped through her fingers like cool water. A sleeveless top sporting a designer label, a one-piece swimsuit and a long, loose gauzy cover-up, for wearing while lolling by the pool. There was even a pair of cute sandals with ribbons that tied around the ankles.

Each in her size.

Each worth more than she'd spend on clothes in a year.

Each mocking her.

Her fury had spiked at the idea of Raffaele ordering them, daring her to wear them.

As if it was any of his business what she wore.

Now they lay, taunting her, a challenge she couldn't ignore.

How had he known what she hadn't recognised in herself? It wasn't as if she were important to him, yet he'd taken time to see her as more than an employee. He'd seen her as an individual. As someone who counted. He'd forced her to understand herself clearly for the first time in years.

The pain of that self-knowledge tore at her.

Gritting her teeth, Lily reached out and touched the swimsuit. The fabric was soft, fluid and silky, frighteningly thin.

It gave nowhere to hide.

Raffa flicked water from his eyes, treading water. Five laps of the bay and his chest was on fire, his legs and arms like jelly. But exertion hadn't brought relief.

All night he'd been haunted by Lily's face when he'd told her to move on with her life, stop taking cover and ignore her scar.

His gut clenched, making him sink below the surface

till he kicked harder. Who was he to tell her how to live? How could he begin to imagine what it was like to be her?

Sometimes his arrogance appalled even himself.

He turned from the headland, back towards the bay, ready for another punishing lap, when a lone figure on the beach stopped him. A figure with pale limbs, long hair and a body clad in bronze. Dawn light caught each supple angle and sweet curve. It burnished the taut swimsuit that clung to Lily's delectable body.

Why had he ever thought it a good idea for her to bare herself?

Testosterone surged, weighting his body, tightening each muscle, turning his lungs into a furnace where each breath was an ache of pure heat.

She was unadorned. He tried to tell himself it was the simplicity of the picture she made that affected him. But he'd seen countless women—clothed, unclothed, in ball gowns and swimsuits, towels and wisps of nothing. None affected him like this.

He took in her ravaged cheek, lit by the morning sun as she shook her hair off her face. The movement was one of impatience, determination, and it made his heart jump.

His lips curved in a proud smile. He hadn't been sure she'd accept the gauntlet he'd thrown down. She could just as easily have nestled further into that protective shell, cutting herself off from the world. From him.

He admired her fierce determination. She was a worthy adversary.

Raffa reminded himself she wasn't an adversary, but an employee.

Except in the oldest contest of all, the struggle between male and female.

He couldn't ignore it any longer. For almost two months he'd pretended Lily Nolan was intriguing because of her prickly ways and quick mind. And her determination not to be cowed by his wealth or position. They were part of

it, but not all. Denial only went so far, especially in a man
who, after years of celibacy, of utter disinterest in sex, felt
the sudden rush and roar of desire.

She waded out till the water was hip deep, her smile
widening with each step. The glow on her face made him
feel like a voyeur, watching an intensely private moment,
yet he couldn't look away. He'd never seen her like this, so
strong and free and elemental.

In a sinuous movement she lifted her hands over her
head and dived. Raffa waited till he saw her begin a strong,
easy stroke. Then he dragged in a rough breath and turned
to the headland. He'd have to clamber over the rocks instead
of sand to get out but she deserved her solitude.

Lily shivered as the warm sea breeze feathered her face, her
bare neck and legs. Despite the blaze of sunshine she was
chilled to the marrow, frozen by apprehension. She'd never
felt more vulnerable since that first day out of hospital.

She'd chosen this chair by the poolside out of bravado,
proving to herself she wasn't the coward Raffaele thought
her.

But it seemed she was. Her joints felt as if they'd been
welded solid with the effort it took to remain here, in full
public view, and wearing so little.

'Can I join you?' The voice, like rich caramel, swirled
around Lily. Beckoning warmth encircled her, coaxing taut
muscles to ease just a little.

Something like relief fizzed in her veins.

He'd come.

She hadn't expected him to.

Or wanted him, she assured herself.

Slowly Lily turned. Raffaele Petri stood on the flagstones, his back to the pool and the outdoor café/bar where
guests gathered. Against the azure of the pool his gold-
toned body, bare but for damp board shorts and a half-
buttoned shirt, glowed. The sun gilded his tousled hair,

but it was his eyes, deep-set and probing, that snagged her attention.

A flare of heat ran through her veins then dropped to eddy in her stomach.

She should be furious with him.

She *wanted* to be furious.

But she was grateful too. He'd ripped the blinkers from her eyes.

She shrugged, stiff muscles protesting. 'Sounds good. With you here they'll forget to look at me.'

More likely the other resort guests would wonder what the most beautiful man on the planet was doing with such an ugly woman. Beauty and the Beast.

She reminded herself she didn't care. That was her mantra as of dawn this morning. She'd given up worrying about the effect she had on others. Or she would, she assured herself, once she got used to being out in public. For now she'd pretend to ignore the prickle across her skin as the weight of so many curious eyes grazed her.

'They're too busy worrying about their suntans to pay attention to us.'

Lily stifled a snort of disbelief. No one could help but notice Raffaele. He hooked a chair close and sank into it, the fluid grace of his athletic body mesmerising.

Yet he wasn't at ease. The smile edging his lips wasn't his usual confident one. It looked lopsided, almost self-conscious.

The idea confused her. She snatched at it greedily, anything to distract herself from her surroundings.

Raffaele was utterly sure of himself. He was powerful, able to get what he wanted with the click of his fingers. Nor did a crisis faze him. She'd seen him work through unexpected and potentially calamitous developments in the office. He'd been unflappable, thriving on challenge.

'Espresso.' He nodded to the waiter who'd materialised

beside them. 'And…?' He looked questioningly at her empty glass.

'Another fruit juice, thank you, Charles.' She lifted her head to meet the waiter's eyes, feeling the sun warm her bare cheeks. In a fit of defiant energy she'd coiled her hair up, using every pin she possessed to secure it. No more covering her cheeks. No more concealment. It had sounded simple back in her bungalow, but here, where everyone passing could see her, she felt exposed.

'You're on first-name terms with the waiter?'

'You disapprove?' She closed her eyes, telling herself she enjoyed the feel of the sun on her face.

'Not at all. But a lot of people don't bother to discover the names of people who serve them.'

'I'm a researcher, remember. You'd be amazed how much I've found out from talking with the locals. But the fact is they're so friendly I enjoy getting to know them.' They'd made her feel welcome despite her nerves in a new place, meeting new people.

'Lily?'

She opened her eyes to find Raffaele leaning close. The blaze of those ocean-bright eyes did odd things to her breathing.

'Yes?'

He paused and she frowned, wondering at his unaccustomed hesitation.

'I apologise.'

Lily stared, watching his lips form the words but not believing the evidence of her eyes or her ears.

'Apologise?' Raffaele Petri? He might not be the ogre who'd once threatened to destroy her business. He might even be kind. But she'd never heard him admit regret.

The line of his mouth kinked in a brittle smile. 'Last night. What I said to you—'

'Don't.' She shook her head, again hyper-aware of the

warmth of the sun on her cheeks instead of the swish of her hair.

'You were right.' The words were thick in her throat, an admission of her own blindness. She should have seen the truth sooner. 'I *was* hiding.' It was the hardest admission she'd ever made.

He nodded, his gaze fixed on her face. A tremor ran through her, her fingers twitching with the almost unstoppable urge to wrench her hair down and conceal herself.

'I know. I wasn't apologising for that. But for the way I spoke to you. I'm sorry. I was angry, arrogant. I should have been more tactful.'

Lily's mouth sagged. No apology for what he'd done, just the way he'd done it. What must it be like to be so utterly sure of yourself?

But he wasn't. She read his wariness and regret. She'd swear that was doubt in his set features. The realisation tipped the world out of balance for the second time in less than twenty-four hours.

'What are you smiling about?' His brow furrowed.

'Nothing. Really.' She paused and dragged in a fortifying breath, watching the waiter place their drinks on the table then leave. 'I… Thank you. I think if you'd been kind I wouldn't have listened. You *made* me listen because you didn't mince your words.'

She owed him so much. Without pausing for second thoughts she reached out and touched him lightly on the back of the hand.

Instantly energy fizzed and crackled up her arm, prickling her skin and drawing the hairs on her nape upright.

Dismay wrenched at her insides. She had an immediate, overwhelming certainty that she'd gone too far. Not because he looked disapproving, but because of the dart and fizz of pleasure making her body come alive in a whole new way. She looked down, *willing* her fingers not to close around his. It took far too long for her hand to obey her brain, yanking back as if scalded.

Her eyes fluttered shut as she sucked in a horrified breath. How could such a little thing be so devastating?

'Lily?' That low voice hummed through every erogenous zone in her body. She had to get a grip. She was twenty-eight, not some teenager.

Except when it came to dealing with attractive men that was exactly how she felt: fourteen and flustered, gauche and totally inexperienced.

Lily snapped open her eyes, forcing herself to meet that stunning blue stare. 'I accept your apology. I hated the way you said it but I'm glad you did.' Her pent-up breath expelled in a whoosh. 'I can't believe I never saw it before.'

'Hey, don't beat yourself up. You're a remarkable woman. You've achieved so much. And, no, I don't just mean your work for me.' He gestured to her cheek. 'Coping with that would tax anyone. You've done superbly.'

'Why are you being so kind?'

'Kind?' His eyes rounded. 'I'm realistic. What you've built for yourself, the woman you are—that took guts and determination.'

He meant it. This wasn't like the well-meaning bonhomie of her family, whose exuberant praise for even the smallest achievements made her feel…not patronised… but as if perhaps those small achievements were the best she could ever do.

Guilt smote her. It wasn't like that, really. Her family had been on her side through the darkest days. She wouldn't have got through what she had without them. Of course they'd wanted to celebrate each small step forward. But eventually she'd become claustrophobic, encircled by their protectiveness.

Yet Raffaele's no-nonsense approach, his confrontational attitude, challenging her to rise above her fear, had made all the difference.

She cleared her throat. 'I could say the same about you. You've come a long way.'

Was it imagination or did the shutters come down on his expression? Strange. She'd never considered he had no-go territory. Raffaele seemed so confident and at ease.

A moment later the impression was gone. He lifted his coffee cup for a leisurely sip, leaning into his chair, one arm looped over the back. The pose stretched the gap of his half-open shirt, revealing a sprinkling of hair across his tightly muscled chest.

Lily blinked, cursing her inability to concentrate. This was the closest she'd ever been to a virile, attractive man in his prime and it tied her brain in knots.

A woman on the far side of the pool stumbled to a stop, staring, before recovering her poise and her dropped beach towel. The fact Lily wasn't the only one responding to Raffaele's stunning looks didn't make her feel better.

It made her feel…possessive. He was here with *her*, even if it was just their business connection and his concern for her welfare that linked them.

'That was another life.' His smile was brief but dazzling, yet Lily couldn't help feeling he used it to distract her.

He didn't want to talk about his past? She could relate to that. She opened her mouth to ask about his plans for this resort, if and when he acquired it from Robert Bradshaw, but he got in first.

'You'll need to be careful of the sun.' He gestured to the filmy caftan of bronze and golden brown she wore over her swimsuit. 'Delightful as that outfit is, there's no sun protection and your skin is like cream.'

Was that a compliment or an accusation? A reminder that she'd lived the last few years immured at home, using work as an excuse not to go out?

To Lily's amazement she felt heat creep under her skin. A heat that had nothing to do with the sunshine and everything to do with Raffaele Petri's heavy-lidded gaze on her body. It had been more than a decade since she'd blushed but that stare was unlike anything she'd ever experienced. Men didn't look at her that way. Ever.

'Where's the hat I ordered for you? You should at least be wearing that.'

It was a sign of her stress that she'd actually forgotten the clothes she wore had been bought by him.

Suddenly the slinky bronze swimsuit felt too clingy. And as for the gossamer-thin cover-up—its light-as-air delicacy against her arms and bare thighs now made her imagine another touch…the touch of trailing masculine fingers.

'I don't need a nanny, Raffaele.' She might have problems going out among people but she was twenty-eight, able to watch out for sunburn.

'Just as well.' His drawl rang alarm bells in some never-before-accessed part of her brain. 'Because I don't feel at all like a nanny.'

His expression jammed the breath in her lungs. Worse, it drew the heat that skimmed her body down into a spiralling vortex.

Lily clamped her hands on the arms of her chair, willing herself not to shift restlessly. But his look was making her feel…aroused. Aware. Awash with longing.

Her nipples tightened into buds and she crossed her arms, hoping she looked annoyed, anything but needy.

It would be excruciatingly awful if he realised how attracted she was. Enough to imagine she read sexual interest in his glance.

'That's another thing. I owe you for the clothes. I know you only sent them as a challenge, to dare me out of my comfort zone, but I have to pay you back.'

Once more his gaze skimmed over her, with the swift precision of a connoisseur. What did he see, apart from her blemished face? A too-pale body that held no allure when compared with the women he knew? Of course that was it. He'd even bought this outfit in shades of brown, surely a sign he saw her as a drab sparrow.

'And for the pleasure of seeing you in them.'

'Sorry?' The screech of her chair scraping back on the flagstones almost obliterated the sound of her shock-diminished voice. Her heart thrummed so hard against her ribs she felt light-headed.

'I said, I wanted to see you in them. You've got a lovely body, Lily. You should be proud of it.'

She shook her head.

'You've made your point about me being a recluse. You don't need to say things that aren't true.' He had no idea how cruel that was. How badly a woman who'd never had such a compliment in her life yearned for it to be real.

She'd spent half a lifetime being told that true beauty was on the inside. But some pathetic, juvenile part of her still longed to be thought pretty. Just once.

'You think I'm lying?' His dark eyebrows steepled together. 'You know me, Lily. I always get straight to the point. These days I tell the unvarnished truth instead of any easy lies.'

He leaned forward, closing the gap between them. His bluer than blue eyes pinioned her. 'You have a beautiful body, Lily, and I enjoy looking at you. *That's* the truth.'

CHAPTER EIGHT

RAFFA WATCHED HER stalk from the pool terrace, along the path through the gardens. Head up, shoulders back, long legs supple and strong, hips swaying in unconscious invitation. She was as alluring as any classically beautiful model he'd known.

More. There was nothing artificial about Lily. From those pert breasts to that searing golden-brown stare she was authentic.

Desirable.

Around the poolside heads turned to follow her progress. Raffa saw women lean close together, whispering, their expressions varying from sympathy to horror.

No doubt about it, Lily had been brave sitting here alone, without even a hat to conceal her scarred face.

But for every female shudder he caught more masculine stares. Some overt, some discreet, all fixed on the delectable sway of her body.

Raffa tried to analyse what it was about her that fired his libido. The swell of her hips? The ripe thrust of her breasts? The long, seductive curve of thigh and calf?

Maybe the way her voice turned to a throaty purr when she was annoyed. Or the curious mix of vulnerability and vivacity that kept him on his toes. Even her prickly defensiveness appealed, provoking him time and again to pursue the woman who tried to disguise herself.

For the first time he was attracted to a woman's mind, her thoughts and character, as well as her body.

Whatever this was, he'd passed the point of hoping it would go away. She'd stirred him out of sexual apathy so profoundly he felt wired, attuned to her as a predator to his prey. Her every shift of mood jangled his senses, under-mining his concentration on the vital deal he'd come here to close. He should be focused on Bradshaw, yet Lily was a distraction he couldn't ignore.

Worryingly, she also aroused dormant feelings—con-cern, protectiveness, caring. Feelings expunged the day his childhood ended. The day Gabriella had been found dead.

Raffa sank back in his seat, winded by the devastating simplicity of what he faced.

For the first time in his life there was no careful con-sideration of pros and cons, of benefits versus risks. Just untrammelled desire, simple and unprecedented.

That explained his less than impressive performance just now. No one hearing him would believe he'd once made a living out of sweet-talking women. He'd known how to pan-der to female fantasies, to become whatever they wanted for long enough to get what he in turn needed from them. He'd been smooth but never obvious. He'd made each one feel special. That had been his gift and his greatest asset.

The question was, had he completely lost his touch?

Raffa was lost in thought when a flash of colour caught his eye. A stream of dark gold as familiar as the reflection he saw in the mirror if ever he bothered to look. Colour as rich as ancient coins, hoarded for a king's pleasure, but instead of cold metal this was a ribbon burnished by the sun, cascading down a woman's back. It rippled in soft waves as she moved.

Emotion clutched his chest, digging talons deep into his heart, squeezing his lungs. His breath stopped on a harsh rasp. She moved again, slender arms pushing her hair over her shoulder in a gesture he'd known from infancy.

Gabriella.

Raffa opened his mouth till instinct, more primitive than logic, stopped him. To call out would break the magic.

He wanted to run to her. Pour out his apologies for not

behaving better, for not appreciating how lucky he was to
have her. For driving her away in frustration that last night.
He was twelve again and desperate. He felt grief and regret, shame and hope.

Till she moved again and the magic was lost.

It wasn't Gabriella.

Of course it wasn't. Gabriella was twenty-one years'
dead. Yet for a moment she'd been vividly alive again.
Raffa's heart sprinted in a sickening, uneven gallop, his
lungs atrophied and he forced his fisted hands to loosen.

The young woman moved again, walking through the
shallow end of the pool, and her walk wasn't Gabriella's.
Her hair wasn't down to her waist and she was boyishly
slim whereas Gabriella had been curvy.

One thing they had in common though. They were both
in their teens. The girl was around fifteen or sixteen, much
younger than the man helping her from the pool.

Raffa was turning away when his gaze sharpened. That
wasn't her father taking her arm. He recognised the fleshy
face and ham-like hands. Hands that lingered on her hips.
Robert Bradshaw. The man he'd avoided since arriving. He had no interest in seeing him till he was ready to
make his move. Making Bradshaw sweat, waiting for that
moment, was a bonus.

But it wasn't the deal on Raffa's mind now. It was Gabriella and how Bradshaw had ushered her aboard his boat
twenty-one years ago, an arm hovering near her waist as
he offered champagne.

The next morning Gabriella was dead.

There was a crash and Raffa looked down to see glass
splintered across the paving where he'd knocked his drink.

Bradshaw heard it too, his head snapping up. Seconds
later he was patting the girl and murmuring in her ear before leaving her.

'Signor Petri. It's good to see you at last.' He lunged forward to shake hands but Raffa avoided the gesture, leaning down to collect broken glass.

'Leave that. It's what the staff are for.' The Englishman turned as a waiter hurried out with a brush and pan. 'About time! You should have been here instantly.'

'It's fine.' Raffa nodded to the waiter. 'My fault.'

Seconds later the glass was cleared and Bradshaw hefted himself into a chair. 'I've been wanting to catch up with you. We've a lot to discuss.' He waved expansively. 'Excellent idea to come here personally to see the resort before we close a deal. It's really something, isn't it?'

Behind his air of ease Raffa detected strain. Good. That was a start. Ideally Raffa would see him behind bars for the rest of his life but, as that wasn't possible, the revenge he'd planned would have to be enough.

'It's peaceful.' He saw Bradshaw frown, dismayed at Raffa's lack of praise. The man was no negotiator, letting his fear show.

'Come to my house and I'll see you get some action.' Bradshaw leaned in. 'Come to dinner. I'll throw a private party. I'm sure you'll enjoy it.'

Raffa was shaking his head before Bradshaw stopped speaking. 'I'm afraid not.' He didn't bother giving an excuse. Let him stew.

Bradshaw's smile grew guarded. 'Later in the week then. Let me know when you're free to discuss business. In the meantime, relax, enjoy.' He leaned close enough for Raffa to smell sweat and expensive aftershave.

'Would you like some female company to amuse you while you're here? It would be very discreet.' When Raffa didn't respond he continued, flicking a glance across the pool. 'A nice, fresh girl. Blonde, maybe? Or redhead? Just say the word.'

Nausea clutched Raffa's belly as he followed Bradshaw's leering gaze to the girl he'd seen earlier. His hands dug so tight into his chair's armrests he'd probably mark the metal like he wanted to mark Bradshaw's face. It was a miracle he held back, a miracle possible only because he knew Bradshaw would pay with everything he had and everything he'd ever wanted, once this deal went through.

'No,' Raffa croaked. 'Nothing. I'm here for peace and quiet.'

Abruptly he levered himself up, barely acknowledging the other man's babble about meeting soon for sundowners at his house.

Raffa nodded and strode away. He told himself his tactic to make Bradshaw sweat could only help negotiations. But the truth was he couldn't stomach being within spitting distance of the man. He didn't trust himself not to do him violence.

CHAPTER NINE

SEEING BRADSHAW LEFT a sour taste in Raffa's mouth. He wanted this wrapped up. But after more long distance discussions with his legal team, he acknowledged there were still matters to be sorted before he brought Bradshaw to his knees. The delay rankled, but at least it had the bonus of making Bradshaw even more desperate.

When Lily knocked on his villa door for their early evening meeting, relief hit like the smack of an ocean wave. Raffa needed distraction from his circling thoughts but more, he'd wondered if she'd show after what had passed between them.

He couldn't explain it but since seeing Bradshaw and that girl at the pool, Raffa had been unsettled, ridiculously on edge as emotions crowded close. Calm evaded him as if the thick skin he'd spent a lifetime nurturing had been scraped raw. He felt… He *felt*! And it wasn't just hatred of Bradshaw.

He told himself he needed the distraction of work.

Yet Lily looked anything but professional in the clothes he'd chosen. An aqua scoop-necked top and wraparound skirt in aqua with a swirl of gold that fluttered enticingly around her legs. She hesitated in the doorway, giving him time to drink her in and to stifle the urge to haul her close. His gaze dipped briefly, taking in the ankle ties on the sandals that accentuated her sexy calves.

An appreciative smile curled inside him, a smile he repressed. She was skittish enough already. 'You're here. Good. We've a lot to get through.'

Predictably, instead of stiffening at his tone, Lily seemed

reassured as she stepped over the threshold and onto the polished wood floor.

'This is for you.' She offered an envelope.

Her resignation? The idea tore his thoughts completely free of Bradshaw and business. His chest hollowed as he made himself reach for it, noting the way she relinquished it as soon as he grasped it.

Had he pushed her too far? She was like a porcupine, raising spiky quills if he got too near. Yet he knew she wanted him as much as he wanted her. If only he could entice her to let down her guard.

Mouth firm, Raffa tore open the envelope. 'Money?'

'For the clothes.' Her voice was as tight as her shoulders.

Briefly Raffa considered admitting it had been pure pleasure choosing clothes for her, ones that suited her and made the most of her delectable body. That if he'd had his way he wouldn't have stopped there. He'd have bought the ivory lace nightgown for starters. Just for the pleasure of seeing her in it, then peeling it away.

'Consider it a business perk.' He held the envelope out to her. 'I insisted on bringing you here.'

She shook her head. For once there was no accompanying ripple of brown silk around her shoulders. She'd pinned her hair up again. Pinned it so tight it was a wonder she didn't have a headache.

Definitely one for gestures, his *piccola istrice*. How sharp, he wondered, were her quills?

'I buy my own clothes.'

'Even if you didn't choose them?' If she'd had her way there'd have been more concealing shirts and baggy trousers.

'I accepted them, therefore I pay.' As she said it her hand rose to her neckline. A sign of nerves?

It struck him anew how difficult it must be for Lily to reveal herself like this. But he knew better than to show his thoughts, much less praise her courage.

'Fine.' He tossed the envelope onto the table where he'd drawn up two chairs. 'Now, let's get started. I want to go over every last detail. Nothing can be missed.'

As ever when they worked, time slid by unnoticed. Lily began to relax as Raffaele focused on business.

There were no kindling glances or personal comments. They were again boss and employee, or more precisely, colleagues. Raffaele recognised the expertise of his team and treated them with respect. Lily thrived on feeling appreciated.

'When are you meeting Robert Bradshaw?' They'd been at the resort two nights and she knew there'd been at least one invitation to dine at Bradshaw's house on the far side of the island.

'In good time.' Raffa's voice was brusque.

'But isn't that why you're here?' Raffaele had driven his team like the devil to prepare for this deal. He'd come here himself rather than delegate. 'You're deliberately delaying?'

One eyebrow rose. 'The time's not right. I'm waiting till he's heard confirmation his play for more capital has failed. Then he'll be more amenable to my terms.'

'What if it doesn't fail?'

'Oh, it will.' Raffa's eyes flashed with an expression that unsettled, until Lily reminded herself they were discussing Robert Bradshaw.

She had no sympathy for the Englishman. Born with wealth, he'd squandered his fortune through excess. His few attempts at running any of the businesses he'd inherited had ended disastrously and now he teetered on the brink of ruin. Not that you'd know it from his lavish lifestyle.

'You're turning the screw?'

Raffa leaned back, linking his hands behind his head. The movement emphasised the heavy breadth of muscled shoulders and taut biceps beneath his casual shirt. Lily dragged her gaze to the old deeds she'd unearthed. But her breath came in shallow little bursts. She didn't feel professional but dizzy and shamefully entranced.

How much longer could she pretend disinterest?

'I've shown my hand by coming here. That's enough. No point letting Bradshaw think he'll get everything he wants.' Venom dripped from Raffaele's tone as he said the Englishman's name, confirming her suspicion of bad blood between the men. Yet her searches had uncovered no link.

'He's desperate for a partner to put up cash to renovate the place. Even he recognises profits aren't what they could be and it's his last money-making asset.'

'So the longer he waits, the more desperate he becomes.'

'Unless he finds another partner. It's a calculated risk not to rush in. The resort is an appealing investment.'

Lily nodded. It was like Paradise. She wouldn't be surprised if at least one of the other companies she'd worked for, De Laurentis Enterprises, was interested.

'But he wants you because you've got the golden touch.' Raffaele's hotels were a byword for discreet luxury that appealed to the seriously wealthy who sought respite from the paparazzi. And who had deep, deep pockets.

'It seems a shame to change the place. It's wonderful as it is.' Her gaze drifted to the white curve of beach framed by lush gardens. To her surprise the bright sky had darkened to indigo, torches lighting the path through the trees. It was later than she'd thought.

'It needs updating to attract the clientele Bradshaw wants.'

'The way the poolside bar has been updated?' Lily pursed her lips. While the rest of the resort had a graceful if slightly worn charm with plantation shutters, airy rooms and individual bungalows, the bar was sleek, black-tiled and ostentatiously modern with vivid neon light displays and uncomfortable, trendy metal chairs.

Raffaele's lip curled. 'Bradshaw's one effort at updating the place. The man's got no sense. The clientele he wants to attract can fly to New York or elsewhere if they want urban modern. They'll come here for premium luxury and privacy. And to experience the Caribbean, its tastes and laid-back style.'

'So what would you do? How would you change it?'

'Reduce the number of bungalows for a start.' He responded almost before she'd finished speaking. 'Keep the best and get rid of the rest. People pay for the privilege of privacy. Remodel and upgrade everything. Each villa would have its own pool, spa, butler and chef. Put in a truly fabulous restaurant on the hill featuring a new twist on traditional local flavours and produce. Bring in the absolute best in everything. Improve…'

'What?' She leaned across the table.

Abruptly Raffaele shook his head. 'It doesn't matter. All that matters is getting Bradshaw to accept my offer.' His voice was harsh, his words clipped.

Lily sat back. It was stupid to feel rebuffed. She wouldn't be involved when Raffaele put his plans into action. He had other staff for that. But she'd been caught up in his enthusiasm. His energy had drawn her, making her want more.

There was no more. Not with Raffaele. Not unless it was legwork for some other project.

She swallowed, realising it wasn't even his vision for the resort that had held her spellbound. It was Raffaele. She'd never known a man so charismatic, so vital. If she reached out a hand towards him she knew she'd feel the buzz and zap of energy radiating from him.

Yet the desire to touch was more than that.

She wanted to touch him the way a woman touched her lover.

Lily stood. 'It's time I left.'

He stood when she did, his expression unreadable. 'There's no rush. I've ordered dinner to be served here.'

Dinner? With Raffaele?

Lily felt the punch of her heart against her ribs. She

imagined them sitting, drinking in the view, sipping wine and feasting on seafood as they relaxed in each other's company. He'd be charming and she'd be witty and insightful and when their gazes locked she'd read heat and hunger and—

'We've finished for the day, haven't we?' Her voice was scratchy. Better that than needy, she told herself. Heat crept up her throat at the thoughts she'd harboured. 'Unless there's something else you wanted me to do.' She made a production of gathering her gear.

'There is, as it happens.'

Her head snapped up as those deep cadences wrapped around her. 'Yes?'

'I want you to dine with me.'

Lily blinked. 'Why?'

'I want your company.'

Her fingers curled around her laptop. She felt out of her depth.

The look he gave her, grave yet knowing, sent a wobble from her chest all the way to her knees. It was the sort of look she'd imagined a man gave a woman he was interested in. It made her pulse flutter in her throat as if she'd swallowed a swarm of bright island butterflies.

Lily had never received such a look before.

She didn't know what to do with it.

Or with the hammering excitement within.

She swallowed hard. Clearly she was superimposing her secret cravings on him. Raffaele Petri had a host of beautiful women to choose from. It was laughable to think he could be attracted to her.

Beyond laughable. It was pathetic.

'It's time I went.' Before she made a fool of herself.

'You said that before.' He crossed his arms over his chest and it struck her for the first time that he stood between her and the door.

Lily spread clammy hands on the table, hoping its solidity would help penetrate the fog in her brain. Help her think straight and stop imagining things.

Except, when she looked up, Raffaele's blue eyes sparked with something that made her belly curl and her nipples bud against her bra. Her skin felt tight, as if the woman inside were bursting to escape.

'It's true. We've finished for the night.'

Slowly he shook his head, the movement accentuating the shadows beneath his high cheekbones.

'I sincerely hope not.' Was it imagination or was his voice thicker, his accent more pronounced? It ran through her veins like warm caramel.

Lily dragged her hands from the table as if its surface was electrified. A large hand snapped out and captured her wrist. Instantly she stilled, all except for the quiver reverberating from her tingling fingers up her arm and down to the soles of her feet.

'What do you want, Raffaele? What are you playing at?' Old habit came to the rescue and her chin jutted. She'd spent half a lifetime pretending to be impervious to hurt.

'What do you think I want?' It was the voice of her dreams, seductive, alluring and full of desire.

Impossible!

She yanked her hand free, stepping out of reach. Her breath sawed through searing lungs.

He was flirting. Sending her that half-lidded look that had turned a single photo into a multi-million-dollar success for a famous men's clothing company.

The impact of it in the flesh, on *her* flesh, was devastating.

'Stop it, Raffaele!' She was almost beyond caring that he might hear the hurt beneath her belligerence. She needed to get away. 'I don't…' She shook her head, wishing she hadn't made a point of pinning her hair up, wishing it could swish around her face, concealing an expression she feared must reveal the yearning in her soul.

'Don't what?'

Don't flirt. She didn't know how. Had no experience of it. Which made this game he played even more cruel.

'What are you afraid of, Lily?' His voice, rough suede, caressed her skin, drawing it to tingling life.

You.

Of you and everything you make me feel.

'I didn't think anything fazed you, Lily. You're so feisty, so focused.'

She cleared her throat to speak as he moved close enough for her to inhale the tantalising scent of warm male skin, salt spice and the sea. But determination wasn't enough. Not when she looked up into ocean-blue eyes. They burned with a heat that beckoned to every feminine instinct she'd spent fourteen years suppressing.

'Is it this you're afraid of?' His head lowered and warmth brushed her lips. The soft caress of perfectly sculpted lips. The fleeting, beckoning taste of Paradise as his tongue slicked the seam of her mouth.

Lily's eyelids flickered, weighted by the desire rolling through her, inexorably growing, expanding, clogging every sense. All she knew was the scent and taste of Raffaele, the heat of his breath on her lips, the pulse of longing throbbing within.

Air brushed her mouth as his lips left hers and for a heartbeat nothing moved. She didn't even breathe.

Lily forced her eyes open. Azure depths captured her and it was as if she'd ventured too far out to sea. Except she wasn't sinking, she was floating, buoyed by an anticipation so acute she felt she'd shatter if he didn't put an end to it and kiss her properly.

'I'm not afraid,' she lied.

She was terrified. Thrilled. Exultant. Curious.

Lily felt her hand settle against the muscled plane of his chest. Beneath her palm beat a steady pulse that seemed leisurely compared with her own wildly careering heartbeat.

He was *real*. Not the phantom lover of her dreams. His flesh was hotter than hers even through his shirt.

His chest rose under her touch, making her aware of the masculine power beneath the designer panache. The air of languid relaxation Raffaele so often adopted was a front, she realised, as sparks tickled her palm, racing up her arm. The man was all potent power.

But he was her boss. He was one of the most beautiful men on the planet, and she—

'Lily.' His voice was so deep she felt its reverberation in her belly. His hand was hard as it clamped her palm to his chest.

She shifted back. 'This is a mistake.'

He moved with her, his thigh brushing hers. Ripples coursed up her leg to the spot between her thighs where a different pulse beat—needy and quick.

'No mistake. Admit it, Lily. This feels *right.*'

His left hand captured her nape, long fingers spearing through her hair to hold her still as his head slanted down.

Time moved in infinitely slow seconds. Slow enough for her to realise that, despite his hold, she had only to turn her head or step back and she'd be free.

But she didn't move. It *did* feel right. More, it felt inevitable. Why pretend when for weeks she'd wondered what it would be like to kiss Raffaele?

His lips touched hers again, once, twice, before settling on her mouth, sealing her breath with his. For a moment he held utterly still. She absorbed the rich, warm scent of his skin, the delicious tang of him on her tongue, the long body hard up against hers, and the gentleness of his hand at the back of her head, cradling, tender...

Then those azure eyes closed, his head tilting as he delved between her parted lips. One swiping caress and sensation shuddered down her backbone and further, weakening her knees. They trembled as she clutched him, drawn by the slide of his mouth, his probing tongue and the waves of need, dark and intoxicating, that buffeted her.

His hand tightened on her skull, the angle of his mouth changed and the kiss grew harder, insistent, demanding. Raffaele drew her tongue between his lips, sucking, and a shot of adrenaline, of *something,* fired in her blood. The pulse between her legs quickened, her nipples against his chest so sensitive she almost cried out as each muffled breath abraded them against him. She was on fire, burning up in a heat he both kindled and promised to assuage.

Was it possible to climax just from kissing?

Lily slipped her hands up to clasp his face, framing hard bone and taut skin, learning sculpted contours as his tongue flicked hers, inviting her to join him, to give in.

A mighty shudder ran through her, a sigh that made no sound in the whirling ecstasy of the moment. A sigh of surrender as Lily let herself go and for the first time in her life kissed a man.

He'd guessed she'd be delicious. He'd expected fire beneath her guarded prickliness.

But still he wasn't prepared. Lily's slender body turned to flame against him, all eager passion and flagrant, hungry need. He felt her shake in his hold, her whole body trembling. But not with fear. Not when she kissed him back with such glorious abandon.

He couldn't get enough, clutching her greedily.

Tongue on tongue, lips against lips, heart to heart, soft belly to quickening arousal—she was all he'd hoped for and more. The scent of sweet pears vied with a tantalising hint of musk and she tasted…he couldn't describe her flavour, other than addictive.

Raffa drew her against his mouth and his groin. How long since he'd felt that urgent spiral of desire? That restless hunger to possess?

For years he'd been celibate, uninterested in women. Yet

Lily, with her shaking hands and clumsy kisses, turned him on more than any practised seductress.

She pressed in, her teeth mashing his lip. Her untutored eagerness was beguiling as nothing he'd ever experienced. Raffaele was used to women blasé about sex, who enjoyed it but were never surprised by it.

By contrast he sensed shock as well as delight in Lily's response. As if all this was new.

Would you touch a woman who looked like this?
Of course you wouldn't.

Her words slammed into him. And the memory of Lily's grave eyes as she'd said it, hurt dragging her mouth down.

In the midst of the maelstrom something inside him stilled, held its breath.

Instinct urged him to take advantage of her eagerness. But some damned part of his brain had begun working, sifting what she'd said, analysing the inexperience in her kisses and clutching hands.

It couldn't be.

No woman got to twenty-eight without being kissed.

His mind reeled. It was inconceivable to a man who'd lost count of his sexual partners well before he was out of his teens. Yet the small, still reasoning part of his brain acknowledged Lily kissed like a virgin.

Shock ground through his belly. Tangled threads of desire and guilt twisted into a jumbled knot that grew and grew till it pressed upon his chest, cramping his lungs, stopping his breath.

He reared back, panting, heart hurling itself against his ribs. He looked down at parted lips, plump and pink. Almost, he slammed his mouth back onto hers as the tide of wanting rose.

But he forced himself to think. To observe.

Her breathing was even more out of kilter than his, her eyes closed. On one side of her face was clear, flushed skin, soft as silk. On the other, the broad, taut brand of healed

flesh. She'd called it ugly, something from a horror movie.
To Raffa it had merely become part of her, like the way she
wrinkled her nose when he said something she disagreed
with. Or the glow in her eyes when she forgot to be cautious and revealed her natural ebullience.

Could it be true no man had got this close because of
her scar?

Or maybe she'd been too defensive to let one near. That,
he could believe.

Her eyes snapped open, searching with an intensity that
made Raffa feel every one of his thirty-three tarnished
years.

He could barely remember being a virgin. He'd never
kissed one in his life.

As for taking one to bed, as he'd aimed to take Lily after
a champagne supper—he shuddered, seeing the awed hope
in her gaze. The innocence, for once unguarded.

She trusted him.

Raffa thought of the things he'd done to get where he
was today, the seedy, *special* arrangements. He was sullied
in ways Lily would never know. Ways that didn't show on
the outside, but were there, a stain nothing could remove.

Aghast, he dropped his hands as a new thought needled.

Had he, at some unconscious level, understood Lily's
innocence? Was he grasping for it as once, years ago, a
jaded businesswoman had lusted after Raffa's innocence
as much as his young body and fair face?

Bile rose in a gush. Acid filled his mouth, obliterating
the taste of her, the beckoning, elusive flavour of innocent pleasure.

What had he ever known of innocent pleasure?

'Raffaele?' Her whisper tugged his libido and his con-
science—two entities that had lain dormant for so long
he'd thought he'd lost both. 'What is it?'

Caution clouded her desire. It happened so fast it confirmed everything he'd wondered about the hurt she'd endured in the past. She'd schooled herself to disappointment.

'You're right,' he croaked. 'Dining together is a bad idea.' He cleared his throat, forcing out the words. 'It's better if you leave.'

She spun away before he stopped talking, was out of the villa within seconds. But not before he saw hurt in her eyes. And the way her head rocked back as if he'd hit her.

Raffa stood where she'd left him, sucker-punched by an unseen blow to his belly at the pain he'd inflicted.

Worse, though, was the knowledge he couldn't fix this. He couldn't be the man Lily needed.

CHAPTER TEN

HOURS LATER, LILY still cringed when she thought of the frantic way she'd clung to Raffaele, begging for more.

One touch of his lips was all it had taken for every defence to collapse, laid waste by his caresses and her desperate hunger.

She'd been so needy she'd thought she'd explode with wanting. Another kiss like that and she'd probably have climaxed where she stood. It almost made the years of waiting worth it, to experience such incandescent pleasure.

Raffaele was a master of the sensual arts. No wonder he hadn't wanted to continue the experiment. She'd been gauchely overeager, lost to everything but the wonder of her first kiss.

Twenty-eight and kissed for the first time!

And the last, if tonight was any indicator.

Lily groaned and swung around to pace the darkened room. There was no danger of tripping over anything. She'd retraced her steps thousands of times in the last few hours, unable to settle while she was so awash with fury, frustration and embarrassment.

Why, oh, why had she let him dare her into taking a risk? Into believing after all these years things had changed and her scar didn't matter?

Had she *really* thought Raffaele was attracted to her? The kiss was all about curiosity on his part and she'd left herself wide open to hurt.

Her ribs seemed to contract around her frantically beating heart. She'd believed Raffaele different. Caring, despite his ruthless streak and patent expectation of always getting his own way. She'd never believed him cruel.

But what he'd done tonight…

Oh, get over it! You were only too eager to kiss the man. You can't blame him for pulling back. Just because you're besotted—

Lily slammed an iron bar across that thought. She was *not* going there. Not now. Not ever.

She was going to do what she always did. Pick herself up, dust herself off and get on with life. Bury herself in work. Strive to achieve.

Except she'd left her laptop in his villa and nothing, not even a tsunami, was going to propel her back there.

Her gaze went to the view beyond the window, the pale crescent of sand and dark glitter of water. There was one way she could expel this restless energy. Spinning on her heel, she crossed the room, reefing off her top and bra. Her skirt slithered to the floor and she stepped out of it, then her underwear, tugging pins from her hair. Naked, she grabbed the new swimsuit, obliterating any thought of the man who'd given it to her as she dragged it on. Of course he hadn't chosen it personally.

Moments later she was closing the door of her villa, breathing the sweet scent of blossom in the resort gardens and the tantalising saltiness of the sea. She took a step, only to slam to a halt as she saw something on her private patio.

Someone, not something.

In the starlight he looked impossibly tall as he vacated the chair and stood.

'How long have you been here?' The words were staccato beats, crashing through the silence. Adrenaline blasted her bloodstream, triggering heightened awareness. She registered the residual warmth of the flagstones beneath her bare feet, the throb of her pulse, the prickle as her flesh tightened, responding to Raffaele's nearness. And the lingering taste of him on her tongue, like a delicacy her memory refused to discard.

In the gloom she made out his characteristic shrug. 'A while. I thought you were asleep.'

Lily hadn't bothered with lights. She didn't want to face herself in the mirror. Darkness had been a refuge.

'I don't want you here.' The words scraped from the bottom of her bruised soul.

'I know.' His voice sounded curiously hollow.

'Then why are you here?' She jammed her hands on her hips, finding comfort in indignation.

'I wanted to make sure you were okay.'

'By sitting here in the dark?' She'd never heard anything so unlikely.

'I didn't want to leave you all alone. I felt…responsible.'

Ridiculous how that stung.

'I'm an adult, Raffaele.' She swallowed his name, hating that even now she loved the taste of it. Lily wanted to rage and curse at the power he had over her. It wasn't supposed to be this way. She was supposed to loathe him.

'There's no need to feel responsible. I look after myself.' For a moment she felt the weight of that drag at her shoulders. The years of being alone, dealing with everything solo. Then she straightened. 'Don't wait up for me. I'm going for a swim.'

One swift step and he blocked her path. 'At night?'

Lily angled her jaw, as if she could meet his eyes in the shadows.

'You're not my keeper. Now step aside. There's no need for this…' she waved her hand dismissively '…show of solicitude. Go away and concentrate on Robert Bradshaw. He's the reason you're here.'

She needed to remember that. Raffaele's focus was business. He was single-minded to the point of obsession with this project. She was a curiosity, a diversion.

'You can't swim now. It's too dangerous.' The words sounded as if they'd been ground out, like glass splintering beneath a twisting boot. 'What if you get a cramp and there's no one to help?'

A writhing, seething, lava-hot surge of anger shot through her, that he pretended to care. She sidestepped and stalked past.

Hard fingers shackled her wrist, pulling her up short.

'Let. Me. Go. Now.'

'Lily, listen to me, I—'

'No.' She swung around, staring up into features now illuminated by starlight, features as flagrantly gorgeous as ever. Lily felt the inevitable lift inside her chest, then the slow burn of shame that she couldn't, even now, eradicate the wanting.

'*You* listen, Raffaele. I may be different to the people you know. I may *look* different. But I deserve respect. I'm not some amusing freak, here to entertain you in your downtime. I—'

'*Per la Madonna!*' The low roar of his voice filled the air, his hand gripping hers. 'Don't talk like that.'

'Why not? It's the truth.'

A rush of words filled her ears, low, fluid, a non-stop litany of what had to be curses, though she couldn't understand the Italian. She'd never heard Raffaele sound so far from the savvy, self-contained entrepreneur she knew.

'You can't think that! It's not true.'

Abruptly weariness gathered her in. What was the point of listening to Raffaele excuse his behaviour?

'I'm not interested, Raffaele. Just go. Leave me be.'

'Lily. I swear it wasn't like that.'

'What was it like, then?' She knew she shouldn't ask. His answer would only rub salt in the wound but she couldn't stop herself.

'It was…unbelievable. Better than I'd ever—'

'No! Don't you *dare*!' Lily reefed her fingers from his, clapping her hands over her ears. 'Don't lie.' She spun away, stumbling down the sandy path towards the beach.

This time it wasn't his hand that stopped her. It was his whole arm, looping around her waist, hauling her back against his tall frame. Heat and muscle burned her back. But it was nothing to the fire roaring within.

'It's no lie.' His breath feathered her neck, stirring her hair. 'Kissing you was the best thing I've done in years.'

Lily shook her head. How was she supposed to stay strong when he used words like that to undo her? Despite her indignation, her knees wobbled. She was in danger of sagging against him.

Deliberately she snorted her disgust. 'Right. That's why you pulled away as if you'd been burned. Why you told me to leave.'

'I told you to leave because I realised you deserved better...than I can give you.'

Her bitter laugh tore the night. 'Better? You have to be kidding.' He kissed like a god. What could be better? 'You just didn't like the way I kissed you back. It reminded you that it was ugly Lily Nolan in your arms.'

Sibilants hissed against her ear as another burst of Italian washed around her, rougher this time. His arm at her waist turned hard as iron.

'Didn't like it? You have no idea.' Gone were the smooth cadences of his seductive voice. Instead it sounded like gravel dipped in burning tar. 'If I didn't like it would I react like this?'

He hauled her back so she was plastered against him. Hard thighs pressed into her and an enormous erection rose between the cheeks of her buttocks.

Lily swallowed convulsively, eyes popping, not just at the impossibility of his arousal, but the sheer size.

In this moment, with only the flimsy fabric of her swimsuit and his clothing between them, she felt her inexperience like a brand. The sensation of him jutting against her created a hollow ache between her legs. Even the liquid heat pooling there couldn't fill the void.

'Does it feel like I don't want you?' He ground against her. The slide of his arousal against her almost bare skin was unlike anything she'd ever known, the rough caress of his voice the most potently seductive sound she'd heard. 'Well, *cara*? Does it? You've been driving me crazy.' This time his lips touched her ear as he spoke, sending shivers of pleasure through her.

'I don't understand.'

'Don't you? You might be a virgin but you're not that innocent, Lily. You can *feel* how I want you.'

The shivers turned to a mighty trembling that racked her from head to toe. She wanted him so badly her skin felt too tight, as if she was going to burst out of it. Need and excitement warred with a lifetime's caution.

She was beyond denying her lack of experience. What was the point? It must be obvious.

'But you pushed me away.' Did he hear the hurt she tried to disguise?

'Of course I pushed you away. It wasn't right. You deserve someone better.'

Yet his arm clamped her to him. His body seared everywhere they touched, branding her. And that hard, swollen ridge against her backside… It took everything she had not to arch back, pressing into him.

'That's the second time you've said that,' she gasped. 'It still doesn't make sense.'

The sound of rough breathing filled her ears. His. Hers. The tumult of her pulse. Finally he spoke. 'You're an innocent. You deserve someone who can treasure that, turn your first time into something special.'

'You can't?' It didn't occur to Lily to play coy. Not with need battering her and Raffaele's breath, his body, his words, an enticement she'd given up trying to resist.

His laugh was short and sharp, off-key. He slid his arm across her stomach as if about to release her and Lily grabbed at it, holding on with both hands. His arm was sinewy, dusted with silky hair, every bit as gorgeous as it looked by daylight.

'I have no experience of innocence, Lily. I'm not the man for you.' There was finality in his words. They struck with the resonance of metal on stone.

'I don't believe you.' Releasing her hold on his arm, she twisted round, breasts to his ribs. He was so hot. So heavy against her belly. The weight of his erection made it hard to think. But she wanted him enough to ignore pride and self-preservation.

She slipped her hand, palm down, between them, curving it round his shaft. To her amazement it jumped in her hand as if it had a mind of its own. Her fingers flexed and tightened and she was rewarded with the sound of Raffaele's hiss of shock.

'Don't, Lily.' Hard fingers dug into her shoulders. 'You need someone special for your first time. That shouldn't be me. It shouldn't be anyone *like* me.'

Hands on her shoulders, he stepped back, creating distance. She felt his loss with a keening desperation.

'Don't go. I want—'

'I want too, but it's better this way. You'll find someone—'

'Don't talk rubbish. There won't be anyone else. There hasn't been and there won't ever be.' Not with her face.

For a long, aching moment she waited for his response but there was none.

Defeated, she pulled away so he had to release his hold or follow her. Of course he let her go.

Exhaustion consumed her. The nervous energy that had kept her wired for hours bled away. She'd never felt so weary.

'Just go, Raffaele. I've had enough. I can't follow your logic. You say you want me but you refuse to take me. You say my looks don't matter, but they do. You and I know they do.' Deliberately she lifted her face so what light there was spilled across her features. 'If they didn't you wouldn't hold back. You wouldn't pretend I could choose to make love with you then tell me I can't.'

Lily heard the defeat in her voice and knew she'd reached breaking point. Swiftly she turned, grabbing the door of her bungalow. 'I've never had that choice with any man and I never will.'

Just once, Lily wanted passion, even if only for a night. She wanted to feel as close as a woman could to a man, to experience physical pleasure at a man's hands. Not out of pity or kindness, but because he desired her as much as she did him.

As if that will ever happen.

Worse still, she wanted that with Raffaele. The man she feared she'd fallen for.

Her shoulders jumped as she bit back a silent sob.

The villa door opened easily and she felt sand under her feet as she stepped onto the cool tiles. But the door wouldn't shut behind her. She looked over her shoulder to find Raffaele blocking it, following her inside.

Desperation rose. 'Please go.' She couldn't stomach more conversation. 'I want to be alone.'

He pulled the door from her hand, closing it behind him with a quiet snick, trapping them in darkness.

'I can't—'

'Shh. It's okay.' Broad hands reached for her shoulders, drawing her to him, filling her with his spicy scent and that terrible, raw yearning.

'It's not okay.' Her voice hit a discordant note and he heard her fight back tears. 'Please, Raffaele. Please leave.'

Her pain tore Raffa's heart. He'd never heard Lily beg. He hated the sound of vulnerability—worse, of defeat. She was stronger than anyone he knew. He wrapped a hand around her back, the other plundering the silken softness of her hair as he held her close.

He breathed in the subtle sweet-as-fruit fragrance of her skin. He couldn't leave her like this, believing her looks had driven him away. It would only reinforce those negative feelings about her scar.

Raffa told himself he was here for Lily's sake. But he was selfish. He'd followed her because he couldn't walk away, despite knowing he wasn't the man she needed.

'I'm not going anywhere. You're stuck with me.'

'But you said...' Her voice was muffled, her lips caressing his collarbone, shooting sensation to his groin.

'What I said was right. I should go. But I can't. I want you too much.'

Later he'd regret this. Lily would too. But it was beyond him to turn back.

He'd never pretended to be a man of honour. Hadn't he spent his life pandering to excess and self-indulgence? Hadn't he built his fortune on the desire for pleasure? Sure, it had been about providing pleasure for others, but he wasn't spotless. He'd learned to grab what he wanted whenever and wherever temptation offered.

He wanted now.

How badly he wanted.

Bending at the knees, he slipped an arm beneath her legs, another around her back, and hiked her up in his arms. She was all sinuous, lissom curves and smooth, fragrant flesh. Her hair spilled over his bare arm and even that notched his need higher.

Her gasp was loud but it barely registered over the racing thud of his heartbeat as he headed for the bedroom. She'd left her shutters wide open and there was enough light to make out the bed.

His leg hit the mattress and he let himself fall, still cradling her, toppling together but twisting so she didn't take his full weight. Even so, the sensation of her half beneath him sent fire scudding through his body.

'You don't need to do this.' Her voice was half shock

and half bravado. Even in the gloom he made out the tight line of her jaw.

Something, a sensation he wasn't familiar with and couldn't identify, curled in on itself, burrowing through his chest. More than approval, more than pride or even protectiveness.

'You're wrong. I need to do exactly this. I tried not to take advantage, I really did. But I'm not cut out for self-denial.' Not surprising when he'd never tried denying himself anything he wanted, not since he'd worked and finagled his way out of poverty, setting his sights on a better life.

'But—'

Raffa stopped her words with his mouth, damming her protest. An instant later she was returning his kiss with a fervour that shattered his last attempt to hold back. The blaze of wanting consumed them, making her writhe beneath him. His thoughts sped to stripping her out of her swimsuit and impaling himself in her welcoming body as soon as possible.

She's a virgin.

Doesn't that mean anything to you?

The thought diverted his thoughts even as he dragged her shoulder strap down one arm, past the elbow she accommodatingly lifted, and off.

A second later her breast was in his hand, perfect, delectable. He lowered his head, licked a peaked nipple and felt her jerk high off the bed. Raffa stretched out his leg to capture both of hers before he lowered his head again to that stiff peak. He'd thought her taste addictive when he'd kissed her mouth, but this…this made him desperate.

'Please.' Her voice was a moan, her hands clutching him as he drew on her nipple, feeling her shift and buck beneath him.

His erection throbbed against her hip. Much more of this and he'd come before he even got naked.

Lily might be a virgin but she was all passionate woman, and a woman already on the brink.

Pride whispered that it was his seductive skills making her so desperate for release. Logic decreed long-term celibacy played its part.

Twenty-eight and virginal. The thought slowed his urgent touch. For him this surge of desire was remarkable, unique, after years of no interest in sex. But for Lily tonight had to be more. He had to make it perfect.

A man as tainted as he shouldn't be the one to introduce her to sex. But he'd do his damnedest to make it special for her.

Which meant tonight would be all about her.

He looped his fingers under her other shoulder strap and again she helped, eager to peel away the clingy fabric so both breasts were bare.

Her sigh of delight spurred him on as he held her in both hands, weighing those delectable breasts, sucking first one then the other, drawing pleasure from her till he thought he'd go mad from the effort of restraint.

The enticing scent of feminine arousal fogged his brain as he peeled her swimsuit down, over her arching ribs and soft belly, past the jut of her hip bones. His hand brushed the silk between her legs and she shuddered. So ready.

Yet Raffa took his time, rolling the fabric down her legs and away before acquainting himself with the arch of her instep, the slim circle of her ankle, the lush smoothness of her calf. When he kissed her knee and moved higher she sighed.

He followed the sound higher to the smooth flesh of her inner thigh, first one leg, then the other. They were trembling around him as he pushed them wider, jamming his shoulders against her as he opened her to him.

'Please,' she whispered in a purr of sound he knew would haunt his dreams from now on. 'I need you.'

His erection throbbed against the constriction of his

clothes. He wanted to rip his trousers away and thrust his way to release.

Which was why he made no move to undress. He didn't trust himself.

Inching higher, he felt her tension rise. There was something he wanted almost as much as to lose himself in her beautiful body. That was to taste the first orgasm she'd ever accepted from a man.

Lily whimpered as he kissed her there, her fingers tunnelling through his hair, her body restless. He'd barely settled at her centre, had merely taken one slow lick when he felt the fine tremor in her body turn to a judder of building ecstasy.

She cried his name in a hoarse gasp as she accepted the pleasure he gave her, returning it tenfold. Her deep quivers of delight, the tang of her in his mouth and the feel of her flexing, strong yet helpless, beneath him were gifts more precious than he expected. And the way she tugged him close, hands and legs pulling him in, enfolding him as if she couldn't bear to let go…

Had he felt this way before?

The answer was a resounding no.

With Lily he wasn't the cynical man of thirty-three who'd long ago lost interest in women, with their avarice and selfishness. Nor the kid who'd had his first taste of sex as a boy toy of a much older woman seeking diversion. He was someone new.

For years Raffa had used and been used. A commodity craved by women and advertisers who weren't interested in *him*. Never once had he felt as real, as honest, as with Lily.

He lay, centred on her, surrounded by her broken gasps, her trembling limbs and clutching hands, and discovered, to his amazement, it really did feel better to give than to receive. He *wanted* to please her.

Of course he wanted her for himself, but equally he

wanted to bask in her rapture as she learned delight in its many forms.

He lifted his hand, gently caressing her damp curls, and felt her jerk beneath his touch, still so sensitive.

How could he resist an invitation like that?

His expertise with women, his intimate, encyclopaedic knowledge of their bodies, wasn't something to be proud of. He'd acquired it as a necessary skill then later used it to get his own sexual satisfaction quickly. But tonight, as he turned that knowledge to seducing Lily, he was grateful for it. Every touch, every kiss, each slide of his body against hers, each murmured encouragement, had the sole purpose of making her first foray into sex memorable.

Gratification filled him with every sigh she uttered, every sob of delight, every climax. Till finally she lay, utterly spent.

His groin was on fire, his erection impossibly swollen, yet he pulled back.

Tonight was for her.

He couldn't quite believe it, but found himself moving to the side of the bed. Time to let her sleep.

'Don't go.'

'You're awake?' She lay so lax he'd assumed she was out for the count.

'How could I sleep?'

'Close your eyes. You'll sleep soon.' Raffa brushed her hair from her hot brow, feeling an unfamiliar wave of tenderness.

Surprisingly strong fingers caught his wrist. In the darkness he caught the glitter of her stare.

'We're not finished. I want *you*, Raffaele. I don't want to be a virgin anymore.'

Raffa couldn't remember denying himself anything he wanted and he wanted Lily with every fibre. But a decent man would leave her for the lover who, some day, would give her not just sex, but the relationship she deserved. A man nothing like himself.

Fingers shackled his other wrist as he made to move. He could break her hold, but her next words stopped him.

'I'm not a charity case, Raffaele. Don't make me feel like one.' There was just enough light for him to make out the movement of her throat as she swallowed. 'I thought you…wanted me too.'

Did she have any idea how close to the edge her words dragged him? Clearly not.

'Or was all this some elaborate attempt not to hurt my feelings?' Pride was in her stretched-thin voice, but pain too, and defiance.

'You've got a lot to learn about men, *tesoro*, if you think I don't want you.' He yanked her hand from his wrist and jammed it against his chest, where his heart galloped.

He caught the way her eyes widened, then she smiled, slow and wide, with the age-old power of a born seductress.

'Then show me.'

Her hands slipped to his trousers, one fumbling at the button and the other tugging the zip, till he had to rear back lest he lose himself there and then.

A moment later he stood beside the bed, drinking in the sight of her spreadeagled there, her hair a fathomless pool spilling out from her shoulders, her limbs pearly.

A man could only resist so much. He wrenched open the drawer of the bedside table, finding the packet of condoms thoughtfully provided for guests. After that everything blurred till he was naked and rolling on protection.

Then he was on her, flesh to flesh, bone and muscle against sweet femininity, and he was shaking as if he'd never done this before. As if it was his first time, not hers, and he was terrified of getting it wrong.

'This could be a little uncomfortable.' His guttural whisper was unrecognisable as he propped himself above her, taking his weight, holding steady at her entrance.

'You mean it could hurt.' Yet she laughed, as if she felt none of the strain weighing his every movement. 'It's okay. I won't break.'

Her hand slipped down, reaching for him, and instinctively he moved, knowing he couldn't last if she touched him now. The glide became a thrust which turned into a surge of power, taking him deep into close, slick space that opened around him, welcoming him.

There was no gasp of pain, no horror, just a moment of resistance then heaven.

Raffa's breath stalled. He tried to breathe, to calm the pulse storming in his blood, the sharp, rising pull of pleasure. Except Lily confounded him. She wrapped her arms about him, lifted her legs and clung on.

'Yes.' The hot sibilant branded his ear as she rubbed her cheek against his. 'Like that. Please.'

That was all it took for Raffaele Petri, renowned for his sexual expertise and stamina, versed in every carnal art and long past the age of impulsiveness, to buck hard against her, shattering with a roar of anguished delight till the world disappeared in a dizzying swirl.

CHAPTER ELEVEN

HE WASN'T SURE what woke him but for once in his life Raffa wasn't eager to get up. He lay, eyes closed, content to enjoy the comfort of lying here, replete.

Usually he was up straight away, diving into each day with a determination to meet every challenge and win. Today felt different. *He* felt different.

He stretched and immediately stilled, registering warm flesh beneath his arm, against his body. Feminine curves, fragrant and enticing.

Lily.

His eyes snapped open and he found himself staring into a serious, questioning gaze of glowing amber, flecked with brown.

Shock buffeted him.

He'd spent the night in Lily Nolan's bed.

He never spent the night with any woman. They got ideas about permanency and relationships, as if they'd shared more than sex.

Memories bombarded, vivid, intoxicating memories of Lily falling apart again and again. And of him, utterly out of control. Him expecting familiar sexual satisfaction and finding something beyond his wildest imaginings.

Raffa sucked in a breath and slid his hand back from the indent of her waist. It was only then he realised he'd clamped one thigh over hers in his sleep, caging her to him.

As if even in sleep he couldn't let her go.

The mighty erection prodding her belly reinforced that.

'You weren't expecting to see me, then.' Her voice was curiously flat, as if she'd ironed out all emotion. But he felt the sudden rigidity in her, saw the brightness dim in her eyes and the hint of a smile die on her lips.

So it started. The games women played. The emotional blackmail they employed.

Deliberately Raffa stilled in the act of drawing his leg away.

'I didn't expect to see anyone. I sleep alone.' There was a hard edge to his words. He resented explaining himself.

'Then you should have left last night. This is my bed. I didn't invite you here, if you remember.'

'I remember.' She'd infuriated him, worried him, turned what should have been simple sex into something complicated. He'd felt like some dastardly villain when he'd sent her away and she'd fled, drawing the scraps of her dignity behind her. Later, when she'd talked of being ugly and not desirable—he'd been torn between hunger and the fear he'd hurt her even more by taking what they both wanted.

She'd made him confront the dark truth at the core of himself, the sense of being tainted, too soiled to touch an innocent.

Yet he had. He'd given her a night of unabated delight. In the process he'd crossed so many boundaries he'd ventured into unfamiliar territory. A difficult, unpleasant place where feelings burgeoned in the pit of his belly. He felt edgy, like the first time he'd left the warren of familiar childhood streets, not knowing what threatened around the next corner.

Now she looked at him like something she'd tracked in on the bottom of her shoe.

'It's time you left. It's getting late.'

Raffa didn't like the memories her words evoked. It had been years, a lifetime ago, since a woman had shown him the door when his services were no longer required.

He felt a burst of that ancient resentment, as if he were a youth again, frustrated anger at himself for letting himself be used, even if it was his only way out of the hole he'd grown up in. Shame that he managed to find physical pleasure when honour dictated he should take none when money changed hands.

Raffa shoved the memories away. It was a place he didn't visit.

'Why?' he drawled, his voice harsh. 'You're ashamed to be seen letting me out of your villa so early in the morning?'

Her eyes widened. 'More like saving your reputation. I'm sure you'd rather not let it be known where you'd spent the night.'

On the words she lifted her hand and pushed her hair off her face, turning her head a fraction so the sunlight spilling across the bed slanted over her scarred cheek.

Instantly, as if a giant fist smashed into his solar plexus, Raffa's indignation disintegrated.

Even after last night, after he showed her again and again how beautiful she was, how much he craved her, Lily didn't believe it.

'You think your face will repel me?' His voice was a low growl. As if she'd let a tiger into her bedroom. His eyes glittered so fiercely Lily felt almost anxious.

There was nothing to be anxious about. She'd had the sort of night she'd never believed she'd experience, discovering intimacy with the only man who could tempt her to let down her guard. She'd loved every minute and would carry the memories for the rest of her days.

Now it was over. Last night's kindness was over. That was obvious the moment he opened his eyes and reeled back.

It was time to move on.

It wasn't as if she'd expected he'd want a *relationship* with her.

'I think it's a new day and it's time we ended this...' Lily didn't have a word to describe last night. Especially as they still lay naked together, his thigh imprisoning her hip and his shaft pressed against her stomach. She kept her hands tucked together in front of her, knuckles touching his chest when he breathed deep, locked together so she couldn't be tempted to reach out.

Yet inside her muscles clenched and released and clenched again, feeling the empty ache she'd never experienced before Raffaele had taught her to want him. She wanted him to fill that void, hold her close and take her to heaven. Being with him, sharing that ultimate intimacy had been mind-blowing.

'You say that because you're scared.'

'Scared?' She looked into narrowed eyes and felt herself fall into those blue depths. 'Of what?'

'That last night was real.'

He stopped the protest rising in her mouth when he lifted one palm to her face, flattening it over the taut, uneven flesh of her scar. Slowly he dragged his hand down, investigating from temple to chin in excruciating detail.

Lily's pulse jittered and danced within a body frozen in shock.

'Don't. There's no need.'

He shook his head and this time she thought she read a softening in that bright gaze.

'There's every need, Lily.' He leaned forward so his breath feathered her lips. As if on cue, her eyelids lowered in anticipation of his kiss. Even angry and hurt, she couldn't help responding.

What she hadn't expected was for him to kiss not her lips but her cheek. Her maimed, ugly cheek.

She reared back, pushing him away, but he was already there, lips skimming her temple, pressing her ravaged face. Not feather-light touches either. These were real, deliberate. She felt each caress as if branded. Everywhere from her cheekbone to her jaw, the corner of her mouth and out towards her ear. There wasn't a centimetre Raffaele didn't touch.

Lily's breath clogged. She couldn't twist away; his powerful body and hands held her still.

Pain built behind her ribs, rising in her throat to scratch the back of her mouth.

Finally, finally he lifted his head and the air rushed from her in an audible whoosh, collapsing lungs on fire till she drew in another breath, this one redolent of spice and musk and Raffaele.

It was too much. More than Lily could take. Moisture pricked the back of her eyes, her throat constricting.

On a surge of desperate energy she shoved him with both hands. She must have taken him by surprise because he fell back long enough for her to tug away, half-sitting, dragging her hair out from between them. She grabbed the sheet and—

'Stop running away.'

Lily stilled, closing her eyes as she sought something like calm.

'I'm not running. I just don't appreciate you pretending…'

'Pretending what? To be attracted to you? To not be fazed by the fact you've got a mark on your face?'

A mark! As if it were a mole or a smudge instead of a stonking great—

'Yes!' The word hissed from her as she rounded to face him. Gilded by the morning light, rumpled and angry and utterly gorgeous—the sight of him cleaved a shard of pain through her middle. 'I don't want you pretending anymore. Even though I appreciate what you did last night. Don't think I don't.'

She'd expected something hurried and perfunctory. Instead she'd been gifted with a night that dazzled her senses and made her poor heart ache even harder for something she couldn't have.

'You're a slow learner, Lily. How many times do I have to prove I don't give a damn for your scar?' He paused, his scrutiny so intense she felt it track over her. Then he shook his head. 'You're hiding behind that, aren't you? You're using that as an excuse.'

'I don't know what you're talking about.' Desperate, she swung away, shifting closer to the edge of the bed.

'It's easier to pretend it's your scar holding you back, than that you're holding yourself back from living. Because you're a coward.'

Lily froze. Even her heart seemed to stall.

What did this man want from her?

How many times did she have to prove herself?

She'd left her refuge and crossed the globe at his insistence. She'd worn the clothes he'd ordered. She'd swam for the first time in years. She'd sat out in public, baring her face and body to all those curious eyes. From the first there'd been something about him that dared her to live up to his expectations. As if he knew she was stronger than even she realised.

And now she'd given him her virginity—begged him to take it, abandoning herself utterly.

'You're pushing me away because you don't want to admit you want more from me.'

Lily squeezed her eyes shut, letting her head sink towards her chest.

How did he know? Was she so transparent?

'Why do you say that?' That croak of a voice wasn't her own.

'Because I feel the same.'

Stunned, Lily spun round. Raffaele's eyes were serious, his mouth grim. As if she got to *him* as he did her!

'I don't understand.'

His bark of laughter scratched like clawing fingernails up her spine. 'Neither do I. But I know this. I'm not ready to walk away from you, and I don't believe you're ready to do that either. This…attraction between us isn't any-where near over.'

Lily frowned, hope and horror vying for supremacy. 'You don't sound thrilled about it.'

'It wasn't what I planned.'

Slowly she nodded. She understood having a plan and sticking with it. Goals, achievements, more goals. It was how she lived her life. Nice and orderly.

Until Raffaele had woken her in the middle of the night with that heartbreaker of a voice. Ever since, she'd been living out of her comfort zone.

And enjoying it, she realised. He'd dragged her, kicking and screaming, out of her refuge and into…life, with its risks and fears and triumphs. He hadn't treated her gently. He'd challenged and instinctively she'd responded.

A firm hand covered her fist where she still held her hair, caught in a long twist.

'Maybe it's time to let go a little. Do something un-planned and see where it leads.'

Was he talking to himself or her?

'I dare you,' he murmured.

'What? To have an affair?' She sounded so prim. So uptight. So unlike the woman who'd melted to his touch.

Raffaele leaned closer, his wide shoulders hemming her in. 'I don't care what you call it but I want more of it. Of you. Unless you're frightened.'

Of course she was frightened. Who knew what would happen if she gave in to her weakness for this man, not just for a night but longer?

A shimmy of heat flared in her stomach. Excitement. Desire. Greed.

And something else in the region of her heart. It couldn't really be love. Not after such a short time. Not for a man so patently not for her in the long-term.

But in the short-term…

'I'm not scared.' At least her voice didn't shake.

A smile lurked in the grooves at the corners of his mouth. 'Prove it. Now.'

Abruptly he released her and rolled onto his back, spreadeagled across the rumpled sheets. With languid grace he lifted his arms to rest his head on his hands.

He was unashamedly virile. Her gaze traced the dip and bulge of muscle and bone, the jut of his erection, the glint of golden hair and the flash of sapphire as he cast her a sideways glance.

'Put your hair up out of the way.'

Lily hated being ordered to do anything. Yet Raffaele's throaty growl was the most delicious thing she'd ever heard. And it told her what she felt was shared. Heat catapulted through her.

One-handed, she groped across the bedside table, finding a couple of hairpins. Seconds later her hair was pinned up haphazardly.

'And a condom. On the table.' The growl grew deeper.

She turned, saw an unopened foil packet in the litter and felt that throb of need again. Her hand was unsteady as she tore it open.

Who'd have thought twenty-four hours ago that she'd be doing this? Shocked laughter trembled on her lips, only to die as she turned back and saw Raffaele watching. He looked relaxed as a cat, sprawled in the sun, yet the atmosphere was taut with expectation.

She opened her mouth to say she'd never put on a condom before, then realised it was superfluous. Raffaele knew and was challenging her to deal with it.

Biting her cheek, she shuffled across the bed, bashful despite the sizzle in her blood. Kneeling over him, she concentrated on her task, diverted by the feel of him, silk over steel. Inevitably she fumbled, hearing his intake of breath.

'Did I hurt you?' An upwards glance caught his jaw clenched and nostrils flared as if in pain.

'Absolutely not. Just—' he paused to swallow '—finish what you're doing.'

This time, as she smoothed the sheath down, she watched his face and realised it was arousal creating that stark look on his face and turning the thighs beneath her to granite.

She, Lily Nolan, was seducing Raffaele Petri, luring him to the brink of control. He wanted her here, wanted her touch, even if it was a little clumsy. Wanted *her*.

Warmth spread through her body, like sunlight coursing through darkness.

Lily rose on her knees and shuffled forward. Still he didn't move, though the muscles in his arms and shoulders flexed. She hesitated, wishing he'd help her, give a suggestion, but of course there was none. This was about her taking charge. The notion was decadently tempting.

Lily held him, bracing one hand on the bed. A familiar hot spice scent filled her nostrils. His scent, she realised, not some bottled fragrance. It lured, beckoned, as if she wasn't already in his thrall.

Slowly she lowered herself till they touched. She caught fire in Raffaele's bluer than blue eyes and the quick throb of a pulse in his throat. Then, watching him watch her, she eased down, eyes widening at the slow, inexorable, amazing sense of him filling her.

It was like last night only different. Exquisite closeness, a fullness that seemed greater than the physical act of sex. It filled her heart, making her blink from an excess of emotion.

Lily felt the sun on her scarred cheek, saw her lover's gaze drink her in and the look in his eyes made her feel triumphant, special, even beautiful.

If she could bottle this moment she would. But already it was over, the breathless stillness giving way to restlessness as she moved against him, her eyelids flickering as flames licked inside her. Raffaele's hands went to her hips, steadying her when she quivered and hesitated, yet letting her set her own rhythm.

In the morning light she was fascinated to read the signs of his arousal. The clench of a muscle in his jaw, the way his chest heaved high, his stifled gasp when she changed her angle and his hips rose, driving them harder together.

Delight beckoned, but so did the idea of pleasing Raffaele, returning at least a little of the bliss he'd given her last night.

Planting hands on his shoulders, she leaned forward. His gaze riveted on the swing of her breasts, the gleam in his eyes as powerfully arousing as the sensation of their bodies sliding together in perfect harmony.

Lily grabbed one of his hands and planted it on her breast. Instantly his fingers moulded, kneading, not gently but enough to send pleasure rocketing through her. Her movements quickened, more staccato than smooth, but it didn't matter because Raffaele's thrusts kept pace, faster, stronger, more abrupt.

Again that fierce triumph filled her. This was something she could do for him. Lily snagged Raffaele's other hand, pressed it against her breast, holding his hands in place with both of hers.

His mouth sagged as he fought for air, the tendons in his neck standing proud. That big, strong body was trembling, on the brink, and it was more exciting than anything that had gone before.

Lily leaned down, holding his gaze. When she was so close she felt his breath hot on her lips she whispered, 'I want to watch you come, Raffaele.'

There was an instant of silence. His heavy-lidded eyes blinked wide then she felt it, the out-of-control buck of his body, the rushed surge inside her turning into a pulsating thrust that ignited the embers of her own climax. There was a muted growl that turned into a rolling roar. His hands kneaded her breasts, sending bolts of rapture from her nipples to her womb where the fire burst its bounds, devouring her as it devoured him.

Together they jerked and shook and shuddered and through it all she was lost in his azure gaze, reading awe that matched her own.

It was only as she collapsed, muscles failing in the wake of such a potent climax, that Raffaele shifted his grip, pulling her head down to his. He bestowed a kiss that tasted different to any they'd shared. It was slow and tender and, as she gave herself up to it, Lily realised the last of her defences had shattered.

CHAPTER TWELVE

RAFFA LOOKED ACROSS the wide veranda of the plantation house to the man he was here to meet.

The man he was here to ruin.

Triumph stirred. Soon Gabriella would be avenged.

Yet he found it difficult to relish the moment when he was distracted by guilt.

He'd made a mistake bringing Lily with him, despite her desire to see the place. He shouldn't have subjected her to Bradshaw. The man's first startled look at her face had morphed into distaste before he belatedly put on a smarmy smile of welcome and became excruciatingly over-solicitous.

It had made Raffa want to throttle him. But beside him Lily had merely stiffened, her face turning mask-like. Raffa knew her well enough now to realise that mask hid hurt but she wouldn't thank him for interfering.

'It's a lovely old house,' she murmured. 'I particularly like the full-length windows and shutters.'

Bradshaw smiled expansively and launched into a monologue about the property.

Its bones were beautiful but it had been let go. Paint peeled on the shutters and even from here Raffa could see blank spaces inside where furniture and paintings had been emptied from the sitting room.

If it had been *his* family home Raffa would have cherished it, not left it to crumble and fade.

The thought caught him up short.

What a joke. Raffa had inherited nothing except his face. And the family trait. Everyone in his old neighbourhood knew the Petri women were saints, suffering long and stoically. For the Petri men were renowned sinners, handsome rogues who enticed beautiful women into motherhood and occasionally matrimony, then abandoned them. Sordid— that was what they were.

No wonder he'd ended up as he had.

'Sorry?' He caught Bradshaw leaning forward in his seat, obviously repeating something.

'Mr Bradshaw was offering you a tour of the house.' Lily's voice had a husky edge that reminded him what they'd been doing just an hour ago.

Bradshaw was unable to hide his eagerness. 'Or perhaps we should go inside and get straight down to business. Leave the ladies to themselves.' His toothy grin widened as a woman wafted through the French doors onto the veranda as if on cue.

Raffa noted her studied pose, her sinuous walk, and felt recognition stir. Blonde, tanned and overdressed, she flashed a diamond bracelet and a come-hither smile.

Olga Antakova. One-time model and would-be trophy mistress.

'Raffa. It's been ages.' Her voice purred but her eyes were ice chips. No doubt she was remembering the way he'd bundled her out of his limo the night he'd found her there in nothing but a fur coat and aspirations to live as a pampered sex toy.

'Olga.' He inclined his head. 'This is Lily Nolan.' His voice was warm as he said Lily's name and the blonde's eyes widened.

'How do you do, Ms Antakova. Or should I call you Olga?' Lily shot him an impatient look as if wondering why he wasn't already off, closing the deal with Bradshaw.

Lily could be almost as single-minded as him. Raffa admired that. He enjoyed the way her mind worked, the unexpected depths she brought to any discussion. Almost as much as the way she all but purred her pleasure when he touched her.

He rose, telling himself it was stupid to delay here, feeling protective. He knew Lily could look after herself.

Deliberately he put down his glass and turned to the man he'd been pursuing for so long. It was time to put his offer on the table. 'Lead on, Bradshaw.'

Olga was speaking, reminiscing about an opulent society event where she'd played a starring role. Lily tuned out, realising all she had to do was murmur occasional encouragement.

She'd been nervous on the way across the island, wondering if she'd hold her own with Robert Bradshaw and his guests. Even knowing she looked her best in her new dress, she'd been daunted. Despite her growing confidence, she still didn't like meeting strangers and the thought of a crowd filled her with nerves. But she'd been determined not to hide away as she'd once have done. Besides, there were only two people here, and Raffaele was with her.

Should she be worried that made her so happy?

This…relationship was short-term, she knew that. Yet being with him, feeling valued as an equal and especially as a woman, gave her a new perspective and a new confidence.

Thanks to Raffaele for daring her to confront her fears. With him she was a woman capable of anything. Even bringing the sexiest, most powerful man she'd ever met to trembling desperation.

So what if Bradshaw averted his eyes from her face? As for Olga, she'd dismiss any woman who wasn't as glamorous as herself.

What concerned Lily was Raffaele. Behind the confident air she'd read deep-seated tension. Was this deal really so vital? Bizarrely she'd wanted to grab Raffaele's hand and reassure him. As if he weren't perfectly able to deal with a lightweight like Bradshaw.

'So, Raffa is your boss?' Olga didn't wait for her answer but kept talking. Obviously she couldn't conceive of Lily as his lover.

Lily shifted in her chair, imagining how she must look to the glamorous Russian, her damaged face in stark contrast to Raffaele's male beauty.

Then the twist of silver around her wrist caught her eye. Raffaele had presented her with the bangle to go with the dress she'd bought on impulse. It was simple yet elegant and she loved it. It felt like a talisman, reminding her how unexpectedly wonderful her world had become.

It was the first time anyone had bought her jewellery. The first time she'd felt comfortable adorning herself. It had felt momentous, a symbol of a bright new start.

But mostly she'd been thrilled by Raffaele's expression when he gave it to her. Not only approval but—

'You two work closely together?' Olga drained her glass and leaned back languidly. Yet there was nothing languid about her eyes. They were like a cat's, watchful, hungry.

'He must trust you to bring you here.' Olga lifted her hand to play with her tousled curls and the band of diamonds around her wrist sparkled in the sunlight. 'You must know if he's ready yet to do a deal with dear Robert.'

Was the woman really so naive as to expect her to betray a confidence?

Olga leaned forward, her voice dropping. 'Robert's been so reasonable. He even offered a forty-five per cent share of the resort.' She shook her head. 'If Raffa is interested he'd better move fast. Others are interested too.'

So that was the deal. A partnership.

Raffaele hadn't mentioned that. He didn't have partners. He delegated day-to-day management of individual enterprises but he was always the final authority.

Could he change to accommodate a partner?

More to the point, why would he? The resort was charming. But what made it so attractive he'd change the habit of a career and take a partner to get it?

'Well? Is he here to make a deal?' Olga's eagerness was obvious. Maybe she really cared for Bradshaw.

'Raffaele doesn't inform me of his plans.'

'That one keeps everything close to the chest.' Olga's mouth tightened and Lily was consumed with a need to know exactly what had been between Raffaele and the Russian woman. 'But you must have some idea?'

Did that wide-eyed look work with men? 'That's not something I can discuss. One of my conditions of employment is complete confidentiality.'

The other woman leaned back, surveying Lily speculatively.

'That's why you won't talk. You're in love with him, aren't you?'

'Sorry?' Lily gaped, horrified.

The blonde looked knowing. 'You're so protective, like a mother hen guarding her chick.' She laughed, the sound grating. 'As if that one needs your protection.'

Lily plonked her glass down, every muscle and sinew twanging with shock.

In love with Raffaele.

Olga had put into words the fear, the dreadful yearning hope that haunted Lily. She'd told herself it couldn't be true, but in her heart of hearts she hadn't been able to deny it.

'You have an excellent imagination to read that from the fact I won't discuss his business.' Lily was proud of her even tone.

'It's not just that. There's the way your eyes follow him when he's not looking. You eat him up.'

Denial stuck in Lily's throat. *Had* she made her feelings obvious? Sickening fear rose that maybe Raffaele had seen her stare at him like that. Except Olga had specified 'when he's not looking.'

Lily shrugged. 'He's the most attractive man I've ever seen. Why wouldn't I look? But, as for anything else? He's not my type.'

'Let's be frank. He's *every* woman's type. You'd have to be blind not to be attracted. And even if you *were* blind, he knows his way around women. He's had plenty of practice using those skills to get exactly what he wants.'

It was on the tip of Lily's tongue to say Olga wasn't in any position to throw stones, but she snapped her mouth shut. It was no secret Raffaele's life was littered with women.

Lily told herself she was grateful for all that experience. She had no one to compare him with but if she was destined to have just one lover, she'd lucked out with Raffaele. The way he made her feel...

That was when she realised what it was she read in Olga's sharp gaze. Jealousy.

'Raffaele rejected you, did he?'

Lily's words halted Raffa in the doorway.

He'd left Bradshaw ringing his lawyer since Raffa had given tomorrow as the deadline to agree to his terms. He'd cut the meeting short, not wanting to leave Lily with Olga Antakova. Unease had been a low thrum in his belly all through the meeting.

What he hadn't expected was to hear Lily take the Russian head-on.

'Reject *me*?' Olga's tone dripped ice. 'As if I'd give him the chance. I have more taste than to fall for a man like that.'

Raffa's lips twitched. No, Olga hadn't fallen for him, but she had tried to catch him the best way she could. And been furious when he'd spurned her. She represented everything he despised in the high gloss, low sincerity world he inhabited. Sex, affection, even friendship were tools to get what you wanted. Commodities. The woman was a million light years from Lily.

'A man like what? Raffaele is incredibly attractive.'

Call him shallow, but hearing Lily's words felt *good*. They kept him where he was, just out of sight.

Raffa was used to the hyperbole of the media, those 'sexiest man' tags, and to fawning women. Yet hearing Lily admit her attraction in her trademark husky voice had a surprisingly powerful effect. Despite their passionate affair she'd never verbalised it, except when she gasped his name in ecstasy.

'I prefer a man with more class.' Olga was giving her best aristocratic impersonation, as if born to diamonds and caviar.

Raffa took a step forward, ready to make his presence known, but Lily's words stopped him again.

'Class? If Raffaele doesn't have that, I don't know who does. He's savvy and successful but he's decent too. And kind. Not every successful businessman can say that.'

Decent? Kind?

Raffa had been called many things but never, to his knowledge, either of those. Formidable, driven, impatient— that was his current reputation, if you discounted the usual flummery about his looks. And before that? No, neither word fitted the younger him.

'You're attracted by his rough around the edges past?' Olga's voice was frosty. 'I prefer a gentleman.'

'By gentleman I assume you mean someone who never had to work for what he's got?' Lily's voice was even but the precise clip to her words gave her away. 'I'm more impressed by someone who's worked hard for what he has. I find that admirable.'

Her words shouldn't matter. Words had long ago lost any power over him. But Raffa felt his heart bash his rib cage in a double-time rhythm that snared his breath.

He'd never had anyone defend him.

Not since Gabriella.

It made him feel... He couldn't describe the hot turmoil

rising from his belly, clogging his chest and squeezing his throat. Emotion clawed his vitals.

'Oh, Raffa had to work. But not in the way you think.' Olga's tone was snide. 'I met someone who's sure she came across him when he was young, in Italy. You'd be surprised at—'

'Reminiscing, are you, ladies?' He strolled onto the veranda, watching Olga start.

He raised an eyebrow, but she said nothing. She dealt in poison, but wasn't brave enough for a frontal attack. Particularly since she hoped he would pour money in her lover's greedy hands.

He looked at Lily, reading anger in her gleaming eyes and taut frame. Raffa put his hand on her slender shoulder, enjoying the way she instantly eased closer.

'Olga says she knew someone who knew you in Italy.'

'Really?' He held the Russian's eyes. 'What was their name?'

She snapped her gaze away. 'No one important. She wasn't even sure it was you.'

Raffa said nothing. He'd be surprised if her acquaintance would come out publicly with her memories. Nor would it bother him if she did. He'd done what he had to escape poverty.

Yet he tasted bile.

He'd had enough of this place. Dealing with Bradshaw, staying his hand instead of grabbing the man and demanding he admit what he'd done to Gabriella was hard enough. Walking back to find Olga baiting Lily was even worse.

'Ready to go?' His hand tightened on her shoulder and she lifted her gaze to his.

'Absolutely.' She turned to the other woman. 'Goodbye, Olga.'

He slid his hand from Lily's shoulder and threaded his fingers through hers as they stepped onto the path.

She stiffened. 'You want them to know we're not just colleagues?' Lily's whisper was for his ears alone.

'Does it matter? I'm not ashamed of you, Lily. Or of us.' Though the thought surfaced that she'd be ashamed of him if she knew his past.

Lily squeezed his fingers and warmth filled him. She was passionate but outside the bedroom she never touched him.

Because she preferred privacy?

Or because she thought he wanted their liaison kept quiet? As if *she* were some shameful secret.

It was people like himself and Olga and Bradshaw who should be ashamed! Lily ought to be nothing but proud of herself.

Raffa disengaged his hand from Lily's and looped his arm around her shoulder, pulling her hard against his side. Her curves slid against him as they walked and once more that sense of rightness as he held her stifled other thoughts.

A swift turn of her head revealed stunning eyes, brown with an inner glow of amber. A hint of a smile tugged her lips and something in his chest rolled over, as if his heart belly-flopped against his lungs, squeezing the air out.

Raffa stopped, turning to face her.

She lifted her chin, eyebrows rising in question as she planted her hands on his chest.

Deliberately, aware they were in full view of the house, he lowered his head and touched his lips to Lily's. Her mouth opened, inviting him into a realm of sweet pleasure. Instantly any thought of the outside world, of proving a point, disappeared.

Only the knowledge there were better places to kiss her made him eventually pull back. Her eyes shone and her husky laugh urged him on as he clasped her hand and turned towards the resort.

By the time they'd followed the path through the gardens to his bungalow, Lily was breathless and his pulse strummed a quickened beat. Usually he enjoyed the view of the crescent beach and clear waters. Today it didn't register.

Digging for his key card, he tugged her to the door. Palm to wood, he pushed the door open and kept moving.

It was shadowy in the foyer but he read the gleam in Lily's eyes. Her breasts thrust out with each snatched breath.

'So, you find me incredibly attractive, do you?' Raffa strove for light-hearted but his voice emerged rough and urgent.

'You know I do.' Lily stared back. 'That's not news. You've known that for ages.'

Not ages. She'd concealed her feelings well behind her prickly exterior. His *piccola istrice*.

'What are you smiling at?' Her palms flattened on his chest, reigniting that slow-burning fire.

'Me.' He covered her hands with his, his smile fading. 'I can't believe how much I need you.' And not just sexually.

Her words earlier had affected him. Her praise of his character had echoed inside with every step they took back to the villa. Each word swelled inside him, taking up all the available space, clotting his brain, filling him with a pleasure as unfamiliar as it was intoxicating.

Raffa couldn't explain it. Didn't want to. All he wanted was an outlet for this…fullness, this feeling he was about to burst out of his skin. It had to be sexual. There was no other explanation.

One step and he backed her against the wall. Another and he was between her legs, his thigh pressing up. He watched the convulsive movement of her pale throat as she swallowed.

Releasing her hands, he cupped her breasts, revelling in the way they fitted his palms. Seconds later she was groaning, her head lolling against the wall as he rolled her nipples between his fingers.

Raffa bent to scrape his teeth along her bare flesh where

her shoulder curved up to that delectable slender neck. Another groan and she slumped into him, hands on his shoulders for support.

Teeth gritted in a feral smile, Raffa tugged at her dress, lifting it, yanking at her panties till they ripped and fell, leaving him in possession of downy softness. His fingers probed, finding liquid heat as her thighs clamped tight around him.

Urgent now, his need a compulsion he hadn't a hope of taming, he reefed at his trousers, wrenching them open, shoving fabric away till he was unencumbered, fully aroused and sliding against slick, delicate folds.

There. He grabbed her thigh and hooked it over his hip. Just…there and—

'Condom.'

At first Raffa didn't register the wisp of sound. Not till she said it again, a hoarse gasp that made him shudder into stillness just as he began a long, slow thrust into Paradise.

Heat surrounded him. Lush softness. Their laboured breathing. And within him that urgency, unlike anything he'd known, to possess, to claim, to brand Lily as his.

Air sawed from his burning lungs then in again as he managed shallow gasps.

He fought for control. His brain ordered him to withdraw, take the precautions he always did, protect them both. But his body was in full-scale mutiny. It wanted completion, now. Not just completion but to claim Lily rough and hard and completely.

Raffa winced as, finally, he withdrew. The sense of loss was so keen it knifed like a blade through his belly.

Dragging in oxygen, he bent and fumbled for his trousers. His hand met Lily's, already in his pocket.

'Here.' She pressed the packet into his hand.

Her eyes were like gems, he realised. Faceted, gleaming gems, with shards of honey-brown fire.

'Quickly.'

He didn't need encouragement, was already ripping it open with his teeth, extracting the condom and rolling it on.

Lily sighed as he grabbed her hips and plunged inside. Heat met heat and desire coiled tight. He tried to give himself time by focusing on her, watching her eyes flicker half closed and her ripe lips part. She keened his name in that raw, beautiful voice he knew he was the only man ever to hear and that was all it took to drag him over the edge. Raffa thrust hard and shuddered, desperate to capture that pinnacle and take her with him.

Or perhaps she took him, the waves of her climax breaking around him with the force of an ocean surge.

How long they stayed there, sagging against the wall, Raffa didn't know. It seemed hours before he had the strength to carry her to bed, collapsing with her in a tangle of slick, spent bodies.

Never had release been so cataclysmic.

Never once had he come near to forgetting protection.

Lily Nolan affected him as no woman ever had. Raffa realised that for the first time a woman had real power over him. Albeit a power she didn't realise she wielded.

He wanted to spurn the idea, tell himself it was impossible. Yet as sleep claimed him he gathered her close, revelling in the way she clung to him, and smiled.

CHAPTER THIRTEEN

How HAD HE ever thought Lily ordinary? Her eyes glowed and the late-afternoon light turned her sun-kissed hair to bronze. They lay side by side on the sand, spent from sex and swimming. The small beach he'd discovered beyond the resort was deserted and they'd made it theirs.

It was hard to believe just a few hours ago they'd been at Bradshaw's house. This felt a world away from his polluted presence.

'Olga called you Raffa. Were you close?' The sharpness in Lily's question took him by surprise. As did the realisation Lily had never once called him by the diminutive. Yet the way she said his name felt uniquely intimate.

'No. Never.' He covered her hand, hating the idea of Lily believing he'd been with the Russian. 'I met her on a photo shoot. Later she invited herself into my limo and tried to seduce me.'

Lily gaped and he had to repress a smile. 'You're not joking, are you?'

He shook his head.

'I suppose women throw themselves at you all the time.' What was she thinking? Even now sometimes, he found her hard to read.

'It's not always about me. Most of them want the lifestyle. Olga wanted money, not me.'

Lily nodded as she stroked a line from his damp collarbone down his chest. Her lips turned up in a smile that loosened something inside him. 'At least I'm upfront. You know I want your body.'

'Then we're equal,' he growled, drawing his hand over her breast, feeling that tug of satisfaction as her breath caught and her eyes dilated. She looked like a sea nymph, temptation for any man.

Desire stirred. But it didn't diminish that other sensation, the one he'd felt when they came back from Bradshaw's house. That strange fullness, as if just looking at Lily created feelings that crammed him to the brim.

Sex hadn't shifted it. Instead it had settled deep inside him, bone-deep. Raffa frowned, moving his hand down to clasp the curve of her waist.

'What's wrong?' She cupped his jaw, her brow crinkling with concern. Unlike other women, Lily really cared about him. It was distracting, disturbing. And it felt frighteningly good.

No one had cared about him since Gabriella. He found it hard to accept. He and Gabriella had been close as blood could make them. They'd clung to each other after their mother died, fighting the odds to stay together.

'Nothing.'

Wide eyes surveyed him. He could almost hear that analytical brain of hers whirring into gear. 'Was it something Olga said? About the work you used to do?'

If only it were that simple. 'Raffaele?' Lily leaned close and he inhaled the scent of sweet pears, saltwater and warm woman. The combination went to his head, the look in her eyes exacerbating that sensation of fullness, as if a king tide rose within him. 'What work did you do in Italy?'

Raffa hesitated, torn between a lifetime of keeping secrets and the compulsion to trust someone as he hadn't trusted since he was twelve. He'd felt unsettled, not himself, ever since taking Lily to visit Bradshaw.

Finally she dropped her gaze, and her hand. 'It's probably time we went back—'

'I had sex with women for money.'

The words throbbed into echoing silence, broken only by the soft shush of a wave and the squawk of a seabird.

Lily's head jerked up. 'No wonder you're so good at

it.' She stopped, eyes widening as if shocked at her words rather than his. 'You must have made a fortune.'

Lily's response was so unexpected he almost laughed. Except memories of those days were too bitter. 'Hardly a fortune. But enough to feed and clothe me and get me out of the slums.' He had to push out each word. This was something he'd never spoken of.

'I can't imagine real poverty.'

Raffa swallowed what he was going to say, that poverty could make you do terrible things, things you regretted.

'You don't mind?' He couldn't read her thoughts but nor could he see revulsion in her features. Then he realised what he'd asked. Was he seeking Lily's *approval*? His brow knotted.

'It's in the past. I have no right to mind.'

Yet Raffa found himself wanting—what? Absolution? Understanding? It didn't make sense.

'When I was eighteen I met a woman who knew someone that needed a model. The one they'd lined up was ill and they needed a replacement quickly.'

'That's how you started modelling?'

'Yes. Through one of my clients.' He used the word deliberately. Testing Lily's reaction?

Why was her response so important? Raffa lived his life pleasing himself, no one else. Yet he found his hand tight on her waist and his breathing shallow as he waited for her to speak.

'Did it take long to begin modelling full-time?'

'No. They liked my look. I had more work than I could handle.' His mouth twisted. He remembered their excitement at the combination of his looks and streetwise aura. As if growing up in the gutter was a bonus.

'So you were only doing…the other for a short time.'

Was that a blush?

'Long enough. I was almost fifteen when I began.'

'Almost fifteen?' If he'd wanted a reaction he'd got one.

Lily's voice rose, her fingers digging into the muscle of his upper arm as she levered herself up to a sitting position. 'That's…that's appalling!'

Something crumpled in Raffa's chest. He didn't bother moving but sank back onto the sand.

'That's child exploitation. Wasn't there anyone to protect you?'

It took a few seconds to digest that her outrage wasn't directed at him. 'I looked older.'

'It doesn't matter how old you looked. You were a kid.' He saw anger etched in Lily's features. Not because he'd prostituted himself, but because there'd been no one to stop him.

'They were bored and I was there. I spent a lot of time around the marina where the fancy yachts moored.'

Lily shook her head, her damp hair sliding across her shoulders. 'Where was your family?'

Raffa jackknifed up to sit beside her, resting his arms on bent knees. 'I had none.'

'I'm so sorry.' The hand on his arm was gentle and there was true regret in her voice.

He could grow addicted to Lily's empathy.

'It was a long time ago.' Yet the ache when he thought of Gabriella was real. 'Our father left when I was a baby. I have no idea if he's still alive. Our mother died when I was nine.'

'You said "our."'

Raffa fixed his gaze on a yacht out to sea, its sails pristine white against the bright water. He never spoke of this. Yet the compulsion to keep talking was strong. What could it hurt?

'My sister, Gabriella, died when I was twelve. After that I was taken to an orphanage but I kept running away. I spent most of my time on the streets.'

'They didn't treat you well?' She leaned closer, her warmth counteracting the chill in his bones as she pressed into his side.

'Well enough.'

'But?'

He looked down to find her gaze intent.

Ingrained caution warred with the desire to let go, relinquish the barrier he'd constructed around himself. Already Lily had breached it, making him experience feelings that defied logical description. It would be easy to distance himself as he always did, except he didn't want to.

'But I was looking for the man who killed my sister.' With the words came an easing inside, as if someone had slashed open thick cords binding his chest.

'Killed?' Shock filled her. She wrapped her hand tighter around Raffa's arm and leaned against his shoulder.

A mighty sigh racked him.

'My sister looked after me when our mother died, or tried to. I was a handful.' Lily heard self-reproach. 'She was patient, honest and *good*. I was wild and she was the one who reined me in. She took the place of our mother but I didn't make things easy for her.'

'What happened?'

'Gabriella took after our grandmother, who'd been an actress in France. She was beautiful. Stunning.'

Just like Raffaele. Lily had wondered how he came by his fair colouring. Even for a northern Italian it was surely unique.

'As long as I can remember Gabriella caught men's attention, but she never returned it. She was reserved. She never went out partying. She never even had a boyfriend.

'Men invited her out but she never accepted. Until that night. She'd met a man who invited her to a party on his boat and this time she went.'

'He was someone special?'

Lily felt Raffaele stiffen. 'No, she went because of me. I'd been hanging around with kids she didn't approve of and I'd been acting up, accusing her of being too strict.

We had a row.' He sucked in a deep breath. 'She was only eighteen herself and trying to manage a boy with the devil inside him. That night she'd had enough. One minute she was telling me why I shouldn't hang about with that crowd. The next she said she needed some adult conversation and she'd go to the party after all. She took off her apron, put on her shoes and headed out the door.'

Raffaele stared out to sea and Lily followed his gaze, knowing he didn't see the beautiful vista before them.

'I followed at a distance. I'd never seen her lose her temper like that and I was worried.' His voice hollowed. 'I should have stopped her.'

'What happened?' Lily needed to know but didn't want to hear.

'She went to the marina where the expensive cruisers were moored for the boat show. I saw her board one where there was a party—people and music and laughter. I figured I'd see her in the morning but she never came home.' A shudder ripped through him. 'Next day she was found floating in the sea. The coroner said there was alcohol and a cocktail of drugs in her system, including one used in date rape. She died of an overdose.'

Lily's breath hissed between her teeth. Horror prickled her skin, making each hair on her nape and arms stand to attention.

'It wasn't your fault.' Slowly she sat up, relinquishing her hold and turning to him. Raffaele swung round, his eyes locking on hers with such intensity she felt scorched. Such pain she read there. Such guilt.

'If it hadn't been for me she'd never have gone.' His voice ground low. 'Despite what the police said, she was an innocent. I knew Gabriella. She'd never been with a man, never had a drink with one before that night. He drugged her and she died.'

'You saw the man she met?'

Raffaele nodded. 'I told the police but they didn't believe me. I gave a description but they said there was no such person to be found.' He snorted. 'As if he'd stay. The cruiser had gone, but I kept looking year after year.'

'That's why you hung around the marina.' And had been spotted by those rich women who thought nothing of taking a young boy's innocence. Lily's stomach curdled. No wonder Raffaele didn't talk about his past. 'But you never saw him again.'

'Oh, yes, I did. Earlier this year.' Raffaele's voice was glacial, the set of his jaw aggressive. 'That's when I discovered his name—Robert Bradshaw.'

Lily goggled, struggling to take it in. 'The same Robert Bradshaw...?' But of course it was the same. The pieces fell into place, the reason Raffaele was so driven with this deal. She'd *known* there was something between the two men.

She read determination in Raffaele's harsh expression and a fierceness that stirred uneasiness.

'How can you want to work with him?'

'It's harder than I thought.' He inclined his head. 'I look at him and I want to wrap my fingers around his podgy throat and squeeze.'

Lily froze at the lethal intent in his voice.

'You can't be sure he's the one responsible for your sister's death. It might have been someone else on the boat.' She wasn't trying to defend him, but Raffaele's ferocity frightened her.

His head whipped around, his stare like the sheen of polished sapphires, cold and merciless.

'It was his boat. His party. He was the one lusting after Gabriella, I saw it in his face. Even if he wasn't the one to dope her, he was still responsible for her safety.'

Lily agreed. He'd invited Gabriella and should have looked after her. From what she'd seen of Robert Bradshaw, he didn't look after anyone but himself.

'So how can you work with him?'

Raffaele's lips turned up in a slow smile that looked...

carnivorous. 'It's worth it. As soon as this deal is done he'll be dead in the water, financially speaking.'

Lily shuddered at his word choice, her mind going to the image of a young woman, golden-haired like her brother, lifeless in the sea. An instant later she was on her feet, arms wrapped around her torso. Despite the balmy air she felt cold.

'You want revenge.'

'I think of it as justice.' He was at her shoulder, his eyes fixed on the distance. He looked as handsome as ever but the lines of that achingly beautiful face were forbidding, as if the man who'd made sweet love to her just an hour ago had been evicted by a stranger. Someone who knew violence and distrust, who'd been used and abused. Who was completely closed off.

Lily rubbed her hands up her chilled arms.

'How will becoming his partner get justice for your sister? Once you renovate the resort he'll profit from your investment and your experience. How is that punishment?'

Raffaele would turn the place into an ultra-exclusive, über-profitable retreat for the rich and famous. It was what he did. That was why Bradshaw was so desperate to bring Raffaele into the equation, holding off other interested parties.

Raffa's smile widened in a way that made her glad it was Bradshaw in his sights, not her.

'That's the beauty of it.' His voice, like velvet over honed steel, scraped her nerves. 'He's so caught up in anticipating a huge profit he can't see anything else.'

'What else is there to see?' Lily stepped in front of him, forcing him to focus on her. His eyes were bright, almost feverish, and their expression made her uneasy.

'Bradshaw is massively in debt.' Lily nodded. That was no secret. 'He's going to give me majority ownership of the whole island in return for money to cover his most pressing debts.'

'Olga said a forty-five per cent share.'

'That's what Bradshaw offered, not what I'll accept.'

They both knew Bradshaw would take Raffaele's terms. He was desperate.

'He'd lose control of the resort—'

'Not just the resort, the whole island.'

'But in return he can rely on you to upgrade the place and make it profitable in a way he can't.'

'So he thinks.' Raffaele's eyes gleamed.

'You can't do it?' Lily had never heard Raffaele doubt himself and it took her aback.

'Oh, I can do it. But why should I?'

Lily frowned. 'I don't follow. Surely that's the deal— that you invest and upgrade the place?'

'You'd think so, wouldn't you? Whereas, in fact, all I'm promising on paper is the cash to meet his immediate needs. That's already a substantial sum.'

'You're not tied in to upgrading the resort?'

He shook his head. 'No. Bradshaw just assumes I'll make it a priority because of the amount I'm spending to acquire it.'

'But you're in no hurry.'

Lily's breath escaped in a rush. It was on the tip of her tongue to ask what sort of businessman Bradshaw was, but she knew the answer. Her research had revealed a man of puffed-up self-importance who lived the good life but had no clue how to fund it apart from spending the inherited wealth others had accumulated.

'What are you going to do?'

'Once he's signed on the dotted line? Absolutely nothing.'

Lily frowned. 'What about your plans to improve the resort?' She'd heard the enthusiasm in his voice when he spoke of turning it into a truly special place to escape.

'Plans? I have no plans.' Seeing her confusion he went on. 'Oh, I've got ideas on what would make the place work.

It's a shame, really, when there's such potential here, but I've no intention of turning it into a profit-making venture while Bradshaw owns so much as a centimetre of sand here.'

'And you're ensuring he can't interest other investors to do that, by keeping the majority ownership yourself.'

He nodded. 'Not only that. The agreement I've given Bradshaw binds us both to seeking approval from the other before beginning any form of redevelopment.'

'So he's hamstrung. He'll have no saleable assets or income.' He wouldn't be able to sell his minority ownership nor could he start a new money-making venture himself.

She spun round, her gaze going to the headland at the end of the beach, beyond which the resort villas were scattered. What would happen to it? She imagined the buildings crumbling, vegetation taking over with no one to take care of them. For if Raffaele wasn't going to run the place for profit he wouldn't bother taking care of it.

Lily whipped around to face him as a thought lodged in her head. 'What about the staff?'

'What about them?'

'They rely on the resort for their work.'

He shrugged. 'They'll need to find something else.'

Lily looked beyond him to the gorgeous, deserted waters surrounding the island. 'There isn't anything else.'

'Then they'll move.' He frowned and bent to pick up their beach towels. 'There's always work elsewhere.'

'You can't mean that.'

Raffaele's frown became a scowl. 'Of course I mean it. My sole intention in buying this place is to destroy Bradshaw. I intend to see it through. There will be no resort on this island. No enterprise of any kind.'

Something plunged hard in Lily's belly. Her illusions falling and shattering?

She'd believed Raffaele a man she could admire. More, she'd thought herself in love with him. She'd suffered through the story of his murky past and terrible loss but now... Distress churned and she had to fight to stand straight, not bend double, nursing pain.

Lily thrust her hands onto her hips. 'Most of them have lived here for generations. They've brought up their children here. There's even a school.'

Raffaele's shoulders rose and fell. 'A little collateral damage. But don't worry, they'll be helped to relocate. It's no big deal.'

Collateral damage. The unimportant consequence of an action.

Lily knew collateral damage. That was what she'd been the day Tyson Grady had decided to make his ex-girlfriend pay for dumping him. He'd got what he wanted. Rachel never got the chance to go out with anyone else. She'd died as a result of the acid he'd thrown in her face. And Lily— well, Lily had suffered for being in the wrong place at the wrong time.

Bile rose in her throat, threatening to choke her. The sheer arrogance of these males with their feuds and their paybacks sickened her.

'No big deal? This is their *home*!' Her breath snagged in tight lungs. She met Raffaele's gaze and saw no softening, just fierce determination. 'Doesn't that mean anything to you?'

'They can make their home somewhere else. What matters is making sure Bradshaw gets his deserts. Ruining him financially isn't nearly enough. Just be thankful I'm stopping there and not taking the law into my own hands.' There was a flash of something dangerous in those blue eyes. A flash that sent a quiver of fear ricocheting through her.

Lily's hands fell to her sides. The fight went out of her. Bradshaw wasn't the only one to be duped, was he? Suddenly she felt cold, despite the warmth of the sun and the sand.

'I thought I knew you,' she whispered. 'I thought you were…' Her throat closed before she could blurt out any more.

She'd thought he'd risen above his pain and his past to become someone special. She'd thought him kind and caring because he'd helped her face her demons. Instead Raffaele Petri was every bit as hard and conscienceless as she'd first thought. How could she have been so wrong?

'Lily? Where are you going?'

She shoved out an arm to stop him when he stepped towards her. Then she was stumbling over the soft sand, clumsy in her haste to escape.

CHAPTER FOURTEEN

DANNAZIONE! TWELVE HOURS and still Raffa couldn't relax. He strode the path to the hill at the island's centre, needing an outlet for the furious energy that hadn't abated since yesterday and that scene with Lily.

Women!

One minute she was blinking up at him, sympathy in those glistening eyes. The next she was staring at him as if he were a monster.

Raffa's flesh crawled at the memory. He'd grown used to Lily's smiles. She'd even taken his part in the face of Olga's antagonism. He fought his own battles, but her defence had plucked at chords deep within, strumming feelings that still reverberated, refusing to disappear.

Bradshaw was the monster. Who knew how many women he'd abused?

Raffa broke through the trees to the summit. The ocean lay below him, awash with sunrise pinks and oranges. Bradshaw's crumbling mansion was lit in gold. In the other direction the resort lay sleeping.

Except someone else was up. A tiny figure crossed the white sand, wading into the water.

Lily. No one else swam at this hour. That was why he'd come inland.

He stilled, chest heaving. It wasn't exertion that made his heart crash. It was realising he'd come here to avoid her.

Raffa frowned. As a kid on the street he'd learned never to turn his back on the dangerous or the unpleasant.

If there was a problem, better to face it than hope it would magically resolve itself.

And she was a problem. Lily, the woman who'd unleashed worrying new forces, new *feelings*.

All night he'd wrestled with a disturbing desire to do something, say something, to banish her scowl so she'd smile at him like before.

How weak was that?

Was he going to stop his plan for retribution because some locals would be uprooted? They'd be better off on a larger island. Simple economics meant a bigger population attracted better services and job opportunities. He'd ensure they got help to relocate. Once they'd moved they'd probably thank him for the opportunities he'd provided.

This is their home! Lily's words echoed in his head.

She was too emotional. If there were problems with the relocation, he'd fix them. He wasn't like Bradshaw, using then discarding people.

Yet, annoyingly, doubt persisted. Just because he had no concept of home, was it possible he underestimated its importance?

Raffa folded his arms. It was sentimental twaddle.

He'd never had any attachment to 'home.' Even when his mother was alive, he'd rarely seen her as she struggled to support them. He'd been raised in a series of miserable rooms, each more rundown than the last. Home was where his sister was, not in cold concrete.

Yet the churning inside didn't ease.

It was like those early days, looking through windows to glimpse the secure, happy lives of other families, knowing they might as well live on another planet for all the similarity between them and him.

Lily made him feel like an outsider again.

He sucked in a breath, inhaling the scent of dew and foliage and flowers. That hint of sweetness reminded him of Lily's tantalising scent, understated yet seductive.

She'd inveigled her way into his life, not just his bed. The realisation welded his feet to the rocky ground.

Lily mattered.

He'd opened up to her, telling her things he never shared. He'd sweated on her reaction to his past then been relieved when, instead of turning away, she'd offered understanding. For the first time since Gabriella he'd had someone on his side. Someone who saw *him*, not just a face or a body. For that brief space he hadn't been alone. It had felt…good.

Raffa hefted another breath, eyes fixed on the tiny spot that was Lily, swimming in the bay.

He'd done more than open up. *He'd trusted her.* Despite the fact trust didn't come easily.

That was why he'd let her into his life. Why it hurt that she'd spurned him.

He'd waited last night for her to knock on his door, apologise for abandoning him and admit she'd been wrong.

He'd missed her.

Raffa's chest burned, his whole body was drawn tight. But worse was the raw ache right at his centre. An ache that echoed the loss he'd experienced when Gabriella died.

It didn't make sense. He'd only known Lily a few months. He felt protective after all she'd been through. He admired her brain and her sass and her indomitability. And her body. And her laugh.

And the husky way her voice broke when he stroked her supple body. And how she snuggled against him in her sleep. Because she wanted *him*, not his money or his reputation.

She cared. Which meant she'd see sense eventually. She was probably looking for a way to mend their argument right now. Maybe she was nervous about apologising. He knew he could be intimidating.

His pulse kicked at the thought.

In the distance Lily emerged from the water and crossed the beach towards her villa.

Raffa turned and started back down the path, his stride lengthening.

* * *

'Lily?' He pushed the door open and entered. The living room was empty, the shutters open to let in the breeze. Her laptop sat open on the coffee table beside a bag of liquorice. Raffa smiled. He'd watched Lily nibble the stuff when she was working hard, particularly if she was nervous.

Was she nervous about confronting him? Was that why she hadn't come to him?

As he crossed the room Raffa heard the shower. He was drawn by the thought of Lily, naked and glistening, of joining her and ending their argument with hot, satisfying sex.

He forced himself to turn away. This was about more than sex. He didn't know what this was between them, but he was determined to find out. And to find out, they had to talk.

Raffa frowned. Such thoughts were a foreign language, unfamiliar and difficult. Unease prickled between his shoulder blades. Did he really want to go there?

Restless, he stalked to the lounge, grabbing the laptop as he sat. Might as well see what updates Lily had done overnight. There'd be something—a nugget of information on the old plantation estate or some snippet about Bradshaw. The deal would be wrapped up in a few hours when Bradshaw signed. Yet still Lily insisted on working. Unless news of his scheme had changed all that. Suddenly he needed to know.

One tap and the screen came to life. Not a report, but an email.

Raffa was about to minimise the document when the title grabbed his attention.

Re: Island Deal—Urgent.

Maybe it was relevant after all. He scanned the text. It was brief. And it sent shockwaves through him.

Your report was excellent. More needed asap, especially on the counteroffer. What can you dig up? Cash bonus if you get me the info and we seal the deal, plus a week as my guest at the resort.
De Laurentis

Raffa gritted his teeth. De Laurentis. The savvy hotel developer who'd caught him out two years ago on that Greek deal. The one he'd outbid for the Seychelles property.

De Laurentis, asking Lily to provide information on a counteroffer for an island resort.

Raffa stared, the text on the screen blurring. There was a roaring in his ears, like the charge of a hundred motorcycles revving in his head. His belly contracted into a seething mass and pain radiated along his jawline as his teeth ground together.

De Laurentis.

And Lily.

Lily feeding De Laurentis information to rob Raffa of the deal with Bradshaw. Robbing him of his revenge.

'Raffaele?'

Lily hoisted the towel higher across her breasts. Her heart careered madly as wild hope rose.

He'd come.

All night she'd tossed and turned, wanting to go to him, wanting things to be as before. But she hadn't because what he planned was just plain wrong. If she went to his villa he'd seduce her with his beautiful body and rich voice and those big, clever hands. With the way he made her feel special.

She swallowed hard.

If she let him seduce her into acquiescence to his scheme she'd feel tainted, as if she'd betrayed the people who lived here. After all, it was her meticulous research that had got him here, poised to take over Bradshaw's business and close the resort.

But he'd come. He was ready to talk.

'Raffaele?' She loved saying his name. She loved—

He swung his head round, those bluer than blue eyes zeroing in and her buoyant lightness faded. It wasn't tenderness or understanding she read in his face. It was something that made her flesh pinch as if an army of venomous ants swarmed over her, nipping and stinging till she felt hot and distressed.

He shoved her laptop aside and stood.

Instantly she was aware of his superior height. Fury radiated from him as clearly as light from a bonfire.

'You've been busy.' His voice was soft. Not soft like a comfortable embrace but lethally soft, lifting the hair on the back of her neck.

'I've been for a swim.' She took a step forward, vowing not to be intimidated by the man she'd come to care for. He was angry because they took different views on his plans but they'd work through that. She'd already decided she needed to speak with him as soon as possible. Emerging to find him already here just made it easier.

'And you found time for work as well. What a busy woman you are.'

Despite her reassuring self-talk, Lily stopped short. She'd heard Raffaele demanding, angry, reassuring, even tender, but never sarcastic.

'You pay me to work.' It was a matter of pride that even though she was having an affair with the CEO, she still did her job.

'And so do others.'

Was that why he looked so grim?

'You know I've got other clients.'

'Not when I pay for your exclusive services.'

Lily's heart stilled then rushed into an uneven rhythm.

The way he said *exclusive services* made her think of something other than her research.

Heat scorched her breasts and throat. She wished she was fully dressed instead of draped in a towel, her wet hair slick down her back.

'The work is all but done. You said so yourself. My staff needed a hand on a project—'

'I pay for your time, end of story. I told you to clear your other work away.'

'I know but—'

'But nothing, Lily.' He stepped around the end of the lounge, stopping square in her personal space.

Normally that wouldn't matter. Normally she'd be reaching for him, eager to run her hands over his shoulders and into that thick hair, tugging his head down to hers.

But the current of energy running between them wasn't like that. This felt dark, troubling. Threatening.

Lily hitched her chin. 'What's the problem, Raffaele? All I've done is answer a few emails and—'

'And what?' It struck her that for the first time in ages there was not a hint of softening in his eyes. They looked hard and cold as rock crystal. 'And sold a report to my rival?'

'Sorry?'

'Don't play coy. I read the email. You're doing business with De Laurentis. You're selling him information, aren't you?'

Lily frowned. What had that project in Thailand to do with Raffaele? As far as she knew, he had no interests in that part of the world.

'I finalised a report for him weeks ago.'

'And now you're sending him inside information.' He leaned close, his breath brushing her lips. 'Have you forgotten the confidentiality clause in your contract? I can sue you for everything you've got and could ever earn if you betray me.'

Lily stared, reading nothing but antagonism and a thirst for blood, her blood, in that big, bold face.

Her throat scraped raw with the force of her indrawn breath.

'You think I've betrayed you?' Understanding dawned. 'You think I used the information you paid me to find and passed it to someone else.'

'Not just someone else. The only serious rival I've got. And not just the information you unearthed.' His voice was like the lash of a whip. 'I've shared things with you—my plans to take Bradshaw down. The fact I'm not going to give him what he wants—a profitable business he can leech off for the rest of his days. I *trusted* you.'

'You honestly think I betrayed that trust?' Lily's head jerked back as if he'd slapped her. 'You think I shared what you told me in confidence?'

She should be furious. Yet somehow all she felt was pain. Pain that he'd think so little of her. That shimmering joy she'd found with him had been an illusion, as insubstantial as a pool of water on a bed of sand.

'What else can I think? You're dealing information to my biggest rival. Or do you deny it's the same De Laurentis who made a name for himself with top class hotels in Italy? The one now investing in coastal resorts?'

'It's the same man, but—'

'But nothing!' As if hearing the way his voice had risen, he paused. When he spoke again his voice was slow, deliberate and barely above a whisper. 'I pay you an exorbitant salary. I expect discretion and loyalty.'

'I have been discreet and loyal.' The same discretion and loyalty she gave all her clients. Which was why she hadn't told Raffaele when she began working for him that she'd already committed to this job. De Laurentis deserved the same consideration Raffaele did. 'There's been no sharing of information.'

'You expect me to believe that? The man says he's desperate for information you can *dig up* on a counter-offer for this resort.' Raffaele didn't move yet seemed to swell, growing taller, more menacing. 'Well? Speak up.'

This was the man she'd fallen in love with.

The man she'd entrusted with her fragile hopes and dreams. The man she'd leaned on as she forced herself from hiding and into the world.

Hot tears spiked behind her eyes. Distress grabbed her throat and she had to work to find her voice. She laced her fingers together, squeezing.

'Despite how it looks, he's talking about another property. On another continent. I didn't tell you because I didn't see a conflict of interest at the time. They're completely separate. But, because of what's happened between you and me, I was about to write and tell him I can't work for him anymore.'

Lily had known that no matter what happened in the future, whether she worked for Raffaele or not, she couldn't work for his competitors.

'You expect me to believe that?'

Lily stared into that stony face, each beautiful line carved as if in granite. Into eyes that sliced through her. She'd swear she felt the cut right to the bone.

She'd turned herself inside out for Raffaele. He'd burst into her life and made her face her deepest fears head-on. He'd seduced her into believing the world could be an entrancing place, that *she* could be someone she'd never dreamed she could be.

He'd made her love him. And, worse, believe he might care for her, just a little.

And now, in one fell swoop, he'd smashed it all. The hopes, the joy, the trust.

That grim face held no doubt or tenderness. She'd made a monumental fool of herself. What had she been—a diversion? A curiosity? Reclusive and virginal and so naive. Someone a little different for a holiday fling.

Pain raked at her insides.

It wouldn't have hurt as much if he'd accused her of being unattractive. But he'd attacked her in the one place she'd always relied on. The one part of her life where she'd been strong and confident and sure of herself. Her professionalism. She'd believed in that when she'd believed in nothing else. And now he tried to smash that too.

'No, I don't expect you to believe it. I can see you've made up your mind, no matter what I say.' She hauled in oxygen and planted her hands on her hips. Somewhere, deep within, dreams were disintegrating, hopes vanishing. But one lesson Lily had learned well—to conceal hurt.

'There's nothing more to say, Raffaele. In the circumstances, I know you won't want me to work out my notice before I resign.'

Silence. Blankness on his features.

What had she expected? Second thoughts? An apology?

'You can resign tomorrow, *after* I close this deal. And know that if you try to pass any more information to De Laurentis in the meantime, my lawyers will make it their mission to destroy you.'

Silently Lily nodded. Words were beyond her. It took all her energy just to stand tall, bearing the weight of each lashing word.

He turned, glanced at the laptop, and she wondered if he was going to smash that too, or take it with him. Instead he strode to the door without looking back, confident in the knowledge no sane person would ignore his threat of legal action.

Clearly he expected simply to walk out of her life, dismissing all they'd shared. As if that, and she, meant nothing.

'You told me about your past.' Her voice was croaky but she knew he heard. 'The way you spoke made it sound like you felt...' She paused, searching for the right word. 'That you felt *diminished* because of what you'd done to get out of poverty.'

Raffaele stopped, his hand on the door. He didn't turn.

'It's not what you did for a living that taints you. It's the fact you haven't learned to trust anyone but yourself. Until you do you'll always be alone.'

She snatched a heavy breath.

'You made me trust you, Raffaele.' Lily almost choked on his name, but fought back despair. 'I hate that you've shattered that trust. But I intend to be stronger than you. I'm not going to let that destroy me. I'm going to get on with my life and not look back.'

For a heartbeat he stood unmoving, then without a word he dragged open the door and strode into the sunlight.

Had she really expected him to listen?

Lily stood in the centre of the room, rigid with shock. A forlorn, disbelieving part of her hoping he'd return when he calmed down.

He didn't return.

She stood so long, not daring to move lest the hurt inside break free and smash her into tiny pieces. But eventually her legs gave way and she staggered to the lounge.

Fifty minutes later she was on the motor launch heading for the next island. Two hours after that she was airborne, beginning the long trip away from Raffaele.

CHAPTER FIFTEEN

AT LAST IT was done. Bradshaw had signed the papers and Raffa was the majority owner of the island.

He should be crowing with delight, or at least smiling with satisfaction. Instead he felt a sense of anticlimax. As if this long-awaited victory wasn't everything he'd hoped for.

There'd been a moment of predictable, if shallow, pleasure when he'd refused Bradshaw's offer of a champagne toast to celebrate their partnership.

There'd been several minutes of gratification as he'd explained precisely why they would never work together. And the fact that he, Raffa, intended to ensure the island would never make a profit to support the man responsible for killing Gabriella.

Bradshaw had blustered and denied and finally pleaded, but the legal documents were watertight. He didn't have a leg to stand on.

Raffa had listened to Bradshaw ranting and threatening, and waited for the welcome surge of pleasure.

It didn't come. Instead he felt unsettled. Something gnawed at his gut. He and Consuela were almost back to the resort when he realised it was because justice, or vengeance, or whatever you named it, couldn't bring Gabriella back. The hole in his heart was still there, still raw. He'd failed her. If he'd been a better brother—

'My legs aren't as long as yours. Do you mind slowing a little?'

He glanced at Consuela, impeccable as ever in a severe charcoal suit. Interestingly, she didn't look like she'd just achieved a major victory either.

'Sorry. I was thinking.'

'Not happy thoughts. I assumed you'd be pleased.'

He shrugged and gestured for her to precede him where the path through the trees narrowed.

'I've got a few things on my mind.' Not just the unexpected sense of let-down but that scene this morning with Lily. His thoughts had circled back to her words time and again, even when signing the all-important contract.

'Something to do with Lily?'

Raffa's eyes fixed on the woman in front of him but she didn't look back, just kept walking.

'Why should it be to do with her?'

'Because when I arrived at the airport I saw her crossing the tarmac to board a plane.'

Raffa stumbled on the perfectly even surface of the path. 'Lily?' He'd only left her a short time ago. 'You're mistaken.'

Consuela stopped and turned. Her expression was neutral but there was something in her eyes he didn't recognise. 'I know Lily, remember? It was definitely her but she didn't see me. She looked…'

'What? How did she look?' Tension hummed through him, drawing him tight.

Consuela's mouth tightened. 'Let's just say that if the security staff hadn't stopped me I'd have gone over and given her a hug.' Her eyes narrowed and now he recognised her expression. Disapproval. Of him.

'But our flight isn't till tomorrow.' Why he said it he didn't know, except he was struggling to grasp the fact Lily had gone. He felt like someone had blasted a gaping hollow in his chest. He braced his feet wider.

It didn't make sense. He should be pleased to be rid of the woman who'd betrayed him. She'd saved him the necessity of travelling with a corporate spy.

Except ever since he'd accused her he'd felt *wrong*.

As if he were the one at fault.

As if he'd missed something.

As if he should have taken time to listen to her protests of innocence.

Doubt had beaten at him from the moment he'd left her but he hadn't let himself weaken and return. He'd had too much on his mind—his plan to exact justice on Bradshaw.

Now he felt as if he'd got his priorities wrong.

'Tell me. Who else was sniffing around this deal? Who else courted Bradshaw?'

Consuela's eyes widened but she rattled off names. Big leisure company consortiums. The ones he knew about.

'Anyone else? De Laurentis?'

'No, but Lily is the researcher. You should ask her.' One perfectly arched eyebrow rose. 'The last whisper I heard was that he had his sights on something in Asia. Thailand, I think.'

Raffa closed his eyes, a sick feeling dragging at his belly. He'd jumped so eagerly at the idea Lily had betrayed him. Had he *wanted* to believe it? Was it easier to believe the worst than try to live with the unsettling feelings she stirred? What did that say about him?

'Raffa! Are you okay? You look like you're going to keel over.'

He snapped his eyes open, finding no comfort in Consuela's concern.

'Speak to me. What's wrong?'

He lifted his face to the sunlight filtering through the trees. Way above was the wide blue arch of sky where Lily was flying away from him.

Realisation skewered him like an insect on a pin. It was an effort to draw breath and his voice, when he found it, was choked. 'I've just made the biggest mistake of my life.'

'So you'd call yourself a digital nomad, Ms Nolan? Working all around the globe? How do you find that?'

Lily smiled at the woman in the dark suit at the front of the audience. 'Lily, please.' She gripped the podium, not with horrible nerves as when she'd started her presentation, but because it was comfortable.

After visiting her family, joining the women's business breakfast group was the first thing she'd done on her return. She hadn't wanted to. She'd wanted to bury herself at home and stay there. Which was all the proof she needed that she *had* to do this.

She'd been shaking with nerves before each meeting, especially today, but came away each time feeling better than before. This was the first time she'd presented and initially it had been tough. Standing in front of all these people, sharing insights into her enterprise, was the test she'd set herself. Proof that she could and would be strong.

Which was a laugh, given how forlorn she felt. Only the determination to keep busy stopped her from curling up and weeping into her pillow. She wouldn't go back to the woman she'd been before Raffaele had forced her to change.

'Like anything, there are positives and negatives. I can work almost anywhere—'

'Just give me the chance to work on a tropical island,' someone said and there was a ripple of good-natured chuckles.

'It had a lot going for it.' Lily's smile grew fixed as an image of Raffaele filled her brain. The touch of his hands, the velvet tone of his voice, the bliss they'd shared, the sheer, dizzying delight.

And the abyss of pain.

She blinked and refocused.

'But it's still work, wherever I'm located, so access to a reliable network is vital. I couldn't risk long power outages, for instance, so I'd give storm season in the tropics a miss.' She forced a smile into her voice.

'And there are benefits to being in an office, face to face with colleagues. I'm currently looking into ways to make that happen regularly, so my team and I aren't always working in virtual isolation.'

'I'm afraid that's all we have time for this morning.' The MC made her way up to the podium, smiling.

Lily was returning her smile when a ripple of unease skated across her flesh, tugging her body to alert.

A whisper coursed through the room. Lily saw heads turn, not towards her as the MC thanked her and the audience applauded, but towards the back of the room.

Lily shook hands, said something suitable and widened her tight smile. But she didn't hear what the MC said about upcoming events. It was drowned by the thump of her pulse as slowly, with a feeling of inevitability, she lifted her gaze towards the rear exit.

Raffaele. Large as life and more gorgeous than she remembered.

Her knees loosened to wobbling jelly, making her grab the podium for support. A mere couple of months wasn't nearly long enough to get over him.

She'd known it was Raffaele from that first prickle of awareness, that familiar soaring sensation inside. Yet she hadn't believed it.

Fate, and Raffaele, couldn't be that cruel.

But it seemed they could.

The MC struggled to get the crowd's attention. But every woman had turned to watch Raffaele, suave and appallingly handsome in his trademark open-necked shirt, casual jacket and pale trousers that emphasised the length and strength of his powerful limbs. Lily's heart slammed her ribs in a stop-start beat that left her breathless.

His eyes met hers and she'd swear she heard a whoosh of flame as her body ignited.

Or was that her paper-thin defences? She wasn't ready to face him. She needed more time to look convincingly unaffected. Despair lashed her.

The MC said something, motioning her towards the side aisle of the auditorium.

Gaze still locked on Raffaele, Lily stepped away from

the podium, forcing her head up and shoulders back. She prayed she wouldn't stumble on those cotton-wool legs but refused to watch the ground. This was the man who'd used then discarded her like a piece of trash. She'd meet him eye to eye with no hint of weakness.

Vaguely she was aware of the audience watching, of excited whispers. But it was the whispers filling her head that nearly undid her. *Cara, tesoro,* and all those other Italian endearments he'd used in that deep velvet voice.

Lily told herself he'd used them deliberately to get what he wanted—the novelty of a twenty-eight-year-old virgin in his bed. Because if he'd meant any of them he'd have listened to her explanation, given her a chance. He'd have believed her.

She stopped close, staring into azure eyes that reminded her how he'd taken her to heaven. Ruthlessly she shut the memory down, licking her lips to moisten her parched mouth.

Instantly his gaze dropped to her mouth and her breath stalled. One look! That was all it took for him to turn her inside out all over again.

'I presume you want to talk with me?' Her voice was steely. She was amazed at how firm it sounded.

His eyes jerked up and she was surprised at how distracted he looked. How far from the determined, decisive CEO who'd ruthlessly cut her adrift.

For a moment he looked about to speak. Then he nodded and held open the door. The whispers grew to excited speculation as the door swung closed behind them.

'You've changed.' He hadn't meant to blurt it out but he was shocked.

Not by the way Lily had held the audience in the palm of her hand. He knew she was capable and a good communicator when genuinely interested in something.

Nor was it her new clothes that surprised him. She

looked good in slim-fitting trousers, heels and an amber
silk top. More than good. He wanted nothing more than the
freedom to run his hands over her body. Explore the sat-
iny skin of her breasts and inner thighs that no silk could
match. Let down her hair and tug her into him.

She swung her head round so their eyes met and there
it was again, that punch to the gut. That frigid glitter. That
total lack of welcome or warmth.

His belly tightened as terror tugged his vitals. It wasn't
new. It had grown familiar since she'd gone. Yet he'd hoped
for a glimmer of warmth.

'Of course I've changed. You taught me a lot.' Her mouth
twisted and he felt searing pain. 'I learn from my mistakes.'
Then the shutters came up.

She looked like a duchess surveying a beggar. Despite
a lifetime pretending not to care, concealing emotions and
revelling in the success and wealth he'd acquired, this time
it mattered. It reminded him of his pedigree of poverty, his
grubby past and every sordid encounter. Worse, it spoke of
the way he'd mistreated her. Her disdain sliced to his soul,
carving through the vast emptiness inside.

How had he thought he had a chance?

'Raffaele?' Her eyes rounded and for a fleeting moment
her hand brushed his. The silver bangle on her wrist caught
his eye and his heart pounded with excitement.

That touch, that moment of concern, and the fact she
wore his gift, were all it took for hope to rise. Not because
he really stood a chance, but because he had to try. He
couldn't go on like this.

'We need to talk.' He quickened his pace, ushering her
from the building. His hire car was parked at the kerb but
she walked on when he would have opened the car door,
her stride biting the pavement.

'Here.' It was a café. Not private. Not what he'd planned.
But he'd take what he could get.

He followed her in, past empty tables and a display of

cakes. Lily hesitated before taking the furthest table, tucked into a corner. Raffa grabbed a seat, wondering if she realised she couldn't get away unless he moved. He doubted it. She looked distracted, her gaze skittering around the room.

There was silence till they'd ordered and received their coffees. Raffa took a sip and moved the cup away.

'Not up to your high standards?' Disapproval laced her tone.

'I'm not thirsty.' He had no idea how it tasted. His mouth was full of the metallic tang of fear. He leaned towards her. 'I'm sorry, Lily. So sorry.'

Her cup clattered back into its saucer, coffee spilling onto her hand.

Raffa heard her hiss of shock as he grabbed her wrist, pulling it towards him, reaching for a napkin at the same time to blot the hot liquid.

'Don't! I'm all right. I—'

Her words stopped when he lifted her hand, pressing his lips to the spot the liquid had seared. Raffa closed his eyes, a shudder of longing passing through him at the taste of Lily, as sweet and enticing as he remembered.

Pain battered his chest.

'I'm sorry. I can't apologise enough. I accused you of something I should have known you'd never do. I wronged you.' His lips moved against her skin, his eyes shut to block out the rejection he knew he'd see in her face.

He'd never thought himself a coward but he was now. He couldn't bear for her to send him away. His grip tightened on her slender wrist, turning her hand so he could plant a kiss on her palm.

She shivered. From horror? Distaste? Or pleasure?

Raffa forced his eyes open but kept them trained on that small, pale hand, noticing the tint of amber nail polish as her fingers curled over her palm.

His beautiful Lily. He'd feared she might withdraw into

her shell again but she was stronger than he gave her credit for. She'd emerged from her cocoon and nothing, not even a lout like him, would drive her back. He was proud of her.

'Why are you smiling?'

'Because you're even more beautiful than I remembered.'

Instantly she tugged her hand. But he was stronger and he'd use any advantage he had, even brute strength.

'Don't.' She sounded choked, not indifferent. 'You've had your fun. Just leave me alone.' Pain pierced at the hurt in her shadowed eyes and the crooked line of her mouth.

'You think I'm here for *amusement*?' Raffa stared. 'There's nothing amusing about my feelings, *tesoro*.'

'Don't talk like that.' Again she tried to free her hand and failed. 'I know it was…diverting to have a woman so different.' Her voice was a rushed whisper. 'But that's in the past. You can't make a fool of me like that again.'

Holding her wrist, he felt her pulse beat a runaway rhythm almost as fast as his own.

'I know you think you can't believe me after the way I rejected you.' He swallowed a knot of guilt and pain at the memory. 'But one thing you must understand. I was never *amused* by you. You were never a *diversion*. You were the most frighteningly real thing to happen to me in as long as I can remember.'

Raffa clasped her hand in both of his. 'No one else has made me feel the way you do.'

To his despair she shook her head, her mouth a mutinous line. 'You didn't feel anything. You turned on me. If you'd really felt anything for me—'

'Oh, I feel, *piccola istrice*. See how much.' He pushed her hand against his chest, spreading her fingers wide over the place where his heart crashed. 'I feel so much I'm terrified you'll turn me away without a hearing. Or that after hearing me out you'll say you're not interested.'

She blinked, an arrested expression in her eyes. 'Not interested in what?'

He shook his head. 'First I need to apologise properly and explain—'

'Not interested in what?'

This wasn't going as planned. He'd worked out what he needed to say, how he'd say it, and she was turning it all on its head. Turning *him* inside out.

'In me.'

Time stretched out like a bungee cord yanked almost to breaking point.

'I've already had you.'

Raffa couldn't prevent the grunt of pain her words dragged out. His chance was slipping away and he couldn't stop it. Panic nudged closer.

'I'm not talking about sex.' The way she shot a glance over his shoulder at the café behind him told him his voice had risen but he didn't care.

'If you're not talking about sex, what then?'

He swallowed, his mouth dry with fear. Had he ever, in his life, laid himself so bare? It went against every instinct of self-preservation to put himself in anyone's power.

'In me. Body and soul. Heart and mind.' He felt her shiver and hurried on before she could stop him. 'I love you, Lily.'

To his horror he saw her eyes well. He reached out and cupped her cheek, brushing dampness from the corner of her eye with his thumb.

'Don't cry, Lily. Please.' It felt as if she'd wrenched his heart out.

'What do you expect me to do when you say something like that?'

He swiped his thumb over her lush lips, feeling them quiver. 'I *want* you to say yes. That you'll stay with me.'

'I can't think when you do that.'

'Good.' His heart soared at the news. For once he did the

decent thing and pulled back. But he stayed close enough to see how the amber at the centre of her irises glowed as if with an inner fire. Always that had been a sign of Lily's pleasure, or excitement. Or emotion.

'How can you love me? You acted like you hated me that morning.'

'And I've regretted it ever since. I couldn't even concentrate on the deal with Bradshaw because I was too busy regretting my behaviour.'

Her forehead crinkled. 'Then why did you? If you loved me—'

Raffa captured her other hand, holding them both tight. 'It won't seem sensible to someone as logical as you, but feeling the way I do—' he swallowed '—loving you, petrified me. I've never loved anyone except my sister and mother. With you I feel *more*. I care about you, Lily. About making you realise how special you are. About your happiness.'

She opened her mouth and he pressed a finger to her warm lips. 'I trusted you with things I've never spoken about to any other person. I felt drawn to you in ways I didn't understand and it terrified me. I think that's part of the reason I reacted so violently to the possibility of you betraying me. It was easier to push you away than put myself on the line and ask you to love me back.' He drew a slow breath, redolent of coffee and sweet pears and warm female flesh.

'I was frightened you'd reject me.'

Reluctantly he dropped his hand from her mouth. He'd run out of words. Which meant facing her judgement. Desperately he tried to read her thoughts, but Raffaele was stuck on her trembling mouth.

'How many women have rejected you, Raffaele?' Her voice was a thick whisper.

Instantly he was defensive. 'Those women in the past don't count. They didn't know or want me. They wanted my money or my body.' He paused. 'Except I suppose they do matter. Why would you want a man who—?'

Lily tugged her hand free and pressed her palm to his mouth. 'Stop right there.'

She smelled so good, like the dreams that had plagued his sleep since she left. He slicked out his tongue, tasting her, and her hand jerked back.

'I don't care about the women in your past.' Was it really possible?

'Then what do you care about?' Was that a softening in her expression?

'Why would you fall in love with me? It's not sensible.'

'I think it's the most sensible thing I've done in my life. Fall for a woman who's generous, beautiful, sexy, honest, and challenges me to be a better man. I've even rethought my plan for the resort because of you.'

To his horror that beautiful mouth wobbled again. 'How am I supposed to resist you when you're so…?'

'In love?' For the first time since he'd arrived he felt his heart lift. 'Desperate? Ready to do anything?'

'Honest.' She shook her head. 'If you really do feel…'

'I do. I love you, Lily. I've been falling for you since the night you seduced me long-distance with that sexy voice.'

Her eyes widened but a smile fluttered at the corners of her mouth. That smile was like warmth on a freezing winter night.

'I've been falling for you since we sat on your rooftop and you listened to me talk about my hopes and dreams. You were so understanding.'

Raffa stilled, all his senses focused on Lily and the words she'd just used.

'Falling for me?' Was it possible after what he'd done?

She nodded and a flush crept up her throat. 'I've been in love with you for ages.' Her whisper all but stopped his heart. Unfamiliar heat prickled the back of his eyes.

'Raffaele?' She put her hand to his cheek. 'Are you all right?'

He cleared his throat. 'I honestly don't know. I've never felt like this.' At least he knew what this feeling of fullness was, of fear and hope. 'I've never loved anyone like this.'

Her mouth widened into the most beautiful smile he'd ever seen. 'Neither have I.'

For the first time in his life he was lost for words. But not for long. Old shame and new regret hadn't quite died. 'I don't deserve you.'

'Nonsense. You're the best thing that's ever happened to me.' Amber fire sparked in her gaze as if challenging him to disagree. 'By far the best thing.' She paused. 'But I have a question. What is it you call me—*picc*…?'

Raffa grinned. He couldn't help it. He'd never believed such happiness existed. Even the prospect of facing his beloved's wrath when she learned he'd been calling her his little porcupine couldn't dim his smile.

'Why don't we go somewhere more private so I can explain?'

'Why don't we?' Lily placed her hand in his and he knew he was the luckiest man in the world.

EPILOGUE

LILY SMOOTHED HER palms down the scarlet silk skirt of her halter neck dress. Her sexy matching sandals slowed her walk to a sinuous, hip-tilting gait.

The outfit had seemed perfect in the resort boutique but she couldn't help having second thoughts. Maybe something a little less obvious would have been better.

'Lily!' She turned to see Pete from the New York office waving a glass from beyond the pool. 'Great party.'

Beside him Consuela, resplendent in a caftan of blue and purple, chatted with the resort's head butler who, with the rest of the staff, had been given this weekend off.

The island was in carnival, all work done by staff brought in for the duration as everyone involved in redeveloping the resort enjoyed a well-deserved party before the opening next week.

Calypso music filled the air and laughing children wove between the adults before jumping into the pool with the maximum possible splashes. Lily laughed too. Raffaele had done something special here. She was proud of him.

After Robert Bradshaw heard what Raffaele intended for the island it had been easy to persuade him to take cash for the rest of his claim to it. According to Raffaele, that meant after he paid off his debts he'd have enough to support himself on the equivalent of a modest wage for a couple of years. More than enough time for him to find an honest job. Though Lily couldn't imagine him working.

Now the island was a shared enterprise. The resort workers whose families had lived here for generations were the principal owners and Raffaele a minority shareholder. It had been a staggeringly generous gesture but it made everyone happy, not least Raffaele, who seemed to think he had to atone for his past.

Lily didn't care about his past, so long as she could help him make his future all it should be.

She wove through the party towards the new restaurant. There was Raffaele in conversation with the head chef. Lily slipped her hand under Raffaele's arm.

Every doubt she'd had about her dress dissolved as he turned and took her in from head to toe. The gleam in his eyes told her everything she needed to know but he said it anyway. 'You look gorgeous.'

His lips were gentle on hers but she felt the way he held himself in check, because she felt the same. When he lifted his head his smile was just for her.

'You'll have to excuse me, Henry,' Raffaele said to the chef. 'There's somewhere else I need to be.'

'Sure.' Henry grinned. 'I'll see you later.'

Raffaele made to pull her closer, but Lily stepped back, threading their fingers together. 'Not here.'

Eyebrows raised, he followed her, patiently waiting as they left the celebration behind and finally emerged on the path behind their private beach. Through the trees stood the shell of what would be their sometime home. Raffaele had offered to relocate to Australia but Lily had refused, for now happy to move wherever business took them.

'What is it, my love?' His voice, that rich-as-caramel caress, wove its magic and she melted into him.

'There's something I need to know.'

'Hmm?' He dipped his head to nibble her neck and Lily's head lolled back, warmth filling her. But still nerves prickled her nape.

She'd planned her words carefully, but they were fading from her brain. Raffaele had the power to undo her.

'I want to know if you'll marry me.' The words shot out before his sensual assault stopped thought.

He stilled. Eyes brighter than the heavens met hers. They

were questioning, stunned. 'You want to make an honest man of me?' The hint of humour couldn't hide his doubts.

'You're already an honest man.' He didn't speak of it but she knew he still felt guilty over his past. Lily threaded her hands through his thick golden hair and pulled his head down. 'You're the only man for me, Raffaele. I want to be with you always.' She watched him swallow hard. 'Unless marriage makes you uncomfortable.'

'No!' He wrapped his arm around her waist, his other hand warm at the back of her neck. 'If you really believe it would work—'

'I *know* it will work.'

'Well, then.' He pressed a tender kiss to her lips. 'We both know I rely on your advice on all important projects.'

'Is that a yes?' Lily's heart skipped.

'You think I'd let you go now?' He shook his head. 'I may have a lot to learn about relationships and feelings but I'm not crazy. Of course it's yes. I want to spend my life with you, *piccola istrice*.'

'I am *not* your little porcupine.' She pushed his shoulders in mock outrage, enjoying how he pulled her close so she felt his muscled body through the thin silk.

'No? But I so enjoy soothing you—' his big hand traced fire down her breast '—till you let down your guard.'

Lily sighed. 'Sounds like a lifetime's project.'

His lazy smile stole her heart all over again. It was brighter than the sunrise and warmed her to the core of her being. 'That's the plan. And I've never looked forward to anything more.'

* * * * *

HIS FOREVER
FAMILY

SARAH M. ANDERSON

To Sasha Devlin, my Spring Fling buddy.
We'll always have Chicago! And when we don't,
we'll always have Twitter!

One

"Come on, Ms. Reese," Marcus Warren called over his shoulder. "It's not that hot."

He paused in the middle of the jogging path to wait for his executive assistant, Liberty Reese, to catch up with him. He looked around, checking for any vans with dark windows that didn't belong. It was an old habit, keeping an eye out for danger. But as usual, aside from some other runners, he and Ms. Reese had the shoreline to themselves. Thank God. The past was in the past, he repeated to himself until his anxiety faded.

Man, he loved Lake Michigan. The early-morning light made the rippling water a deep blue. The sky was clear and warmed by the sun, which seemed to hover just about a foot over the surface of the water. Later today, the heat would be oppressive, but right now, running along the lakefront with a cool breeze blowing in from the water?

This was as close to free as Marcus got to feel.

He checked his Fitbit. His heart rate was falling. "You're not going to let the heat beat you, are you, Ms. Reese?" he teased, stretching out his quads.

Ms. Reese puffed up next to him. "May I take a moment to point out—again—that you're not taking notes while you run?" she said, glaring at him.

But he wasn't fooled. He saw the way the corner of her lips curved up as she said it. She was trying not to smile.

He kept stretching so she could catch her breath. "But I'm talking. That counts for something, right?"

She rolled her eyes and finished off the water. That made him grin. He was Marcus Warren, heir to his father's Warren Investments financial empire *and* his mother's Marquis Hotel empire. He was the sole owner of Warren Capital, a venture capital firm he'd started with his trust-fund money. He owned half of the Chicago Blackhawks and a quarter of the Chicago Bulls, in addition to 75 percent of the pro soccer team, the Chicago Fire. He was one of the richest bachelors in the country and possibly the richest one in Chicago.

People simply did not roll their eyes at him.

Except for Ms. Reese.

She tucked the bottle back into her belt. Then, her fingers hovering over the Bluetooth earpiece she wore at all times, she asked, "So how do you want to proceed with the watchmakers?"

Rock City Watches was a boutique firm that had set up shop in downtown Detroit and wanted a fresh round of investing to expand its operations. Marcus looked at his watch, made just for him. The 24-karat gold casing was warm against his skin. "What do you think?"

Ms. Reese sighed heavily and began to plod up the jogging path again. She was not a particularly graceful runner—*plodding* was the only word for it—but she kept up with him and took notes while they ran. It was the most productive time of day. He did his best thinking while they ran.

Which was why they ran every single day, in rain or heat. Ice was about the only thing that kept them indoors, but he had a treadmill in a room off his office. Ms. Reese could sit at a small desk and record everything and provide her opinion.

He let her get a few feet ahead of him. No, she was not terribly graceful. But that didn't stop him from admiring the view. Ms. Reese had curves—more than enough curves to give a man pause.

He shook his head, pushing all thoughts of her backside from his mind. He was not the kind of billionaire who slept with his secretary. His father had done that enough for both of them. Marcus's relationship with Ms. Reese was strictly business. Well, business and running.

He caught up to her easily. "Well?"

"No one wears watches anymore," she panted. "Unless it's a smart watch."

"Excellent point. I'll invest twenty-five million in Rock City Watches."

Ms. Reese stumbled a bit in surprise. Marcus reached out and steadied her. He didn't allow his hand to linger on her warm skin. "You okay? We're almost to the fountain." Buckingham Fountain was the point where they turned around and headed back.

She gave him a hell of a side eye. "I'm fine. How did you get from *timepieces are a dead market* to *let's invest another twenty-five million*?"

"If no one wears watches anymore, then they become what they once were—a status symbol," he explained. "Only the wealthiest consumers can afford a watch that costs several grand. The timepiece market isn't dead, Ms. Reese. The mass-market timepiece market is. But the luxury timepiece market?" He held out his wrist. "It's a hell of a nice watch, don't you think?" This particular watch went for $4,500.

She nodded. "It'll be great PR, as well. Made in America and all that."

"But they need to accept the realities of the market."

She nodded. "Such as?"

"Marketing and wearables. Let's get back to the Rock City Watch people with requests to see their marketing mock-ups. I also want to set up a meeting to discuss a hybrid device—a luxury watch that can slot wearable tech into the band."

They reached the fountain and she stopped, her head down and her hands on her knees as she took in great gulps of air.

"What else?" he asked.

"You have to make a decision about attending the Hanson wedding," she said in between gasps.

Marcus groaned. "Do I have to?"

"You're the one who decided you should go to this wedding," she told him flatly. "You're the one who decided you should take a date. And you're the one who decided to kill two birds with one stone by scheduling the meeting with the producers of *Feeding Frenzy* the day after the wedding."

Marcus allowed himself to scowl at his assistant. Her lack of sympathy was not comforting. Attending the Hanson-Spears wedding in Los Angeles had not, in fact, been his idea. Who the hell wanted to watch his former fiancée get married to the man she'd cheated on him with? Not him.

But his mother had decreed that Marcus would attend the wedding with a date and put on a happy face so they could "put this unfortunate event behind them." Of course, if his mother had had her way, Marcus would have married Lillibeth Hanson anyway because what was a little affair in the grand scheme of things? Lillibeth came from old money. Marcus came from old money and made new money. Together, his parents had reasoned, they could apparently rule the world.

Marcus didn't see the point. He'd refused to reconcile with Lillibeth and he'd thought his parents had accepted that decision. But then the wedding invitation came.

And the hell of it was, his parents were not entirely wrong about the effects the scandal had had on Marcus's business. To some, his inability to see the truth about Lillibeth until it was too late might also indicate an inability to make good investment choices. So his parents had strongly suggested he attend the wedding to show that everyone was on good terms. And they *strongly* suggested he take a date because it would be an admission of defeat to show up at your ex's wedding alone.

All Marcus had to do was pick a woman.

He looked at Liberty. "What are my options, again?"

"Rosetta Naylor."

Marcus cringed at the celebutante's name. "Too shallow."

"Katerine Nabakov."

"Too Russian Mafia."

Liberty sighed heavily. "Emma Green?"

Marcus scowled harder. He had actually gone out with Emma several times. "Really?"

"She's a known quantity," Liberty explained. "No surprises."

"Wrong. People would think that us dating again is a sure sign of wedding bells." Specifically, his parents.

Marcus had done many things to keep the peace with his mother and father. Hell, he'd come damn close to getting married to Lillibeth Hanson, all because they thought that was best.

He wasn't going to risk that kind of trap again.

"The options are limited and time is running short, Mr. Warren," Liberty said in exasperation. She jammed her hands on her hips. "The wedding is in two weeks. If you insist on attending with a date, you need to actually ask someone to go with you."

"Fine. I'll just take you."

The effect of this statement was immediate. Liberty's eyes went wide and her mouth dropped open and, in a fraction of a second, her gaze dropped over his body. Something that looked a hell of a lot like want flashed over her face.

What? Did she actually *want* him?

Then it was gone. She straightened up and did her best to look imperial. "Mr. Warren, be serious."

"I am serious. I trust you." He took a step toward her. "Sometimes I think…you're the only person who's honest with me. You wouldn't try to sell all the details of a date to the gossip rags." Which had been a huge part of the scandal with Lillibeth. She had capitalized on her affair, painting Marcus as a lousy boyfriend both in and out of the bedroom.

Liberty bit at her lower lip. "Honestly? I don't think you should go at all. Why would you give her the chance to hurt you again?" Her voice had dropped and she didn't sound imperial at all. Instead, she sounded…as if she wanted to protect him.

It was a fair question. He didn't want to go. He didn't want to give Lillibeth the chance to cut him down again. But he'd promised his parents that he'd put a good face on it and make sure the Warren name still meant power and money.

"And for the record," she went on, "I think doing that *Feeding Frenzy* reality show is also a bad idea. The whole problem with Lillibeth was that your private life suddenly became public fodder. Going on television to bid on investment ideas? You're just inviting people to further make a commodity out of you."

"It's supposed to be a good way to build my brand."

Liberty rolled her eyes again, as if that was the stupidest thing she'd ever heard. "Seriously? You've built a successful venture capital firm without being a celebrity. You have plenty of people dying to pitch to you. Heck, I'm surprised we haven't been accosted by a 'jogger' lying in wait to pitch you his million-dollar idea yet."

He tensed at the idea of being accosted by anyone. But no—no suspicious vehicles with armed men were around. The past was in the past.

"But you know what?" Liberty took a step toward him, jabbing at him with her index finger. She could be a formidable woman in her own right. "You do this reality show, that's exactly what's going to happen. You won't be able to run along the lake without plowing through idiots in running shoes who want a piece of your time and your fortune. Don't feed the machine, Marcus. Don't do what 'they' think you should do. For the love of God, do what *you* want."

Marcus. Had she ever called him by his first name before? He didn't think so. The way her lips moved over his name—that was the sort of thing he'd remember. "Maybe I want to take you to the wedding."

It was hard to say if she blushed, as she was already red faced from the run and the heat. But something in her expression changed. "No," she said flatly. Before he could take the rejection personally, she added, "I—it—would be bad for you."

He could hear the pain in her voice. He took a step toward her and put a hand on her shoulder. She looked up, her eyes wide and—hopeful? His hand drifted from her shoulder to her cheek and damned if she didn't lean into his touch. "How could you be bad for me?"

The moment the words left his mouth, he realized he'd pushed this too far. Yes, Liberty Reese was an exceptional assistant and yes, she was beautiful—when she wasn't struggling through a summer run.

But what had started as an offhand comment about a date to a wedding now meant something else. Something more.

She shut down on him. She stepped out of his touch and turned to face the lake. "It's getting warmer," she said in a monotone voice. "We need to finish our run."

"Do you have any water left?"

She looked sheepish. "No."

He held out his hand. "Give me your bottle. There's a water fountain a couple hundred yards away. I'll fill it up."

She unhooked her bottle and handed it over. "Thanks," she said, sounding perfectly normal, as if he hadn't just asked her out and touched her face. As if she hadn't turned him down flat. Somehow, it made him admire her even more. "I'll wait here. Try not to get any brilliant ideas, okay?"

Marcus took off at top speed. He heard Liberty shout, "Show-off!"

He laughed.

The water in the drinking fountain was too warm. He let it run for a few seconds, hoping it'd cool off. As he waited, he looked around. There was a trash can only a few feet away, boxes and bags piled around it on the ground. Marcus scowled at the garbage. Why couldn't people take care of the park, dammit? The trash can was right there.

As he filled the water bottle and debated calling the mayor about the garbage pickup schedule, he heard a noise. It was a small noise, but it didn't belong. It wasn't a gull crying or a squirrel scampering—it was closer to a...a cat mewing?

Marcus looked around, trying to find the source of the noise. A shoe box on the ground next to the trash can moved.

Marcus's stomach fell in. Oh, no—who would throw a kitten away? He hurried over to the box and pulled the lid off and—

Sweet Jesus. Not a cat. Not a kitten.

A *baby*.

Two

Breathing hard, Liberty admired the view as Marcus sprinted away from her. When he reached the water fountain, she turned her attention back to the lake. It wouldn't do to be caught staring at her boss's ass. Even if it was a *fine* ass. And even if the owner had just made one of himself.

Instead, she took the time to appreciate the gift that was this morning. She hadn't set foot in a church in a good fifteen years. But every morning she stood here and looked out on Lake Michigan and gave thanks to God or the higher power or whoever the hell was listening.

She was alive. She was healthy. She had a good job that paid for food and a safe apartment. There was even some money left over for things like running shoes and haircuts.

"Liberty?" Marcus yelled from the water fountain. "Liberty!"

Even though Marcus couldn't see her, she glared at him. What the hell had gotten into him this morning? One of the reasons she worked for him—aside from the insane salary he paid her—was the fact that he treated her as an equal. It was a bit of delusion on her part to pretend that she was on par with the likes of Marcus Warren, but it was her delusion, dammit.

And that delusion worked only because it was just her and Marcus on these runs, both in running clothes. The delusion didn't work when he was wearing a four-thousand-dollar suit and she had on the finest suit she could find on 80 percent clearance at Macy's. And the delusion sure as hell wouldn't work if she accompanied him to a three-day destination wedding extravaganza that no doubt cost more than she'd ever earn in her lifetime.

Someone would see through her facade. It'd get ugly, fast.

"Liberty!" He was even louder this time.

Was he not used to women saying no to him? Oh, whom was she kidding? Women didn't say no to him. Why would they? He was gorgeous, single, richer than sin and eminently respectable. "What?"

"I need you!" he yelled over his shoulder. "Hurry!"

She realized he wasn't standing at the water fountain anymore. He was on his knees by a trash can in the gravel that surrounded the fountain. His shoulders were hunched over and he looked as if—oh, God, he wasn't having a heart attack, was he?

Liberty began to hurry. The three years of daily morning runs with Marcus had given her enough stamina that she broke into a flat-out run.

"Are you okay?" she demanded as she came up to him. "Marcus—what's wrong?"

He looked up at her, his eyes wide with fear and one hand over his mouth. Just then, something in front of him made a pitiful little noise.

She looked down. What she saw didn't make sense at

first. There was a box and inside was something small and dark and moving.

"Baby?" Marcus said in a strangled voice.

"Baby!" Liberty cried with a start. She didn't know much about babies, but this child couldn't be more than a week old. The baby was wrapped in a filthy rag, and dark smudges that might have been dirt but were more the color of dried blood covered its dark skin. Wisps of black hair were plastered to its tiny little head. Liberty stared in total shock, trying to make sense of it: an African American newborn in a shoe box by the trash can.

"It was—the box—it was closed," Marcus began to babble. "And I heard a noise and—baby. Baby!"

The baby opened its little mouth and let out another cry, louder this time. The sound broke Liberty out of her shock. Jesus Christ, someone had tried to throw this baby away! In a box in this heat? "Move," she commanded and Marcus dutifully scooted out of her way.

Her hands shaking, Liberty lifted the baby out of the box. The rag fell away from the impossibly tiny body—no diaper. A boy, and he was caked in filth.

"Oh, my God," she whispered as the baby's back arched and it let out a squeal. His little body was like a furnace in her hands.

"What do we do?" Marcus asked. He was clearly panicking.

And Liberty couldn't blame him. "Water," she realized. "He's too hot."

Marcus held out her water bottle, the one he'd been filling. She grabbed the rag and said, "Soak that in the fountain," and took her bottle.

The baby squirmed mightily in her arms and she had this moment that was almost an out-of-body thing, where instead of looking down at a little baby boy she'd just plucked from a shoe box, she was looking down at William, the baby brother she'd never gotten the chance to see, much less hold. Was this what he'd been like, after their mother gave birth in prison and the baby was taken away to a foster home? Had William died like this?

No. This baby, whoever he was, was not going to die. Not if she had anything to do with it.

"This is disgusting," Marcus said, but she didn't pay any attention to him.

She folded herself into a cross-legged position on the gravel, ignoring the way the rocks dug into her skin. "It's okay," she soothed as she tried to dribble some water into the baby's mouth. "You're a good boy, aren't you? Oh, you're such a sweetheart." The baby turned his head from side to side and wailed piteously. Panic gripped her. What if he wasn't going to make it? What if she couldn't save him? "You're loved," she told him, tears coming to her eyes. "And you're so strong. You can do this, okay?"

"Here," Marcus said, thrusting the rag at her. Except it wasn't the rag—it was his shirt.

She looked up and found herself staring right at Marcus Warren's bare chest. In any other circumstances she would have taken her time admiring the view because *damn*. He was muscled and cut—but still lean. He had a true runner's body.

The baby whimpered. Right. She had much more important things to deal with than her boss suddenly half-naked. She held the baby away from her body. "Drape it over him."

Marcus did as he was told, laying the sopping-wet cloth over the baby's body. The sudden temperature change made the poor thing howl. "It's okay," she murmured to him, trying to get a little water into his mouth. "You'll feel better soon."

"Should I go for help? What should we do?"

Help. That would be a good thing. "My phone is in my pack," she said. He didn't run with his phone—that was her job. "Call 911." She was amazed at how calm she sounded, as if finding a baby on the verge of heatstroke in the trash was just another Tuesday in her life.

Marcus crouched behind her and dug through the fanny pack that held her water, keys and phone. "Got it." She told him her password without a second thought and he dialed. "We're at Buckingham Fountain and we found a baby in the trash," Marcus said way too loudly into the phone.

"Shh, shh," Liberty soothed as Marcus talked to the 911 dispatcher. "Here, let's try this." She dipped her finger into the water and held it against the baby's mouth. He sucked at it eagerly and made a little protest when she pulled her finger away to dip it into the water again.

He latched on to her finger a second time—which had the side benefit of cutting off the crying. Liberty took a deep breath and tried to think. There'd been a baby at her second foster home. How had the foster mother calmed that baby down?

Oh, yes. She remembered now. She began to rock back and forth, the gravel cutting into her legs. "That's a good boy," she said, her ears straining for the sounds of sirens. "You're loved. You can do it."

Agonizingly long minutes passed. She couldn't get the baby to take much more water, but he sucked on the tip of her finger fiercely. As she rocked and soothed him, his body relaxed and he curled up against her side. Liberty held him even tighter.

"Is he okay?" Marcus demanded.

She looked up at him, trying not to stare at his body. Never in the three years she'd worked for Marcus had she seen him even half this panicked. "I think he fell asleep. The poor thing. He can't be more than a few days old."

"How could anyone just leave him?" Now, that was more like the Marcus she knew—frustrated when the world did not conform to his standards.

"You'd be surprised," she mumbled, dropping her gaze back to the baby, who was still ferociously tugging on her finger in his sleep. Aside from being hot and filthy, he looked healthy. Of course, she'd never seen William before he died in foster care, so she didn't know what a drug-addicted newborn looked like. This child's head was round and his eyes were still swollen; she'd seen pictures of newborns who looked like him. She just couldn't tell.

"You're just about perfect, you know?" she told the infant. Then she said to Marcus, "Here, wet your shirt again. I think he's cooling down."

Marcus did as he was told. "You're doing an amazing job," he said as she wrapped the wet cloth around the baby's body. The baby started at the temperature change, but didn't let go of her finger. Marcus went on, "I didn't know you knew so much about babies," and she didn't miss the awe in his voice.

There's a lot you don't know about me. But she didn't say it because it'd been less than—what, twenty minutes? If that. It'd been less than twenty minutes since Marcus Warren had said he trusted her because she was the one person who was honest with him.

She wasn't—honest with him, that was. But that didn't mean she wanted to lie outright to him. She hated lying at all but she did what she had to do to survive.

So, instead, she said, "Must be the mothering instinct." What else could it be? Here was a baby who needed her in a truly primal way and Liberty had responded.

The baby sighed in what she hoped was contentment and she felt her heart clinch. "Such a good boy," she said, leaning down to kiss his little forehead.

Sirens came screaming toward them. Then the paramedics were upon them and everything happened *fast*. The baby was plucked from her arms and carried into the ambulance, where he wailed even louder. It tore her up to hear him cry like that.

At the same time, a police officer arrived and took statements from her and Marcus. Liberty found herself half listening to the questions as she stood at the back of the open ambulance while the medics dug out a pacifier and wrapped the baby in a clean blanket.

"Is he going to be okay?" she asked when one of the paramedics hopped out of the back and started to close the door.

"Hard to say," the man said.

"Where are you taking him?"

"Northwestern is closest."

Marcus broke off talking with the cop to say, "Take him to Children's." At some point, he'd put his shirt back on. It looked far worse for wear.

The paramedic shrugged and closed the doors, cutting Liberty off from the baby. The ambulance drove off—lights flashing but no sirens blaring.

The cop finished taking their statements. Liberty asked, "Will you be able to find the mother?"

Much like the paramedic, the cop shrugged. She supposed she shouldn't have been surprised. After all, she'd barely survived childhood because, aside from Grandma Devlin, people couldn't be bothered to check on little Liberty Reese. "It's a crime to abandon a baby," he said. "If the mother had left the baby at a police station, that's one thing. But…" He shrugged again. "Don't know if we'll find her, though. Usually babies are dumped close to where they're born, and someone in the neighborhood knows something. But the middle of the park?" He turned, as if the conversation was over.

"What'll happen to the baby?" Marcus asked, but Liberty could have told him.

If they couldn't find the mother or the father, the baby would go into the foster system. He'd be put up for adoption, eventually, but that might take a while until his case was closed. And by then, he might not be the tiny little baby he was right now. He might be bigger. And he was African American. That made it that much harder to get adopted.

She looked in the direction the ambulance had gone.

The cop gave Marcus a sad smile. "DCFS will take care of it," he said.

Liberty cringed. She did not have warm and fuzzy memories of the Department of Child and Family Services. All she had were grainy memories of frazzled caseworkers who couldn't be bothered. Grown-up Liberty knew that was because the caseworkers were overwhelmed by the sheer number of kids in the system. But little-kid Liberty only remembered trying to ask questions about why her mom or even Grandma Devlin wasn't going to come get her and being told, "Don't worry about it," as if that would make up for her mother's sudden disappearances.

What would happen to the baby? She looked at her arms, wondering at how empty they felt. "Marcus," she said in a hoarse voice as the cop climbed into his cruiser. "We can't lose that baby."

"What?" He stared at her in shock.

She grabbed on to his arm as if she was drowning and he was the only thing that could keep her afloat. "The baby. He'll get locked into the system and by the time the police close his case, it might be too late."

Marcus stared down at her as if she'd started spouting Latin. "Too…late? For what?"

Liberty's mouth opened and the words *I was a foster kid—trust me on this* almost rolled off her tongue. But at the last second, she snapped her mouth shut. She'd created this person Marcus saw, this Liberty Reese—a white college graduate, an excellent manager of time and money who always did her research and knew the answers. Liberty Reese was invaluable to Marcus because she had *made* herself valuable.

That woman had had nothing in common with Liberty Reese—the grubby daughter of an African American drug addict who'd sold herself on Death Corner in Cabrini-Green to afford more drugs, who'd done multiple stints in prison, who hadn't been able to get clean when her daughter was shipped back to foster care for the third time, who couldn't tell Liberty who her father was or even if he was white, who'd given birth to a baby boy addicted to heroin and crack and God only knew what else.

That's not who Liberty was anymore. She would never be that lost little girl ever again.

She looked back in the direction the ambulance had gone. That little baby—he was lost, too. Just as her brother had been in the few weeks he'd been alive. Completely alone in the world, with no one to fight for him.

Liberty would *not* allow that to happen. Not again.

She opened her mouth to tell Marcus something—she wasn't quite sure what, but something—except nothing came out. Her throat closed up and tears burned in her eyes.

Oh, God—was she about to start crying? No—*not* allowed. Liberty Reese did not cry. She was always in control. She never let her emotions get the better of her. Not anymore.

Marcus looked down at her, concern written large on his face. He stepped closer to her and cupped her chin. "Liberty…"

"Please," she managed to get out. "The baby, Marcus." But that was all she could say because then she really did begin to cry. She dropped her gaze and swallowed hard, trying to will the stupid tears back.

The next thing she knew, Marcus had wrapped his arms around her and pulled her into his chest. "It's okay," he murmured, his hand rubbing up and down her back. "The baby's going to be fine."

"You don't know that," she got out, trying to keep herself from sinking against his chest because Marcus Warren holding her? Comforting her?

The feeling, the smell of his body—awareness of Marcus as a man—blindsided her. Want, powerful and unexpected, mixed in with the panic over the baby and left her so confused that she couldn't pull away like she needed to and couldn't wrap her arms around him like she wanted to. She was rooted to the spot, wanting more and knowing she couldn't have it.

Marcus leaned back and tilted her head up so that she had no choice but to look him in the eyes. It wasn't fair, she thought dimly as she stared into the deep blue eyes that were almost exactly the same color as Lake Michigan on a clear day. Why couldn't he be a slimeball? Why did he have to be so damned perfect, hot and rich and now this—this *tenderness*? Why did he have to make her want him when she didn't deserve him?

He swiped his thumb over her cheek, brushing away a tear she hadn't been able to hold back. "It's important to you?" he asked, his voice deep. "The baby?"

"Yes," was all she could say, because what else was there? Marcus Warren was holding her in his arms and comforting her and looking at her as if he'd do anything to make her happy and dammit all if this wasn't one of her fantasies playing out in real life.

"Then I'll make it fine," he said. His thumb stroked over her cheek again and his other hand flattened out on her lower back. One corner of his mouth curved up into a smile that she knew well—the smile said that Marcus Warren was going to get exactly what he wanted.

And although she knew she shouldn't—couldn't—she leaned into his palm and let herself enjoy the sensation of Marcus touching her. "You will? Why would you do that for me?"

Something shifted in his eyes and his head dropped toward hers. He was going to kiss her, she realized. Her boss was going to kiss her and she was not only going to let him, she was going to kiss him back. Years of wanting and ignoring that want seemed to fall away.

But he didn't. Instead, he said, "Because you're important to me."

She forgot how to breathe. Heck, she might have forgotten her own name there for a second, because she was important to him. Not just a valuable employee. She, Liberty Reese, was important.

The alarm on her phone chimed, startling them out of whatever madness they'd been lost in. Marcus dropped his hand from her face and took a step away before he handed her phone to her. In all that had happened, she'd forgotten he had it.

It was eight forty-five? They'd started their morning run at seven. "You have a phone call with Dombrowski about that proposed bioenergy plant in fifteen minutes," she told him. Despite the heat that was building, she felt almost chilled without Marcus's arms around her.

Marcus laughed. "We're a little off schedule today. We haven't even showered."

Liberty froze as the image of the two of them in the shower together barged into her mind. Normally, they ran back to Marcus's condo, where he got ready while she caught the train to the office. Marcus had installed a shower in the restroom, so she would shower and dress there. She'd get started on organizing the notes she'd made during the run and Marcus would show up by nine thirty, looking as if he'd walked off a red carpet.

There was no showering together. Heck, there wasn't even any showering in the same building. That's how it worked.

But then, before ten minutes ago, there hadn't been any tears or hugs, either. Their physical contact was limited to handshakes and an occasional pat on the back and that was it.

"Shall I call him and reschedule?"

"Please do. Then we'll head back and I'll make a few calls." That was a perfectly normal set of Marcus responses.

Liberty was confident they were going to pretend that the touching and the holding and even the wedding date invitation had never happened. And that was fine with her, really.

But Marcus leaned forward. Even though he didn't touch her again, she still felt the air thin between them. His gaze dropped to her lips and, fool that she was, she still wanted that kiss that hadn't happened. The kiss that *couldn't* happen. "I promise you, Liberty—we won't lose that baby."

Three

It took Marcus the better part of three hours to find the right bureaucrat to deal with. The CEO of Children's Hospital, while sympathetic to Marcus's plight, could not legally provide any information on the baby. He did, however, call Marcus back in twenty minutes with the number of a DCFS supervisor.

The supervisor was less than helpful, but Marcus got the name of the manager of DCFS Guardians, who was responsible for assigning workers to these cases. It took some time to get ahold of the manager, and when he did, Marcus discovered a caseworker hadn't even been sent out.

"We're doing the best we can, Mr. Warren," the tired-sounding woman said. "But we have a limited amount of social workers and a limited amount of funds available to us. The baby will probably be in the hospital for several days. We'll send someone out as soon as we're able."

"That's not good enough," Marcus snapped.

"Well, how do you propose we deal with it?" the woman shot back.

The same way he dealt with everything. He wasn't about to let something like red tape get in his way. Marcus did a cursory web search and discovered that the current head of DCFS had gone to school with his father.

Well, hell. He should have started there. He knew how to play this game. He'd been raised playing an extended game of Who's Who. Political favors and donations were the kind of grease that made the wheels in Chicago run.

It took another twenty minutes to get through to the director's office and an additional twenty before Marcus had the man's personal promise that a caseworker would be assigned within the hour. "Of course, we don't normally keep nonfamily members updated…" the director said.

"I'd consider it a personal favor," Marcus said and in that, at least, he was being truthful.

Because after watching Liberty fold herself around that infant and cuddle the baby until he calmed down? After seeing Liberty's anguish as the baby was driven away in the ambulance? After impulsively pulling her into his arms because she was going to cry and feeling her body pressed against his?

After seeing that look of total gratitude when Marcus had said he'd take care of things?

Yeah, this was personal.

"Give your father my best," the man said at the end of the call.

"Will do!" Marcus said with false enthusiasm. He'd rather his father not find out about this particular conversation or the reason behind it. If Laurence and Marisa Warren knew about this, they'd give Marcus that disappointed look that, despite the decades of plastic surgery, was still immediately recognizable. It was one thing to trade political favors—but to do so for this? For an abandoned baby? Because his assistant got a little teary?

"What do you hope to gain out of this?" That's what his mother would say in her simpering voice, because that's what life was to her. Everything, every single human interaction, had a tally associated with it. You either gained something or you lost.

Warrens were never losers.

And his father? The man famous for his affairs with his secretaries? "If you want her, just take her." That's what his father would say.

He didn't want to be that man. He didn't want to use Liberty because he had all the power in their relationship. He was *not* his father.

Still, his father cast a long shadow. Marcus had gone to the university his parents had picked. His girlfriends had been preapproved daughters of their friends. Hell, even his company, Warren Capital, had been his father's idea. What better way to curry power and favor than to literally fund the businesses of tomorrow?

It had taken him years to loosen the ties that bound him to his parents, but he'd managed to separate his life from theirs. Liberty was a part of that, too. His mother had some friend of a friend she'd wanted him to hire—someone she could use to keep tabs on Marcus. Instead, he'd defied her by hiring a young woman from a family no one had ever heard of based on the strength of her recommendations and her insistence that she jogged regularly.

Marcus had paid for that act of defiance, just as he'd paid for refusing to marry Lillibeth Hanson. He may have lost favor with his parents, but he'd gained much more.

He'd gained his independence.

Still, he couldn't have his parents finding out about this. It simply wouldn't do for them to interest themselves in his life again.

"Mr. Warren?" Liberty stuck her head through his office door. He didn't miss the way that he was "Mr. Warren" again, as if she hadn't called him Marcus by the side of the jogging trail this morning.

"Yes?"

"Mr. Chabot is on the line." Marcus must have looked at her blankly, for she went on, "The producer for *Feeding Frenzy*? He wants to confirm the meeting when you're in Los Angeles after the wedding."

Right. Marcus had spent his entire morning tracking down someone—anyone—who knew about the little baby. He did actually have work to do.

"What did you tell him?"

She notched an eyebrow at him. "I put him on hold." The panic-stricken woman from the run this morning was gone and in her place was his competent, levelheaded assistant. Ms. Reese was impeccably dressed in a gray skirt suit with a rose-colored blouse underneath. Her hair was neatly pulled back into a slick bun and her makeup was understated, as always.

He'd wanted to kiss her this morning. The impulse had come out of nowhere. He'd watched her hold that child and felt her palpable grief when the ambulance had driven off. He'd wanted to hold her, to let her know it'd be okay. And then she'd looked up at him with her deep brown eyes and…

"Thank you, Ms. Reese," he said because what he needed right now was not to think about that impulse or how he'd joked that he should take her to the wedding only to realize he hadn't been joking. Which was a problem. She was an assistant—not part of his social circle. If he showed up with her, people would talk. Marcus Warren, slumming with his secretary. Or, worse, they'd assume that Liberty was manipulating him just as Lillibeth had.

But he wanted to take her. She was safe and trustworthy. And she was the one telling him to do what he wanted.

She gave him a little nod and turned to go.

"Liberty," he said.

She paused for a beat before she turned back around. "Yes?"

"I've made some calls about the baby. I'll let you know when I hear anything."

Her face softened and he was struck by how lovely she was. Underneath that executive-assistant mask was a beautiful woman. He just hadn't realized how beautiful until this morning. "Thank you."

He had nothing to gain by tracking down that baby. The child wouldn't bring him more power or money. The baby boy wouldn't be able to return a favor when Marcus wanted.

But he'd made a promise to Liberty.

He was going to keep it.

The ad mock-up for Rock City Watch drifted out of focus as Liberty wondered about that little baby. It'd been four days since she'd held him to her chest. Was he still in the hospital? Was he okay?

She shouldn't be this worried, she decided as she tried to refocus on the ad. Worrying wasn't going to help anything. And besides, Marcus had promised he'd look into it and she had to have faith that he'd keep that promise to her.

Of course it'd also been four days since Marcus had wrapped his strong arms around her and told her he'd find the baby because the child was important to her and she was important to Marcus.

Since that time, there'd been no hugs, no long looks. There'd been no more mention of the wedding, although that would have to change soon. If he continued to insist on going, he needed to pick a date. A safe date, she mentally corrected herself. Someone who wouldn't look at him and see nothing but a hot body and a huge...

Bank account.

The phone rang. "Warren Capital Investments. How may I assist you?"

"Ms. Reese." The coquettish voice of Mrs. Marisa Warren floated from the other end of the line. Liberty gritted her teeth. So this was how today was going to go, huh? "How is my son today?"

"Fine, Mrs. Warren." But Liberty offered no other information.

When she'd first been hired, Marcus had made it blisteringly clear that she worked for him, not for Laurence or Marisa Warren. If he ever caught her passing information to his parents about his business, his prospects or his personal life, well, she could pack her things and go. End of discussion.

Luckily, Liberty had gotten very good at telling people what they wanted to hear without giving anything away.

"I was wondering," Marisa simpered, "if my son has settled on a date for the Hanson wedding? It's a few weeks away and he knows how important it is."

When she'd first started fielding these nosy calls, Liberty hadn't entirely understood why Marcus was so determined that nothing of his life leak out to his parents. After all, she'd grown up dreaming of having a mother and a father who cared about her. And Marisa Warren seemed to care about her son quite a lot.

But appearances were deceiving. "Mrs. Warren," she said in her most deferential tone because it also hadn't taken her long to realize that while Marcus might treat her with respect and dignity, to his parents she was on approximately the same level as a maid. "I couldn't speak to his plans for the wedding."

"Surely you've heard something…"

Liberty focused on keeping her voice level. "As you know, Mr. Warren doesn't share personal information with me."

She wasn't sure at what point this wedding had crossed from personal to business and back again. When Marcus's relationship with Lillibeth had blown up in the media, she'd read what she could—but he'd never once broached the topic during office hours. It was only when they were running that he'd even touch on the subject—and even that was more about damage control than "feelings" and "sharing."

He'd asked her to prepare a roster of acceptable women with whom to attend this wedding. And then he'd asked her—however jokingly—to be his date.

"Hmph," Mrs. Warren said. It was the least dignified sound she was probably capable of making and, in her honeyed voice, it still sounded pretty. "Have him call me when he's free." She never asked to speak to Marcus when she called his office number. That was the thing that Liberty had realized about that first call. Mrs. Warren wasn't calling to talk *to* Marcus. She was calling to talk to Liberty *about* Marcus.

Liberty knew where her loyalty lay, even if Mrs. Warren didn't. "Of course, Mrs. Warren."

She hung up and finished analyzing the Rock City Watch ads. If Marcus was going to push them as a high-end luxury good, then the ads needed to be slicker. There was too much text talking about Detroit's revival, and the photography needed to give off a more exclusive vibe, she decided.

What rich people wanted was exclusivity. That's what she'd learned in the three years she'd worked in this office on North LaSalle. Not only did they want the best, they wanted to be damned sure that it was better than what everyone else had. It wasn't enough to own a great watch or a fancy car or live in an expensive building. Rich people wanted to make sure that theirs was the only one. She figured that was why they spent so much money on artworks. By definition, those were one of a kind.

This world was all still foreign to her, but after three years she felt as if at least she was becoming fluent in the language.

She was just finishing her notes when Marcus called out, "Ms. Reese?"

"Coming." She grabbed her tablet and the ad materials and walked into his office. This place, for example, was a perfect example of how a rich person simply had to have the very best. Even though Warren Capital was a relatively small operation—Marcus employed fifteen people to handle the finances and contracts—the business was located on LaSalle Drive on the top floor of one of the most expensive office buildings in Chicago. Marcus's office sat in the corner behind walls of glass that gave him expansive views of downtown and Lake Michigan. Warren Capital was the only company on this floor—no one else could claim this view. It was the best—and it was his.

And through sheer dint of will, Liberty managed to carve out a place where she could fit in this world. Sure, it was as an assistant and yes, she had to buy new running shoes every six months. It didn't matter. She loved this office, this view. Everything clean and bright. There were no holes in the wall, no critters scurrying about. If something broke, maintenance had it fixed within hours, if not minutes. The lights were always on and the heat always worked. This office was as far away from the apartment in the Cabrini-Green projects as she could get.

"Your mother called," she said, taking her usual seat in front of Marcus's desk. His office furniture reflected a modern sensibility—black leather seating, glass-topped desks of ebony wood and chrome. Even the art along the wall was modern. Among others, he had an Edward Hopper and a Mark Rothko—names she'd had to look up online because she certainly hadn't heard of them before. Marcus had bought the Rothko for $35 million.

Yes, he had one hell of an impressive...bank account.

"I assume to pump you for information about my wedding plans?" he asked without looking up.

"Correct. She's concerned about your date. Or lack thereof."

Marcus sighed heavily. "I've had an update on the baby, if you're still interested."

"What?" Her heart began to pound as he glanced at her in surprise. She tried again. "I mean, of course I'm still interested. Why wouldn't I be?"

"You hadn't asked."

She blinked at him. "You promised you'd make some calls. I didn't want to bother you."

He gave her a look that was partly amused. But she also thought she saw some of the tenderness beyond why he'd made that promise to her in the first place.

"Liberty," he said in a gentle voice. A creeping flush started at the base of her neck and worked its way down her back. Was it wrong to like how he said her name? Was it wrong to want him to say it some more? "You are not a bother to me."

She swallowed, willing her cheeks not to blush. They were getting off track. "What did you hear? About the baby?"

"Ah, yes." He looked down at his computer. The moment he looked away, Liberty exhaled.

"The baby has been discharged from the hospital."

She gasped. "How is he? Is he okay? Did they find his mother yet?"

"Apparently he's surprisingly healthy, given the circumstances—but no, they haven't located his parents yet." He gave her an apologetic look. "They don't seem to be looking too hard, despite my encouragement. I don't think they'll find the mother."

Liberty didn't know what to think because on one hand,

that poor child—being abandoned and never knowing his parents?

But on the other hand, he'd already been abandoned once. What if they found his mother—then what? There were other ways to abandon a child than just leaving him in a park. That she knew personally.

Marcus said, "I've been assured that the foster mother is one of their best and that the baby's needs will be met."

She gaped at him for a moment before she realized her mouth was still open. She got it shut and tried to remember to look professional. This was probably as good as the news would get. One of their best foster mothers? Personal assurances that the baby would be well cared for? Those were all things she'd never gotten when she was in the system. "That's wonderful. Can I visit him?"

Marcus looked at her in surprise, as if she'd asked for a space pony. "I didn't get the address."

"Oh." She stared down at her tablet. "I just thought…" She cleared her throat and tried to get back on track. "Here's the analysis of the Rock City Watch ad. I don't think it's hitting the target market you were looking for yet. And you still need to find a date for the wedding."

She stood and handed the ad material over to Marcus. Then she turned and headed for the door.

It was better this way. She'd done her part. Marcus had upheld his end of things. The baby was going to be fine.

Besides, what was she going to do? Adopt a child? Please. She worked from 7:00 a.m. until 6:00 p.m., five days a week, and she came in on Saturday to prepare for the next week's meetings. She had to. There was so much about his world that she didn't know and she couldn't afford to be exposed as an outsider, so she did her homework day in and day out.

She was at the threshold when Marcus spoke. "Liberty."

She paused. He wasn't going to ask her to the wedding again, was he? "Yes?"

She turned to face him. The way he was looking at her—it wasn't right. It wasn't normal anyway. What she would give for that look to be right because there was something to it, something that was possessive and intense. It scared her, how much she wanted him to look at her like that.

So she went on the defensive. "You can't want me to go to this wedding with you."

His lips curved into a seductive smile. "First off, aren't you the one telling me to do what I want?"

He couldn't mean that he really *wanted* to take her—could he? "Yes, but—"

He held up his hand like a king. "Do you want to see him again? The little boy."

She gave him a long, hard look. Was this a game? If so, she wasn't playing. "Mr. Warren, you're not going to make this awkward, are you? You'll get me the foster mother's address *if* I agree to attend this ridiculous wedding as your—what, your personal human shield?"

A muscle in his jaw twitched and he looked quite dangerous. Very few people said no to Marcus Warren. But she was one of them. "Just answer the question—do you want to see the baby again?"

She gritted her teeth. "Yes," she said, bracing for his counteroffer.

"That will be all," Marcus said, turning his attention back to his computer.

The dismissal was so sudden and unexpected that she just stood there for a moment. Marcus didn't look back up at her. He didn't acknowledge her continued presence at all. He merely ignored her.

It was not a good feeling.

Four

This time, the DCFS supervisor didn't hesitate to give Marcus the name and address of the foster home. All he had to do was say who he was and the woman practically fell over herself to give him what he wanted.

Well. It was nice that someone was acting appropriately. Because his executive assistant sure as hell wasn't.

Marcus stared at the information he'd written down on a piece of company letterhead. Hazel Jones. He googled the address and saw that it was way up in West Rogers Park.

This was ridiculous. He should be game-planning how to survive this wedding, not diverting his time, energy and accumulated favors for an abandoned baby and his assistant. And yet, here he was, doing just that.

There was nothing to be gained here. He did not need Liberty as a personal human shield and the implication—that he couldn't attend this stupid wedding without one—was an insult to his pride. He was a Warren, dammit all.

He didn't hide from anyone or anything and woe unto the person who tried to stand between him and his goal.

Who, at this exact moment, was Liberty Reese.

He strode out of his office to find Liberty on the phone. She glanced up at him, and the fact that he saw a hint of worry in her eyes only made him madder. What had he ever done to make her afraid of him? Not a damned thing. His father would have had her pinned to her desk by the end of her first month here and if she'd so much as sneezed wrong afterward, he would have done everything in his power to bury her.

And what had Marcus done? He'd treated her with respect. He'd never once laid a hand on her, never implied that her job was in some way connected to her sexuality.

All he had done was ask her to go to a wedding with him. And now she was treating him as if he was some lecherous old man to be feared.

"Yes," she said into the phone. "That's correct. No—no," she said in a more severe voice. "That is not the timetable. That information needs to be on my desk by the twelfth." She notched an eyebrow at him and mouthed "Yes?"

He crossed his arms and mouthed back, "I'll wait."

There it was again, that hint of worry. Okay, so maybe he shouldn't have asked her to the damned wedding. Hell, if he had his way, he wouldn't even be going to the thing.

"No, the twelfth. What part of that isn't clear? *The. Twelfth,*" Liberty snapped at the caller. Marcus grinned. He'd hired her because she was outside his parents' sphere of influence and she ran. But she'd turned into an exceedingly good assistant who was not afraid to push when she needed to.

She rolled her eyes at the phone and then dug through a small stack of papers on her desk, pulled one out and handed it to him.

"Available for the Hanson-Spears wedding" was the label of a column. Below was a list of names and phone numbers.

Marcus gave her a dull look, which she ignored. "Yes. Excellent. We look forward to seeing what you put together." She hung up the phone and took a deep breath. "I have to say that, at this point, the baby-wearables people are not winning any points in terms of organization or professionalism. They may not be ready to move to the next level."

Ah, yes. The company that wanted funding for a line of baby clothes and blankets with smart technology built into the fabric so anxious parents could monitor sleeping and eating habits from the comfort of their phones. The idea was intriguing, but he didn't like to see his money squandered by poor planning. "So noted."

She turned a bright smile to him. It was not real. "Was there something I could help you with?"

He held out the name and address he'd copied down. "Here. It's in West Rogers Park, up on the north side."

Liberty made a small noise, like a gasp she was trying her best to hold in. "I..." She looked up at him and at least for right now, any hint of worry or fake smiles was gone and he found himself looking down at the same woman whom he'd held in his arms beside the jogging path.

She would do anything for that baby, he realized. *Anything.* Even attend a wedding.

He knew it. And given the way her cheeks colored a pretty pink and she dropped her gaze, she knew it, too.

It'd make his life a hell of a lot easier. A plus-one for this wedding in exchange for a little information, and he wouldn't have to worry about finding a media-ready, parent-approved date who wouldn't view the event as a stepping-stone to bigger and better things. He could go with Liberty and might even enjoy himself. At the very least, they could run on the beach along the Pacific Ocean in the mornings instead of Lake Michigan.

She wouldn't be able to say no.

And he wouldn't be any better than his father was.

"As promised," he said and turned to walk back to his office.

He heard her chair squeak as she got up to follow him. "That's it?"

"That's it," he said, sitting down. He felt strange and he wasn't sure why. It wasn't a bad feeling. He stared at the list she'd given him. He'd gone out with a half dozen of these women and he knew the other half. Any one of these women would make a great date to this wedding and appease his mother.

He crumpled the paper up and threw it in the trash.

"You're not going to…" She let the sentence trail off but he could hear the words anyway. *You're not going to force the issue?*

"Insist you do something you obviously don't want to that falls outside of your job parameters? No," he replied, trying to sound casual. He was seriously just going to let this go? If he didn't get a date and he didn't take Liberty, he'd just go alone. Sure, his parents might disown him for it. "Why would I?"

He glanced at her then and wasn't surprised to see her looking as if she'd stepped into a room full of snapping alligators. "That's…thank you."

Even stranger, that made him feel better, as if her appreciation was all that he needed. "You're welcome."

But she didn't leave. Instead, she took another step into the office. "Marcus…"

It wasn't as if she hadn't said his name before. She had. But there was something about the way she said it this time that held him captive.

"I know I shouldn't ask this—but..." She looked down at the paper again as if he'd given her a sheet of solid gold. "Can I leave early today? Just today," she hurried to add. "This won't be a regular thing. I just..."

And he remembered how she'd soothed the baby, how she hadn't just hummed a lullaby but had told that little child that he was loved and he was strong and he could make it. And Marcus remembered how watching her holding that baby had rocked him to his core.

"I'll come in on Saturday and finish up whatever i don't get done this week," she offered, mistaking his silence for disapproval.

He stared at her. Did she think he didn't know she came in on Saturdays anyway?

Liberty went on. "This won't affect my job performance at all."

And he was reminded that he held all the power here and that meant he could gain something from this interaction.

He looked at his watch. It was three forty-five—early by their standards. "Here," he said, holding out his hand for the paper. "Give it to me."

"Oh." The disappointment on her face was a painful thing to see. "Yes, of course." She trudged forward—there was no other word for it—and handed over the paper. Then, without looking him in the eyes, she turned and headed back to her desk.

"Get your things packed up," he said, picking up his phone. He had nothing to gain from this but he was going to do it anyway. Because he wanted to. "We'll go together."

Somehow, Liberty found herself sitting in the passenger seat of Marcus's Aston Martin, zipping up Lake Shore Drive. One minute, she'd been crestfallen that she couldn't immediately go see the baby. The next, Marcus had been hustling her into his car—his very nice car—and personally driving her to the foster home.

She'd never been in his car before. Oh, sure, she'd attended a few business functions with him, but those were either after-hours events when she'd take the El as she always did or business lunches with potential clients when he'd have her order a car big enough for the entire group.

The Aston Martin was his personal car. And he drove it like a bat out of hell. Of course he did, she thought as she surreptitiously tried to grab on to the door handle when Marcus took the curve without braking. He drove as he ran.

"We don't have to go this fast," she said, trying to sound calm. "I'm not in that big of a hurry."

"This isn't fast," he replied and then, the moment they hit the straightaway, he gunned it. Liberty was pushed back into the seat as Marcus accelerated, weaving in and out of traffic. Lake Shore Drive was still mostly clear—it wouldn't fill up for another half hour with commuters. Marcus took full command of the road.

If she wasn't so concerned with dying in a fiery heap by the side of the road, she'd be forced to admit that it was kind of sexy. How often did a billionaire act as her personal chauffeur? Never.

They zipped up the drive in record time and then cut over on Peterson. There, at least, Marcus slowed down.

She was nervous. What if this foster home was one of the best—and it still wasn't very good? She tried to think back to the three homes she'd been in. The first home was fuzzy. It was just after she'd started kindergarten. Less than two weeks into the school year, her mom wasn't there when she got off the bus one day. Liberty had done okay on her own for a few days, going to see Grandma Devlin for food, but before long, she'd been in a foster home.

She didn't remember much, just that it got cold in her

room and that the other girls were mean to her. But she hadn't been hungry and there hadn't been the same kind of screaming and fights as at home.

"Why do you need to see him so badly?" Marcus asked when they got stuck at a light.

Liberty tensed. Were they still in the tug-of-war they'd been in earlier? Or were they back to normal? Since they were out of the office, was this the kind of conversation they might have while they were running?

Marcus glanced at her. "I'm just asking, Liberty," he said, sounding tired. "And it has nothing to do with the wedding."

Oh, if only she could *just* answer honestly. But how would that be possible? Because the truth hurt. And what would Marcus think if he knew the truth about addict moms and foster homes and being an unwanted, unloved little girl? Would he still want to take her to this stupid wedding—or would he look at her and see an imposter who was not to be trusted?

Still, she understood what he wanted to know. It wasn't her deepest, darkest secrets. It was a simple question that was only one step removed from polite conversation. She had to hope he'd be satisfied with her answer. "I had a little brother," she said and she was horrified to hear her voice quaver.

She'd never said those words out loud. Who would she have said them to when she was a kid? Her foster parents? They had enough kids to worry about. Her teachers? That would have only made them pity her more, and she had enough of that. Her friends? *Ha*.

"I didn't realize," Marcus replied. "I'm sorry."

"It's no big deal," she lied because that lie came as naturally to her as breathing air. None of it had been a big deal because she'd survived. She'd thrived. She could afford to ignore her past now.

Or she had been able to. Right until she'd seen the little baby in the trash. Then everything had come back.

She swallowed and tried to get her voice to work right again. "He was born with a lot of birth defects and didn't make it long." Which was a version of the truth that was palatable for Marcus's refined taste.

An uncomfortable silence boxed her in. She could see Marcus thinking and she couldn't have that because if he kept asking questions and she kept having to come up with better versions of the truth, sooner or later she'd either let the truth slip or be forced to tell a real lie. So she barged into the silence and said, "I appreciate you coming with me for this, but it wasn't necessary. You should be focusing on the list I gave you."

"You mean the list I threw away?" There—they were back to their early-morning teasing and banter.

"I have other copies," she announced and was rewarded with Marcus rolling his eyes and grinning at her. "You need to be focused on the wedding and the meeting with the producers, not on taking me to see an abandoned baby."

"Maybe this is what I want to do."

"Be serious, Marcus."

They hit another stoplight. "I am serious. You think you're the only one worried about that baby?"

She stared at him. "You are?"

"I can't explain it," he said in a quiet voice. "But watching you hold him…"

Oh. That was bad. The way his voice trailed off there at the end? The way he sounded all wistful and concerned?

Very, very bad. Damned bad, even.

She was not good for him. She could never be anything more than a valuable employee who got up too early every morning to jog with him. "I can't do anything for your reputation except drag it down."

Marcus didn't even look at her. He kept his attention on

the road, but she saw him clench his jaw again, just as he had in his office earlier. "My reputation isn't everything."

She desperately wanted to believe that, but she knew that in his world, her mere existence would be a scandal. "I'm not good for you," she said in a whisper.

He pulled onto a side street and parked. "I'll be the judge of that."

That was exactly what she was afraid of.

Five

Marcus got out of the car and looked around. He'd only ever lived in the Gold Coast, with luxury high-rises and doormen and valets. He rarely left the downtown area and when he did, it was to see the White Sox play or catch a Bulls or Blackhawks game at the United Center—from his owner's box, of course.

He looked up and down the street at the two-story buildings that stood side by side with older bungalows. Most yards were mowed. Was this a good neighborhood?

"This is nice," Liberty said, sounding shocked.

"What did you expect—slums?"

There was something about the way she avoided looking at him as she laughed that bothered him. She stared down at the address on the letterhead. He saw her hands were shaking.

"This one," she said, indicating a trim little bungalow. It was white with a wall of windows framed in dark wood.

The paint around the windows was a little chipped and the white was grubby, but it didn't look bad. He hoped.

"Ready?" he asked.

She took a deep breath and gave him an apologetic look. "You don't think this is ridiculous, do you?"

He had that urge to once again pull her into his arms and tell her it was all going to be fine. But he didn't. Instead, he told her, "Coming to see the baby? No. I want to do this with you."

Her eyes got huge again, but she didn't say anything. They walked up to the front door of the house and knocked. And waited. Marcus knocked again.

"She knows we're coming, right?" Liberty said. The panic in her voice was obvious. "Should we have—"

The door opened. "Mr. Warren?" Marcus almost grinned at the appearance of the little old lady standing before him. Maybe she wasn't that old, but she was petite, with a crown of white hair cut into a bob and a huge pair of vintage-looking glasses on her nose.

"Mrs. Jones, hello. We spoke on the phone." He offered his hand but she just nodded and smiled. "This is Liberty Reese. We found the child together and we just wanted to see how he's doing."

"It's a pleasure to meet you, Mrs. Jones," Liberty said. She sounded stiff.

"How sweet of you to come. Please, call me Hazel. All my friends do. Come in, come in. Shut the door behind you, if you don't mind." She turned and began to climb up a short flight of stairs.

Marcus made sure to shut the front door behind him, which took a little shove. The entryway contained another set of doors that led both upstairs and downstairs, and he had to wonder if this was a single-family home or if someone else lived in the basement.

Hazel and Liberty finally went through the upstairs door and Marcus followed, shutting it behind him. Then he looked around.

Wow. Once, when he'd been really little, he'd had a nanny who loved *The Brady Bunch*. His parents didn't believe in television, so getting to watch any show was a big deal to him. The nanny—Miss Judy—let him catch a show if he got all his lessons done. She'd make a bowl of popcorn and they'd snuggle on the couch and for a half hour at a time, he'd gotten a glimpse at what normal might look like.

It'd been years since he'd thought of *The Brady Bunch*. But this was like walking into the Brady house. Everything looked as if it was original to the 1960s or '70s—the pine paneling, the vinyl covers over the sofa cushions, the preponderance of autumn gold and orange everywhere. Marcus leaned over to catch a glimpse through a doorway—yes, there were avocado-green appliances in the kitchen.

This was one of the best foster homes in the system?

"He's in the nursery," Hazel was saying. "He's still napping. Oh, they sleep so much the first week or so, but he's starting to wake up."

"Is he okay?" Liberty asked anxiously.

"I think he's perfect," Hazel said as she guided them through a small dining room and past two doorways that led to a bedroom and a television room. The third doorway was the nursery. "I understand your concerns, though. I've had children who were coming off drugs or the like and he doesn't seem to have those problems." She stopped and sighed. "His poor mother. One has to wonder."

"Yes," Liberty said. "One does."

Hazel gave Liberty a maternal smile as she patted her arm. "It's good you've come. This way."

They all crowded into the small room. A metal crib was by one wall and a larger, wooden crib up against another.

There was a dresser with a blue terry-cloth pad on it next to a worn rocking chair. Marcus had to wonder how long Hazel Jones had had these things—since her own children had been babies?

All over two of the walls were pictures of babies, he realized. Old pictures, with the edges curling and the colors faded to a gold and brown that matched the furniture in the rest of the house. There were hundreds of pictures of little babies all over the place.

Next to a window was an antique-looking swinging chair that squeaked gently with every swing. And inside the swing was the baby boy. He was clean and dressed and Marcus swore he'd grown in the past five days, but there was no mistaking that child. Marcus would know him anywhere. How odd, he thought dimly.

Liberty made a noise that was half choking, half gasping. "Oh—oh," she said, covering her mouth.

Hazel patted her on the arm again. "You're his guardian angels, you and your boyfriend. He would have likely died if it hadn't been for you."

"We're not—" Liberty started to say, but Hazel cut her off.

"It'll be time for his bottle in a few. Would you like to feed him?"

"Could I?" Liberty turned to Marcus, her brown eyes huge. "Do we have time?"

As if she had to get his permission. "Of course."

"I'll be right back." In contrast to her slow climb up the stairs, Hazel moved quickly to the kitchen. "Don't go anywhere!" she jokingly called out.

"Is this what you wanted?" Marcus asked Liberty as they stared at the baby.

"Oh, God, yes. He's okay," she said as if she still couldn't believe it. The baby exhaled heavily and turned his head away from the window. Liberty gasped and flung out a hand in his direction and Marcus took it. He gave her a squeeze of support and she squeezed back. "Look at him," she said in awe.

"Is this place okay for him, do you think?" Marcus looked around the room again at the worn, battered furniture. "They said it was one of their best homes…"

"No, it's really lovely." Marcus stared down at her, but she was still looking at the baby. "And it seems like she only has him right now. This is *amazing*."

There was something in the way she said it, the way she *meant* it, that struck him as odd. But before he could ask about it, Hazel said brightly, "Here we are."

He dropped Liberty's hand and stepped out of the way. Hazel handed him a bottle and he took it, even though he had no idea how to feed a baby.

"Does he have a name yet?" Liberty asked Hazel.

"Oh, no. He's still Baby Boy Doe." As if on cue, the baby began to lift his little hands and scrunch up his eyes. "I suppose he should have a name, shouldn't he?"

"William," Liberty said without hesitation. "He's William." She said it with such conviction that again, Marcus found himself staring at her.

"Oh, that's lovely. My husband was Bill. That's a good name." The baby began to fuss and Hazel deftly carried him over to the dresser and laid him out on the pad. She unzipped his blanket-thing—a blanket with arms? Was there a name for that? Hazel began to change his diaper with the kind of practiced motion that made it clear she could do this in the dark, in her sleep. Marcus wondered how many babies she'd changed just like that.

"We never had children," Hazel went on as she got out a clean diaper from the top drawer, all the while never taking her hand off the baby's belly. "But I loved babies so… I was offered an early retirement from my teaching position back in 1988 and I decided that I was going to be a grand-mother one way or another."

"All babies?" Liberty asked.

"Oh, yes. I just love this age. They're such little angels. I can't keep up with them when they start crawling and walk-ing, though." Hazel shook her head. "Babies are just my speed."

Marcus watched as Hazel changed the diaper. She made it seem easy but the mostly naked infant was squirming and then there was the cleaning part and...

Suddenly, he was terrified. It wasn't the same kind of ter-ror he'd felt when he'd opened the box and found this child—that had been stark panic, with a life hanging in the balance. That danger was safely past, thank God. But when Hazel got the diaper on and asked Liberty if she wanted to help re-dress William, and Liberty still looked as if she might start sobbing with relief at any moment, the whole scene was so far outside his realm of experience that he might as well have landed on Mars.

Liberty got his tiny little feet back into the blanket con-traption and zipped him up. "Here we go," Hazel said in a singsong voice as she picked William up. "Dear, why don't you sit in the rocker?"

Liberty sat and Hazel laid the baby in her arms. In that moment, everything about Liberty changed; it was as if he were looking at a different woman. This wasn't his take-charge assistant—this was Liberty, the real woman.

Hazel took the bottle from Marcus and showed Liberty how to hold it. The older woman got a little pillow that had been next to the rocking chair and used that to prop Lib-erty's arms up. "There we go. He's been eating quite a bit, poor dear." For the first time in a while, she seemed to no-tice Marcus. "Oh—would you like a chair?"

"I'm fine," he insisted. He couldn't take his eyes off Liberty and William. There was something about them— something he'd seen that first time in the park…

"You're amazing with him," he told Liberty and he meant it. Yeah, he'd found the child, but it was Liberty who'd cooled him down and got him to stop crying. It was because of Liberty that Marcus had used his clout to make sure the baby got into the best home.

It was Liberty who'd named him.

Then she looked up at him and smiled and everything that Marcus knew to be true about himself was suddenly… not true. Not anymore.

He was Marcus Warren. A trust-fund billionaire, gossip column fodder and a potential reality-television star. He had a business and a reputation to manage. He had to carry on the Warren family name.

And quite unexpectedly, none of it mattered. What mattered was seeing Liberty rock that tiny baby and smile at him with that silly joy on her face, as if she'd been waiting her whole life for this exact moment.

What mattered was knowing he'd made this moment happen. Because he wanted that silly joy on her face. He wanted to be the one who made her smile, who gave her everything her heart desired. Not because it would give him leverage, but because it made her happy.

His entire life had been about accumulation. Things, power, favors—more and more and more. Never enough.

What if…

William's mouth popped off the bottle and he squirmed.

"Oh, is he okay?" Liberty asked Hazel.

The two of them fussed over the baby and Liberty got him burped. Then Hazel took William back and turned to Marcus. "Would you like to hold him?"

"Sure," he said, sitting in the rocking chair. Liberty

propped the pillow under his arm. He tried to position his arms the way she had.

She looked down at him skeptically. "Have you ever held a baby before?"

His face got hot. "No?"

Liberty sighed, but at least she was grinning as she moved his hands into approximately the right position as if it was no big deal to physically rearrange him. But it only made that nearly out-of-body experience he was having that much worse.

What if...

"Here we are," Hazel said, handing William to Marcus. The baby sighed and scrunched up his nose.

Marcus was dimly aware that Hazel and Liberty were still talking, but he didn't really hear them. Instead, he stared down at the child in his arms.

William was so small—how was this human going to grow up and be a regular-sized person? "Hi, William," Marcus whispered as the baby waved one of his hands jerkily through the air.

Without thinking about it, Marcus shifted and held one of his fingers up against William's hand. The baby grabbed on at the same time his little eyes opened up all the way, and in that moment Marcus was lost. How could anyone have walked away from this baby? This must have been what Liberty had felt when she'd held the baby in the park.

They couldn't lose this baby. He'd thought he'd done his part, getting William into one of the best foster homes— but now that Marcus had seen Liberty with him, now that he'd held William himself, how could he walk away from this child?

He looked around the room again. Hazel was a good foster mother for a baby, he decided. But the stuff she had to work with was ancient. Marcus eyed the baby swing William had been in when they got here. The thing looked like a death-trap of metal and plastic.

His phone buzzed in his pocket, which startled the baby. William began to fuss and Hazel swooped in and plucked him from Marcus's arms. "There, now," she soothed.

"Sorry," Marcus said as he dug out his phone. The missed call had been from his mother. This couldn't be good. It was already past five.

"We should go," Liberty said. "Hazel, thank you so much for letting us visit William. This was wonderful. I'm so glad he's got you."

With William tucked against her chest, Hazel waved the compliment away. "You're more than welcome to come back. Just give me a call!"

"Could we?" Liberty glanced at Marcus, her cheeks coloring brightly. "I mean, I'll do that."

"We can come back," he agreed. And he wasn't just saying that—he really did want to see the baby again. More than that, he wanted to see Liberty with the baby again.

Liberty gave him another one of her shy smiles, as if she'd been hoping he'd say that but hadn't dared to ask.

As they walked toward the front door, Hazel followed them. "You two should consider applying for adoption," she said. "A nice couple like you? And because you found him, you might have a better chance of getting him. If they don't find his birth mother, that is," she added, sounding sad. "Poor dear."

Liberty jolted. "I don't—"

"We'll discuss it," Marcus said. He put his hand on Liberty's back and guided her down the stairs. "Thanks so much."

He made sure to shut the door behind them.

Six

Liberty stood on the sidewalk in a state of shock. She knew she needed to pull herself together but she was weirdly numb right now.

"That place was a time warp," Marcus said, stepping around her to the car and opening the passenger door for her.

She blinked at him. Hazel was a warm, loving, capable woman who had only one child in her charge and, by all appearances, would dote on William as if he were her own. That was weird enough, but now? Marcus Warren was opening her door for her. In what world did *any* of this make sense?

"Liberty?" Then he was touching her again, his hand in the small of her back as he gently propelled her toward his waiting car as if he was her chauffeur instead of her billionaire boss. Warmth flowed up her back from where he touched her and she wanted nothing more than to lean into him. "Are you all right?"

No. No, she wasn't. Everything had changed and she

didn't know how she'd ever be the same again. But she had to try. "I can't—you don't have to come back."

Marcus snorted in amusement. "I never have to do something I don't want," he said. "You were right. We can't lose him."

"We?" That word sounded different in her ears now, foreign almost. There was no "we" where Marcus and she were concerned. Not outside the office or off the jogging path. Or beyond her carefully guarded fantasies. "But…"

"Come on," he said, almost pushing her into the car. "Let's get some dinner. We can talk then."

"Dinner?" She couldn't make sense of anything he was saying. *We. Dinner.* "No—wait," she said when he got into the driver's seat. "You don't have to take me to dinner. You should be taking a potential wedding date—not me."

"Maybe I am taking a potential date to dinner."

And they were right back to where they'd been earlier. Well, this time she was not going to mess around. The sooner he realized how radically inappropriate she'd be as a wedding date, the sooner they could get back to their regularly scheduled programming. "Marcus, I'm *not* going. I'm not good enough for you, for that crowd. I know it. Everyone else there will know it. You're the only one who doesn't seem to realize it."

"That's not—"

She cut him off because he had to see reason. She didn't know how much longer she could be this strong. "That's not all. Why would I want to go to this wedding? Why would I want to watch Lillibeth hurt you again? Because you know she's going to try. And everyone will be watching to see how bad it's going to be. You'll be back in the media again. And I don't want to be a part of that. I don't want to be another reason people try to tear you down. I care too much about you to let that happen."

The last part just slipped out. She hadn't meant to say that she cared about him at all, but she'd built up a head of steam. But it was the truth—a truth that she couldn't bury anymore.

"Liberty," he said. And then something horrible and wonderful happened—Marcus touched her. He cupped her face in the palm of his hand.

"I just don't want you to be hurt again," she breathed. And even though she knew she shouldn't, she reached up and held his palm against her skin.

"You won't hurt me. I know you too well for that."

There it was again, that blind trust he had in her. And she knew—*knew*—that if he learned the truth, the whole truth and nothing but the truth about her junkie mom and her unknown father, he would be hurt.

She wanted to lean into his touch, but she couldn't because she was already starting to slip up and if she let herself get swept away in his touch, in his longing looks, something even more damaging might come out of her mouth.

So she shook him off. "If you don't want to, don't. Don't go to the wedding. Don't do the reality show. You said it yourself—your reputation isn't everything. You don't need to do any of that stuff. Do what *you* want."

He stared at her for a moment, but she refused to make eye contact because she didn't know if she could handle it. One searing look from Marcus Warren might break her resolve. So she kept her gaze locked on the windshield.

He started the car and began to drive without answering.

"Please take me back to the office. I'll finish the work I didn't get done earlier."

"Don't worry about it," he said. He sounded distant.

She fought the urge to apologize, to backpedal—to take it all back. She wanted to go back to the way things had been a week ago, when he'd tease her during the run and she earned his respect by being invaluable to his business, when she didn't offer opinions on his personal life and she didn't run the risk of letting the facts of her life slip out at every turn.

But then, that'd mean not finding William—not knowing that he was alive and healthy and cared for. And she couldn't imagine that. She'd seen that baby for a total of an hour and a half and she couldn't imagine life without him.

You two should consider applying for adoption. Liberty would be lying to herself if Hazel's idea didn't sound like a dream come true. She'd long fantasized about Marcus. He was gorgeous, one of the richest men in the city, and she liked him. She hated running but she liked running with him. She liked his jokes and how he treated her and how he'd put that shower in the ladies' room so she could change without going all the way back to her apartment in Logan Square.

And she'd liked the way he looked holding that baby and smiling down at him as if he really did care. It hadn't mattered that he'd had on a suit that probably cost thousands or that William was one burp away from ruining that suit. Marcus had smiled and cooed and held his hand anyway. William was important to Marcus because William was important to her.

She'd spent her entire adolescence and adulthood trying so hard to overcome her abandonment. Her life was built around making sure no one could forget about her again. She worked harder than anyone else. She never stopped working. In college, she'd held down two jobs and carried a full class load and never done anything fun like party or date. Never. She'd passed as white because she could and because it meant she was that much further away from Jackie Reese's life, because passing meant that she had to work only twice as hard to get ahead, not four times as hard.

What if Marcus learned the truth about her? About her mother's criminal history and overdose death? About Liberty's time in foster homes? About how she wasn't really who she said she was?

Would he still look at her and smile as he'd smiled at William? Or would he look at her and see who she really was—a hooker's daughter who lied her way into a better life?

"We're here," he said, startling her out of her thoughts.

She looked up to see that, instead of pulling up to the office, they were in front of a restaurant. A valet in a red jacket opened her door. "Welcome to Alinea."

She turned to Marcus. "Wait, what?"

"Dinner," he said in his nonnegotiable voice.

"Marcus! We can't do this!"

Unexpectedly, he leaned over, his face very close to hers. "We can't? Why can't we?"

"I'm your assistant. You're my boss. I'm not…"

"Don't you dare say you're not good enough for me, Liberty, because it's not true."

Her heart began to pound. He really meant that. Worse, he believed it. He couldn't imagine that she was anything other than what she was. If he knew…

But when he said things like that, she wanted to tell him. She wanted to say yes, that she'd go with him—anywhere with him.

But her reality trumped any fantasy she had. Marcus simply couldn't know the truth. She clung to the only thing she could—their professional relationship. "But I work for you."

He lifted an eyebrow, which made him look like a fox. She felt like a hen, that much was for sure. "I could fix that."

She gasped. "Is that…are you *threatening* me?" She needed this job. She *was* this job. Getting another would mean risking exposure all over again. References would be checked. Questions would be asked. Judgments would be made.

He looked hurt by this. "No—of course not. It's just…" He sighed heavily. "Look, it's been a long day. I'm hungry. You're hungry. I want dinner. This isn't a date, okay? We'll talk business."

"You won't ask me about the wedding again?"

"I won't ask," he promised.

Marcus settled into the booth and watched as Liberty hesitated before sliding in opposite him. The maître d' said, "Mr. Warren, the wine list."

"Thank you, Winston."

When Winston had departed, Liberty whispered, "You come here often?"

Marcus shrugged. "Enough that they have a table waiting for me. I enjoy dining out."

"So," she said in a too-bright voice. "Business."

"Yes," he agreed, staring at the menu. "But first, dinner."

Liberty frowned at the menu. "What's good? I don't even…" Her voice trailed off. "What's haricots verts?"

"Green beans in French," Marcus said with a grin.

"Why don't they just say green beans?"

Marcus snorted. "Like commoners? Please."

Liberty gave him a nervous little smile and he remembered one of her excuses for why she wouldn't go to the wedding with him—because she wasn't good enough.

"What's a foam? A truffle-oil foam? Is that even food?"

"It's more of a taste—a flavor on the palate," he told her. "This isn't the first time you've eaten in a restaurant like this, is it? We've gone to lunches in similar places."

She didn't look him in the eyes. "We've never been here. I'd remember it." As she said it, a waiter walked past with a balloon. He deposited it at a nearby table and the diners popped the balloon and started eating it.

Liberty blanched. "I'd definitely remember *that*. Are they…"

"It's a house specialty." This was wrong, all wrong. At the time, he'd just wanted a nice meal with her, and Alinea was one of the nicest restaurants in the country, with prices to match. "What do you order when we dine out?" He felt bad that he didn't remember. True, when they ate together at a restaurant, he was entertaining clients, but that suddenly seemed like the sort of thing he should know about her.

She blushed. "I usually either order what you order or I order the special."

Why hadn't he ever noticed that before? "But what if you don't like what I order?"

"I'm not picky." She kept staring at the menu as if it were written in, well, a foreign language.

He plucked it from her hands. "What are you in the mood for? Steak? They have a lobster dish that's amazing."

She stared at him as if he, too, had started speaking in tongues. "There was steak on that menu?"

He grinned as the waiter came back. "I'll have the lobster plate and the lily bulbs. The lady will have the *wagyu* plate and the fourteen textures."

"Excellent choices," the waiter said. "May I recommend a 2000 Leflaive Bâtard white burgundy with that?"

"Is that the Montrachet Grand Cru?"

The waiter bowed in appreciation. "It is."

"That'll do."

"If I may be so bold," the waiter said, "we have the pâté sucrée tonight."

"That sounds fine," Marcus said, handing over the menus. He looked to Liberty. "Unless you wanted to try the balloons? They're quite fun. Apple flavored, right?" The waiter nodded again.

Liberty goggled at him. "No, what you ordered is fine."

In other words, she had no idea what he'd ordered. He made a mental note that the next time he took her out to dinner to pick some place more accessible—a nice steak house or something.

"Do I even want to know how much this is going to cost?"

Marcus waved this question away. "It's not important."

"What do you mean, it's not important? Of course it's important. I can't expect you to pay for my dinner."

That made him smile. "Did you think we were going Dutch here?"

"This isn't a business lunch, Marcus. You can't expect me to—"

Actually, he was rapidly losing his grip on what, exactly, he could expect from her. "Liberty, stop, for heaven's sake. That bottle of wine alone probably costs five or six hundred dollars."

All the blood drained out of her face. "And that's not important?"

He knew she was serious but… "What's a six-hundred-dollar bottle of wine to me?"

She still looked like a ghostly copy of herself. "I just—six hundred dollars? When I was growing up…" She stumbled over her words and went silent.

He went on. "Liberty, when you're a billionaire, at a certain point, money loses all meaning. If it were a six-million-dollar bottle of wine, well, it still wouldn't make a big impact in the long run."

He was not making things better, that much he could tell. She looked as if he'd stabbed her with the business end of a wine bottle. "You—you really mean that, don't you?"

"Money is like air. I don't think about it. I don't have to do anything to make more of it suddenly appear. It just *is*." She stared at him, openmouthed. "I understand that most people don't live like that—I'm not a complete idiot," he hurried to add, which did not necessarily improve things. "There's no way I'd expect you to foot part of the bill in a place like this."

He took her in—the pale face, the eyes and mouth wide with shock—and wondered about her life. She'd always been this smartly dressed, exceptionally prepared young woman. Sure, he knew the suits weren't Chanel or Armani, but she'd fit his image of a middle-class woman working her way up.

But was she?

"So," she said nervously. "Thank you for dinner. Whatever it's going to be."

"You're welcome." There was a pause, as if she didn't know what to say next. Frankly, he wasn't that sure, either. "So. We're not talking about the wine."

She gave him a baleful look. For some reason, it made him grin. "No. And we're not talking about the wedding."

"No." He considered. "Are we talking about William?" Because he had some questions for her. And they weren't necessarily fact-finding questions, per se. He had a flood of confused emotions that he hadn't anticipated and didn't know how to process. Tender emotions. It was…odd. He needed to make sense of what he was feeling and he wanted to know if Liberty was feeling the same way.

There it was again, that shy little smile. "I thought we were going to discuss business."

"Fine. Business." He thought back to something that had come up earlier. "Why do you work every Saturday?"

The question clearly caught her off guard. "What? I don't—I mean—you know about that?"

"Of course," he said. "There's very little that goes on in my company that I'm not aware of."

Her cheeks reddened as she stared at the top of the table. "I'm just trying to get a jump on the week." But there was something about the way she said it that didn't sit quite right. Then she looked up at him and gave him a sly smile. "I have this boss, you see—he appreciates an assistant who knows as much as she can about potential clients, market conditions and so on."

"Sounds like a real bastard," he agreed. "But every Saturday?"

She shrugged, as if that were no big deal.

There was something about this he didn't like, but he was having trouble putting his finger on it, which meant he liked it even less. "I don't pay you to work six days a week."

"You pay me a lot," she said and then added, "It's a very generous salary. I don't mind."

"But don't you have a life?" It came out before he realized what he was saying, but there was no taking it back.

Liberty's eyes narrowed as she drew herself up and squared her shoulders.

"I mean," he quickly backtracked, "even I don't spend that much time in the office and it's my business. It's not healthy. You've got to make time to have a social life and—I don't know, go grocery shopping or something."

He did some quick calculations. They ran five mornings in a row and she was basically putting in an extra workday. "You're working sixty-hour weeks, every week. I pay you for forty hours."

"You pay me to do a job. This is what it takes to do the job well," she countered, looking trapped. "And for the record, I have a life. I buy groceries. I shop. I watch television."

"Do you have a social life? Spend time with your family? Do you date?"

Her eyes flared. "Not that it's any of your business."

Maybe it wasn't. He didn't know why he'd asked about her dating, except that he wanted to know. "Here's what I don't understand," he went on. "When I first realized you were working weekends, I thought it was because you were trying to get ahead—which made sense. You'd put in the hours and prove yourself to be invaluable—which you are," he hurried to add because this seemed like a good place for a compliment. "People who work like you do have a plan. They have goals. They stay in a job for a year or two, learn everything they can, and then they move on. They take the next job that can challenge their skill set, the next job that can lay the groundwork for the job after that—they network, build up references, the whole nine yards. They climb a ladder. Yet it's been three years and you're still here with me, fending off my mother and scolding inventors who can't get their shit together. Why?"

"I like this job. It's a good job."

He scoffed at this. "It's not like there's one good job in the world and this is it. What about the time Jenner tried to poach you? He offered to make you his assistant—at, I believe, almost double the salary. And you didn't take it."

Erik Jenner was an old friend of his, going back to prep school. They played golf and talked sports and tried to outdo each other with bigger boats, better cars and everything else. It hadn't surprised him at all that Jenner had tried to poach Liberty for his real estate business. He was surrounding himself with the best talent money could buy.

What had surprised him was that Liberty had said no. Not that she'd told Marcus—Jenner himself had related this whole story with the air of one who had failed in his quest and didn't know why.

Marcus didn't, either.

"I didn't like Mr. Jenner," she countered. That got Marcus's attention. Then she quickly added, "I mean, I didn't like his business model. His real estate developments seemed unsustainable."

"You play it safe, Liberty. You're more than smart enough to go elsewhere and move up the ladder. But you won't take the risk. Are you really content to be my executive assistant for the rest of your life?"

She opened her mouth to answer, but just then their first courses arrived. The waiter explained their dishes for them and instructed Liberty on how to eat hers. She gamely sampled her dish while giving Marcus's lily bulbs the side eye.

"They're good," he told her, spearing one on his fork. "Try one."

He held out his fork to her and, after a moment's pause, she leaned forward. Her lips closed over the bulb and he suddenly realized exactly why he'd asked if she was dating anyone—it wasn't because he was concerned that she was burning herself out.

It was because watching her lips slide off the tines of his fork was close to a holy experience. Her eyes widened as she chewed and then the tip of her tongue slipped out and traced the seam of her lips.

"I don't know how you can accuse me of playing it safe," she said in a low voice, "when you're feeding me bulbs and God only knows what else." She dipped her spoon into her bowl and held it out for him to taste. "I take *lots* of risks."

Seven

Marcus leaned forward, with a glint in his eyes that she wasn't sure she'd ever seen before. "Do you?" he asked, and then took her spoon into his mouth.

Liberty's heart beat so fast that she wouldn't be surprised if Marcus could see it thumping in her chest. Him feeding her? Her feeding him? She stared at his mouth, at his lips. Was it wrong to wonder what it'd be like to feel his lips moving on her body as they moved on her spoon?

Would it be bad if she found out?

She shook her head. That must be the wine talking because right now? This was a hell of a risk. The kind that could put her job in jeopardy. Under any normal circumstances, it would be unacceptable.

But there was very little about today that felt normal. Including this dinner.

Especially this dinner.

Still, she didn't know how to answer him. So instead

she turned her attention back to her dish. She was forced to call it a dish because she simply had no other words to describe it. She wasn't sure that what she was eating qualified as food.

She took a sip of the most expensive wine she'd ever had. "This is good. Weird, but good."

"Next time, we'll go to a steak house," he told her in between bulbs.

"Next time?" Because this dinner walked a fine line between a business dinner and a date. Having more of the same would be decidedly date-like.

She couldn't date Marcus, no matter how wonderful it might be. She wasn't the kind of woman who belonged in a place like this, drinking wine that cost hundreds of dollars and eating things that barely met the basic standards of being edible while also probably costing several hundred dollars. There hadn't been any prices on the menu, which, in her experience, was a bad sign.

She was the kind of woman who considered a five-dollar bottle of wine and a carryout pizza to be a rare treat. If she got really wild, she'd go to the small Thai restaurant a block away and get *pad see ew*.

"The question remains," Marcus said, finishing his bulbs. "You haven't left me. Why?"

"Because." She was aware that wasn't much of an answer. But it was the only answer she had.

Because Marcus was right. She'd worked her ass off to get this position, to get to a point in her life where she wasn't living on the line that divided poverty and extreme poverty. The fact that she'd made it this far? Gotten off public assistance, paid off all her college debt and was finally able to say that she was comfortable? *Valuable?*

Why on God's green earth would she want to risk that?

"*Because* is not an answer," Marcus said. The waiter reappeared, cleared their dishes and refilled their wineglasses. Liberty sipped—slowly.

You haven't left me. That was what he'd asked and she'd truly never thought of it in that light. She'd stayed with a job. She hadn't stayed with the man.

Had she?

She thought back to Erik Jenner, how he'd arrived in the office unexpectedly one day. He'd propped himself up on the corner of her desk and smiled down at her. It wasn't the kind of smile that Marcus gave her—no, this was different. Jenner was attractive and rich—on paper, he wasn't that different from Marcus. But the way he'd looked at her made her uncomfortable.

He'd offered her a lot of money and a lot of responsibility if she'd jump ship. And she'd be lying if she said the money wasn't tempting.

But she hadn't wanted to risk it—any of it. Having a boss who made her uncomfortable. Starting over in a place where people would ask questions about her: where she'd gone to school, who her family was. As tempting as the money had been, it hadn't made up for the stability—the safety—that Marcus offered her.

"I don't want you to work on Saturdays anymore," Marcus announced over the lip of his wineglass.

"It would affect my job performance," she informed him.

"Fine. Then I'm giving you a raise. I pay you now for a forty-hour week. I'll up that by twenty percent."

She choked on her wine. "You'll *what*?"

Oh, that lazy smile—that could be her undoing, if she let it. She wouldn't let it. "Really, Liberty, you need to work on your negotiation skills. A good negotiator would have come back with thirty percent."

"I wasn't even asking for a raise!"

"True. A good negotiator would have used Jenner's job

offer to ask for one. He offered you thirty percent more than I'm paying you with stock options. The benefits package was considerable and you didn't even tell me about it." He wagged a finger at her as if he were scolding her. "I've seen you be a hard-ass with clients for me. Can't you do that for yourself?"

"I don't—" She exhaled.

"Ask me for something," he demanded, leaning forward and pinning her with his gaze. "Right now. Tell me what you want."

Liberty began to panic because she'd had enough wine that she couldn't be 100 percent sure that she wouldn't say something horrible, such as she wanted him. Because she did. This felt like a dream: Marcus Warren sitting across from her in a dimly lit restaurant, offering her what her heart desired. All she had to do was say the word.

She bit down on the inside of her cheek—hard. The pain snapped her out of her reverie. "I want my food," she said in a light tone. "I think your bulb thingies were better than my—my whatever it was."

He stared at her. "Are you afraid of me? Is that it?"

"Don't be ridiculous," she retorted.

"Then why won't you tell me what you want? Come on, Liberty! Do you realize that today, asking if you could leave early to go see William—that was the first time you've *ever* asked to leave work early? That's not normal. People have appointments, stuff comes up. People get sick. But not you."

"Did it ever occur to you that I already have everything I want? I like my job. I like working for you. Nothing has to change."

He gave her a look then that seared her. Heat flushed her, starting low in her back and racing upward like a forest fire. He leaned forward and although she knew she needed to lean back, to break his gaze—to do anything to put a little distance between them—she felt the pull of his body on hers. He was like gravity. That's what this was—an unseen force that guided her every movement.

"What if it's already changed?" He reached out and put his hand on top of hers. His touch was warm against her skin—intimate, even. The air around them felt charged with electricity, and the shock of it all made it hard to sit still. "What if we can't go back?"

The waiter arrived with their dishes and Liberty pulled her hand away and put it in her lap. Marcus had forgotten what he'd ordered, but he didn't care. Liberty stared at her food with open distrust—he couldn't blame her. Her *wagyu* steak looked like charcoal briquettes, complete with embers. The waiter went through the premeal instructions again but Marcus wasn't listening.

What if everything had already changed?

There was no what-if here. Everything *had* changed. Nothing had been the same between them since the moment he'd found that little baby boy and watched Liberty clutch him to her chest. In that moment, he'd seen her differently. She'd been more than his employee then—much more.

Liberty gamely poked at her steak dish. "This is food, right?"

"Eat slowly. The experience is almost as important as the food," he told her, looking at his own plate. Ah, yes—he remembered now. The lobster.

"Eating quickly could be deadly," she quipped as she blew out a smoking ember on her beef.

Why wouldn't she tell him one thing she wanted? Why wouldn't she demand a raise, more perks—anything of him?

I care too much about you. That's what she'd said in the car and that was another moment they couldn't back away from.

He watched her pick at her food. "This is good," she said, diligently forging ahead as if, in fact, nothing had changed.

"I'm glad," he said casually. What if these things were connected? The fact that she cared for him and the fact that she never asked anything of him? Except when it came to William.

Because she cared for that little baby, too.

"What are we going to do about William?" he asked, trying to keep his tone light.

Not that it worked. She paused, her fork halfway to her mouth. He had the urge to lean over and kiss her, but he was pretty sure he'd get a steak knife to the palm if he did that. "We?"

"Yes, we. We're in this together. When do you want to go see him again?"

She took her time answering and he worked on his lobster. Not that he tasted much of it. He was too busy watching her. "I was unaware there was a *we* where William was concerned."

"Of course there's a *we*. We found him. We rescued him. We're checking on him." *You should consider applying for adoption*, Hazel had said, right before she'd called them a nice couple. Was that how they looked to the rest of the world? Is that how the people in the busy restaurant saw them?

He hadn't been in a couple since Lillibeth, and even then he'd felt more like an accessory than a man in a relationship.

"You really are worried about him? About what will happen to him?"

He couldn't help himself. He reached out and took her hand in his again. "I would be a monster if I wasn't, Liberty."

More to the point, he'd be like his parents. They didn't worry about Marcus. They worried about whether they were maximizing the value they could get from him.

A flicker of doubt flashed over her face, but at least this

time she didn't pull her hand away. It stayed there, under his—light and warm. "We should wait a week," she finally said and he didn't miss that *we*. "Otherwise Hazel might start to get ideas. How about next Thursday? That's before you leave for the wedding."

"I suppose I don't have to ask about my schedule."

"You're fine," she said, a half grin curving her lips. Then, her gaze flicked over his body so fast that if he hadn't been watching, he would have missed it. "But the wedding is coming up fast…"

He bristled. "We're not talking about the wedding, Liberty. Not unless something changes."

"Like you deciding not to go?"

"Like you deciding to go with me."

She looked down to where they were holding hands. "I don't think that would be a very good idea," she murmured softly as she pulled her hand away.

He wanted to take her hand back, to hold on to it. He didn't. Instead he said, "I'm not even asking you as my date, you know."

She raised an eyebrow at him. "Oh, of course not. It's a legitimate business expense, no doubt."

"Having you with me when I meet with the producers the next day would be," he defended. "At the very least, you should be there for that. I'll need you to take notes."

That got her. She screwed her mouth off to one side and glowered at him. There was no other word for it. "Fine. But the wedding… Your mother would have my head on a platter, and God only knows what she'd do to you."

He sighed because he knew that was the truth. His parents might very well disown him if he went against the plan in such a public way.

But would that be so bad? For one thing, his parents' ire would be strictly private. They wouldn't dare risk the scandal of publicly disowning him. And if he was disowned, then they might very well keep their noses out of his business—for a while, at least.

"It'd be worth it to me," he told her. "Not to see your head on a platter but just to piss them off."

"I don't want to be the rope in your tug-of-war, Marcus."

"If you came with me, I would do everything in my power to make sure you weren't."

She took in a deep breath. "Why do you want me to go so badly? Why does it have to be me?"

"Because I trust you."

She looked stunned. "Why would you do that?" she asked in a quiet voice.

"Because you've earned it. Look," he said in frustration. "Trust is the one thing in this world that I literally cannot buy. I can't put a price on it. No one can. You can buy loyalty, but the risk with that is that someone else can offer a higher price for the same loyalty."

"Is this just because I didn't take Jenner's job?"

"No." This was going nowhere fast. Why couldn't he make her understand? "It's because you work weekends without letting me know. It's because you run with me every day. It's because you are the only person to tell me to do what I want instead of what you think I should do. It's because you…"

Because you care about me.

Because I care about you.

But he didn't say it. He couldn't, not with the way she was looking at him. "I don't think you should go to the wedding," she said softly. "But then, I don't think you want to go. So it's the same thing."

"It's not." He needed to run—to move. To do something other than to sit here and make an ass of himself trying to explain it to her. "And you? What do you want? You can't want to work every weekend."

She shrugged and dropped her gaze. He could feel her retreating, as if what she wanted wasn't important. But it was.

"Let me ask you this—if this wasn't Lillibeth's wedding, would you go with me?"

She didn't hesitate. "No. I don't fit in your world, Marcus. It's foolish to assume I could."

"But would you want to?"

Her mouth opened and then closed, and he knew the answer was *yes*.

"That's beside the point," she finally said but it was too late.

"What is the point?"

"We work together. We come from two different worlds. This…" She looked around at the people eating taffy balloons and drinking expensive wine. "I don't belong here, Marcus. What I want is what I have—a good job working for a good boss who trusts me."

"You don't want anything else? Something more?" That couldn't be all. Hell, as rich as he was, he still wanted.

He wanted someone he could trust with his deepest secrets, his darkest moments. He wanted a woman in his bed he could trust unequivocally, without worrying about how the story might show up on the gossip sites the next day.

He wanted someone a hell of a lot like Liberty.

Color flamed at her cheeks, but she didn't even blink as she said, "No. There's nothing else I want."

Wouldn't you know, she was the one thing money couldn't buy. "Come on," he said, tossing his napkin onto the table. "I'll take you home."

Eight

Marcus barely glanced at the bill before he paid it, which was enough to remind Liberty of the huge gulf that separated them.

Hell, an ocean the size of the Pacific separated them.

So what if the idea of a three-day weekend with him was exactly what she wanted? So what if he looked at her as if she was the woman of his dreams? So the hell what if she was physically shaking from the effort it took not to lace her fingers with his when he touched her hand?

It didn't matter what she wanted. What mattered was that she was safe and happy and had managed to make something out of her life.

Something foolish like fantasizing about Marcus, how he'd shower her with affection and gifts and make her feel like a princess—that was the quickest way to lose everything she'd fought for. And she wasn't that foolish. She didn't need to be rescued by Prince Charming. She'd already rescued herself.

She needed to get away from him, away from his pleading looks and his demands that she tell him her heart's desire.

"I'll just catch a cab," she said when they emerged onto Halstead. She was having trouble shifting her mental gears from a meal that probably cost a thousand dollars—not including tip—to her one-bedroom apartment wedged into a carriage house behind a two-flat.

Good Lord. That meal had probably been more than her rent.

She clung to that fact when Marcus came up behind her and put his hand in the small of her back, propelling her toward the valet. "I'll drive you home," he insisted.

"You don't have to do that," she said, the desperation growing. Because if he drove her home—all that time in the car together? This situation was rapidly moving beyond awkward and fast approaching dangerous.

"But I want to. It would be ungentlemanly of me to not see you home."

"Why?" Why did he insist on playing with fire?

She knew the answer, of course. It was because the flames would not burn him, not as they would her. He might get a little singed around the edges, but that would be the worst of it.

Men like Marcus Warren didn't face the same set of consequences women like Liberty Reese did. That was just a simple fact of life. He could whisper sweet nothings in her ear and kiss her and then, when the morning regret came crashing down on his head, he could simply fire her.

Well, she didn't think he'd do that, not to her. But she might suddenly have another job offer from one of his friends—Jenner, even—and this time, he'd insist she take it. For her own good, no doubt.

This was why she didn't have romantic entanglements. The risk always outweighed what little reward she might glean from a brief physical coupling.

She could not expose herself, not like that. Intimacy would lead to questions and questions and more damn questions.

She didn't want anything to change. Not at work, not between her and Marcus. She wanted him to stay firmly in his office and her fantasies to stay firmly in her head.

The valet pulled up in the Aston Martin and hopped out. He tried to get Liberty's door, but Marcus waved him off. "I've got her."

Against her better judgment, she sank down into the Aston Martin's seats and tucked her feet up so Marcus could shut the door. She watched him as he walked around the front of the vehicle. What had she done to deserve this? It wasn't just that he was gorgeous, a blond god with blue eyes and a runner's body. It wasn't even that he was so rich that money was little more than air to him.

It was that he looked at her as no one else ever had. Marcus *saw* her. She'd spent her entire adult life—and most of her adolescence—trying to be invisible. Burying herself in her homework so she could get ahead, get out of the projects, get to college—get this job. The only way anyone had ever paid any attention to her was because she was a good student and now, a good assistant. By herself, Liberty was worthless. Well, maybe not worthless. Grandma Devlin had done the best she could, and she wasn't even Liberty's grandmother. She was just a kindly old neighbor who'd lost her own children to the streets and who saw a little girl who needed help.

But Grandma Devlin was the exception that proved the rule. No one else could be bothered with Liberty Reese. She had been invisible to the world—to her own mother. She was valuable only because she made herself valuable.

Maybe too valuable. Did Marcus want her, Liberty Reese? Or did he want what he thought she represented—someone trustworthy and honest, someone who knew her place?

Because he didn't know her, not the real her.

He couldn't. Not now, especially after he'd sat there and told her all the reasons he trusted her.

She would do anything to not destroy his version of Liberty Reese. Anything.

"The address?" Marcus said in a casual tone once he was behind the wheel.

She gave him her address. "It's off of Fullerton." When he looked at her, she said, "Logan Square."

"Ah," he replied, as if he'd ever been there before. She highly doubted he had.

As he drove, she began to panic. What would he say when he saw the run-down two-flat building? When he realized she didn't even live in the building, but in the carriage house out back? Would he start in on how she should ask— no, demand—more of him? And, by extension, of herself?

He simply didn't realize how much she'd already demanded—of herself, of her world. The fact that she'd made it this far was not to be taken lightly.

"This is pretty far from the Loop," Marcus observed as they negotiated Friday-night traffic on the Kennedy.

"It's not that far, really."

"But what time do you have to leave to get to my place for the morning run?" The way he asked it made it clear that this was the first time he'd ever thought of it. "You're at my door at seven every single day."

She fought the urge to squirm in her seat. Point of fact, she was at his door at 6:50 a.m. every day. Then she stashed her backpack of work clothes in a closet where the doorman had reserved a space just for her and waited for Marcus to come down. "The Blue Line is only two blocks from my apartment," she hedged. "It's a straight shot to the Loop and then I catch a bus to your place. It's not bad. At that time in the morning, there's hardly ever any traffic jams."

"Liberty," he said in a stern voice. "I asked you a question. What time do you leave your place?"

She was trapped. "I catch the six oh nine—the train runs every five minutes," she added, as if that somehow made it better.

It didn't. "So you get up—what, at five thirty? Every morning?"

"Basically."

"And you work until six or so every night?"

"Yes," she said, getting irritated. "Do I need to account for my time in between six at night and five in the morning?"

They finally edged off the Kennedy and onto Fullerton. "No, no," he said, sounding lost in thought. "That's not it. It's just…"

"It's just that the rest of us don't have lakefront condos, personal chefs, cars and drivers, and an unlimited budget?"

"I'm not clueless, you know. I realize that very few people live like I do."

"Sure you do—as an abstraction. Have you ever been here? Or to Rogers Park? Ever ventured out of the trendy, safe areas of Chicago?"

His silence answered the question for him.

"This is what I mean, Marcus. This is why I can't go with you to that wedding, why it's ridiculous to think I should even want to. You see me in a specific set of circumstances, but that's not the whole of me. This," she said, gesturing out the window, "this is a nice neighborhood. I have a nice place. I've worked hard for it. But that's not what you're going to see."

He turned onto her street and pulled up to the curb in front of her landlord's two-flat. Then to her horror, he shut the car off and turned to face her. "What am I going to see, Liberty? What am I looking at, right now?"

Me. You're looking at me. That's what she wanted to say. This was a nice place compared with the slum she'd grown up in. This was her getting above her station in life. She'd come up so far that sometimes she looked around and got scared of the heights she now occupied.

Because what he was looking at was a nobody who dared to act as if she were a somebody.

"Money isn't air," she whispered. "Every dollar I make is spoken for. Every grocery trip I make, every lunch I pack, every pair of running shoes I buy is a risk because what if that's it? What if there's no more?"

"Then why didn't you take Jenner's job offer? Why didn't you take a bigger paycheck?"

"Because money isn't the only thing I need from this job."

Damn that truth.

The space between them was already tight. This was not a big car. But there was no mistaking it—that space was shrinking. She didn't know if she was leaning toward him or he was leaning toward her. All she knew was that his gravity was pulling her in and she couldn't fight it any more than she could decide she could fly.

"What else do you need?" he asked in a serious voice. She felt his breath whisper over her skin and she shivered.

"Marcus…" But whatever else she was going to say was cut off as he cupped her cheek in his palm and lifted her face toward his.

"Do you need something else? Something more? Because I do."

In her last grasp at the safety of the way things were, she said, "This will change everything."

His nose touched the tip of hers and she felt his fingers on her skin—pulling her toward him. "What if everything has already changed and we can't go back?"

"I'm not good for you," she warned him even as her

hands moved, touching his face, feeling the slight prick of his stubble against her palm. A sign that he wasn't some perfect god of a man but someone real and warm and hers. Hers, but not for the taking. "I'm *not*."

"Then be bad for me," he murmured against her lips.

All at once, he was kissing her and God help her, Liberty was kissing him back. Her first real kiss. She so desperately wanted to catalog each moment to remember it for all time—she was kissing Marcus Warren!

But any hope of memorizing the moment disappeared under the pressure of his skin against hers. Touching Marcus, tasting him—she couldn't think, couldn't rationalize. This was really happening, she thought over and over. Heat burned through her limbs, making her fall into him.

This was weakness, temptation—things she'd always been above because survival was more important than a kiss. But she'd come to a place where she wasn't on the ragged edge anymore—thanks to him.

His lips moved over hers gently at first and she instinctively opened her mouth for him. She wanted this—him. She was horribly afraid she might *need him*.

When his tongue swept into her mouth, she jolted in her seat. The shock of the intimacy was enough to pull her out of the moment, and the weight of what she was doing hit her like a hammer to the chest. "I can't do this," she sputtered, pulling away from him. She fumbled for the seat belt but she was so disorientated that it took several tries before she clicked the right button.

"Wait—what?" He latched onto her forearm, halting her before she could get the door open. "Can't—or won't?"

She jerked her arm out of his grasp and somehow let herself out of the car. Then she was walking up the sidewalk, her head down and her steps quick. She didn't have his money and, when he touched her like that, she didn't have much air, either.

She heard his car door open behind her but she didn't slow down and she didn't look back.

"Liberty?"

She didn't answer. What could she say? *I want you? I've fantasized about you for years? I would do anything you ask of me—just don't ask me about my past?*

He trusted her. He thought she was honest with him.

If anyone saw them together and did a little digging, she could ruin him.

And she cared too much about him to see him hurt like that.

So she walked away from him.

It was all she could do.

Nine

"Mr. Warren," the security guard said, standing to attention when Marcus walked into the building.

"Hello…" He leaned forward to read the guard's name tag. "Lester."

He knew the guards who were in the lobby every weekday, but he couldn't remember the last time he'd dropped by the office on a weekend. When he worked on the weekend, it was reading reports Liberty had prepared for him from the comfort of his sofa, usually with a game on in the background. "Were you the one I talked to earlier today?"

"Yes, sir," the older man said, still standing smartly at attention. Maybe he was a former military man?

"Ah, good. Is Ms. Reese still here?"

"Yes, sir," Lester repeated. "Ms. Liberty got here at eight thirty, like she does every Saturday."

Marcus got the feeling that Liberty wouldn't have had to look at Lester's name tag. "And she stays until…"

"Three, three thirty," Lester said warmly. "A hard worker, that one."

"Yes," Marcus agreed. He was beginning to realize exactly how hard Liberty worked.

Every Saturday for close to three years, she had worked an extra seven hours.

He definitely didn't pay her enough.

"Thanks, Lester," Marcus said, heading for the elevators.

The ride up to his floor had never felt so long. Hell, the whole morning had been long. He'd wanted to get here first thing, but even he saw the folly of that. If he burst into the office right after Liberty got there, she'd most likely panic and bolt on him.

Just as she'd done last night.

Jesus, this was a mess. And the hell of it was, he wasn't sure he'd do anything different. Well, maybe he wouldn't take her to that restaurant. But everything else?

He'd wanted to go with her to see the baby.

He'd wanted to take her to dinner.

He'd wanted to kiss her.

And what a kiss it'd been. Raw need had coursed through his body at the touch of her lips against his, her skin in his hands. He'd wanted to strip her out of her sensible skirt suit and lay her out on a bed and lavish her with attention until she was crying out his name.

He still wanted that. But he didn't think he was going to get it.

The elevator doors opened and he strode out into Warren Capital's offices. Somehow everything felt different on the weekend. The heat of summer seemed to seep in through the windows and pop music played in the background. He saw an open snack container on a desk.

Liberty was not at her desk.

Marcus stared at the empty chair, not grasping what he saw. She was here. Lester had said so. He peeked into his office—maybe she was in there? No. The place was empty. Where could she have gone?

Then behind him he heard the door to the bathroom open. Before he could turn around, Liberty exclaimed, "Marcus! What are you doing here?"

"I came to see you," he said. And then he *saw* her.

Instead of the woman in the running shorts and a shapeless unisex T-shirt or the woman in the business suits, Liberty stood before him in a short khaki skirt, flip-flops and a sleeveless shirt covered in a brightly colored pattern. The only part of her that was the same as ever was her hair, but even that was different. Instead of her polished buns or sleek ponytails, her hair was messily knotted at the nape of her neck.

She looked young and sweet and everything about her made him want to pull her into his arms and kiss her all over again.

"I didn't expect—I mean, you never come in—oh," she finally said and stopped talking. Her gaze swept up and down his body and he could guess that she was having the same reaction he was. She'd probably never seen him in a T-shirt, cargo shorts and deck shoes. She crossed her arms over her chest and rubbed her bare skin as if she were suddenly cold.

"I needed to come in today," he said, clenching his hands at his sides so he wouldn't rub her arms for her. "I needed to talk to you."

"Is this about work? I'm getting caught up."

"You work every Saturday," he reminded her, wondering why she phrased it like that. "This isn't about work. We have a problem."

"Oh?" she asked drily, which made him grin. "Only one?"

"One big problem, which spawns several smaller issues."

She looked at him wryly. "And that is?"

"You care for me." She opened her mouth to say something, but he didn't give her the chance to deny it. "And I care for you."

"Oh." The word rushed out of her in a burst of air, but that was all she said. She didn't try to talk her way out of it or make excuses.

He couldn't tell if that was a good *oh* or a bad one. "Yes. And you seem to think that it's a problem."

This time, when she exhaled, it was clearly in frustration. "Because it is, Marcus. You saw where I live. You saw how I couldn't even navigate dinner at a restaurant where they know you by name. The only way our worlds ever cross is in this office or on the jogging path. It doesn't matter how I feel about you, and believe it or not, it doesn't matter how you feel about me. It simply won't work."

That answer made him mad. It didn't matter how he felt? How she felt? That sounded like something his mother would say—something she had said when the Lillibeth situation had blown up. It hadn't mattered that he'd been hurting. What had mattered was putting on a good face for the public.

"The kiss last night—are you telling me it didn't matter?"

She touched the tips of her fingers to her lips. "It doesn't change anything."

"The hell it doesn't, Liberty. Did you want to kiss me last night?" Because the thought niggled at him: Had he kissed her against her will?

He wasn't going to prey on his assistant, not as his father preyed on his secretaries.

"That's not important," she said in a shaky voice. "What I want isn't important."

"Don't give me that crap. What you want is just as important as what I want." She opened her mouth to argue with him but he wasn't having it. "Answer the damned question, Liberty. Did you want the kiss?" She looked at him as if he were making for her fingernails with a pair of pliers, but he couldn't walk away from this—from her. He had to know. "Do you want me?"

The silence hung in the air for a beat too long as they stared at each other. "Of course," she whispered, all the blood draining out of her face. "Of *course* I do. But—"

There were no *but*s here. He closed the distance between them in two long strides, pulled her into his arms and kissed her with everything he had. After a squeak of surprise, he was thrilled when Liberty sighed into his mouth, her body molding itself to his.

When the kiss ended, he looked her in the eye and brushed an errant strand of hair away from her face. "Don't tell me *that* doesn't matter, Liberty. It does. Because *you* matter to me."

She closed her eyes and breathed deeply. "It won't end well. I'm not good for you."

She'd said that last night and it'd bothered him then. It bothered him even more now. "But what if I can be good for you? No one cares about me like you do, Liberty. No one worries about what's good for me or what's bad for me. I could disappear off the face of the earth tomorrow and you know what people would mourn? They'd mourn the senseless loss of my money, my looks, my power. My parents wouldn't miss me. They'd only miss being able to use me for their own purposes. You are the one person in this world who would miss me."

It hurt to admit that out loud but not as much as it hurt to know it was 100 percent the truth.

Her eyes widened. "You don't mean that. People love you."

"Do they? Or do they just love what they think I can do for them?" He paced away from her, desperate to move, to think. "You don't know what it was like growing up in my house. Do you have any idea how crushing it is to realize that your parents don't love you? That they wouldn't fight for you, not even if you really needed them to?"

He'd learned that so early. He'd been what, six? Six years old when the men with the guns had tried to take him and his nanny. Miss Judy had screamed and chased the bad guys off and saved him. And what had his parents done? Nothing—except to get rid of his nanny.

Even now, the crushing loneliness of that time filled him with despair. He began to pace.

"I do," she said in a gentle voice, crossing to him. But she didn't try to slow him down. "More than you can know." He paused and looked at her. "But—"

"Don't you dare say it doesn't matter, Liberty. You want to know what doesn't matter? All of this. This office, this company, this life. You're so worried about my reputation and I couldn't give a rat's ass about it." He pulled up short and stared at her. He didn't know where the words were coming from. All he knew was that they'd been building up since last night—since before that, if he were honest. Ever since he'd found that little baby boy—and seen Liberty care for him.

Ever since he'd found someone he wanted to fight for.

And now that the words were coming out, there was no stopping them. "It's not me. It's not who I am. It's what they wanted me to be."

"Who did you want to be?" she asked softly.

He laughed bitterly. "Do you realize you're the first person to ask?"

"You talk like it's too late, like you don't have the power to do what you want. But that's not true, Marcus. It's never too late."

"I thought you didn't want anything to change."

She gave him a long look then, full of heartache and sorrow. "Do you think I'd be happy knowing that I was one of the wardens who kept you locked in a cage of someone else's making? Do you really think that I'd sacrifice you just so I wouldn't have to do something risky?"

"Everyone else would. Lillibeth would have."

"I'm not everyone else and I am *not* Lillibeth." This time, she was the one who crossed to him, grabbed his face in her hands and hauled him down to her lips.

It wasn't an expert kind of kiss, but that didn't matter to him. He wrapped his arms around her and clung to her as she kissed him again and again. His blood sang through his body. Nothing separated them except a few thin layers of clothes. When she nipped at his lower lip, he went hard for her.

He slammed on the brakes before they went too far. "Liberty," he groaned, holding her tight, her chest heaving against his. He felt as if he'd run a marathon in record time.

"I know who you are," she whispered against the sensitive skin of his neck.

"Do you?" Was that even possible when he wasn't entirely sure he knew?

"You're a good man, Marcus Warren." Right now, with her in his arms—her body pressed against his—he did not feel like a good man. "You treat your employees well," she went on, kissing her way up his neck. "You care about a baby that no one else does."

Her teeth skimmed over his skin right below his ear and he couldn't have fought back the groan if he'd tried. His hand slid down her back and he cupped her bottom, pushing her against him so she could feel exactly what she did to him.

He couldn't remember being this turned on.

Oh, sure, he was no innocent. He liked sex. He had his pick of beautiful women, models and actresses and heiresses, all making eyes at him from the time he'd hit puberty. Sex was easy, fun.

Or it had been, once. When had he last been this excited? When was the last time he'd wanted not just sex, but
the woman?

Because this was Liberty. This wasn't just sex. This was
something else entirely.

"You make me feel important," she murmured in his ear
and he was powerless to stop her as she wrapped her lips
around his lobe and sucked.

"You are important," he got out through gritted teeth.
But when she shifted, rubbing against his erection as her
hands began to drift down his backside, he forced himself
to breathe again. "Is this what you want? Because if you
keep kissing me like that…"

She angled his face so she could look him in the eye.
"What I want," she said in all seriousness, "is to get out of
this office."

Out of this office, out of these clothes—yeah, he was on
board with that. "My place? Would you come home with me?"

"It'll change everything," she said, but this time she
wasn't trying to warn him off. Instead, for the first time,
she sounded as if she accepted that it *had* to change, that
staying the same would mean a slow death for both of them.

He held her tight and buried his nose in her hair. "I want
it to. I need it to."

"Then let's get out of here."

Liberty had been to Marcus's condo building, of course.
Every weekday morning she waited for him in the lobby.
But she'd never crossed the inlaid tile line in the lobby that
divided the doorman's territory from the rest of the building,
and she'd certainly never been up to Marcus's floor.

Thankfully, Joey, the usual doorman she dealt with, wasn't
working at noon on a Saturday. "Todd," Marcus said to the
man in the fancy coat.

"Mr. Warren," Todd replied, giving Liberty a little smile.

Jesus, she was doing this, she really was. She was crossing that little line in the tile and getting into an elevator with Marcus.

"Okay?" he asked as the doors slid shut, blocking them off from the bright lobby. He slid his arm around her waist and pulled her in close. "Still okay?"

Yes. And no, but yes. In her dreams, Marcus swept into the office and kissed her and told her how much he needed her and yes, they wound up in bed.

But now? At this exact moment?

This was stupid. This wasn't just a risk—this was practically career suicide. Yes, she wanted Marcus and yes, he wanted her and thank God they were both unattached, consenting adults.

It didn't change the fact that she was initiating a physical relationship with her boss. It didn't change the fact that she'd kissed him back.

But he was right. There was no going back to the way things were. She cared for him and he cared for her and that was a hell of a thing.

"Better than okay," she said, pulling him down for a kiss.

Marcus's lips moved over hers with an urgent pressure as he spun and backed her against the wall of the elevator. "I want you so much," he whispered in her ear as his hands slipped down her bottom. "I want to do everything you like."

Well. There was that. She didn't, technically, know what she liked. Her childhood and adolescence had been about self-preservation and besides, when a girl spent every weekend in the library, who had time for dating?

So she did what she always did—she hedged the truth. Just a little. "I want to see what you've got," she murmured. Then she boldly slipped her hand down between their bodies and over the bulge in his shorts. "Oh, my." Was that all *him*?

"Liberty," he hissed, his hips flexing against her palm. That really was all him, hot and hard and barely contained by his shorts.

The elevator came to a stop. She tensed—what if someone were waiting to get on and saw them?

But Marcus grinned down at her. "Relax, babe. I own this entire floor." He gave her another quick kiss and then pushed away, leading her out into a small room with a door. "I didn't like that the elevator opened up directly into my place," he explained as he unlocked the door. "Too much of a chance that my parents could bribe their way into the building."

He threw the bolt and exhaled in what looked like relief before he pulled her back into his arms.

"We're safe here," he told her.

Then he was kissing her again and for the first time, she let herself get fully lost in his touch. It wasn't the same fall-off-the-edge-of-the-earth sensation that she'd had in his car last night.

"Let me give you the tour," Marcus said, backing her up. She kicked off her dollar-store flip-flops and let him guide her. "This is the entryway." As he spoke, he grabbed at the hem of her shirt and started to pull.

"It's lovely," she replied, not looking at the entryway one bit. Instead, she was studying him. This—this was how they really were. Teasing and talking, just as they did on their morning runs. Except now, they were touching.

"Oh, Liberty," he said in awe as he dropped her shirt on the floor. His hands touched the sides of her waist for a brief second before he started stroking upward, over her ribs. Then he was cupping her breasts, his thumbs brushing over her plain white bra. "Look at you, babe."

Liberty shivered—actually shivered—at his touch. She wasn't clueless, just inexperienced. She'd seen men touch women and women touch men, but she hadn't quite grasped how overwhelming those touches could be.

"Good?" Marcus asked, leaning down to press a kiss to the top of her left breast, right above the bra cup.

"Keep moving," she ordered. She didn't want her first time to be in a hallway.

An image assembled itself for her, of Marcus backing her against the wall right there, lifting her up and wrapping her legs around his waist while he thrust into her.

Okay, right. Not her first time. But maybe her second time. And her third time.

"Hmm," Marcus hummed, his tone light. But he kept pushing her backward, one hand snaking down to her lower back and slipping beneath the waistband of her skirt to brush at the skin hidden there. "And here we have the sitting room. Sometimes, I sit there."

She burst out laughing. "We should maybe try it sometimes. The sitting."

"Want to try other things first," he murmured as her bra strap gave under his expert fingers. The straps slid down her arms and he tossed the bra aside. "These, for example."

He leaned down and took her right nipple in his mouth. Then he sucked.

The sensation was almost too much for her. Looking down and seeing Marcus Warren doing that to her?

But, no, she reminded herself. He was just Marcus.

She threaded her fingers through his golden hair and held him to her. Her head fell back and a low moan pulled itself from her throat. "Oh. The sitting room," she managed to say. "Got it."

"I love this room," he agreed, switching to the other breast.

"It's a great room. Great views." But her eyes had fluttered shut so she could focus on the feeling of Marcus's tongue sliding over her bare skin, of his fingers gripping into her flesh.

A flash of panic popped up out of nowhere as Marcus turned her to the left and continued to back her up. Was this really happening? Or was this a dream? The most realistic, most erotic dream she'd ever had? Maybe she'd fallen asleep at work. She hadn't slept well last night, not after bolting out of Marcus's car. She could be hallucinating this entire thing.

"Dining room," he murmured.

Liberty was only vaguely aware that they were moving through a room that contained tables and chairs. Instead, she was more focused on how Marcus's hands snaked down her hips and how he was pulling her skirt up. "Wait," she said and the moment the word left her mouth, he froze.

"Wait?" In that moment when he stopped, she fell a whole lot more in love with him. It wasn't an act. He wasn't telling her how special, how important she was just to get her in bed. He really did want her and he really did want to do right by her.

"Don't pull it up," she told him. She didn't want a boring khaki skirt bunched up around her middle. Nothing sexy about that. In her fantasies, he stripped her bare. "Just take it off."

"Woman," he growled, relief flooding his face. Whereas he'd been slow and gentle with her shirt and her bra, he jerked at the button at the top of her skirt with an almost savage force.

He didn't even get the zipper the whole way down before he was pushing at the skirt, sliding it over her hips. The fabric hit the ground with a dull *whump* and Liberty took a mental second to thank the laundry gods that she'd put on a cute pair of undies today, white with little pink flowers printed on them and an edge of lace all the way around.

"Office," he said, jerking his head at a doorway.

"Mmm," she hummed, pulling him up and working at the buttons on his shirt. Which was not easy, as she was walking backward and he was sliding his fingertips under the leg bands of her panties and kissing her neck. She managed to get the top two undone before she gave up and jerked the shirt over his head.

"Look at *you*," she whispered, running her hands over Marcus's bare chest. "Do you have any idea how long I've dreamed about this?" She rubbed her thumbs over his flat nipples.

He shuddered into her touch. "I didn't want to be that boss," he said, pivoting her to the left this time. "I didn't want to hurt you."

This was going to hurt, in the end. Not the sex so much—although it might—but falling into bed with Marcus would, in the long run, be bad for both of them.

But not falling into bed with him right now? That wasn't even an option. "Then don't hurt me," she told him, trying to unbutton his shorts.

"Bedroom," he grunted, picking her up. "Bed." The next thing she knew, Marcus was laying her out on a massive bed with crisp white sheets.

Liberty fell back, surrendering herself to the plush softness of his bed and the hard muscles of his body. She touched him everywhere, but it wasn't enough—he still had his shorts on. "I like your bedroom. Nice place."

"Better with you in it." Liberty got the button on his shorts undone but when she went for his zipper, her hands brushing his massive bulge, he sucked in a breath and grabbed her hands. "Slow down, babe. Let me just…"

He pinned her hands to the bed and kneed between her legs. "Let me learn you," he murmured, leaning down and sucking on her nipple.

"Oh, Marcus," she moaned as he kissed and sucked at her. In all the times she'd thought about this, she'd never taken into consideration the wet warmth of his mouth. All that light and heat that flowed around her focused on where his mouth touched her, and her nipple went hard under his attention.

"You like that, don't you?"

"Yes," she hissed as his mouth closed over her other nipple, pulling and tugging until she was writhing on the mattress. *"Yes."*

"You taste so good," he said as his mouth moved lower. He let go of her hands and slid his palms down her sides, hooking into the waistband of her panties. "I want to taste all of you."

He pulled and her panties came off. She was nude before him. She'd have thought that she might feel nervous or self-conscious about this—being naked, having Marcus look at her with that lust in his eyes. But she wasn't.

A strange pressure was building up inside her, like lightning getting ready to strike. She shimmied against the bed when Marcus put his hand over her heart and let his fingertips drift over her midsection. "I'm going to touch you here," he said as his hand moved lower.

"You better," she replied, impressed at how confident she managed to make that sound. He was in no hurry, though, and the anticipation was killing her. She fisted her hands in the sheets.

"Impatient? That's not like you, Ms. Reese," he said with a confident grin.

"I just want to do—" She gasped as his fingers stroked over her sex. "I just want to do a good job, Mr. Warren," she managed to say through clenched teeth as he started to rub her.

"Oh, I have no doubts that you'll do an excellent job, Ms. Reese. You always take care of everything I need, don't you?" His other hand came up between her legs and touched her opening, but he didn't stop rubbing.

"I want to be good for you," she whispered, unable to look away from where he was touching her.

"You are," he said, his voice ragged with need. "So let me be good for you."

One of his fingers slid into her.

"Oh." She sucked in air as he moved inside her and rubbed outside her. "Oh, Marcus."

"That's it, babe," he said, his own breathing coming in hard, fast bursts. "Open up for me."

Then he leaned down and his mouth replaced the finger rubbing against her and he was licking her and stroking into her, and everything about her tightened down until a wave of electricity spiked through her and her mouth fell open in a silent scream of pleasure.

It was unlike anything she'd ever felt. She'd touched herself, but those little pops of release had nothing on the way Marcus had effortlessly brought her to orgasm.

Marcus knew it, too. He looked up from between her legs and stared at her. She was powerless to do anything but stare back as her muscles pulsed around his fingers. "Ms. Reese," he said, but that was as far as he got because Liberty had grabbed hold of his face and hauled him up to her mouth.

This was what she'd guarded herself from for so long—this feeling of his weight pressing her back against the mattress, the feel of his mouth on hers, the sound of her name on his lips.

She was his now. She'd always been his.

But now?

Now he knew it, too.

Ten

The taste of Liberty still on his tongue, Marcus forced himself to push back. *Mine*, he wanted to say as he looked over her body, splayed before him with delicious wantonness. *Mine*.

Condoms. He needed condoms before he lost what little control he had. He managed to get them out of the bedside table as she was pushing his shorts off him, pulling his briefs down and going, "Oh, *Marcus*," when he sprang free.

"Babe," he managed to say, but then she wrapped her hands around him and stroked up, then down, and he lost all thought except the sensation of Liberty's hands on his shaft. He couldn't *not* move. He thrust into her hands and braced himself against the side of the bed and thrust harder.

"Do you like this?" she asked, and he didn't miss the almost innocent note to that question.

"God, yes," he groaned. It would have been easy to just go on and lose it right there in her hands, but he wasn't going to be selfish about this.

He managed to pry her hands away from his throbbing erection and roll the condom on. She watched the whole process with wide eyes. "What position works for you?" he asked, finally climbing into the bed. Before she could even answer, he pulled her into his arms and kissed the hell out of her.

Her hands were all over his body, her fingers digging into his backside—urging him on. She rolled onto her back and pulled him with her. "Like this," she said.

"Anything you want, babe." Her lower lip tucked up under her teeth as he positioned himself at her entrance, and for a second she looked so nervous that he paused. "Okay? Yes?"

"Yes," she said decisively, flexing her hips to rise up and meet him.

Marcus tried to go slowly, tried to hold himself back as he joined his body to hers. It should have been easy—for years, he'd always been able to restrain himself when it came to sex. He'd convinced himself it was because he was a considerate lover, always putting his partner's needs first.

But the truth of the matter was, it'd been safer that way, safer to make sure he didn't get hurt. Even with Lillibeth, the woman he'd resigned himself to marry, he'd never given himself over to uncontrolled passion like this. Maybe because there hadn't been all that much passion in the first place.

He trusted Liberty with his life. And he couldn't hold himself apart from her. Not any longer.

She sucked in a hot breath when he sank home into her tight body, so he kissed her and let the feeling of her warmth surround him.

Then he began to move. Liberty made little gasping noises as she clung to him, her hands digging into his shoulders, her lips on his neck, his mouth. Every so often she would move in a different way and he'd have to pause and realign, but after a while, they learned each other's pacing better and she began to rise up to meet his thrusts.

And he was lost in her. The only thing that kept him from going over the edge was his runner's stamina. He pushed himself past the point of pleasure and pain as his muscles burned and his lungs cried out for more air.

She made a noise high in the back of her throat and then her shoulders came off the bed. She clung to him before she fell back, panting and moaning his name. He couldn't hold back any longer, not when she looked up at him, her eyes glazed with desire and satisfaction.

He groaned through his climax and collapsed, his heart racing. "Liberty," he whispered into her hair. He had things he wanted to say, things he needed to tell her. But he didn't have the words—that's how lost he was.

She leaned back, her gaze searching his face. Then, when he continued to fail to come up with a single sweet nothing to whisper, she kissed him hard.

For the first time in a long time, he felt right. Definitely since Lillibeth's betrayal but even before then. He was safe here.

Liberty lay on her back, staring up at the ceiling. "So… wow."

"Yeah, wow." He grinned. "Just think—we'll have three days to do that when we go to the wedding."

The moment the words left his mouth, he realized that hadn't been the right thing to say. He felt her body tense up, felt her withdraw from him. She cleared her throat. "Um, I need to get cleaned up, I think."

"Through that door," he said, pointing to the master bath. She scooted off the bed without looking at him.

He stared at her retreating form until the bathroom door shut with a decisive click. Bringing her to his place and making love to her *had* changed everything. There was something between them, something that ran deeper and truer than anything he'd ever felt before.

It wasn't a feeling that he wanted on a part-time basis. He couldn't go back to running with Ms. Reese in the morning and working with her in the afternoon and pretend that what they'd had here didn't exist during business hours.

If they were going to be together, they were going to be *together*. Marcus Warren didn't settle.

He hurried to the bathroom down the hall, took care of the condom and cleaned up quickly, and then headed back to the bedroom. He didn't have anywhere he needed to be and there was no way in hell that he was going to let Liberty head back to the office, no matter how much she thought she needed to get ahead.

He was pulling the covers down when the bathroom door opened. Liberty, in all her nude glory, leaned against the door frame, one arm seductively wrapped around her waist. Marcus was glad to see the satisfied little smile on her face, glad to know he'd given that to her.

"Hi," she said in a quiet voice.

He patted the bed next to him. "Come here."

He watched her as she crossed to him. Her body was beautiful in a real way that he wasn't sure he'd ever appreciated before. Lillibeth had had her nose fixed and her boobs enlarged and she worked out slavishly to keep her weight a ridiculous 115 pounds. Lying in bed with her had sometimes been like lying in bed with a bag of bones, all pointy and hard.

Liberty had curves. Her hips were a sight to behold and, as she slid into bed next to him, he was already having a hard time keeping his hands off them. Her nipples were far darker than he'd been expecting, but he liked them, and her breasts, although small, were more than enough to fill his hand.

He pulled her against him and touched her breast. "I can feel your heartbeat," he murmured as he pulled the covers up over them.

She put her hand on his chest. Amazing how even that simple touch warmed him. "Yours, too." She leaned forward and kissed his chest. "So, what happens next?"

"A couple of options. We could stay in bed for the next several days."

She leaned back to give him a sharp look. "You know that's not going to work."

"You're not going back to the office today and that's final," he told her. "I'll fire you if you do."

"Again with the threats," she murmured, but she didn't sound menaced. If anything, she sounded sleepy. Warm and content. And although Marcus didn't nap, per se, he felt his eyelids drifting shut as they snuggled deeper into the covers. "Fine. Twist my arm. I guess I'll just have to stay here with you."

"That's option two—the best option," he agreed, curling his body around hers. He realized he was stroking her perfect little breast, his fingers drawing over her skin toward her stiff nipple.

"What's the third option?" she asked warily.

"I understand why you're nervous about the wedding, so I can call my personal shopper and we can get some things for you. That way you won't have to worry about finding something to wear. Eventually," he added, kissing her bare shoulder.

Her hand covered his as he still stroked her breast. "Marcus… Why do you want me to go so badly?"

"Because." She didn't respond to this unhelpful comment. She just waited.

Now it was his turn to roll onto his back and stare at his ceiling. "Do you know what I wanted to be when I grew up?"

"No." She nestled into him, her hand on his chest, right over his heart. "I take it billionaire investor wasn't it?"

"No. I was actually scouted. I had scholarship offers for soccer, track and baseball from a bunch of different schools with really good programs. Not that I needed the scholarships."

"But coaches wanted you."

"They did. I had an offer from a few teams in Europe to come play soccer. Germany, I remember. There were two teams in Germany that wanted me. There was a bidding war, even."

"Really?" She leaned up on her elbow and looked down at him. "How come I don't know this? I mean, before I took the job, I googled you pretty hard."

"Nothing ever came of it. My parents didn't approve. It simply wasn't done," he said, in a reasonably good impression of his mother's simper.

Liberty winced. "Beneath a Warren?"

That made him smile. She got him in such a fundamental way. He threaded his fingers into her hair. It was coarser than he'd thought, but that just made him like it more—an extra layer of sensation. "Exactly. A few words from my father and the scholarship offers were rescinded. I have no idea how he made the Europeans go away, but he did."

"Wait—what do you mean, he made them go away?"

"I was going to go. I was eighteen and all the college offers disappeared and I had had it. I was going to go to Germany, as far away from my parents as possible, and play soccer for a few years. College could wait, right?"

She was staring at him now, the concern on her face obvious. "So, what—you decided to play professional soccer and because your father didn't approve, he made the team rescind the offer?"

"Basically. I never did know for sure, but I suspect he actually bought the team I chose—for a short while anyway."

"How could they do that to you?" She was genuinely shocked.

He smiled bitterly. "For my own good, they said. To protect me."

"What on earth would they need to protect you from so badly they had to buy a soccer team in Germany?"

"Well…" He opened his mouth to tell her about the men and the guns and losing his nanny, Miss Judy. But the words didn't come. So he didn't answer the question. Instead, he said, "It wasn't to protect me. It was to protect the family name. I went to Columbia instead and Northwestern for business school. It was literally the only option they left open for me. Everything else has been their idea."

She thought about this for a while. "Is that why you hired me? Because it wasn't your parents' idea?"

"Well, that and you said in your interview that you jogged two miles every day."

The corner of her mouth quirked up a bit. "I did, didn't I? I'm a lot faster now."

He grinned at her as he ran his hands up and down her back. "I like running with you. It's the best time of my day. You and me and the jogging path along the lake."

Her smile was wistful, almost. "It's my favorite part of the day, too."

He leaned up to kiss her because that honest touch of his lips to hers said what he couldn't seem to find the words to say.

"I want you to come with me, babe," he told her when the kiss ended. He brushed her hair back from her face and cupped her cheek. "When I'm with you, it's like I can still see that man I thought I'd be once, and I don't want to fall into line and do what I'm told, only do what's good for the family image. I want to fight for you."

She leaned into his touch. "I won't fit in your world," she warned him. "I'm not good for you." But again, it didn't sound as if she was arguing with him. It sounded as though she was accepting this fact just as she accepted that the sky was blue.

"You keep saying that." He leaned up on his elbows to stare at her. "So you're not a trust-fund baby. You keep your private life private and you've got my respect."

She didn't reply, except to look at him with her big, dark eyes.

A whisper of doubt crept into the edge of his mind. She did keep her private life private—so private, in fact, that after three years, he'd seen where she lived only last night.

In his mind, Liberty was this beacon of honesty and respectability, always on time and under budget, outperforming herself every quarter. But what if…

What if there were something she kept hidden, something that could hurt him?

He looked at her. She was lying on his stomach, her chin resting on her hands as she looked right back at him. "Do you really want to know?"

"Only if you want to tell me. The past is in the past, babe. As long as you didn't kidnap or murder anyone…" He paused.

She laughed out loud. "Good Lord, no. I have led a remarkably crime-free life. Never even been arrested."

He exhaled a breath he hadn't realized he'd been holding. She was safe and he trusted her. She was just going to have to get used to it. "You may not be good for Marcus Warren, billionaire," he conceded. "But," he went on, "you are very good for me. Come with me. Let me fight for you."

She broke eye contact first, tilting her head to the side

and resting it on his chest. "No one has ever fought for me," she said in a voice so quiet he had to lean up to catch all the words.

"No one? What about your parents?"

She shrugged. It was a seemingly casual gesture, but he could see the tension in her shoulders. He stroked her bare skin.

"As you said, it's in the past. I don't like to talk about it. But if you want me to tell you, I will."

"You don't have to. It won't change how I feel about you. I want you to be happy."

She traced a small circle on his chest with the tip of her finger. "Is that the reason you're looking out for William? Because of me?"

"Yes. But it's not the only reason. It's..." He sighed. "It's because you care about him, but it's also because when I see you with him—I didn't anticipate how it would make me feel."

She propped herself up and stared at him. "Yeah?"

What if... That's what he'd thought looking at her with that tiny baby, the love on her face obvious. "Watching you hold him, feed him—it's like I was looking at this other life, the path I didn't get to take. Maybe in another life..."

In another life, he might have already married for love, not for power or reputation. He might have a baby, or a bunch of kids, and they'd do normal things such as spend every Saturday running around soccer fields and cooking dinners together, and then he'd help put the kids to bed and pull Liberty into bed and...

"But he's African American," Liberty said, her tone careful. "Does that bother you?"

Marcus shook away the image of him and Liberty and one big, happy family. "It might bother my parents. I couldn't care less."

She continued looking at him, her eyes full of what he hoped like hell was love. Normally, when women made eyes at him, it was because of his money, his looks—or some combination of the two.

But the way Liberty looked at him was different. God, how he wanted it to be different.

"We'll go see him before we leave, okay?" he said. It was so odd. She didn't want anything from him for herself—she was adamant about that. But she wanted someone to fight for the baby. "Thursday. But I'll have my assistant check my schedule."

That got a huge grin out of her. "I think it can be arranged."

"And you'll come with me to the wedding? As my date?" He held his breath because if she said no, he would have to let it drop.

She sighed, a world-weary noise that almost made him rescind the offer. He'd backed her into a corner and it was maybe too selfish of him to ask this of her. "It's important to you?"

"You're important to me."

The corners of her eyes crinkled and he thought she might be smiling at him. Unexpectedly, she rolled off him and sat up on the edge of the bed. He wanted to pull her back down into his arms, but instead, he leaned forward and pressed a kiss between her shoulder blades, high on her back. "Then I guess we have to go shopping. I don't have a thing to wear."

Eleven

"This," Liberty said, staring down at the orange designer bikini covered in huge flowers, "is *ridiculous*."

Cathy, the Barneys New York saleslady in charge of transforming Liberty into a member of the upper crust, met her eye in the mirror of the private dressing room. "The rehearsal dinner has a theme," she reminded her. "Beach Blanket Bingo. Everyone is supposed to dress like something from an Annette Funicello movie."

"Well?" Marcus called out from the other side of the curtain.

"Do I at least get a cover-up?" Something to hide her hips would be nice. Like pants.

Cathy selected a drapey cover-up with an orange-tinted peacock-feather pattern. Liberty slipped it over her head, careful to avoid looking at the price tag. She didn't want to know. Ignorance was bliss.

What didn't help in any of this was the way the space between her legs throbbed gently with every movement, a constant physical reminder of how much things had changed.

After years of fantasizing about Marcus, she'd finally had him—her first. She hadn't had her virginity taken by force or coercion, which had always been a threat when she'd been younger and growing up with very few people to watch over her. She'd given herself to Marcus freely, and he'd done the same.

So why did she feel so damn weird about the whole thing?

Finally dressed, Liberty pushed the curtain aside and strode out into the sitting room. Marcus was reclining on a leather love seat, drinking champagne and generally looking as if he was having fun. Of course he was. He wasn't the one being trussed up like a Christmas goose.

"Like I said, ridiculous. Is this normal? For the entire guest list to be invited to a—a what? A bonfire the night before the wedding?"

Not that she would know what a normal wedding looked like—she didn't. She'd ordered gifts delivered to other people's weddings on Marcus's behalf, but she'd never been to a wedding, normal or extravagant.

Nor had she ever been to a store like Barneys. She'd thought they might be going to one of the stores on the Magnificent Mile, and that alone had been mildly overwhelming—but at least she'd been in Bloomingdale's a few times, stalking the sale rack for those few good pieces that could carry the rest of her clearance wardrobe through.

Barneys, on the other hand, was so far out of her comfort zone that the only thing she could do to keep from hyperventilating was to focus on exactly how ridiculous this entire thing was.

"Who demands that their guests show up in bikinis?" she asked, stalking to the dais in the center of the room so she could model for Marcus.

"You're lucky Lillibeth's not getting married in Vienna like the wedding I went to a few years ago. The dress code for that was lederhosen and dirndls for the women."

Liberty dropped her head into her hands. "I don't even want to know what a dirndl is, do I?"

"Probably not," he agreed. Then he added, "I'd like to see the bikini, please."

She scowled at him in the mirror. "I don't have a bikini body. I won't take the cover-up off at this party."

"You have a body. You're wearing a bikini. Ergo, you have a bikini body," he said. "Besides, if you don't go swimming in the ocean with me, you'll have to stay on the beach making small talk with all the other women who claim they don't have bikini bodies, hmm? I believe there will be surfboards and paddle boards available, as well."

"You don't fight fair." Liberty scowled harder, but she pulled the cover-up over her head. "And what will you be wearing?"

"Board shorts and a Hawaiian shirt. I won't swim in the shirt," he added. To Cathy, he said, "What shoes would you pair with that?"

Cathy disappeared back into the changing room, where racks and racks of clothing had been waiting for their arrival after Marcus had called ahead.

Liberty fought the urge to chew on her thumbnail. She was wearing a swimsuit that probably cost as much as two weeks' rent. Maybe three. "Aren't there sharks in the ocean? Things that sting and bite?"

Marcus snorted, his gaze traveling over her nearly naked body. Liberty didn't know whether to cover up or pose. "Of course. But trust me, the ocean will be much safer than the land."

Cathy reappeared with a pair of gladiator-style sandals in one hand, flip-flops in the other. Liberty dutifully put a foot in each style of shoe and stood while Marcus decided on the flip-flops. And of course the look had to be paired with huge gold earrings and a collar-style necklace and some gold bangles, according to Cathy.

Liberty winced as she was draped in finery. And she kept right on wincing as she spent the next hour and a half trying on dresses suitable for a beach wedding. If all the clothing had been pretty, that might have been one thing. But some of it wasn't pretty. Some of it—like a maxi dress that looked as though it'd been sewn out of old curtain sheers, as if she'd attempted high fashion on her own—was just hideous.

Finally, Cathy picked up a bright coral dress that was sleeveless with an asymmetrical hem. The neck was a high twist halter that tied in the back in a huge, drapey bow.

The dress was *pretty*. More important, Liberty didn't feel like an imposter in it.

Marcus knew it, too. When she walked out into the sitting room, he sat up and whistled. "Wow," he said in what sounded like awe.

"That color is fabulous with her skin tone," Cathy agreed warmly. "And since she'll be walking on the beach…" She scurried back for the gladiator sandals.

Liberty examined herself in the mirror. The dress made her seem tall and elegant—willowy, even. The color was good with her skin—she was glowing.

It didn't look like her. It looked like some alternate-reality Liberty, one who'd had a normal childhood, and a loving set of parents, and hadn't had to claw and fight for every single thing.

For the first time in a very long time, Liberty realized how much she resembled her mother. Not the woman who couldn't stay clean and out of jail, but there'd been one time…

"Mama, why do you look so pretty?" That was what

Liberty had asked. She must have been around nine. Mama had gotten clean during her first stint in prison and she'd been trying.

"I've got a date with Prince Charming, baby girl, and he's going to save me from…this," Jackie had said as their neighbor from two floors down had zipped Jackie into the borrowed pencil skirt and Grandma Devlin had unrolled the hot rollers from her hair. Mama had had "good enough hair," as she'd called it. She'd claimed her mother was half-white and that was why Liberty's hair was so good. No mention was made of Liberty's father, who was probably white, as well. But that was only Liberty's guess. They didn't speak of her father. Ever.

"Real proud of you, sweetie," Grandma Devlin had said as she teased a curl into a voluminous wave.

It was the only time Liberty had ever glimpsed the woman her mother could have been, if only she'd tried to save herself instead of expecting someone else to do it for her. Her date hadn't saved her. Maybe nothing could have.

And now here stood Liberty, wearing a four-thousand-dollar dress that was made of the softest silk and feeling as if she was trying to be something she wasn't. Was this how her mother had felt that night? In three days—or, more specifically, after three days at this destination wedding—would Liberty still be swept off her feet by a prince who promised to fight for her?

Or would she be right back where she started, waiting for life to smack her down for daring to get above her station?

Marcus stood, breaking her reverie. God, she didn't want life to smack her down again. She didn't need this Prince Charming to rescue her—she could save herself. But was it wrong to want more out of life than to just survive? Was it wrong to want something more than just an afternoon or a long weekend with Marcus?

He was looking her over and she struck a pose, mimicking the way she'd seen models stand.

"Do you like it?" he asked.

She smiled at him in the mirror. He was plunking down God-only-knew how much money on a wardrobe for her. He could just decree it was fine or not. But he still asked her opinion. "I do, actually. It doesn't feel like a costume, you know?"

"Cathy, I'll need a new tie," he said when she came back into the room.

"You went with a linen suit, correct?" Cathy said, which made Liberty look at her sideways.

"Yes," Marcus said, clearly unsurprised that the saleslady would recall his clothing options.

"I think we have something that will complement her outfit beautifully," Cathy said as she hurried from the room.

The moment the door was closed, Marcus stepped up onto the dais with Liberty. "You look gorgeous," he told her, leaning forward to press a kiss against her bare shoulder. He caught her eye in the mirror and slid his arm around her waist. "You do fit in my world, you see? You fit with me."

"It's just the dress," she said, feeling a little weird because she was wearing a gown and he was still in cargo shorts. "It's a great dress."

"It's not the dress. It's you. Babe, I know this makes you nervous, but what's the worst that will happen?" She gave him a suspicious look in the mirror, which made him grin. "You'll be your normal confident, capable self, and we'll have some fun together and *maybe* a few bored, vicious people make snide comments. So what? There's nothing inherently scandalous about you."

She swallowed. There'd been a moment this afternoon,

lying in his arms, listening to him tell her his deepest secrets, that she'd wanted to tell him hers.

And he'd said the past was the past. So it wouldn't matter that Jackie Reese had been African American or an addict or a hooker in her free time. It wouldn't matter that Liberty was a foster kid. None of it would change his opinion of her, right?

Maybe she was foolish, but she desperately wanted to believe that. He hadn't asked for details, so she hadn't told him. It wasn't dishonest because she would tell him if he asked.

"I know how these things go," Marcus went on, his fingers drifting over her bare arms. "I've weathered worse, remember? It'll only be a few short days and then people will move on to the next scandal."

She could still stop this. She could come down with the plague or something—anything to make sure that her past couldn't be used against him.

But she'd backed herself into a hell of a corner and she had no choice but to brazen it out in a pretty dress. Still, she gave him one final out. "Are you sure about this?" she asked even as she leaned into him. "It's not too late. We could just spend the three days in bed here."

He turned her into his arms and looked her in the eye. "We still have time before the trip, if you want to come home with me."

"You mean, spend the night?" She'd be lying if she said the idea didn't appeal to her. A night curled around Marcus? Waking up by his side in his gorgeous home, the lake spread out beneath them?

It was like something out of a fairy tale.

He cupped her face. "Yes. It's fine if you don't but…" Then he lowered his lips and kissed her. Her blood began to pound and the space between her legs throbbed even harder. It wasn't a bad thing, that throbbing. If only he'd touch her there again, take some of the pressure off her body as he'd done earlier… "I want you to stay."

How could she refuse? "I'll need to go back to my apartment at some point before work on Monday," she said in a quiet voice. "I'll need my running shoes. I have this boss, you see…"

His eyes lit up with hope—and excitement. "We can stop by after this, then grab some dinner."

"Not at that fancy restaurant?"

"No," he quickly agreed. "Let's get some takeout and watch the sun set. Just you and me. Let me show you how good I can be for you."

"Here we are," Cathy announced loudly as the door cracked open. Liberty jumped and tried to step clear of Marcus, but he didn't let her go and Cathy didn't come rushing in. "This tie will match her dress perfectly, but I brought a few others, just in case. I've got pocket squares and sock options, as well."

Marcus barely looked at the ties before giving his approval to the first one. Then, stepping off the dais, he said, "I think that we're ready to move forward."

Twelve

This time, when Marcus and Liberty got out of the car in front of the little bungalow in Rogers Park, they held hands as they walked to the door.

It was a brilliantly hot Thursday afternoon, one of those days that's so warm the sky is no longer blue but a nearly colorless gray. It was the kind of day when Liberty stayed at work as long as she could. She was lucky she had a window air conditioner in her apartment, but air-conditioning wasn't cheap. She ran it only when she was home.

Of course, she hadn't exactly been at home much in the past six days. And she hadn't been working late in the office, either. Instead, she'd spent nearly every moment with Marcus.

The whole week had a dreamlike quality to it. Dining out at nice—but not too weird—restaurants with Marcus. Going to see a White Sox game Tuesday evening. Even the morning runs were different. She ran faster because instead of having to catch the train to work to shower, she raced Marcus back upstairs to his home and they showered—together.

But the thing about dreams was that they always ended sooner or later. And since they were flying out on Marcus's private jet early tomorrow morning for that wedding—the wedding she had a completely new wardrobe for—she was afraid that the ending would definitely be sooner.

And it would be no one's fault but her own.

The door popped open before Marcus could ring the bell. "Mr. Warren!" Hazel Jones stood in the open doorway, beaming a megawatt smile at them. "Ms. Reese! Oh, it's just…" Her voice trailed off as honest-to-goodness tears formed in her eyes.

"What's wrong? Is William okay?" Liberty demanded, releasing Marcus's hand and rushing toward the older woman.

She was surprised when Hazel pulled her into a hug. "It's just the most wonderful thing ever!" she said in a quavering voice. "William's fine, just fine. Do come in."

"I trust everything was delivered satisfactorily?" Marcus asked as Hazel began her slow climb up the flight of stairs. Liberty paused and looked back at him.

"What did you do?" she asked in a whisper as he pushed the door shut.

Marcus winked at her. "You'll see."

"I know you called," Hazel was saying, "but I had no idea you meant to replace it all. And when the men showed up! Oh, my heavens!"

"Replace *what*?" Liberty whispered at him. But his only response was to place his hand on her lower back and propel her forward.

"William's just waking up," Hazel said as she disappeared into the nursery. "Oh, those men did such a quick job—I hardly had to worry about a thing!"

"What…" Liberty walked into the nursery and her words died on her lips.

The walls were the same, with all the curled and faded photos of tiny babies tacked up. But the rest of the room?

Gone were the rickety metal swing and the metal crib. Gone was the dresser that doubled as a changing table and the second crib. The ancient rocker that had barely rocked wasn't there anymore, either.

Everything was brand-new. There were two sturdy wooden cribs finished in a high-sheen gloss. Instead of threadbare cotton sheets, there was new bedding and, Liberty was willing to bet, new mattresses. The swing was up-to-the-minute and the rocker was so clean that it practically glowed. The changing table was an actual table now, with stacks of diapers underneath. The dresser next to the table matched the cribs and the rocker.

"This is simply the most thoughtful thing anyone has ever done for me," Hazel said, clasping her hands in front of her as if she were giving thanks to God.

"It was nothing," Marcus said warmly, moving toward the crib where William was beginning to fuss. "You're doing so much good in this world, helping these babies out. I just wanted to make your life a little easier."

Then, as Liberty stared at him, he leaned over and picked William up—correctly, even, supporting his head and everything. "Hey there, buddy," he said in a soft voice. "Did you grow? I think you grew!" He tucked William into his arms and began to sway gently from side to side. "How do you like your new swing?"

Something clenched in Liberty's stomach, some need she couldn't even name. As she watched, completely dumbstruck, William blinked and focused on Marcus. His little mouth opened and he made a sighing sound. It was a noise of contentment.

A hundred images flooded her mind—images she knew she couldn't have, but she wanted anyway. A baby—not just any baby, but their baby. And Marcus would be right there with her. He wouldn't disappear and abandon them. They'd get up in the morning and load the child into the jogging stroller and they'd all run together and then, when he got older, they'd spend Saturdays at the parks, playing soccer and baseball. Afternoons on the beach, trips to the museums.

What she wanted more than anything else in the world was a family—with Marcus, with William, with babies of their own. A family where no one had to hide from drug dealers or pimps or even overbearing parents. A family where they had lots of good food and a nice place to live and they never had to worry about tomorrow. A family where everyone was happy and laughing and smiling.

She'd always wanted that, ever since she'd realized that other people had it.

But now? Watching Marcus coo at William?

She wanted that with them. The wanting was so strong that she couldn't even seem to breathe.

"Those men—they even washed the bottles!" Hazel was saying. "I never! They put everything together, took all the old things away and even organized the drawers!"

Marcus turned to her. "Was everything acceptable? Is there anything I missed? I don't really know what a baby needs, so I had to take the salesman at his word."

"My heavens!" Hazel wiped a tear of joy from her eye. "It's so much more than I could give the little angels." She turned to Liberty. "Did you help pick out the clothing? So thoughtful, to send clothing for little boys and little girls."

Liberty realized that her mouth was hanging open to her chin. She shook her head, trying to make sense of all of this.

Marcus, who had just spent maybe ten thousand dollars on a weekend wardrobe for her, had at some point spent another God-only-knew how much on a complete nursery, in-

cluding bottles and clothes. And all for an abandoned baby
boy he had no earthly reason to care for.

"No," Liberty finally said, her voice weak. "He did this
all."

"Why," Hazel said, turning her attention mercifully back
to Marcus, "you're just a guardian angel, aren't you?" William made a high whining noise in the back of his throat.
"Oh," Hazel said, "he's hungry. I'll go get his bottle and
you can feed him."

"Okay," Liberty said. Somehow, despite the fairy-tale
qualities of the past six days, this took the cake. When Hazel
was out of earshot, she turned to Marcus. "*When* did you
do this? *How* did you do this?"

The man had the nerve to look pleased with himself as
he sat in the chair and began to rock William. "I wanted it
to be a surprise. Before I came to find you at the office last
Saturday, I made some calls."

"*Why* did you do this, Marcus?"

He gave her a long look. "You have to ask?"

"Here we are," Hazel said, bustling back in. "Oh, just
look at the two of you," she added, beaming down at William and Marcus. "Don't they make a handsome pair?"

"They do," Liberty agreed automatically.

The panic hit her like a Mack truck barreling down the
highway at seventy miles an hour, and suddenly she couldn't
breath. This was all well and good, this little delusion she
and Marcus were enjoying. All of her private fantasies were
not only seeing the light of day, but Marcus was proving to
be better than she ever could have dreamed. She knew sex
was fun—why else did people do it so much? But being in
bed with Marcus, where she could pretend their world was
just big enough for the two of them—that was one thing.

But this? Him sending professional baby people over
to revamp Hazel's house? Him taking her for a wardrobe

makeover so she could fit into his world—no, not even that. So she could fit into a very specific social setting, complete with cheating ex-girlfriend and overbearing, borderline abusive parents?

No. Not only was this not going to work, was this going to fail—it was going to fail epically. Marcus may think that a few vicious people might whisper behind their hands at this wedding and then people would move on, but Liberty knew the truth. People didn't move on from something like this.

She'd come so far. She'd literally, figuratively and metaphysically pulled herself up by her own bootstraps through the sheer force of her will and a promise she'd made to Grandma Devlin all those years ago—she would save herself. Because no one else would do it for her. Not her mother, not her nonexistent father—not even Grandma Devlin could save Liberty from her own mother or from foster care.

But Liberty had gone too far. She'd fallen in love with a billionaire—someone so far above her station that she shouldn't have even been able to see him, much less talk with him, work with him—run with him. She'd gotten too close to the sun and when the truth burned bright, she would fall back to earth and her carefully constructed life would fall with her.

For so long, that had always been the worst thing that could happen to her—someone would learn the truth and she'd be out of a job, back on the streets, struggling to start over once again. But now she knew the real truth.

Marcus looked up at her as if he could sense her racing thoughts. "Liberty?"

"I'm sorry," she said, her voice shaky. Because she was. When she fell, she wouldn't just lose her job. She'd lose Marcus. She'd hurt him because he was naive enough to think that he could trust her.

"I asked if you two had discussed applying for adoption." If a little old lady could do puppy-dog eyes, Hazel was doing them right now. "William would be lucky to have two loving parents like you." She sighed happily. "Such a handsome family you'd be."

Marcus looked at Liberty as if he were expecting her to come up with some sort of reasonable response to this statement, but she had nothing. So he finally said, "We're still thinking about it."

Oh, God—he *was* thinking about it. She could tell from the way he gazed down on William's little face as he happily drank his milk.

And just as she'd stood in front of that mirror and seen a different version of her mother—a path not taken—she knew that right now, Marcus was looking at a different version of himself, one where he found a way to make her fit into his life and a way to make this baby fit into his life and just like that—*poof!*—they were this instant family that was supposed to live happily ever after.

He thought he could make it happen, just as he'd made this nursery happen. He was rich and powerful and he could bend reality to his will because his illusion was that he was in control of his own life.

He would hate her when she took that away from him.

He looked up at her and there was no missing it—the way his face relaxed into that peaceful smile. The way his eyes lit up when he caught her gaze. Even—oh, God—even the way he leaned down and pressed a tender kiss to the top of William's fuzzy little head.

She was shaking with want, with need, with the wish to make this fantasy reality. *I don't want to wake up*, she decided. *If this is a dream...*

She was in love with her boss, one of the richest, most powerful men in Chicago.

No, that wasn't true. It had been, once, but not anymore.

She was in love with Marcus, with a man who cared for a baby boy he didn't have to, who'd once almost run away to Germany just to be free. She was hopelessly in love with a man who used his power, his influence, to pull her up next to him, instead of lording it over her.

If only there wasn't a wedding or a reality television show. If only they could go on ignoring the rest of the world.

But they couldn't. She had to end this charade before it destroyed both of them. She couldn't go to the wedding with him and that was that.

"I think Liberty needs to cuddle a baby," Marcus said, half to her and half to William.

So she took the infant in her arms and sat in the finest rocker money could buy and tried to stop looking as if she'd been flattened by a semi.

She gazed down at the baby boy in her arms. William. Her William, her second chance to redeem her mother's greatest mistake. She hadn't been able to save her little brother, hadn't had the power or the money or the skills to keep that baby alive. He'd never been anything but a ghost of regret that haunted her. But here this baby was, just as alone and lost as William had been.

Except for Marcus, his guardian angel.

What would happen to William when she and Marcus ended? Would Marcus still invest this kind of money and time in the baby? She didn't want to think that he'd punish her by punishing William. The child was innocent.

But she couldn't risk that. She couldn't risk losing another William, not when she had the power to save him this time.

She looked up at Marcus, who was making good-natured small talk with Hazel about cribs and diapers and babies.

She hadn't wanted anything to change. She hadn't wanted to risk the comfortable life she'd made for herself. And if they hadn't found this tiny baby in a shoe box by the trash, maybe they would have gone on as they had, Marcus gently teasing her during their morning runs and Liberty working every Saturday and their worlds crossing only in safely defined ways.

But everything had changed.

And there was no going back.

Thirteen

Liberty paused at the top of the stairs, her hand on the railing that led down to the beach. She just stood there for a moment, her eyes fixed on some point way out in the ocean.

"Beautiful," she murmured, turning a strange smile in Marcus's direction.

"Yes," he agreed, slipping his arm around her waist and pulling her into a light hug. They needed to get going. They'd delayed arriving for the Beach Blanket Bingo party as long as they could. They were quickly becoming unfashionably late and that would create its own set of problems.

But he didn't want to ruin this moment. Liberty was framed by the bright blue sky and the deep blue ocean. The salty breeze whispered softly through the sands on the private beach on Catalina Island, blowing the strands of her hair around her neck. He wanted to bury his face against her and let those hairs play over his skin.

No, he didn't blame her for not hurrying down to the beach.

He looked down to where the party was in full swing. Even though it was only three in the afternoon and the sun wouldn't set for hours, the tiki torches burned bright and the bonfire was already going. Easily a hundred people were lounging in the sand, getting drinks from one of the two bars that had been set up on opposite sides of the beach, or sitting around the bonfire. From this safe distance, it looked like fun. But he knew better.

He gritted his teeth and said, "Are you ready?"

She turned a quick smile to him, but he didn't miss the glimmer of fear in her eyes. "There's no going back, is there?"

"We'll go down, make the bare minimum of polite greetings, and then we'll hit the water, okay?" He pointed to where a cabana had been set up close to the water. "See all the boards? I'll get you a paddle board and we'll be out on the waves in fifteen minutes—twenty, tops. And most people aren't out in the water. It'll be just us."

She took a deep breath. "I'm going to hold you to that," she said, tugging her cover-up down over her bottom before she started down the steps.

"You look great," he told her again. He'd been telling her that ever since they'd gotten on the plane early this morning because she'd been extremely nervous. She'd tried to hide it, but he'd seen right through her confident smiles and stiff shoulders.

She'd spent the plane ride with her hands glued to the armrest. She hadn't said much of anything when they'd landed in Los Angeles to refuel and she'd said even less when they'd taken off to fly to Catalina Island, where Lillibeth's wedding was being held on the private lands owned by the Wrigley family. Liberty had turned an unnatural shade of green when they'd landed on the tiny airstrip carved into the top of the highest point on Catalina four hours ago. He'd never seen a single person drink so much ginger ale at one time in his life.

"You're just saying that because I'm mildly terrified," she said in an almost normal joking tone.

"I'm not. You're gorgeous independent of your fear level."

They made it to the bottom of the stairs, where she waited for him. "Fifteen minutes," she murmured, linking her hand with his.

"You'll fit in," he promised.

But as they strolled down the beach, approaching the bonfire—complete with pig roasting on a spit—Liberty's apprehension began to affect him.

It only got worse when Lillibeth caught sight of them and waved. In the space of time it took for her to make her way over to them, he realized he should have listened to Liberty. He shouldn't have come. To hell with putting on a happy face and showing the world that Lillibeth hadn't actually trampled on his heart and, by extension, trampled on the Warren name.

He'd thought he'd been making an acceptable compromise with his parents by agreeing to come to this wedding, but now? With the woman who cheated on him and publicly humiliated him strolling toward him wearing nothing but a tiny little white string bikini and a whole lot of gold jewelry?

Bad idea. This wasn't saving face. This was rubbing his face in his failures.

"Marcus, darling!" she cooed, as if he were a toy poodle. "Where have you been? You're looking marvelous."

"Lillibeth," was all he got out before she was planting kisses on his cheeks. He shot a helpless look at Liberty, who rolled her eyes. "This is quite…something."

She slid her arm around his waist and leaned her head against his shoulder as if Liberty wasn't standing a foot away. "Isn't it? I wanted something private and intimate." The tips of her fingers brushed against the buttons on the

front of his garish pink-and-blue Hawaiian shirt. "Somewhere we could all just relax and…see what happened."

Warning bells went off in Marcus's head—was she flirting with him? Was that even possible? The bride flirting
with the man she sold out to the press the night before her
own wedding?

But then again, this was Lillibeth. She had not proven
herself to be the most trustworthy of significant others. Of
course she could be flirting with him. He wondered if her
groom knew—or cared.

In a panic, he looked at Liberty. She was outright glaring
at Lillibeth. Well. At least they were all on the same page.

Lillibeth looked up at him, her limpid blue eyes composed
into some variation of regret. "I'm so glad you came. I feel
terrible about how it ended between us, you know. I hope that
we can—" she lifted one of her smooth shoulders in a shrug
and then, unbelievably, lifted on her toes and leaned toward
him "—make amends."

"I don't think that's possible." Marcus removed Lillibeth's
arms from around his waist and moved to Liberty's side. She
looked as if she was going to erupt at any moment. He took
her hand in his and squeezed it. "Lillibeth, this is my guest,
Liberty Reese."

Lillibeth blinked in confusion, as if she couldn't believe
he'd say no to her. "Wait—Reese?" When Lillibeth's eyes focused, they zeroed in on Liberty like a heat-seeking missile.
"Ms. Reese? You brought your *secretary* to my wedding?"

"It's nice to see you again," Liberty said in the kind of
voice that made it clear it was anything but nice. "And actually, I'm an executive assistant."

"Really, Marcus," Lillibeth said, her nostrils flaring in
a most horselike manner, as if she'd stepped in something
unpleasant.

Marcus felt Liberty tense but before a catfight could break out, the situation got a whole lot worse.

"Marcus!" a high-pitched voice called out over the beach. Marisa Warren, draped in a sheer caftan that was blindingly lime green, sauntered up to them, a cigarette in one hand and a drink in the other. "There you are, you naughty boy!"

"Mother," he said, turning his head so she could kiss him on the cheek. This was fine. This was going according to plan. They'd get this over with, and then he and Liberty could hit the water. "Where's Father?"

Marisa waved the hand with the cigarette dangerously close to his shirt. "Oh, he's around, I'm sure."

Translation: he was probably screwing around. Jesus, was this entire wedding party going to devolve into an orgy? What happens on a private island beach stays on a private island beach? He felt nauseous.

Marisa's gaze passed over Liberty, categorizing and dismissing her in the blink of an eye. "Dear," she said, dropping her voice to a more conspiratorial whisper that did nothing to prevent Liberty from hearing every word she said, "I was so hoping to see you with Emma Green. She's such a darling young woman…"

"Oh, I love Emma," Lillibeth added, smiling at Marisa. "She'd be great for Marcus, don't you think?" The two women shared a friendly smile.

Liberty's grip tightened on his hand to the point of pain. "No," Marcus said in a fierce whisper. "I'm here with Liberty."

"Your secretary?" Lillibeth said, trying to pull off an innocent tone and failing completely.

But it worked on Marisa—too well. Her gaze cut back to Liberty with renewed interest. "Your *what*?"

Marcus pried his fingers out of Liberty's grip and slipped his arm around her waist. "Mother, you know Liberty."

"What are you doing, Marcus?" Marisa hissed in a whisper, as if everyone else were listening in. Gone was the soft, delicate voice she used in public. Instead, her tone could cut glass. He knew the warning when he heard it, but he refused to buckle. "We agreed," she said, dropping her cigarette and digging her fingers into his upper arm, "that you were going to bring a suitable date to this event."

"Liberty is perfectly suitable." Lillibeth made a highly unladylike snorting noise. "She is my guest," he said, shaking his mother off. "I am a grown man, Mother. I can see whomever I want."

For a moment, her mask of social acceptability snapped back into place. "But, darling, what do you think can be gained from this?" she said, looking at Liberty as if she weren't a woman, but a thing. A bargaining chip.

He stared at his mother. "I thought I might try being happy. Isn't that enough?"

Marisa's face twisted into a mask of rage. "You are an embarrassment to the Warren name," she threatened as if he were still eighteen and a flight risk.

But he wasn't eighteen, not anymore. He was not afraid of her, of any of them. "You're doing a fine job of that yourself," he replied, pointedly looking at her glass.

Marisa's eyes blazed with righteous anger. "I am trying to protect you, *dear.*"

And he was six again, holding his nanny's hand, and crying as he stood in front of his parents and told them about how the men in masks in the big black car had pulled up next to them on their way home from the park and pulled out guns and threatened to take them away the next time. How his nanny had yelled and scared the bad guys off. Marcus had asked if they were going to call the police because the police were the good guys who'd catch the bad guys.

That's when his parents had exchanged a look and said, "Dear, we can't risk the Warren name. We'll protect you."

And two days later, Miss Judy—the woman he'd spent most of his six years with—had been gone and Marcus had been very much alone.

All to protect the Warren name.

He was only dimly aware that he'd taken a step toward his mother, dimly aware that he'd dropped his arm from Liberty's waist. Marisa took a step back, her eyes widening in alarm.

"Protect me?" He barked out a harsh laugh. "Is that what you tell yourself so you can sleep at night? You don't care about me. You never have."

"That's not true!" Marisa gasped.

"Isn't it? You got rid of my nanny for protecting me. And Father—he made all those scholarship offers disappear. He made the offer from the German soccer teams disappear. How was *that* protecting me?"

"German soccer teams?" Lillibeth asked in genuine confusion.

Marisa shot Lillibeth a hard look. Lillibeth crossed her arms and took a step back, her head down. She may well cower before Marisa Warren, but Marcus wouldn't cower. Not anymore. "We are in public," Marisa said in a harsh whisper, her gaze darting around.

"That's all that matters, isn't it? What the public thinks. God, what an idiot I've been. To think, after all this time, I'd been telling myself that things would get better if I just did what you wanted. If I went to school where you wanted me to, if I started the company you wanted me to—if I slept with the women you wanted me to."

His mother gasped. "Marcus!"

"It never mattered, did it? No matter how hard I tried to be the perfect Warren, it was never enough. Well, I'm done pretending we're a happy family because we never have been and we never will be. You wanted me to marry her?"

he went on, jerking his chin back in Lillibeth's direction. "Why? So we could spend the rest of our lives making each other as miserable as you and Father make each other? *No*."

"That's not why," Marisa said and this time, he heard a note of desperation in her voice. "Be reasonable, Marcus."

"Be reasonable?" He laughed again. Heads turned in their direction, but he didn't care. "You mean, do as you're told, Marcus—right?"

"That's not what I said. Please, Marcus," she begged, her eyes huge. "People will talk."

"Like Lillibeth talked to the press? She hurt me and yet you insisted I take her back, insisted I make amends—the only reason I'm here is because it was the lesser of the evils. Let them talk. They can't do any more damage than she's done, than you've done."

"Hey!" Lillibeth protested from somewhere behind where he now stood.

"Be quiet," Liberty snapped. "You sold your story. You sold him out."

"Funny coming from you," Lillibeth fired back. "Who the hell are you? Just a secretary trying to sleep your way to the top. You're nothing."

"That's executive assistant and I'm a hell of a lot more to him than you'll ever be."

Marcus felt a welling of pride for Liberty. She would not be cowed, either. But more than that, she was defending him. God, he loved that woman.

"Marcus, everything we've done was to protect you," his mother offered weakly. "You don't understand. We just wanted to keep you safe."

"No, you just wanted to control me. I'm nothing but a pawn to you. I'm not here for her," he said, jerking his thumb at Lillibeth. "I'm not here for you. I'm not here for Father and I'm sure as hell not here for the Warren family name.

I'm here with Liberty. Stay out of my life." He turned to Liberty. "You were right. Let's go."

"Marcus, you *will* stay," his mother demanded. "You came all this way—it would be a scandal."

He stopped and made eye contact with Liberty. "What do you want to do?" she asked in a soft voice.

Honestly? He didn't want to admit that his mother had a point. It wasn't a great point—but storming out of here less than ten minutes after he'd arrived would make people talk.

"Fine."

He took Liberty's hand and turned back to Lillibeth. "Congratulations on your nuptials," he said as he pulled Liberty after him. Without looking back, they walked down to the water's edge.

Liberty barely had time to kick off her shoes and tug her cover-up over her head before Marcus was hauling her into the water. They walked straight out into the waves, hand in hand, and they didn't stop until the water was at her chest and she was beginning to panic.

"I can't swim," she reminded him when a wave jumped up and smacked her in the chin.

"Here," he replied, turning and scooping her into his arms as if she weighed nothing.

She let him and the water carry her as she looped her arms around his neck. She rested her head against his shoulder as he turned and began to walk parallel to the beach.

They were silent until Marcus stopped. They had moved far past the actual beach—maybe a hundred yards from the last cabana. They were, as promised, completely alone on the edge of the ocean. The other guests who were in the water were so far away she couldn't hear them splashing in the water.

Confident they wouldn't be seen or heard, Liberty leaned

back to look up at Marcus. His face was drawn tight, but she couldn't tell if it was sorrow or anger. The two emotions blended together too completely to see where one left off and the other started.

What had he said about a nanny? Whatever it had been, it had hit a true nerve with his mother. Liberty wouldn't have thought she could ever feel anything for Marisa Warren, but in that moment, the older woman had looked her age, haggard and worried. She'd looked like a mother who truly did care for her son.

One thing was clear. Liberty wasn't the only one with secrets.

"The past is in the past," he said in a tight voice, his eyes focused on a point so far in the distance, she wasn't sure human eyes could actually see it. "That went well."

"Swimmingly," she agreed.

Marcus looked down at her, a small grin on his face. "You can't swim."

"And yet, here we are. I believe I was promised a paddle board or something," she added.

"Later." His grin faded. "You stood up for me."

"I just backed you up. Your flank was exposed." But then she thought of how Lillibeth had looked when she'd called Liberty a nothing—vicious and victorious. And that woman hadn't been wrong. Liberty was a nobody. No name, no family. And in this crowd—where a mother would throw her son under the bus for the sake of the family name—being a nobody who came from nobodies was a cardinal sin. Liberty would never be forgiven, no matter how industrious or smart or loyal she was.

It was bad enough that he was sticking his neck out for her with his mother, in front of all these people. She just couldn't bear the thought of him realizing how much of a nobody she really was.

God help her, she never should have let it get to this point, where Marcus Warren was cradling her in his arms in the Pacific Ocean.

But she hadn't been able to help herself. He cared for her and she was terribly afraid she might love him, and if that meant she might have to beat the hell out of a debutante bride, then so be it. And he didn't ask, so she didn't tell him.

"Thank you for standing with me. For being here with me. This is why I wanted you here, Liberty. Because I knew, deep down, that this was how it was going to go." He sighed heavily and looked out onto the ocean. "Because this is how it always goes and I need things to change—"

"Hello?" The voice boomed off from their left, interrupting Marcus.

Dammit! She wanted to hear what Marcus was about to say. Scowling, Liberty twisted in his arms to see Erik Jenner paddling toward them on a surfboard.

Jenner waved and Liberty couldn't help but note that he looked relieved to see them. "Are you two hiding over here?"

Yes, Liberty thought, frowning at him. Why did it have to be Jenner—someone who knew that she was Marcus's assistant?

She was in no mood to have to tell one of the most powerful real estate moguls in Chicago to shove off. But she would, dammit. Friend of Marcus's or no.

"Jenner," Marcus said, his voice dropping in register. And just like that, he was back to being Marcus Warren, Billionaire. "How are the waves?"

"Lousy. This whole beach is pretty subpar," Jenner said. His casual tone didn't match the way his eyes were darting between Marcus and Liberty.

She was still in his arms. And he was in no hurry to set her down.

"I thought she was going to get married in Hawaii," Jenner went on after a moment's pause. "Better beaches there." When Marcus didn't reply, Jenner leaned forward and addressed Liberty. "I'm Erik Jenner. We've met, right?"

"We have. Liberty Reese." Liberty reached over the surfboard to shake his hand.

Jenner's eyes went wide as he said, "Ah," in a long exhalation. "I didn't recognize you out of your suit." He shot Marcus a knowing look. "That certainly explains *that*."

Marcus's eyes narrowed in challenge. "Comments?"

"None," Jenner said quickly. "Who the hell am I to judge? But your mother—"

"No," Marcus interrupted. "Don't tell me. I'm sure she's having heart palpitations or something melodramatic. Hence we're all the way over here."

"Fair enough." Jenner looked from Liberty to Marcus again. "So."

"So," Marcus echoed.

Liberty floated in Marcus's arms. She didn't know what, if anything, she was supposed to say right now. Lillibeth and all her vitriol she could handle. But Jenner was a friend of Marcus's. Guy friendships were not Liberty's specialty.

Marcus was the one who broke the silence. "Listen, Jenner—do you still need an assistant?"

"I might," he said hesitantly. "Why?"

Liberty looked up at Marcus in surprise. "Why?"

Marcus looked down at her, his eyes full of tenderness. "Things have changed."

"Marcus," she said in a low voice, "what are you doing?"

"Trying to make sure your boss isn't taking advantage of you," he whispered back.

"I thought you told me you couldn't survive without her," Jenner said, his tone cautious.

Marcus grinned at Liberty. "I can't."

She saw then what he was doing and she loved him for it.

Anyone else might have tried to keep her closer—keep her in his office and his bed. Or anyone with as much money as Marcus had could have easily told her she could quit her job and stay at home and he'd pay for everything. And it would be tempting. To be his? To not have to worry about money, about security?

But that would mean that Liberty would be a kept woman—as long as he wanted to keep her. That would mean giving up everything she'd fought for to hope and pray a man would marry her and take her away from her life.

That would mean she would be no better than her mother, who refused to save herself on the off chance a prince might do it for her.

That's not who Liberty was. And, God bless him, even though Marcus didn't know about her mother and her princes and everything Liberty had done—every lie she'd told—to get where she was today, he knew that she would always need her job, always need the security it promised.

He didn't need to know about her past. He understood her anyway.

"I have a job open. It's not as an executive assistant, though. That position was filled. I need an office manager. More responsibility, more involvement in the business."

"I know someone," Marcus said, still grinning at her. "Great people skills, amazing at organization. A quick learner." Her cheeks flushed, but she couldn't help it. "She's got amazing recommendations, too. She's worked for the best."

Jenner snorted. "Man, you are *gone*."

In the distance, a gong sounded. An honest-to-God gong. Talk about pretentious wedding accessories. They all looked up the shoreline.

"Luau," Jenner said. "I guess that means we have to go back and eat a pig."

Hearing the note of resignation in his voice, Liberty

looked at him. Out here, in his swim trunks, sitting astride a surfboard, he didn't look like the real estate mogul who'd tried to woo her away from Marcus. He looked like a regular guy—attractive, yes, but there was something about him that gave her the impression he didn't want to be here any more than she or Marcus did.

"I guess we do," Marcus agreed. "Hey, can we borrow your board? I promised Liberty."

"I can't swim," she explained when Jenner looked at her. "I hope that's not a job requirement."

Both men laughed at that and some of the melancholy tension dissipated. "Sure." Jenner slid off the side. "But after we suffer through this, I'm coming back out. You guys are welcome to join me."

"You're not going to give me and Liberty any crap, are you?" Marcus asked, helping Liberty up onto the board.

Jenner let go and held up his hands in surrender, which made the board shift underneath Liberty. "I'm not your mother, man." Jenner looked back up the beach and added, "Someone in this crowd should get what they actually want."

"We all should." He looked at Liberty. "Ready?"

Ready? For what? To go back and face a mostly hostile crowd who thought of her as nothing more than a secretary who was trying to snag her boss right out from under their noses?

No, that wasn't right. Was she ready to go back and stand by Marcus's side, protecting his flank while he defended her right to exist? Was she ready to do what it took to protect him—to protect them? Even if that meant taking a position with Jenner's company?

"Yes," she said, trying to paddle without falling over the side of the board. "I am."

Fourteen

When they returned to shore, Lillibeth stayed well clear of them, which suited Marcus just fine. He and Liberty ate enough of the roast pig to be polite and then got boards of their own and headed back out into the ocean. There weren't really any decent waves here but, given how Liberty squealed as she rode out the smaller waves, Marcus knew this was all she could handle. He stayed within easy reach of her at all times, but she fell off her board only twice.

When dusk draped itself over them, he and Liberty sat on their boards, holding hands as the golden sun dropped below the surface of the waters. "And I thought sunrise over Lake Michigan was something," she said, her voice reverential.

"It's beautiful out here," he agreed, stroking his thumb over her knuckles. "I'm glad we came. It was worth it to share that with you."

She turned a smile back to him, but it faded with the last red streaks of light as she turned to look at the beach behind them. "I suppose we have to go in."

"We can stay out," he said because he really didn't want to go back in. Out here, floating in the ocean with Liberty by his side, he didn't have to deal with Lillibeth or his mother's guilt or anyone's side-eye glances.

But he knew that, sooner or later, they'd have to face the reality waiting for him back on the beach.

"Marcus," she said in that teasing tone, "may I remind you for the fortieth time today that I don't know how to swim? So being in the ocean after dark seems like a particularly bad idea?"

"Fortieth? Is that all?" He tried to grin, but he knew she was right.

"I've made it through a whole day of not drowning," she quipped. "I'd hate to ruin my streak at this point. Besides, it's getting colder."

Without realizing it, his gaze dropped to her chest. He could just make out the stiff peaks of her nipples straining against the wet fabric of her bikini top. Yeah, they could get out of the water—and skip the bonfire entirely. "Come on," he replied. "But we don't need to hang out. They're all just going to get drunk anyway. More drunk," he corrected himself.

"I'd rather be in the hut with you," she said, catching his eye and giving him a sly smile.

He laughed. He wouldn't necessarily call it a hut. It was a cabin—a rustic cabin. Three walls, a bed, a small bathroom and expansive views of the ocean—and that was it. There wasn't even a shower—that was up at the big house, where most of the wedding party and the less intrepid guests were staying, including his parents. The estate had a few of these small cabins scattered around, complete with thatched roofs and open views of the ocean.

And a sense of privacy. Their cabin was down a rocky path, maybe three hundred yards from the rest of the estate.

They made it to the shore without a problem and dropped off their boards. It didn't take long to see that he'd been right—the bartenders were still pouring and the DJ had started playing thumping club music.

He looked around. Trust-fund babies, hedge-fund managers, debutantes and minor celebrities, all partying together under the haze of the bonfire's smoke in an alcoholic daze. This was his crowd. These were his friends.

But were they? Had he ever been happy with them? Or had it just been a never-ending game of one-upmanship and drinking?

He and Liberty gathered up their things and began the long walk back to their hut. Tiki torches marked the path, so at least they weren't stumbling around in the dark.

Then a voice called out behind them. "Marcus?"

His mother.

He almost kept going. But Liberty was the one who stopped and turned back. And since she was holding his hand, he had little choice but to do the same.

His mother was still in her lime-green caftan. The shadows the torches were throwing over her face made her look older than he'd ever seen her before. It was almost like looking at a ghost of a woman he'd known in a previous life. "Yes?"

She didn't reply until she caught up to him. "Marcus, I have something I need to tell you."

"I'm sure you do. That doesn't mean I need to hear it. Come on, Liberty." He started to turn but his mother latched onto his arm.

"Don't you turn your back on me, young man. I am still your mother. And…and I owe you an apology."

That tripped him up, so much so that Marcus physically stumbled. "You what?"

Marisa stepped into him, touching his face with the palm of her hand. It was almost a tender gesture. But Marisa Warren didn't have a tender bone in her body. "You don't understand what your father and I have done to protect you."

He stiffened. He didn't want to do this, didn't want to deal with the guilt and the burden of being the one to carry on the Warren name—at all costs.

She went on. "That's our fault. Perhaps we did our jobs a little too well."

"Yes, of course. You were obviously Parents of the Year." He tried to turn again but she wasn't letting him go.

"I didn't realize you remembered that nanny," she said, halting him in his tracks for a second time. "I'd hoped you'd forgotten about her."

He stared down at her in shock. "Forgotten about Miss Judy? I was almost kidnapped and she's the one who saved me—not you, not Father. And what did you two do? You didn't call the cops. You didn't find out who was behind it. You got rid of her. And you left me all alone."

Beside him, Liberty gasped in shock.

"But, dear," his mother said in a pleading tone, "that's not what happened." She sighed heavily, as if the truth weighed on her. Marcus didn't buy her act for a minute. This was nothing but manipulation, pure and simple. "She was the one who organized the fake kidnapping."

Marcus recoiled in disbelief. Miss Judy? The one who'd given him baths and taken him to the park and read him stories at night? The woman who'd make a big bowl of popcorn so they could watch *The Brady Bunch* together? The one who'd loved him? "I don't—*what*?"

"Why do you think we fired her? She staged the whole thing."

"How…" He was so surprised that he couldn't even form the words. All he could see was the woman with the graying streaks in her hair and the warm smile on her face. "She wouldn't have. She cared about me!"

Marisa shook her head. "She might have. But desperation makes people do funny things. We had a private eye investigate what happened. Why would kidnappers be scared off by a woman screaming? It didn't make sense."

He reached out behind him for Liberty. When her hand slid into his and he felt her step closer to his side, the panic that was building in his body eased back enough that he could try to think again. "Why should I believe you? Because you've lied to me before. You've told me what you thought I needed to hear to get me to do what you wanted. Why is this different?"

His mother gave him a long look. "You should believe me because it's the truth. What do I stand to gain by telling you this? You're going to be very mad at me, I know. I just... I never realized that you hated us for that. I thought we'd made it clear that we were doing what was best for you."

"Yes, you made it quite clear that I was not to worry about it. That doesn't mean I was able to stop the nightmares."

A look of guilt stole over his mother's face. "She was in trouble. She needed money. The day after the attack, we got a ransom note—we were to pay a million dollars or next time, we wouldn't be so lucky. It was a scam—she'd get the money and look like the hero. I'm just sorry that she saw fit to use you as a means to an end."

Confusion rolled through him—that and anger. His whole life spent checking over his shoulder for vans—all for nothing. "Why are you just now telling me this? Why didn't you have her arrested? Why did you let me live my whole life thinking there were people out to get me?"

His mother took a step back. "You were a child," she said in a pleading tone. "What was I supposed to tell you? That the nanny you loved had put you directly in harm's way? That she'd arranged for her brother-in-law and his friends to don masks and use real guns to scare your father into giving them a million dollars?"

"Yes," he said through gritted teeth. "You should have been honest with me."

Marisa scoffed. "You wouldn't have understood then. We didn't want to subject you to the police, to a trial—and, yes, the publicity. You were six, Marcus. You would have forever been the boy whose nanny tried to kidnap him. People wouldn't have treated you like a Warren. They would have treated you like this thing to be pitied. No," she said decisively. "We did the right thing."

"You only cared about the Warren name." That's what he'd spent the past thirty years thinking—they loved the name and the power that went with it. Not him. Never him.

His mother looked incredulous. "Of course we did. Your father was involved in high-level negotiations with the Saudis for oil then and our first thought was that the negotiations had gone sour. We couldn't risk showing weakness."

"You let those people go because you wanted to save face for a *business deal*?" That he could believe. That was exactly what his father would do.

Unexpectedly, her expression turned dark. "We *ruined* those people for what they did to you. Their hands were not clean and we dug every single misdeed of theirs up. They went to jail for other reasons, but you can be damned sure they knew we had put them there. No one messes with a Warren."

Part of him wanted to believe her, wanted to believe that his parents had actually cared enough about his well-being to mete out punishment as they saw fit. And there was a time in his life when he might have bought everything she said, hook, line and sinker.

But he wasn't that naive little rich boy anymore. And this woman no longer held that power over his life. So he drew himself up to his full height and glared down at her. "And I'm just supposed to believe you? All those scholarships that Father made disappear? Was my life in mortal danger then, too?"

His mother waved those questions away as if they were mosquitoes. "Wanting to run off and play soccer? Do you know how embarrassed your father was?"

"Yes, I can clearly see how I've been nothing but a massive failure my entire life. Well, get used to disappointment, because I'm done. I always did everything you wanted—the schools, the girls, the company. Now I'm going to do what I want and I dare you to try to stop me."

"Oh, Marcus, please—you're being melodramatic." Anything sympathetic about his mother disappeared in the flickering light of the torches. "Do you not see what we did for you? You're one of the most powerful men in Chicago. You could run for office. You *can* do whatever you want. That's what we gave you. The world is yours."

Marcus heard a strangled-sounding noise and realized it had come from his own throat. "Run for office?"

"Now," his mother went on, as if she'd won and he'd lost and everything would go on as it had. "It's unfortunate that you decided to go public with your little affair, but at the very least, we're on a private island. This can be suppressed. No one needs to know you were dallying with your assistant." She straightened the collar on his shirt. "Nothing needs to change. You're still a Warren and that means something."

This was it. This was the rest of his life right here. His mother might claim that she had no ulterior motive telling her little story about his nanny, but he saw through that lie. She was trying to pull him in, trying to make him trust her.

"...Emma would be a perfect choice," his mother was

saying, as if Liberty were nothing more than set dressing. "From such a good family."

"No."

"No?" His mother paused. "Well, there are other options if Emma doesn't work for you."

"I'm with Liberty," he said.

"Yes, well, just keep it quiet," Marisa said impatiently. "That's what—"

"No," he insisted, louder this time. "No, Mother. You don't get to pick. You don't get to dictate my life anymore. I didn't want Lillibeth. I don't want Emma. For God's sake, I didn't want to come to this wedding and have to put on a good face all because it fits some twisted version of what the Warren name stands for." His mother opened her mouth, but Marcus cut her off. "I'm with Liberty. I'm not going to cheat on her and I'm not going to use her and I'm sure as hell not going to cast her aside because you think I can do better. I want her and I'm damned lucky that she wants me."

His mother glared at him. "You're being difficult, Marcus. Do you really think she—"

"She's the only person in my adult life who has cared about me. Not about what I could do for her, not about what I can buy her—but about me, Marcus. I want someone who's honest with me, who would never lie and cheat. I want the one thing money can't buy. I want her love. And if that means I'm not protecting the Warren name, then so be it."

His mother's eyes narrowed to slits; she looked like a snake on the verge of striking. No, she wasn't going to let him go that easily. "This is exactly why we didn't tell you about your stupid nanny. You always were a fool. You—"

"I," he interrupted, jerking his arm free from her grasp, "am going to do exactly what I want."

Lesser men had cowered before that look of intense

hatred. But Marcus would not give. "Are you, now?" It wasn't a question, but a threat.

No, she wasn't going to let him go at all, if she could help it. "I am. And if you try to interfere? I will do everything in my power to drag the Warren name through the mud. You think we lost face when Lillibeth sold me out? You have no idea how much damage I can inflict."

That got his mother's attention. Her eyes widened and she physically recoiled in horror. "You wouldn't *dare*."

"Try me and we'll find out."

They stood in a furious silence for a moment, trying to outglare each other. "I am very disappointed," his mother said softly, the simper back in her voice. "Very disappointed."

"So am I. God knows that when I have children, I won't treat them like pawns in some game that's rigged from the start." He turned, still holding Liberty's hand. "Goodbye, Mother. Don't look for me at the wedding tomorrow. I won't be there."

"Marcus?" Marisa called after him. "Marcus, this is not acceptable!"

But he didn't stop, he didn't try to figure out what twisted definition of love his parents had been using for the past thirty-some-odd years. Maybe they did love him and this was the only way they knew how to show it.

No, that was a cop-out because he'd grown up in that world, and even he knew that wasn't love. That was control. And he was done being their puppet.

Everything had changed.

And now he was free.

He began to run.

Fifteen

She had to tell him the truth. And she would, just as soon as he stopped sprinting along the dimly lit path—and pulling her with him. Liberty stumbled to keep up in her flip-flops. Somehow, she managed to keep her balance. But that was only physically.

Emotionally, she wasn't sure she'd ever find her balance again. How was she supposed to make sense of what she'd just heard? No, what his mother thought of her wasn't a huge shock. Nor was it shocking that what Marisa Warren had a problem with wasn't that Marcus was sleeping with Liberty, but that he'd gone public.

But… He'd almost been kidnapped as a kid? By his nanny? And his own parents—people who should have loved and protected him at all costs—had…well, she couldn't make sense of it. They'd put the perpetrators behind bars—but completely ignored Marcus while they did it? They'd kept him locked away from the world, as if it'd been *his* fault?

Her own mother had been a horrible person. Liberty knew that. Jackie Reese had been a sheep without a flock, lost in a hell of her own making. She'd ignored Liberty for drugs and men for years and years.

But no matter how bad it'd been—and Lord knew it had been pretty damn bad—Liberty had always had hope. She'd had Grandma Devlin teaching her to read. As shitty as the foster homes had been, the foster parents had fed her three squares a day and made her go to school. There had always been the promise that if Liberty put her head down and worked her ass off, she could save herself.

But Marcus—with all his money and all his power—had never had that hope. All she wanted to do was pull him into her arms and tell him it was going to be all right.

If only that were the worst of it.

But it wasn't because he really was going to fight for her. He really was going to risk everything—his name, his fortune—for her. He'd promised her that and he was going to keep his promise.

She'd tried to tell him that she wasn't good for him, that she'd hurt him. But he hadn't listened.

Well, that had to change, starting right now. She'd tell him about her childhood, about her times in foster care, about all those lies she lived with. He'd understand. After all, he understood how much she needed to make sure William was okay. It hadn't mattered to Marcus that William was a lost baby boy. Marcus would see that Liberty had done what she needed to in order to survive.

They crested the small hill in front of their cabin hut. He didn't even break stride as he ran up the single step that led inside. He only stopped when they reached the raised platform that held the bed.

Hands linked, they stood there for a short second, both of them panting from the run. His head was down and she knew he was hurting. And she knew telling him that she wasn't exactly the woman he thought she was would hurt him even more.

But she couldn't be yet another woman who lied to Marcus Warren. She was better than that. She had to be, if she wanted to be good enough for him. "Marcus," she began, trying to find the words. *I'm black—but I've been passing as white my entire adult life. My mother was an addict and a hooker. And I'm in love with you.*

"Don't talk," he said gruffly, turning and yanking her into his arms. Before she could react, his mouth crushed down onto hers.

It was not a tender kiss, not when his teeth clipped her lower lip. But she didn't pull away, didn't do anything but tilt her head to give him better access. She could taste the desperation on his lips—the confusion, the despair.

"Marcus," she said, pulling back enough that she could form the words. "I need to—"

"Don't want to talk." He jerked at the clasp of her bikini top and savagely pulled it off. The cold air hit her chest, still damp with ocean water, and she shivered when her nipples went tight. Then his mouth was against her bare skin, sucking her nipple into his mouth. "Let me take care of you."

"Marcus…" This wasn't about him taking care of her— she needed to take care of him. She needed to protect him. But his mouth was on her body and he was yanking down her bikini bottoms and sliding his hands up between her legs and…and she couldn't fight the rising surge of desire.

Still, she knew this wasn't about her. It wasn't. This was about him and dammit all, she needed to do something to tell him that she'd be here for him, however he needed her. "It's going to be okay," she said because that's what he needed to hear. Because that was what she'd always wanted to know when she was being thrown around by her mother's fate. She reached for his board shorts and began to pull them down. "Everything's going to be okay."

"Stop talking." He pushed her back down onto the bed and grabbed a condom. Before she'd even gotten his shorts all the way off, he spread her legs and plunged into her with a savageness that she'd never experienced before. She gasped as he filled her completely in one sure stroke, her body shuddering to take him in.

He paused, hovering over her, his head down. He was breathing hard, although she didn't know if that was from the sprint back to their hut or from the conversation with his mother or what.

"It's okay," she murmured. She ran her fingers through his hair, trying to lift his face so she could see him. They'd been lovers for only a week now and she was still getting used to the feeling of Marcus's body joined to hers. "It's okay, baby." She wasn't sure if she was telling him or herself.

She expected him to move—but she didn't expect him to grab her hands and hold them over her head. Then his mouth closed over hers again and he furiously kissed her as he began to thrust.

For the first time, she was completely at his mercy. He'd spent the past week making sure that she was comfortable, that she was okay with what was happening. Any sweetness was gone, however, as he drove into her harder and harder.

If it'd been anyone else, she might have been scared. But this was Marcus and she was his. She'd always been his.

But more than that, he was hers. This raw coupling, this furious need? This was how much he needed her. So instead of trying to reassure him, instead of struggling to get her hands loose so she could touch him, she gave herself over to him completely. This was what he needed and she could give it to him.

He shifted and held both of her wrists with one hand and then grabbed at her bare breast. He pinched her nipple with just enough pressure to make her gasp and, when she did, he covered her mouth with his.

He shifted again, slipping his free hand under her left leg and holding her thigh up so that he could thrust deeper. Electricity filled the air between them, making her skin prickle as her climax began to build. "Yes," she hissed at him. "Oh, yes, Marcus."

"Babe," he groaned, his teeth scraping over the sensitive skin at the base of her neck. Then he pushed back and reached down between her legs, his fingers finding the place where she needed him most.

He pressed and thrust into her, and Liberty couldn't control herself any more than she could control the storms. Her climax broke over her like a clap of thunder. Marcus thrust a few more times before he froze. Then, groaning, he fell forward onto her.

She pulled her arms free of his grasp and hugged him to her. She didn't say anything, though. She didn't need to. She just needed to be here for him.

They lay tangled together, breathing hard, for several minutes before Marcus leaned up on his elbows, a sheepish grin on his face. "Okay?"

"Okay," she agreed. "More than okay." Except she needed to tell him. And she hadn't yet.

Before she could get her mouth to form the words, Marcus said, "Before I had you, I didn't know I could fight back, babe. But I'm going to fight for you—for us. You and me and even William."

The mention of the baby shocked her out of her little speech about mothers and prison and foster care. "William?"

Marcus rolled over and pulled her up into his arms. "I think maybe we should try to apply for custody. Together."

She sat bolt upright. "We should *what*?"

His smile this time was more confident—the smile of a man who knew what he wanted and was used to getting it. This was, after all, Marcus Warren—and very few people said no to him. "I know I'm screwed up and I know my parents probably aren't done with me yet. But it doesn't matter what they think, what anyone thinks, I'm not going to hide you and I'm not going to let you go. I'm going to fight for you, Liberty." He touched her face, his fingertips trailing over her cheek. "I can give you anything you want. And you want William."

"But—I work. I *need* to work. And what about Jenner?"

"I know it bothers you to carry on an affair with your boss. I'm not that fond of the circumstances myself. My father is notorious for sleeping with his assistants, and I want to be better than that. I want us to be on a level playing field."

"But—the baby?"

He shrugged. "We can hire a nanny or you can take some time off. A year."

She stared at him openmouthed. "But…"

"There are no *but*s here, Liberty. I want you. I think I've known that for a long time. I want to wake up in the morning with you in my arms and I want you in my bed every night. You are the one person I trust and I can't imagine life without you anymore. Come live with me." He sat up and touched his head to hers. "Come be my family. You and me and William."

"Marcus…" *I'm black. My mother was a convict.* "You should know—"

He shook his head. "No, I don't want to know. Really, Liberty—it doesn't matter. I can't change your past any more than I can change mine. It doesn't matter any more than my mother's version of what my nanny did matters. It's

over and done and I'm not looking over my shoulder anymore. I know what I need to know—that I love you and I
want you," he whispered, his thumb stroking over her cheek.

She couldn't. She shouldn't.

Then he said, "Let me be your family, Liberty—that's
what I want. Be my family. Be mine."

And how was she supposed to say no to that? If the life
she'd been born into truly didn't matter to him, then it didn't
matter to her. Jackie Reese was dead and gone, and so was
her grubby little baby girl. The woman she was now—that
was who mattered. She mattered because Marcus loved her.

"That's what I want, too," she told him.

He began to laugh, a happy noise that couldn't be stopped.
And she laughed with him.

Because she wanted to.

Sixteen

"Why are we doing this again?" Liberty stopped in front of the nondescript building that held the offices for the producers of *Feeding Frenzy*.

It'd been two days since they'd left Catalina Island early Saturday morning—hours before the Hanson-Spears wedding had been scheduled to take place. Since then, they'd been ensconced in a suite at the Beverly Hills Hotel, feasting on room service and each other.

Marcus had no idea if Lillibeth had actually gotten married or what his mother had told people about their absence. And what was more, he didn't care. "We have a meeting. It would be rude to bail."

Liberty made a noise of frustration. "I didn't think meeting with reality-show producers was a good idea before we got involved," she said. "And now? I think it's a *really* bad idea."

"I'm not going to do the show," he said, holding her hand as they headed inside. The fact that she was arguing with him made him smile. He couldn't have this kind of honest conversation with anyone else. Just her.

"Then why meet with them at all? You don't have to do this."

"Look." He stopped and turned to face her. "My parents are insane."

"No argument here," she replied, wrinkling her nose.

"But," Marcus went on, "they're right—to a degree," he hastily added when Liberty rolled her eyes. "I do have a business image to maintain. So this isn't about building my brand name. This meeting is more about keeping investment options open. I'll listen to their pitch, politely say it's not for me and who knows? Maybe in a year or three, someone remembers this meeting and they reach out to me with an investment opportunity." He squeezed her hand, hoping she'd see that this was a good compromise. After all, it would be foolhardy to close the door on potential investments. That was his whole business. "I could make movies."

"You could do that anyway. You're Marcus Warren," she reminded him, trying to look stern. But he saw the way the corner of her mouth curved up into a tiny smile. "You can do whatever you want."

"Speaking of that," he murmured, pulling her in closer. "What do you want to do after this? We can see the sights or…" He pressed a kiss right underneath her ear and was rewarded when she shivered.

They'd get this meeting out of the way and then they'd take another day or two to do whatever Liberty wanted. And after that, they'd head back to Chicago and he'd start working on assembling the necessary paperwork to get custody of William.

Liberty would move in, of course. And if she didn't like his place, they'd get a new place, one that was theirs and not just his. And he'd have to get a ring. "Or we could fly to Vegas and get married."

Liberty jolted against him. "Marcus…" she said in a quiet voice. "Let's—let's get through this first."

He looked at her—was that reluctance in her voice? But she gave him a huge smile, as if maybe getting married was exactly what she was thinking, too. "Think about it—but no Beach Blanket Bingo. That's final."

She laughed and he laughed with her. This was right. This was his life on his terms.

They were shown into a conference room. Liberty sat beside Marcus, her tablet out. He smiled to himself as she slipped back into her role as executive assistant as if nothing had happened. The only thing that seemed different about her was the business suit he'd bought for her. Everything else was the same.

The show staff filed into the room. In general, they were all slightly rumpled looking. Rick Chabot, the producer of *Feeding Frenzy*, introduced himself and his coproducers, assistant producers and executive assistants—seriously, how many people were in this entourage?

Finally, all the hands were shaken and they all sat down, Marcus and Liberty at one end of the table, Chabot and his crew at the other. "Now," Chabot said in a different tone from the one he had just used to introduce half of Hollywood. Marcus shot Liberty a look, but all she did was shrug. Chabot was studying his own tablet. "Let's get down to business. You and Ms. Reese are a couple, is that correct?"

"Yes," Marcus said in what he hoped was a casual voice. He'd just spent five minutes introducing her as his assistant. Where the hell had this guy gotten that information?

"That's going to be a problem for *Feeding Frenzy*," Chabot went on, without bothering to look up. One of his group tapped his arm and tilted a screen in his direction.

Chabot nodded and continued. "Gotta be honest with you, Warren—part of your appeal is your availability. You're hot, you're rich—you've got to be single for this show. Someone with her background isn't going to send the right signals to our target viewers, especially not women."

"Excuse me? What background?" He looked at Liberty and was surprised to see that she'd turned a ghastly shade of green.

Chabot studied his tablet before turning a critical eye on Liberty. "Is this correct? Your mother was a convicted drug mule and hooker? She died of an overdose?"

A different person leaned over and pointed at the screen. "Is that a picture of Liberty with her mother? But is she…?" The producer turned the tablet around so that Marcus could see the photo of a young girl, clearly Liberty, standing in front of an apartment building with a gaunt-looking, light-skinned African American woman.

There was a moment of total silence. Marcus knew he needed to say something—it was completely unnecessary to blindside Liberty like this. And it was patently untrue.

Except…

Except Liberty wasn't denying it. She wasn't doing anything—maybe not even breathing. If everything Chabot had just said had been a lie, Liberty would have laughed it off. She wouldn't just be sitting there, looking as if she'd been shot.

Because it wasn't a lie, Marcus realized.

"Where are you getting your information?" Liberty managed to ask in a strangled voice.

"We received an email," Chabot said. "We vet all our candidates thoroughly so we followed up." For the first time, he looked up at Liberty. "It's not personal, you understand."

"No, of course not," she mumbled.

"Now—you have a child you gave up for adoption, is that correct?"

That got an immediate response out of her. "What? No."

Chabot scrolled. "A boy named William? Is that not correct?"

Marcus gaped at her. She couldn't possibly—could she have?

"I do not have a child," Liberty said firmly. "Your source is mistaken."

"We're selling a specific image here—wealthy, powerful," Chabot went on as though Marcus gave a flying rat's ass for what he was saying. "Now, if you two were already married, that might be one thing, but if we're going to take this to the next level…"

He said other things about image and selling, but Marcus didn't hear him. All he could do was stare at Liberty. She did not meet his gaze.

Her mother was African American? An addict? And a hooker? Why hadn't she told him? She couldn't possibly think that it mattered to him, could she? Or had there been another reason she'd kept that part of her hidden?

No, not even hidden. She'd lied to him. And for what? She had to realize that her race was a nonissue to him. But what would she have gained by making him think she was something she wasn't?

I'm not good for you. That's what she'd said, over and over. All those times she'd tried to convince him not to take her to the wedding? Not to do this stupid reality show?

Was this what she'd tried to tell him? Was *this* what he'd said didn't matter?

"…market share," Chabot was saying. "And you can be listed as a producer, of course."

He'd rather gouge out his eye with a rusty spoon. "Well," Marcus said, standing up before he quite knew what he was doing. Because this mattered. This history—he couldn't wrap his head around it. He'd thought...well, he'd thought wrong.

All he knew was that there was no way in hell he was doing anything that would take him to "the next level." He shuddered at the mere thought. What did that even mean? His face on lunch boxes? Did people even have lunch boxes anymore? He didn't know and he didn't want to find out. "We'll be in touch," he lied. Then he turned on his heel and walked right out of that crowded room.

He didn't know if Liberty followed him and he didn't wait around to find out. He didn't want to hear her excuses. He'd heard it all before—from his mother, from Lillibeth. From everyone who wanted a piece of the Warren name, the Warren fortune—but not him. Never him.

They all told him what they thought he needed to hear. To "protect" him. No doubt Liberty would say the same thing. She'd been trying to protect him from the truth—but why? So it could be used against him? Or had there been something more to it? Something sinister?

Idiot. That's what he was. A fool of the first-class order. Because people always wanted something from him. His money, his power, his body—but not him. Never just him. He'd thought Liberty was different. But was she? She'd pushed back against coming to the wedding with him, against this meeting—and she'd made it sound like it was because she was worried about him.

But he saw the truth. She'd been protecting herself and her secrets. How many more did she have? Was this just the tip of the iceberg?

There was always a cost. Everything was a transaction. And if you didn't gain something you lost.

God, he was tired of being the loser. And this time, it was no one's fault but his own.

He realized he was already outside. He didn't remember walking out of the conference room or down the hall.

"Marcus," Liberty said in a soft voice behind him that, yes, had a tinge of fear to it. He could hear her footfalls now as she hurried to catch up.

He kept going. He had a car around here somewhere, a car with a driver. The guy couldn't have gone far.

"Marcus, wait—please."

He didn't want to. He didn't want to give her another second of his time. But he didn't know where his car was and he had no idea where he was going. The confusion metastasized into rage. This was his fault—because he'd dared to be a real man with her.

He didn't feel as real anymore. "Why?" He turned on her. "Why, Liberty?"

She stood before him, her eyes painfully wide. She looked awful and the foolish part of his brain that hadn't gotten the message that she was not to be trusted, she was not safe—she was just like all the rest—wanted to pull her into his arms and tell her it was going to be all right.

It wasn't, though. So he did no such thing.

"I…" She swallowed, clutching her tablet to her chest. Her bag gaped open on her shoulder. She looked as if she'd run after him. Maybe she had. He didn't care. "I called for the car. He's coming right away."

"That's what you have to say? That's it?"

"I didn't—we should—" Her back stiffened. "Can we at least wait for the car? If I'm going to be humiliated for the second time in less than an hour, at least I'd like it to be in private."

"Oh, yes—sure. We wouldn't want any more public humiliations, would we?"

For a moment, he thought she was going to bend. Her

chin dropped and her shoulders hunched and she looked small and vulnerable.

Fine. Good. She could just look that way. It was a trick, a play on his feelings. Well, he'd show her. He'd stop having feelings. That was his mistake; he saw that now. He'd allowed himself to care about someone. Her. He should have learned his lesson after Lillibeth a little better.

But then Liberty rallied. She straightened up and glared at him. "Can we wait for the car, please? Or is it going to make you feel better to put me in my place with an audience?" She glanced around them with an exaggerated motion.

Yes, people were milling around. No one was paying them a lot of attention, though. "You know what? It's not. It's not going to make me feel any better. But how tender of you to pretend you care."

"I do care," she responded, the fire lighting in her eyes. "Don't you dare imply I don't."

The rage in his chest built, swirling back on itself like a hailstorm picking up speed. God dammit, he could do some damage right now. He could leave a wake of destruction in his path and watch the world burn.

"You're a fine one to be talking about daring. When were you going to tell me? Or were you going to wait until we'd adopted that baby? Until we had children of our own?"

"William is not my child." She paused, as if she was collecting herself. Or was she just trying to get her story straight? "He couldn't be. You were my first."

"You were a *virgin*?" he roared.

She flinched as if he'd slapped her. Heads around them turned. If people hadn't noticed them before, they sure as hell did now. "Marcus—the car—"

But the storm of rage kept on swirling and he couldn't fight it. "And you didn't feel like you should have mentioned that at some point?"

"I tried," she snapped. "I tried to tell you about all of it. You're the one who said the past was the past, and my past didn't matter any more than yours did. You're the one who cut me off. So, yes, I did feel like I should have mentioned it at many points. And I didn't because you didn't want me to."

"Because I thought you'd gotten your heart broken or you had to, I don't know, work your way through college—something common like that! I never imagined you were passing as white and hiding this! Because that seems important to me. I was going to marry you, for God's sake! I wanted to have a family with you! I trusted you with everything, Liberty. Everything. Things I've never told anyone else because I love you. And you didn't. You obviously didn't trust me at all."

"Marcus," she pleaded as tears started to drip down her cheeks. "I wanted to tell you but—"

"No. If you'd wanted to, you would have." Her tears were not going to move him. Not even a bit. "And you know what? It doesn't even matter. I don't care."

"You...don't?" Her chest hitched up as her eyes swam.

"An honest conversation, Liberty. That's all I wanted. That's what I thought I was having. I mean—is it all a lie? Did you even run?"

She flinched. "No. I never ran before I met you."

Everything he thought he knew about her was based on a lie. The past three years, their morning run together—that time had saved him. Because he had Lake Michigan and Liberty and the freedom to run, he'd been able to get past Lillibeth's betrayal. He'd been able to deal with the pressure his parents put on him.

He didn't think he'd be able to run his way out of this storm. "Nothing but lies. And why? Was it just so you could trick me into marrying you? So you could have a piece of the Warren name?"

That got a reaction out of her. "Don't be ridiculous, Marcus. I hate your name and I hate what your family has done to you because of it." The force of her anger pushed him back a step.

"Then why? And I want a real answer, Liberty. No more lies."

"Why? Have you ever tried being a black woman in this world? We aren't all born with a collection of silver spoons to choose from, Marcus."

He wasn't going to be relieved that she was fighting back, that he'd always loved how she argued with him when most everyone else would tell him what they thought he wanted to hear. The Liberty he'd loved had been a lie.

"Yes, my mother was black and yes, my father was probably white. I don't know. All I know is that passing meant I only had to work twice as hard to get out of the gutter instead of four times as hard. So yes, I passed. Yes, I let everyone think I was a middle-class white girl. I'm not about to apologize for what I had to do to survive."

"I don't want you to apologize for surviving, dammit."

"Then what do you want from me?"

"I wanted the *real* you, Liberty."

Her eyes flicked behind him. "The car is here. I'll be happy to tell you what it was like growing up with a hooker junkie for a mother and being bounced around from foster home to foster home—in the damned car, Marcus."

"No, I'm done. I'm *done*, Liberty. Do you realize that I risked everything for you? I stood up to my mother for you, I bailed on commitments for you—I would have done anything for you." His voice caught in his throat but he ignored that. "I would have fought for you, Liberty."

She looked at him with so much pity in her eyes that it made him physically nauseous. All his rage seemed to blow itself out and suddenly he was tired.

He'd wanted things to change and change they had. Why hadn't he considered the option that they might change for the worse?

Because it got worse when she stepped in closer to him and laid her palm against his cheek and, fool that he was, he let her. He should push her away and put her in her place and make sure she knew that no one screwed over a Warren. No one. "I didn't want you to fight for me," she said, her voice soft and gentle. "I wanted you to fight for yourself."

Her words hit him like a gut punch. What the hell was she talking about? Of course he fought for himself! He was Marcus Warren, dammit all!

But before he could tell her that, she turned and, head held high, walked off. He thought she was heading for the front gate, but he wasn't sure. "What are you doing?" he called after her.

"Take the car. I'll make my own way home."

"That's it?" For some reason, he didn't want to watch her walk away. It wasn't that he wanted her to stay—he didn't. He just…he wanted the last word. He wanted to do the walking, dammit.

She stopped and looked back at him and he was horrified to see she was crying again. "That's all there can be. We both know it. Maybe we always did."

"Sir?" Marcus started. The driver was standing next to him, looking deeply concerned. "Sir, would you like me to get the young lady?"

That's all there can be.

"Can you get me another car here within ten minutes?"

"Yes, sir."

Marcus nodded toward Liberty's retreating form. "Take her wherever she wants to go."

That's all there was.

And she was right, damn her. They both knew it.

Seventeen

If Liberty knew where her mother was buried, she'd go to the graveside. She had so many questions and for maybe the only time in her life, she felt as if her mother might have had some answers.

Or at least, one answer. Was this what Jackie Reese had felt like when her prince in polyester failed to rescue her?

Not that Liberty had wanted Marcus to rescue her. But for a few days—less than two weeks—he'd been her knight in shining armor, ready to take on all comers to defend her from the cruelties of the world.

Liberty didn't know where her mother was interred. For that matter, she didn't know where Grandma Devlin had been buried, either. Liberty had no connection to her childhood. She didn't see people from the projects. She didn't have any old friends who kept her up-to-date on the neighborhood gossip. Hell, there wasn't even a neighborhood anymore. Most of the Cabrini-Green projects had been leveled to make way for trendy new housing, the likes of which all her old neighbors would've never been able to afford. Maybe that was the point.

Her old life was so far removed from the person she'd willed herself to be that it didn't seem as if she could be both versions of Liberty Reese. And being Jackie Reese's daughter was not the better option.

So she'd stopped being Jackie's daughter. That hadn't been a chapter—it'd been a completely different book, one that was finished and done and had no other bearing on her life now. As Marcus had almost come to believe, the past was past.

Except it wasn't. Liberty would never be free of Jackie.

She hadn't lied to Marcus. Okay, well—she had maybe bent the truth. But that wasn't the real problem.

No, Liberty had lied to herself. She'd convinced herself that Jackie Reese's daughter didn't exist and, as such, wasn't important. That's what little Liberty had always felt like back then. Unimportant.

But the woman she'd become? That Liberty was *important*. She was valuable because she made herself valuable. She worked harder and longer than anyone else. She had saved herself. To hell with princes.

She had no prince. In fact, she had no one.

Well, almost no one. Two days after she'd walked away from Marcus Warren, she knocked on Hazel's door and waited. She should have called before she came, but she'd been afraid that Hazel might not have let her come over. The older woman still might not let her in, but Liberty was desperate. She knew that this William was not the same as the little brother who had died all those years ago, unwanted and unloved. But this baby, here and now, felt like her only living connection to a past she'd tried to bury.

"Yes? Oh, Ms. Reese!" Hazel's large eyes looked up at

her through her thick glasses. "I wasn't expecting you or Mr. Warren today." She peered around Liberty, looking for Marcus.

"Actually, he's not here," Liberty said. There. She'd managed to keep her voice surprisingly level. She could do this.

"Oh." Hazel gave her an odd look, but Liberty ignored it. "May I see William?"

"Of course, dear. Come in. Mind the door."

Liberty entered and followed Hazel up the steps. Tomorrow, she was going to go into Marcus's office after hours, when she knew he wouldn't be there, and clean out her desk. Then she was going to start applying for jobs. She wasn't even going to bother contacting Erik Jenner. That was too close to Marcus.

She was unemployed and starting over from scratch for the second time in her life. Which had led her to one unavoidable conclusion—this would be her last visit with William. She couldn't afford to let herself get any more attached to the child than she already was because she could not afford the child and if she did get a job, she didn't know where she'd wind up. It'd be for the best if she weren't in Chicago anymore. Too many versions of her past here.

"...Ms. Reese?"

Liberty shook herself out of her thoughts. Hazel was standing just inside the nursery, a look of concern on her face. "I'm sorry?"

"I asked if everything was all right." She peered at Liberty with owlish eyes. "With you and Mr. Warren."

Oh. That. "I don't..." But her words trailed off as she saw William rocking in the brand-new swinging chair that Marcus had bought just for him, and her chest felt as if it was going to collapse back into itself. The whole room was a giant reminder of how very much Marcus had cared—for William, for her.

This was going to hurt more than she'd thought it would.

She understood that he felt betrayed. She couldn't blame him for that. But what stung even more was that he'd promised to fight for her—and he hadn't. It hadn't mattered how valuable she'd made herself and it hadn't mattered how much she truly cared for him. All that had mattered was that she hadn't fully disclosed the most painful parts of her life.

"I don't think that Mr. Warren and I will be able to apply to adopt William," she said, plucking the infant out of the swing. William made a small mewling noise as Liberty tucked him against her chest. His tiny body was so warm, so fragile.

"Dear, I'm so sorry to hear that. You two… I had hoped…" Hazel's voice trailed off.

Yeah, they'd all hoped. Liberty sat down and stared at William's face, trying to commit every last detail to memory. She'd come so close to being able to hold on to this child—to being able to hold on to Liberty Reese. But she'd flown too close to the sun and what went up had to come back down. "I came to say goodbye." She said it more to the baby than to Hazel.

William blinked up at her, his tiny little mouth stretching out. She desperately wanted to think that he knew her now, that the sound of her voice or the smell of her skin was familiar to him. That, somehow, he'd remember there once had been a woman who loved him so much that she'd risked her safe, comfortable life for him.

And Marcus said she never risked anything.

"Will you take our picture together?" she asked, shifting to retrieve her phone. The company phone, with all the company communication on it. She'd have to bite the bullet and get her own phone after this. She couldn't keep Marcus's property. And the dresses—those would have to go back, too. Part of her wanted to return them herself or sell them—that money could carry her for months while she hit the job market.

But that would be another level of dishonesty. Marcus would assume that she'd been with him only for the money. As much as she was worried about her financial future, she couldn't bring herself to lower his opinion of her any more.

Hazel cleared her throat and took the phone. With some fussing, she managed to take a few pictures. "You belong together," she said, handing the phone back.

"I know." It was only after she'd said it that Liberty realized she didn't know whom Hazel was referring to— Liberty and William? Or Liberty and Marcus?

"Dear," Hazel began delicately. "It might be best—for the baby—if you kept visiting for as long as you're able."

"Really?" Oh, how Liberty wanted to believe that. But was Hazel telling her what she thought she needed to hear?

"Oh, yes. He knows you, you know. And he's still settling in after that rough start..." Hazel looked at her hopefully. "I know it can't be a permanent thing. When you're a foster mother, everything is in a constant state of change. Babies come and go, and all I can do is try to give them the best start I can. He's already lost his mother. They haven't found her, you know. I don't think it'd be good for the little angel to lose you so soon, too."

Liberty's throat started to close up. "I'm—" She had to pause and take a breath. "I'm going to be looking for a new job. I might have to move soon."

"I understand. But even for a few more weeks..." She looked at William and smiled. "They know when they're loved. Trust me, it makes such a difference later on."

Wasn't that the thing that had saved her? Grandma Devlin had loved her. She'd never been able to take Liberty in, but knowing the older woman was right down the hall with a cookie and a story and a hug—that she'd be there when Liberty left the foster homes—that was what had kept Liberty going throughout a hellacious childhood.

"All right," Liberty agreed, trying her hardest not to sob and doing a lousy job of it. "If you say so."

Hazel made satisfied noises and bustled off to get William a bottle. When Liberty and the baby were alone, she leaned down and whispered, "I love you, William. I always will."

He sighed against her cheek.

And Liberty let herself cry.

Marcus waited at the office the next day and the day after that, but Liberty did not show up. He took that to mean that she didn't intend to come back to work. Fine. Great. He needed a new assistant and that was inconvenient, but whatever. He'd work around it.

This did not explain why he left explicit instructions with the security guards to call him the moment she came back. She'd left all of her things, after all. She'd be back. And when she did finally show up...

Well, he'd know about it.

He didn't want to speak to her again. But when his phone rang at nine fifteen at night and Lester the security guard was on the other end, telling him that Liberty had entered the building, Marcus still hurried down to his car and took off for the office.

As he drove, he wondered what the hell he was doing. He didn't need to confront her. He'd pretty much said what he needed to say. He was just...making sure she didn't walk off with office supplies or change all the passwords out of spite. That was all.

She wasn't there. "You just missed her," Lester said, sounding sympathetic.

Marcus noticed that the older man wasn't meeting his gaze. "Is that a fact?"

"Yes, sir," Lester said. He had nothing else to add.

Marcus went up to the office anyway—just to be sure. Liberty's shower supplies were missing from the bathroom. Her area was as neat as a pin, as always—but the drawers were empty. He checked.

She was just...gone. It was almost as if she'd never even existed.

Then he saw it—her company phone sat on the corner of his desk and underneath it was a small white envelope with *Marcus* written in Liberty's neat hand across the front.

He didn't want to read it.

But that's exactly what he did.

Marcus,

I will never forgive myself for the pain I have caused you. This was never my plan. I didn't want things to change because I thought I had everything I needed. I was wrong about that, too.

I think it's best for me to move on. I won't take the job with Jenner, so you won't have to worry about explaining anything.

Please don't hold any of this against William. None of this was his doing. I just wanted something better for him than what I had.

I hope you figure out what you want and you fight for that. Not for me, not for your parents—for you, Marcus. If there's one thing life has taught me, it's that you have to save yourself. No one else is going to do it for you.

Thank you for everything. The last three years have been a gift I don't deserve.

Love,
Liberty

He picked up her phone. He didn't know why he remembered her password and he didn't know why he entered it.

The phone didn't open up on the home screen. Instead, it opened up on the last app that had been used, and Marcus wasn't ready for what he saw.

There was Liberty, looking as if she hadn't slept in days. She had William in her arms.

The sight of the two of them—it tore right through him. Because he'd spent the past two weeks allowing himself to think of a different life from the one he had. He'd pictured running in the morning with Liberty as they pushed the jogging stroller. And later, Saturdays at soccer parks and movies on the couch and silly songs and dancing around. Taking Liberty to bed at night and waking up with her in his arms in the morning.

He had everything he wanted, he told himself as he stared at that photo. He didn't need her. He didn't need kids. He absolutely did not need a big, happy family.

And what the hell was she talking about? He was Marcus Warren and that meant something. That's what his mother had said and she was right. She was…

Marcus froze, his heart suddenly pounding so hard he was afraid it would rip right out of his chest. *His mother.*

She and his father—they'd hired a private investigator who'd dug up enough dirt on his old nanny to put her and most of her family in jail.

She was very disappointed in him.

And suddenly, Liberty's past had appeared out of nowhere.

He grabbed his phone out of his pocket and, before he could think better of it, dialed his mother. "Marcus, darling," she cooed. "How are you? Are you all right? I've been so worried about you."

He didn't even have to ask the question—she'd already answered it. No one else knew that Liberty was gone.

But she knew. Of course she did. She—she and his father—had been behind the breakup.

There were, however, a few questions remaining. "How long have you known?"

There was an unnervingly long pause before Marisa Warren cleared her throat and said, "Known about what, darling?"

"About Liberty. About her past."

"Really, Marcus—you've got to be smarter about these things. Once you're settled down with the right kind of woman—"

"Answer the damned question, Mother. How long have you known about her?"

"Why, since you hired her, dear. You didn't really think I was going to let a nobody with no name and no family just ingratiate herself into your life without finding out something about her, did you?"

Why was he surprised? He shouldn't be. And he wasn't going to give his mother the satisfaction of thinking she'd one-upped him. "So let me get this straight—you dug up all the dirt you could find, or thought you could find—on my assistant and then sat on it for three years?"

His mother didn't reply.

Keeping his voice level was the hardest thing he'd ever done. But he wouldn't give her the satisfaction, dammit. "You've been waiting this whole time for the chance to use Liberty's past against her, haven't you? Not even against her. Against me. You sat on this information for three damned years because you knew you could use it to keep me in line, didn't you? *Didn't you?*"

So much for keeping his voice level. He didn't care. No one was around to hear him. He was completely alone because he'd fallen right into the trap without even realizing it had been set for him.

He'd done exactly what his mother wanted him to do. He'd pushed Liberty away.

"You're being ridiculous, Marcus. Think of what she could have cost you. And that baby? What were you think—"

He hung up. And when she called him right back, he turned his phone off.

Everything had a price and you either gained or you lost. That was the game he'd been raised to play. You gained favors and cashed them in when you needed them. Failure to do so meant you lost the game—you lost face, you lost business, you lost your name. Winners or losers, that's who made up the world, and Warrens were always winners. Always.

Except the game was a lie. He wasn't a player. He was a pawn. He was never supposed to win anything. He was nothing more than a favor to be accrued or cashed in. Everyone wanted something from him.

Except for Liberty. She hadn't asked him for anything. Not even a recommendation. And she would do anything for that baby. Including risking her job—and her heart.

If there's one thing life has taught me, it's that you have to save yourself. No one else is going to do it for you. That line from Liberty's note jumped out at him.

He hadn't thought he needed saving. He hadn't realized he had to fight for himself. He wasn't some helpless newborn. He had the ways and means to accomplish what he wanted.

But had he? Or had he just gone along with his parents to get by? He saw now what Liberty meant—what she'd always meant when she'd told him not to go to the wedding because he didn't want to, not to meet with the producers because he didn't want to.

All this time, she'd been telling him to fight for what he wanted.

He picked up her phone again and looked at the picture of Liberty and William. He loved her—he loved them both. What he'd wanted was a family. Liberty and William and more babies—one big happy family. His forever family.

He knew what he wanted.

Now he just had to fight for it.

No one was going to stand in his way this time.

Eighteen

"Ms. Reese? This is Trish Longmire of the One Child, One World charity."

"Hello," Liberty said, stopping in the middle of the sidewalk and fiddling with her new phone so that she could hear better. She had about two blocks to go before she got to Hazel's house. This was her third visit this week to feed and cuddle William.

She tried to think—had she applied at this organization? She'd sent out a lot of résumés, but she didn't recognize the name. The sun beat down on her head and she began to sweat. "How can I help you?"

"One Child provides basic school supplies to children living at or below the poverty line and grants to upgrade classroom technology at schools in need, primarily schools on reservations."

"A noble cause," Liberty said. Education had saved her from crushing poverty, after all. "But I have to ask—what does this have to do with me?"

"The Longmire Foundation has given us a considerable endowment and a mandate to get computers into classrooms."

The Longmire Foundation? That name she recognized— Nate Longmire was the Boy Billionaire of Silicon Valley who'd made headlines when he'd married a young woman no one had ever heard of from…

Oh, God. "I'm sorry—did you say Trish *Longmire*?"

Trish laughed. "Yes. We're expanding our efforts. I'd like to offer you the job of our urban outreach coordinator. You were highly recommended."

"But—who? I haven't applied for the job!" she said, her voice squeaking. Was this happening?

"Marcus Warren," Trish said, although Liberty should have guessed—who else could it be? "We need someone who's comfortable in both underprivileged classrooms, and organizing and attending fundraising events. I understand that you can personally attest to the value of a good education in changing your circumstances, but you've spent the last three years singlehandedly managing Warren Capital," Trish went on. "That makes you uniquely qualified."

"I—am?" Liberty cleared her throat. She needed to be making a better impression here. But she'd spent years— *years*—hiding her childhood. And this woman was telling her it was an asset? "I am, of course. Qualified, that is. I, um…" she babbled. "I'm sorry. This is quite unexpected."

"I understand. I'd like to fly you out to San Francisco next week so we can work out the details, if you're interested in the position."

"Of course. That would be—San Francisco. Yes!"

She and Trish exchanged emails, and then the call ended. Liberty sagged against the parking meter, staring at the screen of her new phone. What had just happened? Had Marcus really called up the wife of another billionaire and recommended Liberty? For a job? For which she was "uniquely qualified"?

She hadn't seen him since the blowup in the parking lot a week and a half ago. She hadn't heard from him, either—not so much as a peep. True, she hadn't exactly left her new number or anything but...

It was over. She'd kept the truth from him and he'd broken his promise to fight for her and that was that. That's all there could be.

Wasn't it?

On shaky legs, she managed to walk the rest of the way to Hazel's house. The shocks just kept right on coming, though, because Marcus's sleek Aston Martin was parked out front.

Oh, God. Marcus was here. Liberty was physically a hot mess—she'd sweat through the back of her tank top and her hair was frizzing. And Marcus was here. With William.

Oh, *God*.

But before she could bolt, the door swung open and there was Hazel, all big smiles. "Ah, Ms. Reese—Mr. Warren is waiting for you."

"He is? How did he know when I'd be here?"

"Oh," Hazel said, shooing her inside and waiting until Liberty hip checked the door shut, "he called shortly after your last visit." She scurried up the stairs with more energy than Liberty had ever seen out of her. "William is so glad to see him again—you can just tell."

Liberty stared at Hazel's back. Maybe none of this was real. Maybe she'd fallen getting off the bus and hit her head and was currently hallucinating. That would be almost as plausible as a job offer out of the blue and Marcus cuddling a happy William.

Stuck somewhere between panic and disbelief, she followed Hazel upstairs and into the nursery. What was Marcus doing here? What was he doing, period?

Oh. He was playing with a baby, that's what. Marcus Warren, one of the most powerful men in all of Chicago— if not the nation—was sitting on the floor of Hazel's nursery, making circles with William's legs and going "whee!" And William? He was kicking his little legs in what looked like sheer joy every time Marcus paused.

"She's here!" Hazel crowed in victory.

Marcus paused mid-*whee* and looked up at Liberty. "Hey, William," he said, carefully turning the infant around. "Look who's here."

William's legs kept right on kicking and his plump arms lifted in her direction. Hazel was right. William did know her.

"Marcus?" she managed to get out. "What did you do?"

That grin—that was the look he always got on his face when he didn't take no for an answer. And he was looking at her. When she didn't pick William up, he tucked the little boy against his chest and surged to his feet. "Hazel," he said, leaning around Liberty, "could you give us a moment?"

"Of course!" Hazel clapped—actually clapped—before she hurried to the kitchen. Liberty heard humming.

"Marcus," she said again, trying to sound stern. "What are you doing?"

The smile dimmed a bit. "Visiting William. Asking Hazel about what I need to do to apply for custody."

Liberty's mouth dropped open, but she quickly got it closed again. "Custody? Why would you do that?"

"Because I want to," he said simply.

"And—the charity? I just got a job offer—in San Francisco? What was that about?"

He shrugged, as if personally getting her a job was no big deal. "You need the work. I know you. I know you won't be happy if you don't have something to manage."

"But…why? Why did you do that for me? My past—you're done. We're done."

"About that." He shifted William in his arms and pressed a gentle kiss to the top of William's fuzzy little head. "I've been thinking about what happened and I owe you an apology."

She didn't even bother trying to get her mouth closed this time. "But—"

"No *but*s. Hear me out. Did you stop and wonder about how those producers knew so much about you? Do you remember Chabot saying they'd gotten an email?"

"I…guess? But so much happened—I didn't think…" But now that he mentioned it, that had seemed odd. "Who?"

"Well. It turns out that my mother had you investigated back when I first hired you and she'd been…saving these details, shall we say, until she could use them to her best advantage."

Liberty gasped, her hand against her chest. The violation was a physical thing, one that made breathing hard. Marisa Warren had known the whole time. "She *what*?"

There had been hundreds of opportunities for Marisa to use that information, too. She could have demanded that Liberty do what she wanted or she'd expose Liberty and all her little lies. But she hadn't. She'd waited for three years.

Marcus nodded grimly. "It was a lousy thing to do to you. You didn't deserve to be ambushed like that. She wouldn't deign to apologize, so I'll do it for her. I'm so sorry, Liberty."

"You're apologizing for her?"

William made a little noise and Marcus adjusted his hold on the baby. "And for myself. I should have listened to you—you were right. The whole weekend was a disaster and I…" He sighed. "I acted like a Warren. And that's not who I am. I want to be better for you. If you'll give me a second chance, I'll be better."

Liberty looked at the tiny baby, her second chance to make things right. "There's something else I should tell you, though, Marcus. The last time my mother went to prison—she went three times—and I was in my third foster home, she had a baby. He was born addicted to God only knows what. He didn't live past three weeks. I don't think he ever had a name. I never saw him. But I named him William because it was a good, strong name. Just like I named this baby."

"Is that all? Because if we're going to make this work, Liberty, I need you to be completely honest with me."

Were they going to make this work? Was that what he was doing here? For the first time, she began to hope this wasn't a dream. If this were really happening... "I don't like to run. But I do it anyway because I get to do it with you. Not at first—at first it was just because I needed a job. I needed to make myself valuable and if that's what it took, then that's what I did. I needed to be someone important, Marcus. And then, when I actually became that person, I couldn't untangle myself from all the little lies I'd told. I wanted to tell you, I did. But I was so afraid that if I did, you wouldn't look at me and see the woman I'd made myself into—all you'd see was Jackie Reese's daughter, and I didn't want to be that person ever again. I never did it to hurt you. I never tried to trick you. I tried to tell you. I just..."

He nodded, as if he truly did understand. "You just did it to survive."

"Yes," she agreed weakly. "I hope you can forgive me."

"Oh, babe," he said. Somehow, he'd gotten closer to her. With William cradled in one arm, he reached out and cupped her face. "Only if you can forgive me. That producer caught me off guard, but that doesn't excuse my actions. I made a promise to you—that I would fight for you, that I would protect you—and when the shit hit the fan, I didn't."

"You didn't," she said. She couldn't get her voice any higher than a whisper, though. Marcus Warren, the billionaire, was apologizing—to her. "You said it didn't matter, but it did."

No, that wasn't right. Because this was just Marcus. He was a little messed up, but he was a good and honorable man trying to make things right.

"It doesn't matter. Does knowing my nanny might have tried to kidnap me matter to you? Or the fact that I almost ran away to Germany—does that matter?"

"Of course not. That's not who you are now."

"Just like your mother's past isn't your present—or our future. I know I haven't earned your trust, but I'd like another chance." He slid his hand down her neck and pulled her in closer. "This time, I won't fail you."

Please don't let this be a dream. Or, if it was, Liberty didn't ever want to wake up. "But I'm a nobody. Why would you do that for me?"

"Because," he said, his lips curling up into a smile. He leaned down and, without squishing the baby, touched his forehead to hers. "The smartest, kindest woman I know told me to figure out what I wanted and go do it. Not because anyone else thought I should, but simply because that's what I want. So that's what I'm doing."

"But…me?" The baby sneezed and they both looked down at him. Liberty touched the top of his head with her hand. "And William?"

"I want you—both of you. I want to be a big happy family." He tilted her head back and stared down into her eyes.

"But you just got me a job in San Francisco."

That made him grin. "No, I recommended you for a job as an urban coordinator. They're branching out. As Nate explained to me, not all Native Americans live on reservations. And we happen to live in Chicago, which is urban. But even if you can't be based here, we could go together. We can start someplace new. I'll be happy anywhere—as long as I have you." He lowered his face to hers. He was going to kiss her, she realized—and she wouldn't have it any other way.

"I'm not good for you." She whispered the words against his lips. "I'll always be the daughter of a convicted criminal. People will always talk."

"Then be bad for me. None of that matters. What's important is you and me and what we know is true. Marry me, Liberty. Be my forever family. Let me prove that I'll never stop fighting for you—for us." He glanced down at William, who was watching this whole thing with big eyes. "For all of us. Right, buddy?"

William cooed.

"Oh, Marcus." Then there weren't any more words because she was kissing him and he was kissing her and they were trying not to squish the baby in between them.

"Is that a yes?" he asked.

"Yes." She lifted William from his arms and then leaned into Marcus as he pulled her against his chest. "*Yes*. I'm yours. I always have been."

"And you always will be."

* * * * *

LET'S TALK
Romance

For exclusive extracts, competitions
and special offers, find us online:

- facebook.com/millsandboon
- @MillsandBoon
- @MillsandBoonUK

Get in touch on 01413 063232

For all the latest titles coming soon, visit
millsandboon.co.uk/nextmonth